Praise for *An Evening of Long Goodbyes*

"In this very funny and ultimately very moving first novel, indolent Irish aristocrat Charles Hythloday is forced to do the unthinkable—give up his love of gimlets and old movies and get a job. A seamless, memorable combination of farce and social commentary."
                    —*Booklist* (starred review; Best Books of 2004)

"[A] comedy of the highest caliber."   —*The Sunday Tribune* (Ireland)

"Paul Murray manages to fit a brilliant social novel in the small spaces of a farce, without ever losing his lightness of touch or his sense of humor. The result is something unique. Murray starts with Wodehouse (and does him proud), but ends somewhere entirely his own—somewhere very, very funny and surprisingly touching."
                    —ARTHUR PHILLIPS, author of *Prague*

"One of the most entertaining and laugh-out-loud Irish yarns of recent years."   —*Irish Independent*

"If Wodehouse's Bertie Wooster were plopped into the twenty-first century, his adventures might resemble those of Charles Hythloday, the buffoonish hero of Murray's insouciant romp. . . . Murray's blend of drawing-room comedy and postindustrial hilarity is deft and jaunty, and well-timed snippets of foreshadowing keep the story moving briskly. . . . Witty and satirical . . . this is a breezy, highly entertaining read."   —*Publishers Weekly* (starred review)

"Murray has a good comic voice, and Hythloday . . . is well worth knowing as he navigates Dublin's high-tech job market, lands a job in a bread factory frosting cakes and begins to learn the hard task of being human."
—*New York Post*

"A hilarious, rich, and satisfying novel."
—*The Times Literary Supplement*

"A lyrical, satirical tour-de-force, a huge, hilarious elegy. A surreal and very funny festival of truths, fictions, luck and love. How can this be a first novel? A triumph."
—ALI SMITH, author of the Man Booker Prize finalist *Hotel World*

"A deft, funny, and ultimately quite moving debut about the strenuous and determined efforts of a young Irish aristocrat to evade all contact with the real world. . . . Riotously funny from the start, the sharp edge of the author's satire turns this tale into something very different from comedy by the end and reveals Murray as a master of narrative sleight of hand."
—*Kirkus Reviews* (starred review)

"This likable shaggy-dog story is full of poignant humor and colorful . . . characters. . . . [Their] struggle to embrace life in all its complexities will endear the Hythloday siblings to readers. Strongly recommended."
—*Library Journal*

"The deliberately absurd plotting and Charles' droll narration wring smiles."
—*Entertainment Weekly*

"You can't go home again—not after the old pile's been converted into a showcase for dreadful lumpen drama . . . not when the Bosnian cook's extended family turns out to be living secretly on the grounds; and certainly not when the miles of bandages about your head cause people to upset their drinks. . . . Paul Murray's laugh-laden debut . . . is thankfully more like four or five long evenings' worth of companionable reading."
—*The Village Voice*

AN EVENING OF
LONG GOODBYES

RANDOM HOUSE TRADE PAPERBACKS NEW YORK

A NOVEL

AN EVENING OF LONG GOODBYES

Paul Murray

2005 Random House Trade Paperback Edition

Copyright © 2003 by Paul Murray
Reading group guide copyright © 2005 by Random House, Inc.

Published in the United States by Random House Trade Paperbacks, an imprint of The Random House Publishing Group, a division of Random House, Inc., New York.

RANDOM HOUSE TRADE PAPERBACKS and colophon are trademarks of Random House, Inc.

This work was originally published in the United Kingdom by Hamish Hamilton, an imprint of the Penguin Group (UK), in 2003. It was published in hardcover in the United States by Random House, an imprint of The Random House Publishing Group, a division of Random House, Inc., in 2004.

Brief excerpt from *Laura* copyright © 1944 by Twentieth Century Fox. All rights reserved. Used by permission.

Excerpt from "Over the Rainbow" by Harold Arlen and E. Y. Harburg, copyright © 1938 (renewed 1966) Metro-Goldwyn-Mayer Inc., copyright © 1939 (renewed 1967) EMI Feist Catalog Inc. All rights controlled by EMI Feist Catalog Inc. All rights reserved. Used by permission of Warner Bros. Publications U.S. Inc., Miami, FL 33014.

LIBRARY OF CONGRESS CATALOGING-IN-PUBLICATION DATA

Murray, Paul.
    An evening of long goodbyes : a novel / Paul Murray.
        p. cm.
    ISBN 978-0-8129-7040-1
    1. Inheritance and succession—Fiction. 2. Brothers and sisters—
Fiction. 3. Children of the rich—Fiction. 4. Film historians—
Fiction. 5. Biographers—Fiction. I. Title.

    PR6113.U78E94 2004
    813'.6—dc22   2003058451

www.atrandom.com

Book design by Barbara M. Bachman

147429898

To Miriam

AN EVENING OF
LONG GOODBYES

A black wind was blowing outside the bow window. All afternoon it had been playing its tricks: scooping up handfuls of leaves and flinging them over the lawn, spinning Old Man Thompson's weather vane this way and that, seizing rapaciously at Bel's ruby leather coat as she battled down the driveway to her audition. Now and then, from the rear of the house, I would hear it shriek through the bones of the Folly, and I'd look up from the TV with a start. If this were Kansas—I remember thinking—it might have been the beginnings of a terrible Twister; but this wasn't Kansas, and what the wind blew in was worse than witches or winged monkeys. For today was the day that Frank arrived at Amaurot.

It was after four but I was still in my dressing gown, recuperating on the chaise longue in front of an old black-and-white movie that starred Mary Astor in an array of hats. I'd been out the night before with Pongo McGurks and possibly overdone it a little, insofar as I'd woken up on the billiard table with a splitting headache and wearing someone else's sarong. By now, though, I was feeling much better. In fact, I was feeling particularly at one with the world, supping at a bowl of special medicinal consommé that Mrs. P. had made for me, thinking that no one wore a hat quite like Mary Astor—and then I caught my first sight of him, it:

a large, vaguely humanoid shape shifting about behind the glass frieze that looked onto the hallway. It didn't fit any of the shapes that should by rights have been there—not Bel's slender figure, nor Mrs. P.'s squat domestic trapezium: This shape was bulky and distended, grotesquely so, like one of those self-assembly IKEA wardrobes I'd seen advertised on TV. I raised myself up on my elbows and called out: "Who's there!"

There was no reply; and suddenly the figure was gone from the glass. I put down my consommé with a little sigh. I am not so vain as to think myself, in the general run of things, any more heroic than the next fellow; still, a man's home is his castle, and when Swedish furniture decides to have a wander through it, one must take the appropriate measures. Tying the belt of my dressing gown and picking up the poker, I stole over to the drawing room door. The hallway was empty. I cupped a hand to my ear but heard only the sound of the house itself, like an endless exhalation of air echoing between the high ceilings and wood floors.

I was beginning to think I must have imagined it; but I seemed to remember someone telling me about a rash of break-ins recently, so just to be certain, I continued down the hall. There were plenty of nooks in which a miscreant could hide. Holding my poker at the ready in case he tried an ambush, I checked the library and the recital room—slowly twisting the knob, then swiftly thrusting open the door—to find nothing. Nothing lurked behind the Brancusi Janus; no one loomed beneath Mother's sprawling poinsettia. On an impulse I tried the double doors of the ballroom; they were locked, of course, as they always were.

Relieved, I was on my way to the kitchen to have a cursory look around and also to see if there was anything by way of biscuits to follow the consommé, when a noise came from behind me. I spun round just as the door of the cloakroom burst open—and there, lumbering toward me, was the hideous Shape! Without the benefit of frosted glass between us, it was even more gruesome—my nerve quite failed me, the poker freezing midswing—

"Charles!" cried my sister, ghosting up suddenly at the Thing's shoulder.

"Haugh," the Thing snarled, before I recovered my wits and caught it a good blow on the temple, sending it tumbling to the floor with a thud which rattled Mother's china collection clear in the next room.

There was a moment of silence. Outside the house the wind snapped and howled.

"God, Charles, what have you *done*?" Bel said, hovering apprehensively over the stricken beast.

"Don't worry, he's still breathing," I reassured her. "Anyway, it's no more than he deserves. Breaking into someone else's house like that—it's a good thing you weren't here on your own, Bel, he's a vicious-looking brute."

"That's *frank*, Charles," she moaned.

"Yes, it is, and I wish you hadn't had to see it, but the fact is that this is the world we live in, and—"

"No, you idiot, I mean that's *Frank*, he's a—a friend of mine. We're going out this evening." She knelt down to examine the creature's forehead. "If he regains consciousness."

"Oh," I said. Through the door I glimpsed Mary Astor dancing a daring Charleston in a man's trilby and wished—not for the first or the last time—that I could step into the screen and join her.

"Is that all you can say, 'Oh'?" Bel half-rose again, the better to chastise me. "The poor guy takes an afternoon off work just to give me a lift back from that stupid audition, and then before I can even offer him a drink, you—you *assault* him."

"I thought he was a burglar," I protested.

"A burglar," Bel repeated.

"Well, there's been that rash of break-ins," I said, "and"—there was really no nice way to put this—"he does *look* like a burglar, Bel, you have to admit. I mean, look at him."

We turned our attention to the figure on the floor. He wore a denim jacket, a grubby white shirt, and nondescript brown shoes. He was very large and, in some unplaceable way, lumpy. His head, however, was what really fascinated me. It resembled some novice potter's first attempt at a soup tureen, bulbous and pasty, with one beetling eyebrow, a stubbly jaw, and less than the full complement of teeth; to describe his ears as asymmetrical would be to do asymmetry a disservice.

"What do you mean, 'disservice'?" Bel exclaimed when I pointed this out to her. "Charles, you practically *kill* someone and all you can think to do is stand around criticizing his ears? What's *wrong* with you?"

"It's not *just* his ears," I said. "Think about it. Can you imagine what Mother would say, confronted with *that*?"

"I know quite well what she'd say," Bel said sourly. "She'd say that she felt quite faint, and could someone please pour her a glass of gin."

"Mother's nerves are no laughing matter," I reproved her, but she was already heading for the kitchen, reappearing a moment later with a tea towel full of ice cubes just as her creature was coming to its senses.

"Janey," it said. "Fuck."

"Are you all right?" Bel asked, after hauling it with both hands up to a sitting position.

"I dunno what happened," the creature said. "I was lookin for the kitchen and I must have got lost cos then I was in this room with all these coats and then it was like somethin *hit* me . . ."

"You had an accident," Bel told it, glaring icily in my direction.

"Well, all in the past now," I said. "You could probably do with a drink, though. A cognac, maybe? Or actually, I was just going to make myself a gimlet, if I can tempt you . . ."

"A cup of tea'd be lovely," the interloper said, dragging itself up off the parquet and, leaning on Bel's shoulder, limping into the drawing room to sink down in my place on the chaise longue.

"Tea. Certainly," I said graciously, as he picked up the remote control and Mary Astor's smiling eyes were replaced by a straggly trail of dogs running about.

There was no response when I rang the service bell, and I was staring hopelessly at the range of kitchen cupboards when Bel came in. "Where does Mrs. P. keep the tea?" I said. She opened a door rather abruptly, nearly clipping my nose, to reveal a cabinet of glazed pots. "Do you think he wants Earl Grey? Is it a bit early?"

Bel sighed heavily, took a box of Band-Aids from a drawer, and left again.

Maybe he'd be better with Lapsang Souchong, I pondered, but then I decided I had been right the first time and carried in the tray with a plate of Mrs. P.'s *amuse-bouches* left over from the other night. Our guest was delighted with these and shoved them in fistfuls into his cavernous mouth. The tea, however, was less to his satisfaction. "Isn't there any milk?" he asked.

I rolled my eyes at Bel, who flounced out of the room again with yet more sotto voce imprecations. Now the two of us were alone. I could feel him looking at me, and I knew the poker was within his reach. I kept my eyes fixed firmly on the television screen. The key was to show no fear. After a long, strained silence he addressed me. "Follow the football at all?" he said.

"No," I said.

"Oh," he said. He cleared his throat. "So . . . do youse live here all alone?" He had a thick Dublin brogue that made everything he said sound vaguely menacing.

"Hmm?" I said. Menace or not, I was becoming hypnotized by the dogs on TV. They were racing around their track at full pelt, despite appearing not to have been fed for several days; a small electric rabbit was leading them a merry dance. Frank repeated his question.

"Oh, yes, it's just the two of us at the moment, and Mrs. P., of course. Father passed on a couple of years ago," gesturing at the photograph on the wall, Father with that Westwood woman at a fashion thing in London, "and Mother has been unwell lately—nerves, you know. Quite a trouper, though, never complains."

"Oh, right," said Frank. He ruminated over this, then his mouth contorted itself into a sinister leer. "I'd say you've a bit of crack in the gaff though, without the oul pair knockin about?"

I didn't understand quite what this meant, but it sounded like he was insinuating something unwholesome. "What?" I said.

"Parties, like, you must have a good few parties and stuff."

"Oh, oh yes." I relaxed. "We do. That is, I do. Bel usually prefers to mope about with her drama friends. It's been pretty quiet lately, now that I come to think of it. But we've had some high times, all right. Back in April, for instance, a close friend of mine—Patsy Olé, maybe you know her? Everybody knows Patsy—"

He looked at me blankly.

"She's gone now, anyway," I continued, annoyed to hear a quaver in my voice as I said it—"India, Grand Tour sort of a thing, you know.

Where was I? Oh yes, that night, absolute mayhem. This one chap, Pongo McGurks"—I leaned forward conspiratorially—"arrives at the stroke of midnight with an *entire deer*, bagged it over at the Guinness place in the mountains, and we . . ." I stopped, judging from his uncomprehending gaze that there was no point continuing this anecdote. We returned our attention to the greyhounds' pursuit of their small, indigestible prey.

"So who's this Mrs. P., then," he asked suddenly, "your auntie or something?"

"Mrs. P.? Oh no. She's the help. Bosnian, you know. Or is it Serbian? An absolute treasure, anyway. As I always say to Bel, if there's one good thing to come out of all this fuss in the Balkans, it's the availability of quality staff . . ." The words died away on my lips: once again I found myself trailing off in the stare of those unblinking eyes. This fellow was like some kind of after-dinner black hole. My anxiety began to mount again. Where was Bel anyway? What was she doing leaving me at the mercy of this primate? Did she want me rent limb from limb and stuffed up the chimney?

"Excuse me a moment," I said, getting to my feet and tracking her down to her bedroom, where she stood contemplating her shoe rack.

"Charles, for God's sake, no one's going to stuff you up any chimneys," she said. "I'm trying to change here, do you mind? I'll be back down in a minute."

"Well I do mind," I said. "As a matter of fact I mind very much. I thought you'd just gone for milk."

"*Charles*"—Bel turned, waving her hairbrush impatiently—"can't you just not be weird for five minutes, and just talk to him until—"

"I've tried talking to him," I said, drawing aside the curtain to see the wind still careering over the long grass. "Everything I say just gets sort of . . . *absorbed.* It's very off-putting. And then I worry that he'll get hungry, and mistake me for a brisket."

"Well if you'd simply allow me to get dressed, then I— Come to think of it, are you planning to put on clothes at all today? Or have we reached a new stage in your seemingly interminable decline?"

"What decline?" I said. She stomped barefoot past me to the chest of drawers. "What's that supposed to mean?"

"I mean," she said as she pulled out a series of frilly items, held them up for scrutiny, and dropped them on the floor, "that you've been cooped up in this house for I don't know *how* long and you're beginning to—"

"Beginning to what? Beginning to what, exactly?"

"It just seems like more and more often these days I haven't the slightest idea what you're talking about." She tossed a slip and a pair of slate blue moccasins onto the bed. "I seem to recall you making a lot more sense than you do at the moment."

"Well that's absolute poppycock," I retorted, "because for a start I was out last night. Pongo McGurks is going off to London to work for his old man, we went to the Sorrento for valedictory gimlets—"

"I see, that would explain the strange dream I had of the pair of you dancing around on the lawn at four in the morning . . . Were you wearing grass skirts? Please tell me you weren't wearing grass skirts." She opened her wardrobe. "Anyway, it doesn't matter, my point is could you please try and act like a normal human being and just . . . be *polite*."

"All right," I said. "But if the circus comes looking for him, I'm not going to be answerable."

She took a dress from the wardrobe, turned to the mirror, and shook out her hair aggressively. "Haven't you anything better to do than stand around annoying me?" she said.

"Well, yes, as a matter of fact, I was watching a film with Mary Astor and hats—"

"We're going in a minute," she scowled. I was about to make another witty remark, to the effect that if I didn't leave the house much it was probably because everywhere else was full of people like Frank; but catching sight of her eyes in the mirror I decided to hold my peace. Bel put up quite a show, but she wasn't nearly so tough as she liked to make out. I knew how long she took to apply her mascara, and if she started to cry the pair of them would be here all night. The audition mustn't have gone well.

"I never asked how you got on today," I said casually. "Did you get the part?"

"No," she mumbled, tilting the cheval glass and holding the dress up against her. "It was *awful*, it was for an ad for some company selling doors over the Internet. I'd never read anything so *asinine* in my whole life. The idea was that me and this guy who's supposed to be my boyfriend are in an apartment having this huge fight—I mean he's shouting at me and insulting me and just being a bastard for about two minutes, until I storm off and slam the door behind me. And then the slogan is 'Doors. It's good to leave.' Isn't that poisonous?"

"Still, that was your first one in a while, wasn't it?" I said. "Something better's bound to come along."

"Mmm." She flushed. "Charles, I really do have to change now, do you mind?"

"I mean something that you actually want to— You're not wearing moccasins with that dress, are you?"

"Charles, I'm *changing*, would you please get out?"

I retreated without further comment and went downstairs to fidget in the kitchen until I heard her descend the staircase and rejoin Frank.

"Don't wait up," she called from the hallway.

"Ha!" I returned, but they had already gone.

It might seem that I was being a little hard on my sister, but with Mother away at the Cedars I felt it was my responsibility to look after her. Bel was twenty-one, three years younger than me, a strikingly pretty girl with Father's pale blue eyes and Mother's autumn-leaf hair and a streak of recklessness, a dismissive impatience with her own life, that she'd inherited from no one. In June she'd finished at Trinity, where she'd taken a rather indulgent degree in Drama—"Bel study Drama," Father had sighed as he signed the check, "there's coals to Newcastle for you"—which wasn't entirely fair, because while she did have a tendency for melodrama and a keen sense of any injustice that pertained to herself, she wasn't really the flamboyant type. Although acting was her passion, in college productions she'd always preferred to work behind the scenes, designing sets or editing scripts, and any time she got onto the stage her roles were swallowed up by her own shyness.

Ever since her finals she'd been at a loose end; the void bothered her, I could tell. Over the last months, she'd gone through a series of male companions of diminishing quality, even by her haphazard standards; the rest of the time she'd spent closeted away in her room, listening to Bob Dylan records and smoking joints out the window into the evening air.

"It's time off," I'd counsel her. "Just enjoy it. Slow yourself down a little, like I do."

"It's not time off," she'd say. "It feels like *Purgatory*. Stuck out here on my own in the middle of *nowhere*, cut off from everyone I know, just *waiting* I don't even know what for, and I have no money, and I'm nothing, I feel like a *zero*—"

"You've only been finished a month. It's a transition period, that's all. I don't see what you're so worried about."

"I'm worried that I'll turn into *you*," she'd wail, and return despairingly to the endless pages of computer programming jobs in the appointments section of the newspaper. Which was a pity, because that summer we enjoyed beautiful stretches of sunshine, and the grounds had rarely looked so fetching. With Mother away, I was free to stroll around at my leisure, admiring the verdant tint of the oak leaves, the fleecy flowers of the horse chestnut, the tall amaryllis and columbine; it was a peaceful time, and in spite of what Bel had said, I felt unusually contented, although naturally from time to time I thought it would have been nice to have a companion for my rovings—a wolfhound, perhaps, or a setter, to wag along beside me as I tramped over the grass and curl up at my feet as I sat under a tree with my Improving Book.

After Bel and Frank departed, I spent a good half hour massaging the chaise longue to remove the dent Frank had left in it. I was feeling dinnerish but there was still no sign of Mrs. P. I was standing at the window waiting for her when I saw the postman roll drunkenly up the path. One of the disadvantages of living where we did—the house was on the coast, two miles of devious road from Dalkey village—was that the postal services found it hard to bring themselves to deliver; on rainy days, or days when it looked like it might rain, or days before or after days when it had rained, you could forget about it. But it had been relatively clement lately, and the postman, a white-haired geezer of untrustworthy aspect, had evidently decided to take a chance. I opened the front door just as he was bending to the letter box with a sheaf of correspondence.

"Morning," he said, the brazen untruth of which knocked the wind out of my sails and with it the lecture I had been preparing for several days to give him; instead I just snatched the mail from his hand and slammed the door, and he sauntered off whistling across the lawn, which is not meant to be walked on except by the peacocks.

I glanced cursorily through the letters. Nothing for me, a few official-looking things for my sister, several others addressed to Mother with a similar red stamp, special delivery or something. I put these aside for Bel, who was in charge of family correspondence while Mother was indisposed, and turned my thoughts back to the whereabouts of Mrs. P. I hadn't seen her since lunchtime and by now was getting weak with hunger. What I'd said to Frank had been no exaggeration: Her bonhomie and excellent cuisine had carried the household through some difficult times. Yet recently she hadn't seemed quite as devoted as usual. She'd been keeping rather erratic hours, and she seemed preoccupied, as if her mind was elsewhere. I hadn't said anything to Bel yet, but the truth was that I was getting a little worried. I wondered if she hadn't something troubling her—or worse, if she had simply come to the end of her useful days and was ready to be put out to pasture.

On the upside, by this time my hangover had dissipated, so I went down to the cellar to pick out a bottle for dinner. I liked the cellar: The air down there was cool and rarefied, and clung to one damply in a comforting way, like a blanket over the shoulders; and all around the dim light glinted crimson, mauve, and burgundy on the bottles, rainbows within rainbows, one of the few unalloyed joys of my father's life. Of late, it had to be said, the ranks were looking somewhat depleted. It had been a rather frenetic few months—all the old crowd together again, those fabulous, foolish parties merging into one another like the giddy, breathless space between night and day. In retrospect I suppose it had all the hallmarks of a Last Hurrah. I wondered if everyone had known it except me.

Not that it mattered; none of it had come to anything, not the flings nor the booze nor the girls with peacock feathers in their hair. Patsy Olé had been the one I was after: Patsy Olé, who was suave and pretty and didn't give a damn, and who, like all girls that are suave and pretty and don't give a damn, always had a string of fellows groveling at her heel.

She was one of those girls, furthermore, who enjoyed the strife and hatred she engendered among her suitors at least as much as the relationships themselves, and as such was quite amenable to conducting two or more romances at the same time. And yet, on certain nights, she and I had seemed on the verge of something quite . . .

I roused myself. She was in India now; we were all probably better off. I selected a bottle and returned to the kitchen. It was easy to get caught in the cellar. If I wasn't careful I could end up mooning about down there for hours, getting myself covered in cobwebs.

My stomach was really beginning to hurt now, and Mrs. P. remained AWOL. This was ridiculous. I couldn't be expected to hang about all night. There was a Gene Tierney double bill on television later that I'd been looking forward to for ages. I decided I would teach Mrs. P. a lesson by cooking my own meal.

The larder presented some difficulties initially. The fish needed gutting, the meat cutting, the vegetables peeling, slicing, sautéing. But then I chanced on some beans in a jar and, thinking that one could not go wrong with beans, put them in a pot with a cupful of rice. I waited until some steam began to brew over the water, then drained it and put it on a plate and took my meal into the dining room. It was quite edible if you ate it quickly enough between swallows of wine, and I was rather proud of myself. I dined alone, watched over by the somberly ticking clock and a moth that fluttered atmospherically against the shade of the lamp by the long mahogany table. Afterward I made myself a gimlet and returned to the drawing room and the by-now-restored chaise longue.

The first half of the double bill was the negligible *Heaven Can Wait*, in which Tierney has only a small part as Don Ameche's saintly wife; but it was followed by Otto Preminger's magnificent *Whirlpool*, in which her curious combination of magnetism and vacuity, so suited to Hollywood's purposes that she might have been constructed in some Burbank lot, was exploited to its fullest: Drawing in the viewer as at the same time she retreated from the plot, fading and fading until, Siren-like, she had pulled you right into the picture just at the moment that she disappeared from it, so you found yourself alone in the space where she should have been, in the shadows and spiderweb of Preminger's cruel machine.

I watched a lot of old movies, and from the first time I saw her, Gene Tierney was my favorite star of that era of true stars. Although she's largely forgotten now, in her time she was regarded as the most beautiful woman ever to grace the silver screen. But her beauty took the form of a smoldering, purely feminine darkness, without the reassuring masculinity of a Bacall or the frivolity of a Hayworth, and it seemed to terrify the moviemakers; they would cast her resolutely against type, as a dullard housewife or a good-natured ninny or a cartoonish Arabian princess, roles devised to restrict and minimize the awesome power of her face, emphasizing instead her natural and deep-rooted uncertainty. Critics and industry, even as they fell in love with her, insisted unanimously that she couldn't act. (Of *Whirlpool*, for instance, in which she plays a kleptomaniac taken advantage of by an unscrupulous psychoanalyst, one reviewer said: "It is sometimes difficult to tell from Miss Tierney's playing whether she is or is not under hypnosis.") Preminger was the only director who seemed to understand her and what she meant to those who saw her; in his and her best film, *Laura*, she spends most of her time dead, appearing on screen in the form of a painting and in the flashback testimony of the suspects for her murder.

I'd seen both films before, though, and drained by the exertion of making dinner, I dozed off. As I did so I experienced the curious sensation, not for the first time in recent months, that in some inexplicable way the film was watching *me*; I slept tormented by bad dreams, in which vampiric images of women enticed me, withholding focus and changing at the last minute into hideous monsters that grinned toothlessly and made meaningful gestures at a vast chimney lined with empty bottles. I woke to the sound of voices at the door and a new, more crippling pain in my stomach. The voices belonged to my sister and the Thing and had distinctly romantic undertones, but I found myself unable to get up and intervene. "Cease," I cried weakly, but my voice cracked and my head swam and I lay there powerless in a pool of sweat. In the corner the muted television showed pictures of people in some kind of makeshift campsite—thousands and thousands of people, weeping and lamenting. Then, in one of those moments of extreme clarity that nausea brings, I perceived that my cocktail glass had been removed from the table. Mrs. P. was back! With the last of my strength, I pulled on the bell rope, and its clang echoed distantly around me as I passed out of consciousness.

When I came to again—parched, pain rampaging through my intestines—I was in my bed. The little bedside lamp illuminated two anxious faces, my sister's and Mrs. P.'s (the latter looking a shade guilty, I noted, no doubt realizing that it was effectively through her negligence that I had been forced to poison myself), and one gormless and oblivious face, which belonged to Frank. Biting her lip and putting a hand on my shoulder, Bel asked if I was all right.

"Beans!" I gasped.

"What?" she said.

"I think he has eaten many kidney beans." Mrs. P. shuddered. "Many kidney beans not cooked."

"Beans!" I cried again deliriously.

"Oh for heaven's sake," Bel said. "Charles, listen carefully, did you soak the beans before you cooked them?"

"Of course I didn't soak them," I said. "What are you talking about?"

"What do you think?" Bel said to Mrs. P. Mrs. P. threw her hands in the air and turned away, speaking agitatedly in Bosnian, or whatever it was.

"They did seem rather crunchy," I recalled.

Frank gave me a wink. "On the batter, eh? Hair of the dog's what you want."

"What?" I said, then "Oh," as he produced a hip flask. The thought of putting my lips where his had been repulsed me, but I would have done anything to rid myself of this mortal agony, so I steeled myself and swallowed a mouthful of very cheap whiskey—and it worked, in that soon I was copiously throwing up into a silver champagne bucket. After that I felt a little better, better enough to request a moment in private with Bel.

"Charles," she said, sitting beside me and stroking my brow, "when are you going to learn to stop being such an idiot?"

"Never mind that for the moment," I snapped. "I'd like to know what's going on."

"Well, we came home and found you rolling around the floor, so we—"

"Not that, damn it, Bel—that Frank, what is he doing back here?"

Bel drew back. "What do you mean?" she said.

"I mean, I've never laid eyes on him before today, and already he's spending the night? Just because Mother isn't here doesn't mean the house can be turned into a—a *bordello*, you know."

She flushed a deep scarlet. "How dare you," she said coldly.

"I'm only thinking of you," I said. "I'm just trying to stop you doing something you might regret. One of us has to keep a level head, after all."

"My head is perfectly level, I assure you."

"Well, is it, though," I said.

Bel stood up. "What do you mean, 'is it, though'?"

"I mean, you're not in good form. You said it yourself, Bel. You're feeling bereaved. You're ticked off because you're not with your pals in college anymore. You've been like this all summer. It's perfectly under-standable. But there comes a point where someone has to step in and take charge. Because the fact is that bereaved or extremely sad people often reach out for support to the wrong places. Their heads are clouded, you see, so they make these ferociously bad decisions—"

Bel's teeth ground audibly. "Charles, how dare you say what you just said and then presume to think you know how I feel. God, if anything's pushing me to make bad decisions and do something I'll regret, it's—"

"I'm simply thinking of your welfare. Can't you just sit down and listen for a moment?" I winced and pressed my hand to my side as a flame of pain shot up from my gut. "I mean, who is this Frank? That's what we have to ask ourselves. What does he want with us?"

"*I* know who he is, *I'm* what he wants with us."

"Ah, but do you? I mean he could be anyone, he could be a—a serial killer, or a very well-disguised master criminal after the family fortune—"

"Why do we keep having this conversation?" She directed her ques-tion to the ceiling. "Why are you like this every time I bring someone home? You snipe and you complain till I can't face it anymore—it's *in-supportable*."

"Well," I said, "it's because you have such uneducated tastes"—

adding hurriedly as she looked about set to hit me, invalided or not, "Because you're such an exquisite creature, Bel, you deserve so much better."

"Charles, two minutes ago you basically called me a prostitute."

"No I didn't."

"You did, you said I was turning the house into a bordello."

"I didn't mean it like that," I said. "I only meant, you know, you shouldn't be wasting your time on imbeciles. I know how hard it is to find the right person, but that's no reason to exhaustively work your way through all the *wrong* people. You seem to be living your romantic life by some kind of process of elimination. It's like matching a Louis Quatorze armchair with one of those plastic patio tables. It simply doesn't work."

"Oh, I see," Bel said. "I'm an armchair, is that it?"

"A Louis Quatorze armchair," I qualified.

"And my boyfriends are patio tables."

"Actually," I remembered, "this one's more like one of those self-assembly Swedish wardrobes."

"I worry about you," Bel said, getting up and pirouetting angrily in the pool of light thrown by the lamp. "I seriously do. I think you have real demons to struggle with, Charles. Every single relationship I have you do your best to destroy. You make every boy I bring home feel uncomfortable and you make me look like I come from some sort of uppity *zoo*. No one is good enough for you. Kevin was too badly dressed—"

"The sandals? The socks?"

"Liam was too Scottish—"

"Oh, but *so* Scottish, Bel! Come on, the *bagpipes*? The interminable quotations from *Braveheart*? Anyone who's *proud* of coming from Scotland obviously has issues—"

"David?"

"Duck-walk."

"Roy?"

"Repressed homosexual."

"Anthony?"

I scratched my head. "Picayune," I said.

"Thomas, what about him? How did he offend you?"

Why do birds sing? Why is the sky blue? Thomas, the alleged body artist, who looked like he'd fallen face-first into a bag of nails: I refrained from comment, contenting myself with a supercilious chortle.

"But haven't you ever considered," Bel went on in an ironic tone, "whether the problem might not be with you? Have you ever thought to yourself, why am I so obsessed with my sister's love life, isn't that a bit unhealthy, especially when the rest of the time I do nothing except wander around the house drinking Father's wine and watching television and romping around with singularly stupid girls who haven't a hint of brain in their pretty little heads like that awful whatshername who sounded like a bullfight, even as I criticize my unfortunate sister for her attempts at a normal, real relationship and a real actual life—am I"—she heated up and started stamping about—"am I going to spend the rest of my life hanging around Amaurot doing nothing but spy into other people's affairs as if I *owned* them when in fact it is none of my *business*?" Trembling with fury, she turned to look at me, as if expecting a response.

"Are we still talking about me?" I said.

"*Yes,* Charles," bringing her foot down thunderously.

"What—you're suggesting that instead of trying to protect and care for my family I should be out working in some sort of a—a *job,* is that it?"

"In a nutshell," Bel replied.

I was confused. "This isn't how the conversation started out," I averred.

"Maybe not," Bel said. "But it's high time someone told you a few home truths."

"Actually, I think I can feel another nauseous spell coming on," I said hurriedly.

She said it anyway: She was remorseless, telling me that while possibly by some tortuous logic I was misconstruing my meddling behavior as paternal, or protective, in actual fact it was intrusive and stifling, "and the only reason you do it is that you don't have anything else, because for the last two years you've been either sitting around here on your own or drinking with your good-for-nothing friends and basically living without the remotest concept of *adulthood* or *maturity*— Well, I've had enough, Charles. I don't care anymore if you don't go back to col-

lege. I don't care if you want to ruin your life. But I don't see why you should get to ruin mine as well. If you're going to be a failure, fine. But please fail on your own time."

"Failure?" I yelped. "Someone has to preserve the family tradition, don't they? Someone has to keep the flag flying."

"Father never took a day off in his life," she said contemptuously. "Flag indeed."

"Yes, but he didn't work his whole life so that his children would have to—to also work," I parried, "and besides, I don't understand what you're getting so het up about"—although it was pretty obvious; Bel was relentlessly introspective and probably suffering from terrible guilt over this Frank character. "I don't see why a few kindly meant words of advice have you sending me out to work shelling *peas*, or putting tops on jam jars in some hideous mechanical *barn*, standing all day at a conveyor belt, the roar of machinery in my ears, not even a chair to sit on and the endless gleaming jars rolling inexorably toward my little lid-placing device—"

"I'm talking about responsibility, Charles, about living like an actual human grown-up person—"

"This Frank of yours, I suppose *he* works, does he?"

Bel halted midstamp and adjusted the strap of her dress. "He works," she said evasively.

"Well? Brain surgeon, hot-air balloonist, third violin . . . ?"

She cast down her eyes. "He has a van," she said.

"A *van*!" I exclaimed, triumphantly jabbing a finger in the air. "A *van*! And any idea as to what he puts in this 'van'? Opium? Elephant tusks? Well-intentioned but misguided young girls from good families?"

"It doesn't *matter*!" she shouted. "God, I knew I shouldn't have bothered trying to reason with you."

From outside, the querulous creak of the weather vane rose over the wind. I sighed, sat up in bed, and turned back the cuffs of my pajamas. The thing was, I wasn't just trying to annoy her this time; I really did have the uncanny feeling that with Frank she had crossed some kind of a line. "Bel," I said earnestly, "I'm sorry if I'm harsh with you. You're grown up, you've finished college, you can make your own decisions.

But although I may not have a respectable job in a jar factory, I have seen a thing or two. And this Frank . . ." I racked my brains for a more diplomatic, more palatable expression for my fears, but I couldn't think of one. So I took a deep breath and came right out with it. "Are you familiar with the figure from Yiddish mythology known as the Golem?"

Bel looked puzzled but suspicious.

"The Golem, according to legend, is a creature composed entirely of clay—or in certain cases," I couldn't resist adding, "putty, seemingly—"

"Here we go," she declared heavily, cutting me off. "Here we go!"

"Come back!" I cried, stretching my arms after her. "Come back, for pity's sake! I'm not joking, Bel. What I am about to tell you could be of the utmost importance to both of us!"

She paused in the doorway, then with a slight, acidic nod of the head, coolly bade me continue.

I am not by nature a superstitious man, and the next day I wondered if the kidney beans were to blame for the wild thoughts riding roughshod through my mind that night. Looking back on it now, though, I can see that I was part right, at least: that the coming of Frank did mark the beginning of our downfall—although each of us had many, many contributions of our own to make. "The Golem does not think for itself," I told Bel. "It is an automaton, animated by mystical powers—usually malevolent, it has to be said."

"Charles, it's late. Have you a point to this, other than pretending that the reason you don't like Frank isn't that you're a snob and a sociopath but because he's some kind of a mystical being sent to corrupt me?"

"I know it sounds outlandish," I said. "But I don't know how else to explain this sense of *foreboding*. None of your boyfriends ever made my skin actually crawl before." I shuddered, imagining the dark slab of Frank driving his van down crepuscular suburban streets, eyes gleaming emptily as he awaited the call from his master . . .

Bel's shoulders slumped. "Then it appears we are at an impasse."

"Almost literally," I said, picturing Frank moonlighting as a roadblock or a small dam.

Bel sighed and sank wearily onto the foot of the bed. "Charles," she said, "it's quite obvious that in Mother's absence the power has gone to

your head. I don't know what's going to come of it, or if there's anything I can do about it. But I know that I can't go on like this. We have to sort something out if we're going to keep living here with any semblance of normality. So though I do this with a bad conscience, I propose we make a pact."

"A pact?"

"A pact." She rubbed her eyes with the edge of her hand. "If you let this relationship take its course, without any more complaining or allusions to Jewish mythology, I hereby promise that if—*if*—Frank and I then break up, I'll—I'll stay in for three months before seeing anyone else. How's that?"

"That sounds very cynical, Bel," I said, surprised. "I mean, I just want you to be happy."

"Charles, just tell me what it will take to get you to leave me alone."

"Hmm," I said. Cynical it might have been, but I was rather taken with the novelty of this arrangement. Usually my arguments with Bel ended in her hurling something breakable at me. The sad truth was that she was going to see this fellow whether I liked it or not. At least this way I would be offered some kind of recompense—something, for instance, that under normal circumstances she would never be persuaded to do . . .

"All right," I said slowly. "Three months, and . . ."

Her eyes narrowed. *"And?"*

"And you also have to introduce me to that friend of yours. That Laura Treston."

"Laura Treston?" Bel repeated disgustedly. "She's not my friend, I haven't spoken to her in— Wait a minute, what made you suddenly think of *her*, anyway?" I made an indistinct coughing noise and smoothed some bumps out of the eiderdown. Bel groaned and tugged her hair. "Oh, Charles, you haven't been going through my old yearbooks again, have you?"

"I had to check something," I mumbled.

"I wish you wouldn't do that, it's creepy and morbid, those photographs are from four years ago at least, those girls are practically still *children* . . ."

"Be that as it may," I said gruffly.

"I mean, none of them looks the same now. A couple are *dead*, even."

"Coming back to the matter at hand," I said.

Bel groaned again. "Don't make me call her, Charles. She's so *boring*. The last time I talked to her I practically had to be drip-fed espresso for the rest of the week."

"Those are my terms," I said. "Take them or leave them."

She surrendered. "Fine," she said. "Fine. I'll call her tomorrow, and you'll promise to leave Frank and me alone. Promise?"

"Where is he now?" I sat up. "I hope he's in the spare room, Bel."

"Starting now."

"All right, all right, I promise." I stretched out my hand; she shook it, and the pact was sealed. She went off yawning to her room, and I laid down my head, thoughts awhirl like galaxies.

Bel's yearbooks had been a secret vice of mine since my girlless schooldays, when I'd spirit them away from the pile under her bed and bring them in to show my classmates and be hailed as a hero for the day. We would gather behind the cricket pavilion and huddle round in the glow of the pages: boggling at the sheer number of faces and names and possibilities, rating every single girl out of ten, speculating on their sexual proclivities, imagining lights-out in the dorms and the pillow fights that, if we knew anything about girls, must surely ensue . . . And before long a silence would fall, as each of us drifted off into his own private reverie—lost in the photograph, this seeming Elysium where our feminine counterparts dwelled beaming or scowling in black-and-white rows, distant and unknown to us as stars.

And that was where I first encountered her—one summer's day when, with nothing to do, I had stolen into Bel's bedroom on an ongoing and fruitless quest for her diary and instead found the new yearbook, and sitting on the bed cast my eye over the rank-and-file of twelve-year-olds, until suddenly I stopped and caught my breath; and my lust gave way to something purer, translucent and doomed as a wish. Those eyes, that mouth, the thrilling glimpse of throat through the school blouse; that array of tresses—hazel or blond, it was hard to tell—that hung so magnificently still . . . With a strange sense of destiny

I'd traced through the block of names at the bottom of the page—Audrey Courtenay, Bunty Chopin, Dubois Shaughnessy—until I arrived at hers: Laura, Laura Treston.

Ever since then, although the fates had conspired to keep us from meeting, I had followed her progress in the yearbooks, each one bringing a new metamorphosis; in the pillow fights of my dreams, it was the throw cushions of her breasts more than any others that shook and resounded with the light thump of feathers. Even now, years after school had ended and she had gone I knew not where, she lived on in my heart like a hologram. The Patsy Olés of this world could come and go; this, I felt sure, was to be my grand love story.

Bel herself never appeared in the class photographs, nor in any other photographs for that matter. She'd always been sensitive about her looks; whenever photos came back from the chemist after a family occasion she would invariably grab them first, and look through them compulsively, and put them down disappointed two minutes later, saying sadly, "I look like *that*? Why didn't someone *tell* me . . ." I never understood what she got in such a fuss about, because even then you could tell she would be pretty—but the girl in the pictures evidently didn't match up to the girl she was in her imagination, and she began to dread them, these moments that didn't die away but came back to haunt her in all their objective, inescapable truth. So, at the age of twelve, she'd decided she would simply no longer allow herself to be photographed. In school she'd engineered ways to get out of it, coming down with ever more extravagant ailments on Photograph Day (the nuns who taught her were old and doddery and always fell for her painted-on measles, lesions, yellow fever). In family portraits, she'd feature as a blank space, a decentering, inexplicable inch of room furnishings beside Mother, Father, and me. To this day, the moment a camera appeared, Bel seemed to vanish into thin air.

I was too excited to get back to sleep, and for an hour I lay there happily considering my new life with Laura. But as the night wore on the excitement curdled, and I began to be tormented by doubts. That everything should fall into place this way: suddenly it seemed too neat, too easy. Should I have turned down the pact? Had I sold Bel down the river? And then I thought I heard noises, and I couldn't reassure myself that it wasn't him, stalking deadly through the halls and corridors, making sure all was quiet before beginning his maleficent enterprise.

Chiding myself, I put on my slippers and went out to the landing. But all was silent, save the distant clanks and rumblings the house made in its sleep, and somewhere a clock ticking to itself. There was no one in the bathroom, although there was an unfamiliar stench. I drew the curtains in Mother's bedroom, then went to the door of Father's study. And there I paused, seized, as I turned the handle, by memories, as if they had been waiting there coiled inside the metal. They were from when I was very small, before he started locking the door, and I would come to see him with a glass of milk or a snail or my homework (*norway has alot of fjords, nobody does much there*) and find him brooding in the recesses of his enormous chair; how the room had seemed enchanted, with its vertiginous walls of arcane books and ledgers, the murky carpet that he wouldn't let Mother change, the obsequious plaster head waiting hopefully on its plinth—the room like an alchemist's lair, that both was and wasn't part of the house, where Father both was and wasn't with us . . .

"What's this about, Dad, *bones?*"

"*Cheek*bones, Charles, see some people don't really have 'em, and these colors—"

"And what's this?"

"Ah, well, that's a chemical formula, is what that's called, this fellow here's a stearate radical and— No, don't touch that, Charles—"

"Oops, sorry."

"Doesn't matter. Look, there's Mother out in the garden, I wonder if she needs a hand," steering me gently but firmly out the door . . .

Nothing in the room had been touched since his death. Everything was as he had left it, as if he'd just stepped out and would be returning momentarily: the vials of dyes and tinctures, the color charts and cross sections; the desk overflowing with magazine cuttings of tempestuous models in hair and dresses already passed out of fashion, like spirits that had been called into being for that moment alone, sprung like flames from shadows before disappearing back to that essential realm where it was forever 1996. The only addition was the portrait that Mother had installed—opposite the window, so that he could continue to enjoy the grounds and gardens, this empire he had built from nothing. Or not quite nothing; our family traced its lineage back to the first Norman conquerors, although some regrettable dalliances with the local peasantry over the centuries had somewhat thinned the bloodline, perhaps accounting for an occasional lassitude in judgment such as exhibited by my sister. Standing in the moonlight, leaning back with my arms rigid against the desk, I studied the aquiline nose, the thinly smiling lips, the ruddy cheeks. It had been painted posthumously, from photographs, but the picture really captured the spirit of my father, a man devoted to life in his own inspiring if inexplicable way.

I'd almost forgotten why I came in at all when by chance I spotted something unusual. Two red dents in a velvet square: two pieces of Father's coin collection mysteriously absent. Frank! So that was his game—start slow, no one will notice, until the whole house was cleaned out! I pictured him at one of those vile suburban pubs, sitting at a faux-marble tabletop, drinking a fizzing lager with his fence, satellite television blaring above them as they laughed and clinked glasses in their porkpie hats. Now from downstairs came the sound of a cupboard opening. In a fury I rolled up my pajama sleeves. Just let me catch him in a fresh act of thievery, I would settle his hash for him, Golem or no!

I padded softly down the stairs. I took the poker from the drawing room, then saw a faint glisten of light along the wooden floorboards of the hall; I whirled about in the eye of the sweeping staircase, glancing from one shut door to the other, and then a noise! I pounced, poker high, through the scullery door—and checked myself just in time, so that Mrs. P. was dealt only a glancing blow, although unfortunately enough to bring the silver tray she was carrying crashing to the floor.

"Young Master Charles!" she cried. "You are giving me the heart failure!"

"Oh, yes, sorry Mrs. P., didn't think you'd be about this late—"

"Yes," she faltered, "I am—I am making the breakfast . . ."

I picked up a tender sliver of pheasant from the floor. Morsels of roast potato clung to it alluringly. Making breakfast at three in the morning? And no ordinary breakfast either—on top of the pheasant, or rather beside it on the floor, was a heavenly looking soufflé and a bottle of rather fine Armagnac. It looked like someone was in the running for a first-class breakfast in bed. And there could be little doubt as to who that someone would be—the poor thing was still upset about the kidney bean debacle; indeed, now that I looked at her properly, I could see the rings that worry and tiredness had left on her simple rustic face.

She protested, but I would not hear of her making another breakfast at this hour; I told her to forget about the kidney beans and go directly to bed as soon as she had cleaned up the floor.

She bowed gratefully, and I left the room, marveling at her diligence even if increasingly concerned about her mental stability—I mean to say, pheasant for breakfast? In all the excitement, the Frank conundrum went clean out of my head; and it wasn't until some time later that I noticed the disappearance of the ottoman, and the ornamental teapot.

CHAPTER TWO

Perhaps it might seem that Bel had a point, about me not having a job, I mean. To the casual observer it may have looked like I was living a life of indolence, compared to the noisy industry with which the city to the north was ripping itself to pieces. It was true that, after a brief but regrettable entanglement with Higher Learning, I had fairly much confined my activities to the house and its environs. The simple fact of it was that I was happy there, and as I didn't have any skills to speak of, or gifts to impart, I didn't see why I ought to burden the world with my presence. It was not true, however, to say that I did *nothing*. I had several projects of my own to keep busy with, such as composing, and supervising the construction of the Folly. I saw myself as reviving a certain mode of life, a mode that had been almost lost: the contemplative life of the country gentleman, in harmony with his status and history. In Renaissance times they had called it *sprezzatura*. The idea was to do whatever one did with grace, to imbue one's every action with beauty, while at the same time making it look quite effortless. Thus, if one were to work at, say, law, one should raise it to the level of an art; if one were to laze, then one must laze beautifully. This, they said, was the true meaning of being an aristocrat. I had explained it several times to Bel, but she didn't seem to get it.

Our house was called Amaurot. It was situated in Killiney, some ten miles outside of Dublin, a shady province of overhanging branches, narrow winding roads, and sea air. Most of the houses had been built in the nineteenth century by magistrates, viceroys, military and navy men; in recent years, however, the area had become something of a tax haven for foreign racing-car drivers and *soi-disant* musicians. But it still possessed a sequestered elegance, an arboreal hush: I would not have lived anywhere else. On bright mornings I might take a walk up to Killiney Hill, climbing mossy steps under canopies of ash and sycamore; at the top stood the Obelisk, a monument to the kindness of the landed gentry to the local peasants during the famine year of 1741, from where you could look out over the half-hidden rooftops to the blue mountains and the golden sickle of the beach. Beside it was a little ziggurat, and the legend was that if you ran around each level of it seven times your wish would come true. But neither Bel nor I had ever managed to make it to the top; and even if we had, we would have been too dizzy to wish.

Amaurot was big and hundreds of years old, and it seemed to me while Bel and I were growing up that as long as we were there nothing bad could ever happen to us; the world outside could go up in flames and we would continue to play, safe in the shadow of the high stone walls. As far as we were concerned, Amaurot *was* the world—and it belonged to us, like the waves belonged to the sea, or certain shades of blue to the sky.

The house was set on a promontory, bordered on two sides, at the bottom of steep hills, by the sea. At every hour of the day you could hear it whispering or roaring, slipping from jade to amethyst to gray to deepest black; I loved it as the companion to my thoughts and the ear to which I disclosed my desires. A long avenue swept proudly over the lawns back to the road; ancient trees rubbed shoulders with saplings and wildflowers along the perimeter. To the rear of the house were the vegetable garden, which had gone to seed rather in recent years, the apple and cherry trees, and a small rivulet that bore frogs down to the sea. This was where Bel and I had spent most of our childhood, in the long grass and pine needles.

Bel had been a recalcitrant playmate. She went through long periods of not talking to anyone; instead she'd read, for days on end, her bare legs dangling from the windowsill. But she had a gift for invention, and on days when she jumped down from the ledge to join me in my stick fort, all of the fabulous ideas that she nursed over her books came bubbling out as complex adventures which I had to struggle to keep up with.

She liked to read about Russia, and Amaurot often doubled as the Winter Palace. Sometimes we would be orphaned children of the czar, fleeing the clutches of the evil Revolution, crossing invisible wastes on phantom troikas; sometimes she would be the diffident, entrancing princess and I the dashing suitor trying, with difficulty, to win her over. I would be called Karl, and Bel, Tanya, after the heroine of Pushkin's *Eugene Onegin*, which she had fallen in love with at the age of eight. (In fact, even when the toys had been put away forever and the games forgotten, she hung on to this name: to her friends at school, she was Tanya until well into her teens. "Christabel" had been Father's idea, after a Coleridge poem—a murky and rather depressing thing about nymphs and vampires, which breaks off abruptly at a point of confused identities and general malaise. She couldn't stand it. "It's not just the fact that nobody can *spell* it," she would fulminate periodically, "but he never even got around to writing the happy ending. I mean, couldn't they have named me after a poem that someone had actually *finished*, would that have been too much?" Eventually, "Bel" was arrived at as a sort of compromise, and Father became the only person to call her by her full name.)

Mother thought she might be a genius; I overheard her talking to Father about it sometimes. "The way she reads!" she'd say. "The library is looking positively bare, she's smuggled off so many books."

"I was thinking perhaps we should get a billiard table for it," Father said.

"And such an imagination!" she went on. "The things she comes out with, really—"

"Hmm . . . You don't think she might be a bit overimaginative, do you? She does seem to spend an awful lot of time in this dreamworld of hers."

"That's a sign of intelligence, Ralph. That girl will go places, believe me."

"Hey, Your Highness," I'd say to Bel, listening in on the windowsill, "escaping from these sorfs is making me hungry, I think there are apples in yonder wood, yonder . . ."

"You can't say 'Hey' to a princess, Charles," jumping down, "and it's *serfs*, not *sorfs* . . . ," and we'd steal through the gap in the hedge to Old Man Thompson's garden and throw sticks up into the branches, until apples began to thud around us and, inevitably, Olivier, his sinister German manservant, appeared on the veranda: "Herr Zompson! Zey are scrumpfing our apfeln!"

Old Man Thompson would come hobbling out, waving his cane, yelling, "After 'em, Olivier! After 'em!" and we'd shriek and run away as Olivier gave chase—a spindly black spider in his tight PVC suit—and burst back through the gap just in time, Old Man Thompson howling from the other side, "Bloody children, I'm going to call your father up, you bloody . . ."

I don't know if he ever did call Father up; I don't know that it would have done him much good anyway. Father could be a difficult man to get through to. He was full of unfulfilled romanticism and willful, unspoken delusions; he spent long hours at the office or in his study, and only the husk of him was brought home to us at the end of the day. Through the evening he'd maintain a weary, benevolent silence, and address us only to deliver abstract lectures, or ask disinterested questions about school. But sometimes he would take walks out through the trees to the hillside, to look down at the flying vapor of the sea, and bring Bel and me along with him; we would fidget restlessly while he gazed into the darkness, and then, just as we were wondering what the point of all this was, and how long we would have to stand there doing nothing while valuable television-watching time was being eaten up, he would turn to us and without introduction launch into a poem from memory, spooky verses about lonely lovers and capricious fairies, tricking specters and murmuring seas. And as our faces turned pale with not-understanding, and we tingled with the haunting, equivocal magic that crackled around the poems, he would chuckle out, "Yeats, children. Yeats would have liked to be up here with you and me, on a night like this." And before we could express our indifference as to the presence or otherwise of Yeats, he would be marching off again, back to the house.

Father had been a master cosmetician. In the skin of the human face he divined what a Renaissance master might have seen on a blank canvas: the possibility of a transcendent beauty. Though the Renaissance master painted to testify to God's greatness, while my father, one of those agnostics who spends his life doing battle with the God he doesn't believe in, worked more out of defiance, as if to say, *Where you have failed, I succeed; I can lift people up out of your squalid Creation.* He had worked with all the greats—Lancôme, Yves Saint Laurent, Givenchy, Chanel—inventing unguents, balms, and lotions to retard the ravages of the sun, to preserve the black sparkle of mascara from rain and tears, to maintain the bloody red kiss of the mouth through a thousand bloody red kisses; to soothe, to rejuvenate, to enhance and restore, in short an act of such great love for the human race that, through his cosmetics, the years could be rolled back and the tale of anyone's life—written always in lines, scars, desiccation, no matter what they say about the beauty of wisdom and life's rich tapestry—could be untold.

His death was more than two years ago now; it followed a long, wasting illness which had caused him great suffering. In his last days he had faltered badly. His mind had slipped, and he misused his art. He tried to disguise the desecration the disease had left, and thus, by his thinking, counteract it. "There's no escaping it," he'd been fond of telling us when he was well, "the way you look defines who you are. You might argue for your soul, or your heart, but everyone else in the world will judge you on your big nose or your weak chin. Six billion people could be wrong, but you'll never get them to admit it." And so the makeup was caked on with trembling fingers, layer upon layer; he lay in the half darkness like a sad, syphilitic Pierrot, his gaunt cheeks stained concavely with rouge. For a time the house teetered on the verge of becoming some kind of hospice *Cage aux Folles*, everyone flapping about in hysterics and occasionally French accents. It was a mercy when he died and we could restore him in our memories to what he had been before all this mortal vaudeville. I can still hear his last words to me, with a crumbling, crooked finger beckoning me out of the shadows to kneel at his side: "Son . . . the world is cruel," he'd whispered. "Always . . . moisturize . . ."

Although before his death Father's was the mood that generally prevailed in the house—a sort of brittle otherworldliness, an ethereally edged detachment, as though saying to the world, "We will indulge you for the moment, but bear in mind, please, that as soon as Father's work is done, we will leave you"—Mother had always been the steelier of the pair, strict about correct behavior and what she called "breeding." She knew just about everyone there was to know and was forever flying about to lunches and gallery openings and book launches and dinner parties, with or without Father in tow. In later years especially she became more and more independent of him, and ran the show in the house as he receded from it.

Shortly after his death, however, she too began to disintegrate. It happened gradually but unmistakably, a slow, irresistible shutting-down, until eventually she wouldn't go out at all, or even take telephone calls. At the same time she exhibited a sunniness that was quite out of character. Bel and I constantly found ourselves cornered in silly, chatty, endless conversations with her. She'd rabbit away to us with gossip about the neighbors or vague plans to take a holiday or work that needed doing round the house—whatever came into her head, like a kind of domestic Reuters, tickering constantly in her armchair in the drawing room. It was a side of her that we hadn't known existed, that (we presumed) used to be bounced off Father and now came babbling through to us. We didn't know quite how to respond, and it wasn't even clear that she was listening when we did, because she was drinking all the time, martinis for breakfast and whiskey sours to see in the evenings, drinking and talking, talking and drinking. Finally, one night, the situation came to a head.

Over the years, she and Bel had developed quite a fiery relationship, which could be ignited by the most trivial things. I didn't know what lay at the heart of it, but I had my suspicions. Before we were born, Mother and Father had been quite the stars in Dublin dramatic circles—never professionally, of course, but they were certainly well known—and now some kind of showbiz rivalry seemed to have arisen between Mother and Bel. It was funny, because for the first years, when Bel was still in school, Mother had been very encouraging about her acting ambitions. Then, suddenly, she changed. Suddenly—almost overnight—

she seemed to resent them; suddenly she was full of needling opinions and advice, far more than Bel was happy with. "Every great actress has an inner core, on which all her performances are hung," she'd say—most of her pronouncements were along these metaphysical lines. "Your trouble, Bel, is that you have still to find your inner core."

That, I conjectured, was the source of the bad feeling; that was how it was even before Father got sick. In the months that followed his death, it deteriorated to the point where they could create a fight out of almost anything. Mother would accuse Bel of forgetting things, or neglecting things, of selfishness, narcissism, disloyalty, deceit. At first, Bel was so surprised that she simply took it; but after a while, when everything she did incurred a criticism from above, she began to retaliate. Bel's practice, when she was hurt, was to shout and scream abuse of every kind until whoever it was went away; the fights got ugly very quickly. One night about six months ago, I arrived home to find Bel standing in the hallway with a face quite drained of color. Her hands were shaking; Mother was nowhere in sight. She refused to tell me what had happened. All she would say was that, after a protracted discussion, Mother had agreed that she wasn't herself, and that perhaps she needed some time on her own to think. The black car that had passed me in the driveway belonged to the nice people from the Cedars, taking her away for an indefinite stay.

Which is how the house came to be under my care, and whatever Bel said, I had to work hard to keep its inscrutable momentum, to tie the disparate elements together in some semblance of order—Mrs. P.'s wandering mind, Bel's pathological insistence on controlling every aspect of her life, the eccentricities or criminal tendencies of whoever she was seeing at the time, and the house itself, the centuries of stonework and timber, that had its own whims and bad moods to be coaxed through. It was I who kept it all ticking, who stayed in all day just to center things a little, give them a bit of focus; it was a tough job, and no one thanked me for it. I couldn't be expected to get things right all the time, either; that is, what happened afterward wasn't entirely my fault, whatever they tell you.

—

I ROSE EARLY the next morning, in spite of all the excitement the night before. The vet was coming to look at the peacocks, which had developed an infestation of some kind, and I had to let him into the garage. The peacocks were my responsibility. Father had looked after them when he was alive—he was the only one who actually liked them—and they had been somewhat neglected since. I had had a peacock flap built into the door of the garage where they lived, so they could come and go as they pleased, and other than embarrassing visits from the vet, we didn't have much to do with each other most of the time. I felt a little guilty about this, but really it was their own fault: They were the most unrewarding creatures, bone-stupid and filthy, with little sense of loyalty or gratitude, and they got infestations at the drop of a hat if they weren't paid constant attention.

The vet examined each bird and doused them with some sort of powder; then as usual he started getting cross about their living conditions and exhorting me to change their sawdust more frequently to avoid future infections, et cetera. "And *feed* them, Mr. Hythloday, they're *animals*, they need to eat every day, not just when you remember—"

"Yes, yes," I said; it was a little early for exhortations, and frankly I think we were all secretly hoping that they would die off quickly and we would be rid of them. I can't think of any other reason that I should have been left in charge of them, apart from the practical one that the garage was the only area of the house to which Mrs. P. did not have a key. Even Mother found the peacocks a little over the top, and Bel reserved a special loathing for them—all her Drama friends had turned Marxist in their sophister year at Trinity, and they gave her a fearful time about them.

The reason Mrs. P. didn't have a key was that the peacocks shared the garage with what was probably the most beloved of Father's *objets:* a 1930 Mercedes, a pristine, bottle green Grand Prix racer. It had been a gift from the German ambassador, who lived nearby; Father had developed a special hypoallergenic balm for his daughter, who suffered terrible eczema. He'd never driven the car—in fact, none of us was quite sure whether it could actually be driven—but he'd cleaned it obsessively every Sunday afternoon, buffing vigorously with chamois and beeswax for hours on end. When he was finished, he would stand arms folded at the garage door, watching the light spill over the metal as behind him the sun sank below the trees; and these liminal moments, reflecting on the stationary Mercedes, were among the few times when you could say with any degree of certainty that my father looked genuinely happy.

After the vet had gone I wandered into the kitchen, where Mrs. P. was scooping scrambled eggs onto two plates of soda bread and smoked salmon.

"He's still here, then," I said.

"Yes, Master Charles, you must hide from your sister, she is very, very busy."

"Busy, what's she busy about?"

"I don't know, she get up early too, say where is my scrambled eggs please, I must prepare—"

"Prepare for what?"

"I don't know, Master Charles, but she is very—how you say—stress?"

"Just a second, Mrs. P.—who owns those pants?"

"Pants, Master Charles? I see no pants."

"There, poking out of that basket." How could she not see them? They were the most enormous underpants I had ever seen.

"Oh, yes, I see, those pants."

"They're not Frank's, are they?" I didn't like the idea of Frank's delicates mixing it with mine.

Mrs. P. rubbed her chin slowly. "No, Master Charles, they are a . . . a present."

"A present?"

"Yes, Master Charles"—she nodded—"a present for you, I buy."

Surely this wasn't more penance for last night! Couldn't she just let it go? This was the sort of thing I meant earlier, about her seeming distracted; these pants, furthermore, could quite comfortably have fitted three or four Charleses in them. "That's a very touching gesture, Mrs. P., but really, I don't expect you to buy me presents. Anyhow, I already have plenty of underpants."

"Oh yes, Master Charles, but it's in shop, is special offer, I think only, ah, is bargain for Master Charles, but then I see, is too big—"

"Yes, well, not to worry, you can bring 'em back later, or something."

"Later, Master Charles, I bring them back to the shop."

"That sounds like the best plan, all right." I found myself speaking to thin air as she bustled away with the tray. "I mean, thanks anyway."

Whatever they were doing, Bel and Frank kept a low profile for much of the morning, and in keeping with the terms of the pact I refrained from investigating. Passing by her door at one point, however, I couldn't help but overhear Frank talking about a countess. I wondered what Frank was doing knocking about with countesses, and whether it was anyone I knew, and without meaning to eavesdrop, I lingered there momentarily. But the conversation soon turned to appearing in court, which seemed more in his line, so I continued on my way.

As a matter of fact, I was feeling unusually purposeful after my early start. I passed a fruitful hour at the piano working on the bridge for a song I was composing, entitled "I'm Sticking to You."

You may say that we're all through:
I'll tell you that I understand;
You can cry, and say goodbye,
But as you leave I'll take your hand—

For I know that you need to be free,
But I can't let go so easily,
A girl like you's a damn hard thing to leave,
So . . .

I'm sticking to you
Like gum on your shoe,
Like a cheap tattoo, like the Chinese flu,
Or a nasty cough
You just can't shake off—
Oh darling, I'm sticking to you.

That was merely a warm-up, however. The double bill I had fallen asleep during last night had reawoken an idea for a project. I returned to my room and searched amid the clutter under the davenport until I located an old shoe box. Inside, beneath a wasting elastic band, were pages and pages of biography, reviews, snatches of Hollywood gossip, photographs and stills—all of them relating to Gene Tierney, her life and work. I had been assembling these odds and ends for the longest time, without ever quite knowing why. There was something about her that set her apart, that seemed to speak to me. More than any of her contemporaries', her life seemed entwined with the actual, intangible stuff of cinema; every detail had the quality of a fairy tale, or its opposite. The more films I saw, the more cuttings I assembled, the more I felt this vague, nagging desire to do something for her—to write something or make something or at least to sort these fragments into some kind of sense.

She was seventeen when she was discovered—backstage on a Warner Bros. set, like a figment of Hollywood's imagination. She was on a guided tour of the studio with her mother, brother, and sister, one stop on a grand cross-country vacation they made that summer, driving eight thousand miles from their home in Fairfield, Connecticut, to California and back again (the girls brought so many clothes they had to hitch a trailer to their car). Here, on the set of *The Private Lives of Elizabeth and Essex*, starring Errol Flynn and Bette Davis, the director stopped shooting to come over to tell Gene she ought to be in pictures. It wasn't just a line: he sent her for a screen test right away, and the following day Warners offered her a contract.

Her father, when he heard the news, was not enthused. He had stayed in New York that summer to work. Howard Tierney was a powerful insurance agent, though, like everybody's, his fortunes had dipped in recent years. He didn't think much of Hollywood, and he thought even less of Warners' $150-a-week contract. In those days, young ladies of breeding—the Tierneys were society—were expected to finish school, marry a Yale boy, and live in Connecticut; any actorly tendencies were to be confined to the ball and the country club. But Gene was his favorite, and he told her that if after making her debut she still wanted to act, he would do everything in his power to help her find a job on the Broadway stage.

He was as good as his word. Every Wednesday, instead of going into the office, he and Gene caught the 8:15 train into the city to meet agents and producers. After bit parts here and there, she finally landed a part in a hit play, and Darryl F. Zanuck, the head of Twentieth Century–Fox, flew out to see her. He signed her up immediately. Her father brokered a deal with Fox worth five times what Warners had offered. He formed a company, the Belle-Tier Corporation (Gene's mother was called Belle), to represent and promote his daughter and to administer her future earnings.

Gene flew to Hollywood in 1939 on the maiden transcontinental flight; somebody gave her a plaque when she got off the plane. She was handed over to the Fox publicity people to be given the starlet buildup: to be photographed at nightclubs, by the pool, on the beach, to be interviewed and profiled while they thought about changing her name and decided what "type" she was—a Penny Singleton, a Deanna Durbin; it was important to look like somebody else. She began work on *The Return of Frank James*, with Henry Fonda; she spent night after night alone in the projection room after the shoot, watching films, trying to teach herself how to act.

I spent the next few hours going through my discontinuous notes, trying to put them in chronological order. Reading over them made me sad; perhaps everyone's life is sad when you know what will happen next. It seemed to me that in every atom of information—in every snippet of biography, in every publicity still—you could descry the whole trajectory of her life and the forces that would destroy her. Even when you went right back to the beginning, to when everything was full of promise and hope, they were there, like traps waiting to be sprung.

By twelve o'clock I was feeling quite fatigued. I put the notes back in the shoe box, pledging to return to them sooner rather than later, and went to see if Mrs. P. felt like rustling up some crumpets. On my way I passed Bel's door again, and happened to pause there, to get my bearings, so to speak—only to find them talking about exactly the same thing as earlier on. Frank was on about his countess again, saying that she was very wealthy, and then stopping and coughing for a while, and then saying that she was easygoing morally and had married a man who wasn't of noble birth, which seemed a bit rich coming from him. He appeared to have developed a speech impediment overnight; he stumbled over every second word and spoke in a maddening, leaden monotone. Bel got upset and started fretting about how she couldn't sleep. She kept calling Frank "Uncle," which I took to be some kind of odious pet name. She sounded odd, as if her voice were a borrowed dress that didn't quite fit right.

"Yes," Frank said. "Yes. You are quite right. It is dreadful. My God."

"Could you go a bit faster?" she said.

"Yes yes you're quite right it's—"

"Stop, Frank, maybe we should go back a bit—how about 'My dear little child'—"

"All right . . . you're not just a niece to me, you're an angel, you're—Bel, I can't understand a word this bollocks is sayin, is he tryin to ride her or what? Cos like if he's the uncle you wouldn't think he should be tryin to, like, give her lengths."

"Oh for God's sake," she said despairingly.

"Unless," he mumbled to himself, "he was one of them uncles that's just like married to her auntie, I s'pose then it'd be fair enough . . ."

"Look, it doesn't matter, Frank, you just have to *read* it— Oh, this is hopeless, I'm *never* going to get this right."

She was teaching him to read, that was what it was!

"Bel?"

"What?"

The poor thing sounded quite exhausted and it wasn't even lunchtime yet. Perhaps she was realizing that she'd bitten off more than she could chew.

"I reckon if you were my niece, I'd want to give you lengths."

There was a moment of outraged silence; I blushed at the door on her behalf.

"Give you a ride on the oul train, like . . ."

Oh, for shame! I was on the point of bursting in and rewarding his discourtesy with the back of my hand when—to my horror—I heard Bel burst into laughter: "Oh, you," she said, and there was a creaking of bedsprings. Suddenly I felt queasy; I beat a hasty retreat before things took a turn for the tactile.

"WHAT DO WE *know* about Mrs. P.?" I said next afternoon, laying my book down.

Across the table, Bel was crimping her eyelashes with some sort of metal contraption. "Hmm?" she said.

"I mean, she's been here with us for—what, two years? Three? And yet we don't *truly* know what makes her tick."

"You're not going off on one of your paranoid delusions," she said, inserting the top lashes of one eye between two steel prongs.

"No," I said impatiently. "I just think it odd that someone should live in one's house for so long and remain a veritable stranger, albeit a cherished and well-paid stranger. Do we—are we giving her enough attention? Should we be, you know, talking to her, and so forth?"

"What's brought this on?" Bel said curiously.

"Nothing," I said. "But everybody needs love, though."

She cackled unflatteringly. "Maybe you should have a bed-in?"

"Well, haven't you found her a little . . . unbalanced lately? Take the business with the kidney beans. She keeps making these bizarre gestures of atonement. Yesterday she bought me *pants.*"

"I don't think there's anything unbalanced about her wanting to make it up to you, Charles, except that it was entirely your fault, of course—"

"Yes, well, you didn't see the pants. Anyway, it's hardly appropriate, is it, buying underwear for one's employer—unless . . ." A terrible thought struck me. "Good God, Bel, you don't think she's developed some sort of obsession with me? I mean, she's not trying to seduce me, is she?"

"I'd say she probably knows all it takes is a half bottle of Jameson and a Wonderbra . . ."

"I'm being serious. There's other things. The other night—at a quite ungodly hour—I caught her making me breakfast. I can't fault her dedication, obviously, but she was preparing what looked like a full pheasant. Isn't that a little strange?"

She raised her eyebrows thoughtfully. "Not really. Not for you. Not when you remember your lobster breakfast phase, and your foie gras phase, and that *atrocious* Moroccan concoction—"

"Yes, yes . . . But lately I've been quite frugal. I take just a croissant and the cricket pages."

"Yes, but only because *lately* you've been hungover every morning. I do wish you'd curb your drinking, Charles, have you seen the wine cellar? Of course you have, silly question. But it looks like it's catering for a whole shedful of rakes, not just you."

"Well, better a rake than a hoe, as I always say. That's quite enough, anyway. Kindly return to your maquillage."

She made a face and began to dab her nose with a powder puff. Bel always took great care with her appearance: Most of her clothes came from charity shops, but her look—penniless Parisienne student circa 1968—was artfully constructed. I wondered how Frank prepared for a night out. One suspected that once he had hidden the bolts in his neck he was satisfied.

"I was talking about Mrs. P. I simply feel we ought to make more of an effort. She's getting on and she needs our support. Polite inquiries, suchlike. I daresay she's got a few rum stories from that place she's from, what is it, Bosnia?"

"I daresay."

"What's it like, Bosnia? Do you know anything about it?"

"For heaven's sake, Charles, it was only on the news for about three solid years—"

"Well, which one is it? Is it the one with the chaps with those funny hats?"

"I can't believe you. Don't you know anything about current affairs?"

"Hardly my cup of tea."

"Oh, *genocide* isn't your cup of tea, is it?" she said sarcastically, pulling a miniature pencil over her eyebrows. "One wonders whose cup of tea it is."

"Well, I don't recall *you* doing much about it," I retorted. "I don't recall *you* . . . collecting bottle tops, or—or writing stern letters to the UN."

"Collecting bottle tops," she said, reaching for an emery board. "The great humanitarian. That's priceless."

"Well, it seems to me," I objected, "that the only reason you know about these things is to lord it over me. In fact, it seems to me that that's the only reason anyone knows about these things, so they can act superior and have heated discussions in pubs and make everyone else feel guilty for not watching more television."

"You go and talk to Mrs. P. then"—Bel scowled—"and I'm sure she'll be delighted to share in your informed opinions. Maybe you can swap traditional recipes, you can give her kidney beans à la Charles—"

"So where's Frank bringing you tonight, then?" I said, as the gloves appeared to be off. "Badger baiting? Mud wrestling? Are you going to drink cans in a field?"

"The pact!" she cried, outraged. "The pact!"

"Habeas corpus," I countered. "The pact isn't sealed till you fulfill your half."

"I called her," she protested. "She gave me her work number and said she would be delighted to hear from you any time."

"Well, *that's* no use!" thumping my hands on the table. "You know I hate using the phone." In fact, I abhorred all modern gadgetry—*gadgets*, even the word had an ignoble ring to it. "Couldn't you call her back and tell her to come over here?"

"What are you, an invalid? I'm not your lackey."

Maybe Mrs. P. would call her—but no! The pact had not been honored, and I was going to make a stand. "The pact has not been honored," I told her, "and until it is, we remain in a state of war."

"War?"

"So I must insist on joining you tonight as chaperone."

"Charles," she warned, glaring at me through her black-frosted eyelashes.

"I insist."

"Every day you plumb new depths, do you know that?"

"Be that as it may," I replied peaceably. "So where are we going?"

"GO ON, ASK ME HOLE, you useless fucker!" Frank was shouting abuse at the top of his voice, between dips into a bag of coagulated chips. "Go on, you shitbag, run, for fuck's sake!"

I chuckled to myself. My hound, Jasper, had turned out to be a superb brute, and had left Ask Me Hole and the pack trailing in his wake.

Bel's choice, meanwhile, the insipidly named Piece of Lightning, seemed to have given up the ghost entirely.

Ascot it wasn't, but the proprietors of the dog track had made a brave effort to lift it above its inherent squalor. There was a well-lit bar with a long glass window from which one could look down on the action; mixed in with the luckless reprobates gambling away their welfare were several groups of normal people. Frank, however, had eschewed the bar as for "ponces," and dragged us out to shiver in the stands with red-eyed, desperate types as whippet-thin as the dogs to whom they had entrusted their fortunes. None of them was quite as terrifying as Frank himself, though, and I was oddly comforted by his presence. They all seemed to know him, anyway: throughout the races a litany of Mickers, Antos, and Farrellers approached to pay their respects—"All right, Francy, how's your wobbly bits?" they would say, or "Howya, Frankie, get up the yard, ya bollocks."

He seemed to have grown even larger in the open air; beside him Bel looked small and pinched, her eyes glowing sparely like cold blue moons. I don't know if she was still sulking because I'd insisted on coming along, although Frank didn't seem to mind, or if she was ashamed of me seeing him in his natural milieu, or if it was something else entirely, but she'd hardly spoken two words all night: she kept her face buried deep in her muffler and her eyes locked on the track. After asking her twice if she was all right, and offering her a chip, Frank had left her to her silence. We'd discovered I had a hitherto untapped gift for picking winners, and I had risen several notches in his estimation.

"Who'd you fancy for the next one?" he said respectfully, "Up the Duff or Gordon's Couscous?"

"Neither," I replied. "Look at them there in their pens. These are dogs whose spirits have been snuffed out. They might be fast, but neither of them has the self-belief to actually win. Take a look at Meet the Wife, on the other hand. Note the calm gait, the proud, lofty bearing. A regal dog. That's where I'd put my money. If you ask me, he's already won it."

"Right—here, Bel, you'll have a flutter, won't you?"

"I don't have any money," came the icy response.

"I'll spot you, come on."

"It's all right," she said flatly, not looking up.

"Ah, go on, look, I'll put a bet on for you. Meet the Wife is Charlie's tip, I'll put a fiver on him—"

"No!" she exclaimed, suddenly animated. "I don't want Charles's tip." She unfolded her track sheet and studied it, white-fingered in the frosty light of the floods. "I want to bet on this one. Number Four."

"An Evening of Long Goodbyes," Frank read over her shoulder. "I dunno, what d'you think, Charlie?"

"Well," I said evenhandedly, "they're nice odds if he's any good at all. Number Four, where is he anyway?"

We scanned the track. The trainers had brought the dogs out and were leading them up and down the grassy area in the middle; sleek coats gleamed, pink tongues quivered athletically as they went through their paces. "I don't see Number Four though—oh."

Number Four, wearing an unflattering chartreuse jacket, was sitting alone on the chewed-up grass, despondently licking his testicles. "Hmm, I don't know, Bel . . ."

"That's the one I'm betting on," Bel said adamantly.

"Would you not listen to Charlie, Bel, he always wins."

"You're here with me, not Charles, and anyway I thought you were going to spot me, why are you so concerned who I bet on?" Her jaw thrust out palely against the first flecks of rain blowing down and backward from the roof of the stand.

"It's just it has such a stupid name . . ."

"They all have stupid names, Charles."

A barrage of noise from the loudspeaker signaled that the race would be commencing shortly. The dogs were locked into their traps.

"Yes, but names are important, you have to pay attention to them." I said this with a curious certainty, for here at the dog track, I was finding my senses awakening to the resonances of seemingly superficial things, the intricate spectral machinery of Luck . . .

"Here, youse, the race is startin," Frank said. "I'll put a fiver on him anyway, all right?"

"I don't think it *is* a stupid name," Bel said, ignoring him. "I think it's romantic."

"It's a *dog*, that's why it's stupid. I mean, if it was a song or a book or something, that'd be different, but who on earth names their dog An Evening of Long Goodbyes?"

"Ponces," Frank chipped in. "You get some posh benders down here fancyin themselves as trainers, as a hobby, like, prob'ly cos they can't afford a horse. Their dogs are always crap."

"Exactly. There's a time and a place, Bel. Not everything can be theater—"

"Why not?" she said, coloring. "Anyway, there's more to it than winning."

"Depends who's paying for it," I returned.

Frank sighed and shrugged and went off to the plate-glass hatch to place the bets—perhaps with a forlorn glance over to the far side of the stand, where his down-at-heel pals merrily drank their cans—leaving us to stare furiously into the thickening sheets of rain, starting as the gun went off and the electric rabbit began another lonely circuit . . .

After Meet the Wife's storming victory, Frank took us to a local inn to celebrate. Bel's mood improved once we had left the track. None of us mentioned An Evening of Long Goodbyes, whose race had been so catastrophic that, by the end, neither Frank nor I could summon the will to gloat. He had begun badly, getting his head stuck in the gate and having to be extricated by the stewards, and continued with a series of humiliating and distinctly uncanine trips and stumbles, disgracing himself beyond redemption in the third lap, when his muzzle came off and, to the boos of the crowd, he abandoned the race to leap over the hoardings and snatch a hot dog from the hand of a small boy.

The pub was seedy and glum and my white wine arrived in a diminutive bottle with a screw-off lid. My sister joined Frank in a conciliatory Guinness, and as they clinked glasses I looked about at my fellow drinkers. Was I the only one in evening wear? These chaps were a uniformly rough-looking lot, and many of them, I realized, were directing unfriendly stares at me.

"Quite an ambience, this place," I laughed nervously.

"We come here a good bit," Frank told me, "don't we, Bel?"

"That's right," Bel looking me straight in the eye. "It's our favorite pub."

I sighed inwardly; I came up against this kind of attitude quite often in my dealings with girls in general, and Bel in particular. They love to flirt with transgression; give them a lout who breaks the odd window and they will pull each other's hair out for him—without ever diluting or moderating their own careful delicacy, needless to say. Sometimes Bel reminded me of an E. M. Forster heroine, traipsing about the jungle in a ball gown, with a full set of china and embroidering work for the evenings. What was she looking for, I wondered, in her lonely dallyings outside her own realm, while keeping that same realm locked tightly up inside her.

"Well, I like it here too," I said to annoy her. "We should do this more often. I like the company of the working man. Good, honest folk, enjoying their time for reflection after a hard week in the jar factory."

"You always get a deadly scrap in here," Frank said. "Last week me and me mate, right, saw these two scumbags we know, and we go up to them, straight in with the dujj, and bop! I loaf one of them, and then I see his mate's got me mate on the ground and he's stampin on his head, so I grab this bottle, and smash, right between the fuckin eyes. The both of them fuckin legged it."

I absorbed this silently.

"I was just laughin," Frank added.

"Aha," I said.

"That's one of the cunts there," he said, raising his voice. "See that cunt sittin at the bar? The poxy little fuck? That's one of the cunts we done."

The cunt in question was a short man with a crew cut and a long fresh scar down his jaw. As Frank spoke he turned his head slowly in our direction. An interchange of baleful stares ensued. Caught in the middle, I rubbed my nose and coughed and was beginning to hyperventilate when, mercifully, the cunt bowed his head. Frank snorted victoriously. Bel let out a worried coo.

"Ah, don't mind him," Frank assured her. "Sure he's only a cunt. Anyway if there was any bother you'd have Charlie and me to protect you, wouldn't you?"

"Ha ha," I said, but this was my cue to go. "Look, I forgot, I have to, um . . ."

"See a man about a dog?" Frank chortled, the meaning of which escaped me; Bel smirked triumphantly as I put on my topcoat and hastened outside in a cold sweat to hail a cab.

It was a long ride back, and at the door I bade farewell to a sizable portion of my winnings. But I didn't care, it was such a relief to be home. I closed the door and leaned back against it thankfully. The rich aroma of cooking floated up to me, and I went into the kitchen, where Mrs. P. was just that minute taking a tray of cinnamon buns out of the oven, piping hot with the sugar frosting still sizzling on their golden tops. My entrance took her by surprise—in fact she practically jumped out of her skin, only this time the tray acted as ballast.

"Buns," I said, ignoring this. "I'll just pinch one, if I may—"

"Hmm yes," she recovered in time to swerve nimbly away, moving the tray just out of my reach, "but, Master Charles, they are for your dear mother in hospital."

"She won't mind," I said, deftly stepping around to her tray side.

She reversed. "Now, Charles, please to think of your poor mother."

"Look, give me a bun," I said bluntly.

Pursing her lips, she proffered the tray. Tearing off a mouthful of delicious steaming sponge, I remembered my plan to save Mrs. P.'s failing mental health through love. "So," I said, chewing and swallowing, "what's it like in that place, anyway?"

"What?" she said.

"You know, where you're from," I said, taking another bun. They really were very good. She hadn't made cinnamon buns in ages.

"Well . . ." She frowned. "It was very nice, yes. When I was a little girl. Now, of course, there are many troubles."

"But it was nice when you were little, eh?" I said.

She put the buns on the counter behind her and folded her arms meditatively. "Oh yes," she said, and her expression quite changed, making her look twenty years younger, her amber eyes taking on a happy, nostalgic glaze not unlike two frosted cinnamon buns. "When I was little, we lived in the country. My father was a painter, and the house is filled always with the loveliest colors. Each day my sister and I bring wildflowers home for him to paint—"

"Yes, yes," I said, as this line of questioning didn't show much promise. "But it's in a bad way now, is it? Lots of explosions, houses burning down, sort of thing? Like on the news?"

"Now," frowning down at the ground, "everything is changed. Like you cannot even think. The explosion may stop, the burning, but . . . Like this plate," she picked up one of Mother's Wedgwood dinner set from the dresser and traced her finger around the intricate design on the rim, "if I drop, is gone. Smash up into little pieces. You can glue it together, but the pattern, that leads into itself at every place, is still broken, disappears forever. Houses and families, friends who talk at the market, children who sing and shout in the street, men who build, eat sandwiches in sunshine, look at pretty girls—all pattern lost and disappear like—"

"Well don't break the plate," I said hurriedly, snatching it from her upheld hand. Midnight breakfasts were one thing, but willful plate breaking was another matter entirely. Really the woman seemed quite disturbed. Possibly I ought to call the chap at the Cedars to come and have a look at her. "What about your family?" I said, attempting to lead her on to more peaceful topics that might be less of a threat to the crockery. "What about them?"

She was about to reply but halted and regarded me curiously. "Why do you ask me this?"

"No reason. Just, you know, I don't know much about you. Seems odd, doesn't it? I mean you live here—"

"Many, many questions," she said.

"Well, global village, you know, hands across the sea, what—"

She didn't understand. "Many questions," she mused to herself, then looking back at me said in an unfamiliar, bitter tone, "In Yugoslavia, men come with questions. Is not good, when they come."

So I was the secret police now, was I? "Look," I said, "you can just answer the question, or not. Tell me about your wretched family or don't. I don't care. I'm just trying to be nice. I know all about it already. I watch the news."

"You want to know about my family?" she shouted angrily. "Fine. Five years ago, my husband is architect, I give the legal aid, we have two sons in university and a girl who wants to be famous actress. Now there is nothing. House gone, money, we hide and we run—" She covered her face with her apron. Little cotton ducklings danced up and down where her nose had been.

I hadn't even known she had children. "Where are they?" I asked, as gently as I could.

"—and now I cook you buns!" Mrs. P. sobbed, and ran out of the room.

What could I do? I couldn't follow her; she was the help, after all; her personal life wasn't really any of my business. Possibly paying attention to Mrs. P. hadn't been such a good idea after all. We truly didn't know the first thing about her—she'd just turned up one day, responding to an advertisement that had, we discovered subsequently, mysteriously appeared in the window of the local newsagent. As it happened, though, Mother had been thinking of getting a new maid, the last one, a fetching little French au pair, having left some months before following a misunderstanding with Pongo McGurks at our Christmas party— perfectly innocent, of course, but you know au pairs. And so Mrs. P. had joined the household. By then Father was already very sick, and no one had ever got around to asking her about her past. It hadn't occurred to me until now that she might have preferred it that way.

Pensively I ate another bun, then took the tray up to Father's study. I ate tentatively; one could no longer be sure of the cooking's soundness, that was the thing. They tasted fine, but who knew what madness might throw into the mixing bowl? And if not now, what of breakfast tomorrow? Elevenses? Lunch? Tea? Dinner? Supper? And the day after that, the deadly game of Russian roulette would continue, with each spoonful another spin of the chamber . . .

Deciding a glass or two of wine might steady my nerves, I went back downstairs to the cellar. Hmm. I could see what Bel meant. The stocks really had taken a beating recently. Was it possible that I could have put away this amount on my own? Or could it be that I was getting help from another quarter? I clenched my fists and swore. Frank! I could just see him, laughing soundlessly in the back of his rusty white van, rocking back and forth as he swigged from the neck of a bottle of Marsanne. Or at the dog track, the green rim poking from the collar of his windcheater as he frittered away the proceeds from our ottoman. Or—a new thought struck me. Maybe it wasn't Frank at all! Maybe Mrs. P. had drunk the wine! Maybe she was a Secret Drinker, like that laundrywoman of Boyd Snooks's he'd found asleep in the dog basket! Wouldn't that explain why she was acting so strangely? Unless of course it was only a symptom of her collapse . . . Great Scott, we were living in a time bomb!

I grabbed a soothing premier cru and returned to the study. There was only the ghost of a moon outside, but I left the light off. I sat at the desk, poured a glass, and raised it to Father's portrait—just in case there might be some vestige of his spirit still hanging around among the toxic oils and leads that could give me a sign, point the way out of my quandary. But the glass was filled and emptied until there was nothing left, and I remained in the dark.

I turned to the window and looked out at the Folly, half-hidden by night. The Folly was my idea; it had occurred to me on one of my strolls around the grounds that we hadn't got one, and as no one else seemed to be doing anything about it, I had called in the builders. That was almost a year ago, but the tower, to be the glory of our estate, was still nowhere near finished. The builders hadn't been in all week; possibly they were on strike, they were always on strike for one reason or another. Unlike most builders one hears of, these ones were very moral. They would go on strike at the drop of a hat, in support of the nurses or the bricklayers or some other branch of laborer, or often on more general humanitarian grounds. "We can't work," the head builder would tell me in the kitchen of a lunchtime, "until the UN does something about Indonesia, it's getting ridiculous" ("It is," I'd agree, as they went off to picket the Nike shop in town); or they'd down tools on a Tuesday morning, telling me, "It's the whole Kurdish thing, Mr. Hythloday, it's unconscionable, and the U.S. is just making things worse" ("I know," I'd say with a sigh as they gathered up their placards and set off for the Turkish embassy); and every week the Palestine question took a new turn to prompt a day off.

"Basically, it would be wrong of us to work while this sort of thing is going on," they would argue, and they had a good point; however, the world didn't seem to be improving, and consequently the Folly was going very slowly. I still wasn't allowed to enter it, and they weren't sure exactly when it would be safe enough to do so. Yet in a way, I almost preferred that they did it like this; as I looked out at its skeletal form, I could perceive already its proud upsurge, its noble future. "Liberty!" it seemed to cry. And tonight, just as I was about to look away, I saw something: an angelic face peeping out from one of the narrow windows. It was a very beautiful face, painted in the choicest grays and silvers of the clouded moonlight; it saw me, smiled and waved. I waved back, whereupon it disappeared.

I should explain at this point that this sort of thing wasn't entirely new to me. In recent months I had had quite a few supernatural experiences. My theory was that without Mother here to distract me with her nagging, I was more receptive to communications from the spirit world. I've mentioned the eerie feelings I had had watching late-night films— i.e., the unshakable sense that the films were watching me. Often the Visions were of a more hostile variety. Leaning from the window after a long night, attempting to assuage my spinning brain, I had on more than one occasion seen huge, goblinlike figures, not dissimilar to Frank, lurching about in the shadow of the Folly or lumbering with silent menace across the lawn. Whether these manifestations had always been resident in Amaurot or whether they had only arrived recently in some sort of premonitory capacity, I didn't know. But whichever line you took, this particular Vision seemed propitious. I mean an angel was a definite step up from a goblin, for one thing; symbolically speaking, it surely meant that the Folly (representing me, Charles, and also the family line in general) would continue to rise and transcend the intrusions of the brutish world (symbolized by Frank, if you want).

I tipped an imaginary hat to Father, by way of thank-you for the good omen, and returned to my room in a much more optimistic frame of mind, and it wasn't until I tried to sit down on it that I realized the chair to my writing desk wasn't there. "What now?" I said to the ceiling, which had risen to prominence in my new horizontal position.

Picking myself up, I scoured the room for it, and then the landing, but it was nowhere to be seen. This was exasperating. It wasn't a costly chair, it wasn't even an attractive chair; it had come down from the attic after its predecessor succumbed to woodworm. Its theft revealed a hitherto unsuspected degree of stupidity in the malefactor. There were lots of nicer things in the house to steal, and it was most bothersome that he should settle on this worthless item just as I intended to sit on it. At that very minute I heard them come in and, sniggering to each other, climb the stairs to Bel's room. I had half a mind to go and confront him there and then: Indeed I had put on my slippers and was halfway to the door when the horrible image of interrupting him and Bel in the middle of *something* appeared in my mind, and my legs quite failed me. The room began to list, like a ship in a storm; knees buckling, I staggered into the armoire, then back the way I had come as the room tilted to the other side. I lay down on the bed and covered my eyes. This had to end. We couldn't go on like this; my stomach, for one, couldn't bear it. Action had to be taken: definitive action.

CHAPTER THREE

The next couple of days were peaceful enough. Bel was out most of the time, and she took her Project with her; when at home they tended to stay in her bedroom at their reading lesson. The day after was when all the trouble with the bank first materialized, and things really started to cave in; though the morning began so sweetly, with Mrs. P. waking me just before noon with the telephone on a tray.

"Hello?" I said, after establishing that this was not a murderous ruse on Mrs. P.'s part.

"Hello," an unfamiliar voice said. "Charles?"

Heart pounding, I scrambled out of bed to my feet. It was a sultry voice, throaty, at once refined and scandalously suggestive; it could have come from a thousand black-and-white movies—the fallen dame in the barroom asking for a light, the heiress with the detective parked on a shadowy driveway, the trembling young widow pleading for help from the embittered ex-marine. A monochrome voice that could belong to only one person.

"Laura," I said with a strange, thankful calmness, a sense that one thing had ended and a new one was beginning.

"Yes," she said. "Your sister called me last night, she said you had something you needed to discuss with me . . . ?"

Damn that Bel, she would make nothing easy for me. "That's right," I said. A moment of blissful tension elapsed.

"So what is it?" Laura said.

What was it? I could hardly tell her she'd caught my eye as a twelve-year-old while I was paging through my sister's yearbook, it might give her the wrong idea, and I didn't want to jump the gun with any talk of destiny. "Um . . . ," I said.

"Christabel told me," she interjected delicately, "you were interested in insurance?"

"Yes," I said, seizing on the words. "Yes I am. Very interested. Insurance, in all its, ah, forms, and, um, wonders . . . it—it enthralls me . . ."

"She said you were interested in insuring a vase," Laura said slowly, as if guiding someone of limited mental ability.

"Vases, yes, that's it, I have a vase and I'd like to insure it. I was wondering if you'd care to come over some night and discuss it? Over dinner perhaps? Say this Saturday?"

She was doubtful at first. "Couldn't you just come by the office?"

"No," I said, "because there's actually more than one vase, you see, in fact there's several vases, much too many to carry to the office—and anyway I prefer to do business over dinner. That way, ah, no one gets hungry."

"Oh," she said. There was a long pause. I waited, quietly grinding my teeth and berating myself. *That way no one gets hungry*—what on earth was I thinking? Was I still crippled by the fallout from the Olé incident? Would I never be able to speak to a woman again?

"All right," Laura broke in. "It's not normally how we do things, but you are Christabel's brother, after all."

"Yes," I said fatuously, resisting the urge to jump up and down weeping tears of gratitude. "So I'll see you Saturday? Eightish?"

"I suppose," the voice crackled. "Oh, but I'm lactose intolerant, okay? So, like, I can't eat anything with lactose."

"Certainly, certainly . . . don't give it another thought," I said and replaced the receiver. For a few seconds I remained there in the moment's afterglow, not yet ready to yield up its immediacy; then, with a whoop, I raised my fist to the air. Victory! True, I hadn't presented myself in the most flattering light; I may have come across as a tad eccentric, or deranged. But what mattered was that she had accepted. Once she was inside the house, where I controlled all, everything would fall into place: for she would see that here was a world waiting to be remade as she desired—mountains moved, seas emptied, lactose banished to the ends of the earth—it would all be for her, and she would understand straightaway that we were meant to be.

I went into the breakfast room to deliver the good news but found myself confronted by Frank in a state of partial undress on the far side of the table, which rather spoiled the moment. "All right, bud," he greeted me, stretching back in an uninhibited, vaguely postcoital yawn that exposed his flaccid white belly. I shuddered. How could Bel endure to look at *that*, indeed to feel it slapping greasily against— But no. She had honored the pact and I had got what I wanted—now the détente must be respected. Swallowing my disgust, I gave him as unhostile a nod as I could manage and pulled out a chair at the table.

Bel was sitting slumped in front of a pile of opened letters. She looked rather agitated; her cheeks had a high color and her hair was frazzled as though she'd been tugging at it, and when I asked her pointedly who had eaten all the marmalade she didn't reply. I changed tack and told her about Laura. "Funny that she's in insurance, though. I hardly thought she'd be the type, did you?"

"Mmm," Bel said, continuing to glower into her pile.

"Is there any more marmalade?" Frank said.

"I mean, bit funny, isn't it?"

"Not to anyone who knows her," she snapped. "Why, what did you think she did?"

"I don't know," I said truthfully, although in my imagination I'd sort of pictured her walking around a big, empty house, gazing melancholically out at the rain with a cup of black coffee in her hands and slow jazz in the background, more or less on a full-time basis.

"Whatever. Listen, Charles, there's something I want to talk to you about." She turned in her seat to look directly at me. From the far side of the table I heard Frank chuckling as he ate his toast.

"Yes?" I said, suddenly feeling uneasy.

"How long, exactly, have you been leaving letters in the String Drawer?"

"Why . . . I don't know." I was usually at home when the postman came, so it was generally me who separated the post; taking personal correspondence up to our respective bedrooms and leaving family business in the String Drawer for Bel to look at at her convenience. I didn't see what she was driving at, or why her face was taking on that disconcerting brick-red hue. "A few months, I suppose."

"And were you thinking of *telling* me at any stage?"

"Telling you what?" I said, confused. "I mean, it's your, well it's sort of your cubbyhole, isn't it?"

"What gave you the impression," she said, "that the String Drawer was my cubbyhole?"

I didn't like her tone and was about to retort when I realized that I had no idea what had given me that impression. We must have had some prior arrangement, I thought, racking my brains; although it was not beyond the bounds of possibility that I had stuck the afternoon post in there one day after some lunchtime drinks and latterly *assumed* that there had been a prior arrangement. Whatever had happened, the String Drawer was where family-related correspondence had been going more or less since Mother left for the Cedars. Now that I came to think of it, I had wondered recently why Bel was letting it build up so.

"Well?" she said.

"Well what?" I said. "You've found them now, so let's just be happy with that, and not start blaming each other—"

"Charles, have you *seen* these? Do you know what they are?" She waved a sheaf of the envelopes with the funny red stamp on them. "Do you?"

"Special delivery?" I hazarded. Frank stifled a laugh. "Well how should I know? All that's your department, that's always been the way."

"One of my many departments," Bel said in a scornful aside to Frank. "Charles handles Food and Wine, and the rest is left for me."

"As long as you keep handlin me." Frank leered. She lapsed into a shy smile, and I glimpsed her stockinged toe nudging his white sock under the table; I experienced a sensation of utter displacement, as though the earth had shifted on its axis and everything had toppled over. This must have been how Louis XVI felt, I reflected, when he was taken from his prison cell and led to the scaffold, and understood for the first time that this noisy, shouty bunch of nobodies were actually serious about their Revolution business.

"Well, what are they so?" I half-shouted, in case she had forgotten I was there.

"They're from the *bank*, Charles!" Bel shouted back, banging the palms of her hands on the table. "From the bank, from the building society, from our solicitors, from other people's solicitors. But mainly from the bank."

A cold shiver went down my spine. "I wonder what they want," I said.

"What do they ever want?" Frank mused dolorously. "You won't catch them wastin stamps askin you how you are."

"Money. They want money. There's bills in here going back for months, from the phone company, the electricity, the television people." She flung the pages about desperately. "But they're the least of our worries. The big one is the bank. Our mortgage repayments are in arrears, serious arrears. They're talking about foreclosing."

This took a moment to register with me. *Mortgage, foreclose*—these were words with which I was not wholly familiar, rarely being encountered in polite society, except in murmured stories told in the midnight hours, in the same tone one might use for cancer or abortion; horrible things that, outside the confines of one's demesne, were happening to luckless strangers. "I didn't know we *had* a mortgage," I said.

"Charles"—Bel pulled at her hair frustratedly—"this *Hythloday empire* you're always going on about didn't come from nowhere. It's built on *credit*. None of it's *ours*, not really. It looks like Father borrowed an absolute fortune, the sums they're talking about here are just—just *astronomical*—" She sat back in her chair, making slits of her eyes. "I *knew* something like this would happen. Mother's just let everything go to hell since he died, I don't think she's even *seen* the accountant since the funeral . . ."

"But . . ." We had company, so one didn't want to be vulgar. "But, I mean—we're still *rich*, aren't we? Can't we just pay them what they want and they'll leave us alone?"

Bel got up and started throwing her hands around. "What goes on in that fucking head of yours? When you're not drunk, what's happening in there?"

"Well, don't swear," I pleaded, not feeling very well.

"Father was a *chemist*, Charles, a *scientist*, not an *emperor*, not fucking Charlemagne. Even very good scientists don't get paid enough to afford a place like this, haven't you ever thought of that?"

"He had his investments"—for some reason I felt the need to defend Father here—"his assets, that sort of thing—"

"Well, where are they? Where are they, Charles? I mean I just don't know what he was thinking. Even if he hadn't *died* I don't know how he was intending to repay it all. And since then we've had no income proper and this colossal inheritance tax and all these new demands on the finances, Mother's clinic and your alcoholism and that ridiculous Folly and we seem to be spending a ton on groceries at the moment for some reason—"

I bit my lip. "What are you saying, exactly?"

"There isn't enough, Charles. There simply isn't enough to pay them back." She rested her head on the back of her chair, as if overcome by fatigue; sunlight streamed through the Chantilly curtains and picked out golden strands in her hair. At that moment my conversation with Laura seemed to be terribly far away. "Right now the only thing I can think of to do is sell off some of our shares. I mean, that'll get us some time, at least."

"Ah, yes, the shares," I said neutrally.

"Mine're still all bound up in trust, so we'll have to use yours," she blinked at me with red eyes. "We can split the difference later."

"Right. Good." I decided that now was not the best time to tell her about my run of bad luck at the baccarat table a few months ago. Instead I put on a false smile and told her not to worry.

"They're reasonable people, bankers," I said. "And we've given them loads of money over the years. They must have forgotten it's us, that's all. I mean I'm sure no one ever lost a house because they'd put the letters in the wrong cubbyhole; that's absurd. I can go and talk to them today. It's a storm in a teacup, you'll see."

"Ha," remarked Frank, who had been occupying himself with an extensive excavation of his aural cavities.

"What, 'Ha'? What do you mean, 'Ha'?" I rounded on him; the whole thing was his fault, sort of.

"Me ma was plagued by them fuckin banks her whole life," he said into his teacup. "Never had a penny to her name but they'd be sniffin after it—she used to have this joke, What's the difference between banks and the devil?"

Bel and I looked at him.

"In Hell they won't cut off your heatin," he said.

"Is that a joke?" I screeched at last.

He shrugged. "It's about as funny as banks get," he said.

"Well, I'll go and talk to them," I said and left them to their sock rubbing, which might calm Bel down at least. I didn't like her to get upset. She might not have looked it, but she was a ferocious worrier: She could tie herself into knots over the most inconsequential matters. She had always been like this, even as a small girl. When other children were busy believing in Santa Claus and Tooth Fairies, she became obsessed with the idea that every time Father and Mother left the house they would never come back. She never said anything to them; but as soon as she saw the car pull out of the driveway, she'd go to her room, sit very still, and think Positive Thoughts about them until they had safely returned.

That was just one instance of what was even then a broad spectrum of worrying. She also worried about losing things. She worried about things breaking or running out. She worried about robbers and dangerous drivers. She worried about what would happen to her dolls when she died. She had a whole host of worries on behalf of the animal kingdom— what would they eat in the winter, where would they sleep if people kept putting buildings everywhere, whether they would be all right crossing roads by themselves. All these were as nothing, however, compared to the Herculean bout of worrying provoked by the arrival of our one and only household pet, not counting the peacocks, which I didn't: a springer spaniel, a loving if excitable fellow who in the end wasn't around long enough even to be given a name.

Almost as soon as it was in the door, Bel diagnosed the anonymous dog, unsuspectingly brought home as a gift for us by Father, as suffering from a dizzying array of existential terrors. It was, in retrospect, a clear case of transference: as if the appearance of the dog had allowed her to open the floodgates, so that all of the dread that had accumulated inexplicably within her small soul could come pouring out. For the two weeks it lasted in Amaurot, she devoted herself to acting as mouthpiece for the anguished dog. She stayed up night after night, not sleeping, pacing around the house with the dog trotting amiably at her heel, relating its woes to anyone who would listen. She worried that it was lonely. She worried that it was hungry. She worried that it was being overexercised, or not exercised enough. She worried that its collar itched. She worried that it might start thinking it was a human but feel bad because it had fur instead of skin. She worried that it was unfulfilled. She worried that it felt naked, missed its parents, was afraid of the dark, fretted about being able to speak only in barks, was ashamed of its fleas, didn't understand why it had to sleep in the pantry. At school, she continued to voice her fears, which separation from the dog only made worse. Before long, the other children in the class were so upset that the teacher was spending the whole day just trying to reassure them as to the welfare of our pet. Finally, one afternoon, the school principal rang Mother up and suggested in a weary voice that something really ought to be done; before Mother could reply the phone had been passed over to a tearful Bel, who asked Mother to put her on to the dog, please—and that's when Mother snapped. When we came home that day the dog was gone. Mother wouldn't say where, only that it had been "relocated." She refused to discuss the matter any further.

Strangely enough, Bel received this news quite calmly, and soon she seemed to forget about the dog entirely. Maybe it had served its purpose. Her anxiety had miraculously disappeared; she started attending Speech and Drama classes after school, and immediately that was all she could talk about; she grew, romantic turbulences aside, into a happy teenager. I suppose that for all of us that was a sort of Golden Age. The family prospered, everything seemed secure; I shocked Father by gaining captaincy of the school cricket team, and thanks to the unpopularity of that sport in Ireland we even won a few matches.

Bel was in her late teens when she started acting up again, just as I began my short career in university. The doctor called them Hysterical Episodes. For a period of about seven months she suffered these Episodes almost every other week. They were quite terrifying to witness: shaking and tears and vomiting and voices. She would lie on the bed sobbing and begging us to help her without being able to tell us how, what was the matter, what these forces were that were attacking her. The doctor hadn't been overly concerned; by now he was more interested in Father, whom he had sent into the hospital for tests. Bel's kind of instability was quite common in girls of her age, he told us. It was little more than a rather extreme manifestation of adolescent confusion—a natural side effect of growing up, complicated by her propensity to doubt and overanalyze, by her volatile relationship with Mother, and Father's waning health. The best way to look at it was as a period of adjustment; some people adjust to the real world more easily than others. He tried her on different dosages and different medications, he gave her time off school. Eventually she was back to normal, and everyone was pretending it had never happened. Father's condition had spiraled downward, the house was full of white coats and strange machinery—there simply wasn't space to keep worrying about Bel too.

But I couldn't forget. Sometimes, if we were having a fight, or if something had upset her, I would think I saw it—the hysteria, the terror—shivering, eclipselike, at the edges of her, waiting for its moment. It seemed to me that, wherever it came from, it was too fundamental a part of her now ever to truly go away. That was why I badgered her about her boyfriends, that was why the unsettled, mercurial mood she'd been in lately bothered me, like that curious gathering of electricity an epileptic feels before an attack. She might have put it all behind her—I knew she hated being thought of as delicate, or precarious—but to me the memory was still fresh. The fear, that was what I remembered primarily: those horrible mornings of convulsions and terrorized, unfocused weeping, and in her eyes the fear so huge and formless that it robbed us both of speech.

THE BANK WAS situated about a mile and a half away, in the middle of a shopping center. I set out to see the manager that very afternoon. I was sure Bel was making more out of this business than she needed to, but I knew I wouldn't have a moment's peace until it was sorted out; also, it provided a useful cover for another matter I needed to take care of. Pact or no pact, furniture was still disappearing; I wanted to see if I could find some background information on our Golem friend.

I rarely ventured that far from home. Bel took this as another instance of my "feudal outlook." "You see yourself as Lord of the Manor," she'd say, "and these people are your vassals, and you don't want to rub shoulders with them in case you catch something." But that wasn't it at all. Watching from the backseat of the cab as lofty sea roads and shady avenues gave way to the encircling suburbs, I was gripped—as I always was—by a sense of claustrophobia and threat. The shopping center frightened me, the alien, prefabricated meanness of it: the cut-rate hair salon, the boutiques of bleak pastel frocks, the newsagent's whose staff were in a state of perpetual regression—seeming to be skipping whole rungs of the evolutionary ladder, so that pleases and thank-yous had gone south long ago, and I expected to go in someday soon and find them gnawing bones and worshiping fire. As vassals I doubt they'd have been much good to me.

The newsagent's, however, was where I was headed now, debouching from the cab onto newly laid faux cobblestone and gingerly edging my way through a Walpurgisnacht of middle-aged women with bleached hair, mock-leather jackets, and yodeling children. Across the road, a huge billboard dominated the skyline. IRELANDBANK: WE PLEDGE UNTO YOU, it said. 100 WAYS IN WHICH WE ARE MAKING LIFE FOR OUR CUSTOMERS BETTER AND BETTER. Which seemed to augur well for me and my predicament, but then beneath the letters was a picture of the amassed Irelandbank staff, waving mirthlessly up at the camera. There were thousands of them, a silent army clad in uniform blue jackets, the appalling tailoring of which made them all the more menacing.

The window of the newsagent's was cluttered with Day-Glo flash cards; I scanned down through advertisements for nannies, lawn mowing, kittens, maths grinds, until I found what I was looking for.

THE ALL-SEEING EYE.
MARITAL INFIDELITY? EXTORTION?
CONSPIRACIES AGAINST YOU IN THE OFFICE?
THE ALL-SEEING EYE SEES ALL.
HAVE YOUR SUSPICIONS CONFIRMED

AND YOUR MIND SET AT EASE.
GOLD-SEAL GUARANTEE OF SUCCESS.

I took down the number and went in search of an unvandalized call box.

"Hello?" a cautious voice answered, low and mumbly as if unwilling to divulge the slightest hint of identity.

"Is that the All-Seeing Eye?" I said.

"Maybe," the voice said.

"My name is Charl—"

"No names!" the voice interrupted urgently.

"Fine then, my name is . . . is C, and I need your help."

"Marital infidelity? Extortion? Conspi——"

"No, no, none of those. There's a chap in my house stealing my furniture."

"Oh," the All-Seeing Eye said. "Are you sure it's not marital infidelity?"

"No," I said. "It's my sister's boyfriend."

"Ah," it said salaciously. "Want a few pictures, do you?"

"No, look here, Eye, are you going to help me or not?"

"Come to my office," the Eye said. "One eighteen, the Savannah. Come alone. The All-Seeing Eye takes cash and all major credit cards."

"Fine," I said.

"Photo development is extra, though, and the All-Seeing Eye reserves the right to hang on to negatives it likes . . ."

He gave me directions to his office, which was in fact more of a small semidetached house in an estate of identical semidetached houses not far away. I rang the doorbell, and after a series of unlocking noises, the door was opened by a familiar figure: none other than our dilatory postman, the one who smelled of gin and only delivered post when he felt like it.

"What!" I said.

"C?" he said.

"But you're the—"

"No names," he said, and after a furtive look around motioned me inside. The hallway was filled with great billows of steam, into which he quickly disappeared. I followed as best I could and arrived in an even steamier room, where after stumbling around blindly for a moment I bumped into something. It emerged presently as a table, with a post bag of mail sitting on it. On either side of the bag was a pile: one of opened envelopes, the other presumably their former contents—hundreds of sheets of handwritten and printed correspondence.

Gradually, through breaks in the vapor clouds, I was able to piece together the rest of my surroundings. We were in a kitchen. The windows were fogged with condensation; on the cooker and counter, several kettles and saucepans were on the go at once, with sealed envelopes resting over each on makeshift tripods of Blu-Tack and cocktail sticks.

"Tea?" he said from somewhere.

"What's going on here? Is this people's *post*?"

"I'll put on a kettle," the postman said, abruptly appearing and disappearing again into the fog. I sat down at the table and looked through the damp pages. *How is Uncle Harold's new leg? . . . We regret to inform you that your application has been unsuccessful . . . These girls are beautiful and discreet . . . Dear Bazzer, Mother died today . . .*

"I mean, what are you doing?" I asked in disbelief.

"Well, I suppose it started as a hobby," the postman said over his shoulder, "and then it grew into something more. I like finding solutions to problems. Answers. Life is full of questions. Only the privileged few have access to the answers."

"But you can't—"

"It's really amazing what people will say in their letters," he mused.

"And this . . . this heinous intrusion into people's privacy is what you call detection, is it?"

"You may not like it," he replied, setting a cup in front of me and sitting down, "but it means that I can give you a Gold-Seal Guarantee of Success."

"Hmm," I said.

"Let's talk business," he said. "Actually, when I saw you at the door there I thought you must have come about your mortgage difficulties."

"Did you," I said.

"Yes, thought you might have been wanting to fake your own death or something. Not unusual, people in your position."

"Not that it's any of your concern," I told him haughtily, "but the mortgage is a minor matter, a simple crossed wire. As a matter of fact, I'm just on my way to see my bank manager and sort it out."

He smiled at me indulgently. "Sure," he said. "Of course you are. I suppose the repo men won't be needing this, then." He plucked from the pile a single sheet headed with the Irelandbank logo, a sort of euro-sign-meets-swastika affair, and passed it to me. It was addressed to a debt collection agency, stating that the bank now had legal authorization to take "the next step" and that the collectors could begin shortly with their "recovery."

"Quite so," I swallowed. "A trifle."

"So you've come about your sister," he said, grinning.

"Yes—listen here, Eye, kindly remove that lascivious expression when discussing my sister, if you please."

"All right," he said amiably. "Fine-looking girl, though. Shame that company didn't take her on. I'd have thought she was a shoo-in." He exhaled ruminatively, crossed an ankle over his thigh, fiddled about with the hem of his trouser leg. "Takes the wind out of your sails, a knockback like that," he added as an afterthought.

"I don't know what you're talking about." His omniscience was starting to irk me; it was like meeting the Wizard of Oz or something. "And I don't want to know. I'm not especially pleased about taking this course of action, and I'd appreciate it, Eye, if we could keep to the matter at hand and you would at least pretend not to know all there is to know about my family."

"Fair enough."

"And another thing, don't you have a name? I can't keep calling you 'Eye,' it's confusing."

"Okay." His eyes narrowed and he rubbed his jaw. "Call me . . . MacGillycuddy."

"All right then." Carving a niche of air for myself from the steam, I told MacGillycuddy the whole story of Frank's sudden and mysterious appearance in my house: his murky past and equally murky present, his baffling success with Bel, the disappearance of various household items, the sinister rusty white van.

"I don't quite get why the van bothers you so much," MacGillycuddy said.

"Because no one knows what's *in* it, that's why." I told him about the time Frank was driving us to the greyhound race, when I had surreptitiously managed to peek into the back and seen dimly, through the smeared grille, what looked like mounds and mounds of *garbage*.

"That's unusual, right enough," MacGillycuddy admitted.

"It's more than unusual. The man's a *sociopath*. I mean I don't know if you're familiar with Yiddish folklore at all, but—well, perhaps we shouldn't get into that now. The sad fact is that my sister has a *thing* for sociopaths, and if I don't keep an eye on him he'll run off with the whole house and her to boot."

"So you want me to . . ."

I told him that I wanted him to find out everything he could about Frank: who he was, what he did, what had happened to my chair. "Basically, anything incriminating," I said.

"No bother," MacGillycuddy said. "Child's play. Give me twenty-four hours." Having scribbled out my number and a check for his retainer, I rose to leave.

"Say hello to your mother for me," he winked. "Good to have her back."

I was tempted to pursue this, but the sight of his eagerly rubbing hands was enough to warn me away from opening any more Pandora's boxes. I wished him good day and opened the door.

"And the repo men!" he called after me.

I made my way back to the shopping center sunk in thought. So they'd already called in the repossessors; that seemed rather unsporting of them. This interview might not be the formality I'd expected. I took a deep breath and stepped through the doors of the bank.

It was a long, windowless chamber, with a rather elegant fan depending lifelessly from the low ceiling. A painted wooden counter ran down the left-hand side, bearing pens on chains, transaction dockets, leaflets about car loans, tracker bonds, inscrutable investment schemes. To the right, beside a small row of uncomfortable chairs, a louvered door led off to another room, to which one went for cash, lodgements, and so on. Two pictures hung side by side on a prominent area of the wall. One was an anemic landscape of a soothing sun glinting through trees. RELIABILITY, it said underneath in big, sincere letters. The other was somewhat more fanciful, depicting a tropical island with dolphins frolicking soothingly just offshore. QUALITY SERVICE, this one said.

At the back of the room, a man in a badly tailored blue jacket was smiling at me from behind a desk. His arms were folded, and he was sitting at the exact midpoint between his computer and a fake-looking potted plant. He looked rather as if he had been sitting like that all day, smiling placidly; a sign saying INFORMATION hung above him, with an arrow pointing down at his head.

"Good afternoon," he said pleasantly, when he saw I had finished my examination of the dolphin picture.

"Ah, hello," I replied with a whimsical brightness, as if I were just passing a few idle minutes on my way somewhere else.

"How can I help you today?" he inquired. He was a nondescript-looking fellow, with a kindly, roundish face and a little hyphen of a mouth.

"Oh, just a small thing," I said breezily, waving a couple of red-stamped envelopes at him. "Just a few final-notice things we seem to have got by mistake."

"Ah," he said. "Mind if I have a quick look at them?"

"Not at all," I said. "Be my guest."

"Why not take a seat," he said, "Mr. . . . ?"

"Hythloday—Charles," I said. "Thank you."

He scanned through the pages expressionlessly while I whistled something in keeping with the relaxed but respectful mood we had established and tried to imagine what he might look like away from his desk—cheering on a boat race, or frowning thoughtfully over a jar of pickles in the supermarket. He slid his chair over to the computer and began to tap at it. He tapped for a good three minutes. "Oh," he said at one point, briefly pulling back from the screen. I leaned casually over to one side, but I couldn't make out what was on it. I continued uneasily with my whistling.

"Well, Charles," he said eventually, "it says here that we haven't received any mortgage payments from you in over six months."

"Yes, that's right," I said in a businesslike manner that might make this sound like an explanation.

"It looks like we've been trying to contact you about it for some time," he continued, still gazing into the computer screen. "Didn't you get our letters about legal action?"

He was trying to keep up his friendly tone, but I could tell that he was hurt, as though I had deliberately misled him. I explained that the letters had been misfiled in the String Drawer, but this didn't cut much ice.

"The String Drawer," he repeated to himself, laboring to understand.

"It's not just string," I expanded, "there's other stuff in there as well: thumbtacks, Sellotape, that sort of thing."

"Yes," he said, placing his hands on the top of his head and leaning back his chair. I felt like a heel.

"Well, Charles, that could happen to anyone. But unfortunately that doesn't change the fact that we have a bit of a problem here."

"Do we?"

"Yes—unless, of course, you're going to tell me that you have in your wallet the sum of"—he named the sum with a jocular laugh—"in cash, ha ha"—but his eyes implored me to give him *something*, not to let a dreary, mundane old debt scuttle the friendship that was budding so beautifully between us. My heart sank a little more. Coincidentally, the figure he'd named bore some resemblance to the amount I'd lost playing baccarat that spring, on somebody's yacht one day with Pongo and Patsy and Hoyland Maffey. How insubstantial it had seemed then, in the simmering belowdecks; after too many Kahlúas and with Patsy pressed against my arm, when she wasn't outside playing some juvenile hide-and-seek game with Hoyland, that is. It hadn't seemed to matter whether I won or lost; she'd clutched my elbow and laughed and cheered me on, little pearl earrings shining out of her ebony bob; and the cards all looked the same anyway, smiling in the light that washed in through the picture window, as the croupier swept up another pile of chips . . .

"There must be something we can do," I said.

The bank official chewed his ballpoint pen pessimistically. "Charles, I don't know," he said. "I just don't know."

"The family has *assets*, though—I mean, it's not as if we're down to our last few pennies. This is just a temporary thing. Couldn't we sort out a . . . a loan, or a moratorium or something? At least until I can talk to

Father's accountant, and he can . . . he can divert funds from our dividends . . ."

The bank official looked up at me with a weary little smile; he knew I didn't know what I was talking about. "Charles," he said, "that would be all well and good. I would love to do that for you, Charles, and if it were personally up to me, you're right, arrange a moratorium, that's exactly what I'd do. But you see, I have to look after the bank's interests too." His eyes looked earnestly into mine, hoping that I would understand. "It's so far behind, and the sum is so large, and—though I personally believe you do—on paper I can't see that you have the collateral to pay this off. I want to take care of this for you, Charles, but I have to make sure that the bank gets a square deal."

I swallowed, looking helplessly back at him. Didn't he think he could trust me? Did he think we were some crowd of snaky con men, trying to take advantage of the bank's good-heartedness? In a fatuous slip of mirror beside the fake-looking potted plant I caught a glimpse of my hands wringing and wondered curiously whose, what they were.

"The thing is, Charles—you see, the mortgage as it stands seems somewhat *irregular*. That's what really bothers me." The pen went back in his mouth.

"Oh yes?" distractedly mopping my brow.

"Yes. You see, normally, Charles, how a mortgage works is that when the first party passes away—Mr. Ralph Hythloday, that's, that was your father, I assume?"

I nodded.

"I'm sorry," the bank official said quietly.

"Thank you," I said. For a moment we reflected in silence.

"Anyway," he resumed, "what usually happens is that, on the occasion of the borrower's death, the life insurance is put toward outstanding debts. For some reason, that hasn't happened in your father's case."

"No?" The atmosphere in the room was unbearably close; I glanced hopefully up at the fan.

"No . . . And then when I go back further, I find that the original *structure* of the loan was . . . well, I've never seen anything quite like it. The payments are totally irregular. And they come in from somewhere new practically every time. Look," turning the screen round to me, "this is just in the last four years. Instead of us simply debiting your father's account, the money's paid in by this company on this date, and a different company here, and then there's nothing for months, and then this lump sum from this bank which I have to say I'm not familiar with. Do you know who any of these people are?"

"Assets?" I croaked weakly. My head was spinning and I could make no sense of the numbers dancing up and down on the screen. Why wouldn't he let me go?

"I don't know who set this up," he was saying, "but it's most irregular, most irregular."

"So what should I do?" I said feverishly, simply to bring this to an end. "You can't give me a loan, you say, and you can't give me any more time."

He looked at me with a sorrowful, stoical expression. "Charles, my hands are tied," he said. "If you can find your family's accountant, and if he can make head or tail of this—well, then, maybe we can work something out. But as it stands . . . the debt *will* have to be called in."

"Meaning the house will be repossessed?"

"That's the standard operating procedure, yes." He brooded behind a steeple of fingers.

"I see." That was the bottom line. I reached behind me for my jacket and got to my feet. "Well," I said, reverting to the breezy style I had begun with, as if none of this were really important anyway.

"Yes," the bank official followed suit, "thanks for dropping by." He stretched over the desk to shake my hand.

"Thank *you*," I said without quite knowing why, and made my way to the door.

"Oh, Charles?"

"Yes?"

"Why not have one of these?" He took something out of a drawer and held it out to me.

"Thanks," I said, taking it. It was a key ring. The plastic tag had the Irelandbank logo on one side and the legend "We Pledge Unto You" on the other, with a metal ring attached to it on which, presumably, I could hang the keys of the house I no longer owned.

"You're welcome," he said warmly. "Mind how you go."

I saw Mrs. P. as I passed the supermarket, deep in conversation with a foreign-looking woman. The woman wore an identification badge and was selling magazines. "Mine are in one little room," she was saying, "above a butcher's shop, we pay and pay, and when he say, oh, police, is trouble, we pay more—" I covered my face with my hand and slipped by them, breathing stinging, shallow breaths. What was happening? What did they mean, those irregularities? Could it really be so complicated that they couldn't begin to sort it out? Because it seemed to me to be so obvious: it was Father, he had assets, there was plenty of money, there had to be— Gasping, I leaned against a mock-Corinthian pillar, flooded by nightmarish images: hordes of machine-stitched blue suits pouring into the house, dismantling it with their dead Golem eyes, rebuilding it as a luxury aparthotel, a leisureplex, the eighteenth hole of a crosstown golf course . . .

There was nothing more I could do here, however. I detached myself from my pillar and, deciding a walk home might calm me, I headed up Ballinclea Road and through the iron gates of Killiney Hill Park. But instead of calming me, the pathways—my pathways, which I had trodden a thousand times—seemed to curl indifferently away from me; the trees bowed with the wind like elders shaking accusing heads, the birds screeching and yammering as if raising an alarm. And the mountains, and the sky, and the dark gorse and gray-blue rolling sea, they remained steeped in the clouded afternoon, withholding their beauty from me as from an undeserving passerby.

Soon it began to rain, and by the time I got to Amaurot I was thoroughly soaked. Ascending the driveway, I saw the house appear through a shifting veil of precipitation. Already I seemed to feel its weight on my shoulders. "I can't do it!" I whispered inwardly. "You're too heavy!" And the house, even as I got closer, retreated further back into the rain.

It was pouring now. I went into the kitchen in search of a towel. From the window I saw Mrs. P. making her way in the direction of the clothesline, tucked discreetly in the lee of the Folly, with a basket of washing. Covering my head with one of Bel's theater monthlies, I chased out after her. "What are you doing?" She froze, her shoulders leaping up around her neck. "Give me that basket," I said, taking hold of it. "You can't hang clothes out in the rain." She handed over the basket without a word. I looked through the contents—blankets, towels, sheets, once again those fearful underpants, capacious with dread and mystery— everything already dried and pressed. "Go inside," I directed sternly. Mrs. P. looked as if she were about to cry. "Go inside and go to bed. You're not well. I'm suspending you from your duties until we get you a doctor."

And then she did start to cry. I set the basket down on the ground and, taking her arm in mine, led her back to the house. She sobbed and sobbed, and as we walked over the wet grass I felt for all the world as though I was leading a prisoner to the scaffold. In the kitchen I sat her down and made some tea.

"What's *wrong*?" I demanded. "What's *wrong* with you?" But she just waved her hands in front of her face, before giving way to a fresh stream of tears.

I stood at the sink and looked out at the rain and the sky, the same stolid gray as the bricks of the tower. Suddenly I felt smothered in there, as I had in the bank. "I need to think," I said, going to open the back door. "Will you please go and get some rest?"

Mrs. P. looked like she hadn't slept in weeks, but she leapt up and dragged me back from the door. "Please, Master Charles, don't go back outside!"

"I have to get the basket," I said. "The clothes are getting wet."

But she didn't hear. "It rains," she kept saying, "you catch cold."

"All right, all right . . . ," sitting down again at the kitchen table. "Happy?"

"Good." She wiped her cheeks and pretended to be cheerful again. "Now, everything is good. Here we are, safe and dry. I make you hot chocolate and you watch television, yes?"

Try as I might, I couldn't persuade her to lie down until she had in- stalled me on the chaise longue, with a cup of cocoa resting on the floor where the table had been. As luck would have it, there was a movie on: *The Killers*, a.k.a. *A Man Alone*, handsome old Burt Lancaster murdered in flashbacked increments by faithless Ava Gardner. I eased my head back and tried to immerse myself in that world, the bare dark apart- ment where Lancaster sat and smoked, waiting for the assassins to come. But I couldn't do it. I was thinking of the impossible mortgage, the exhausting interview with the bank official. It seemed to me that it all came back to Frank somehow: that after all these years, all Father's fortifications, one little cancerous cell of reality had at last slipped through; and now, inexorably, it was metastasizing.

Bel and Frank entered with a great commotion an hour later. Frank was holding his jaw, across which a big purple bruise was spreading. Bel fussed about him, bringing him iodine and cotton wool from the bathroom.

"What happened?" I asked.

"Uh ugh," Frank mumbled, "or ucksh ake."

"It was the cunt," my sister translated. "Do you remember, Charles, the cunt from the pub?"

Remember? The cunt's knobbly white face had been etched into several of my many nightmares in recent times. Bel explained that he and his mates had followed Frank home from work and ambushed him on his way to meet her; indeed, had not the postman been making a tardier round than usual, it might have gone worse for Frank. As it was, Bel had had to take him to Outpatients to get his ribs taped up.

"I gugga figh ag ugh," Frank expostulated now, making to rise from his chair, "ah ick izh ughing ead ih."

Bel pushed him back. "You're not going anywhere," she told him. "It can wait. You're in no condition to kick anyone's head in."

His eye rolled whitely, like a fallen horse's: and for a split second, before the Golem dead calm reasserted itself and he sat back, it was disconcertingly like looking into a mirror. I recognized the same besieged humanity that shrieked bansheelike through my own heart; and for that split second I felt a sympathy for the poor beast, and wondered if it might not be better if we were all of us Golems: obedient, unquestioning, impervious to pain.

I left them and went to the breakfast room, where the various threats and notices still lay on a corner of the table. I seated myself and read them through with masochistic glee. The principal players were numerical: account numbers, rates of interest, amounts outstanding, dates from long ago. These were the figures whose tale was spun over the headed pages; we were mentioned in passing, in the third person, given only bit-part, transient-sounding roles as "occupants." I read the last one, and as I laid it facedown on the table I experienced a sensation of utter dislocation, as if all this were happening light-years away, in a parallel, contradictory universe. But it was succeeded by a kind of a supercharged *hereness*, a phantasmagorical awareness of my familiar surroundings: the heavy drapes hanging drowsily, the quietly babbling patterns of the wallpaper, the grandfather clock and the tea chest resting innocent in their shadows like sleeping children about to be orphaned. I thought of Amaurot and all the other great houses, those great hearts that strained now to keep beating with the thin blood of modernity, built for a simpler time when men wore hats and ladies wore gloves, silver was polished for guests, fires roared in hearths . . .

In the hallway, Frank was gibbering incoherently into the phone, like a chimpanzee general declaring a state of emergency. Through the door, Bel was sitting off to one side with her chin resting on her hand. I looked at her, and looked back out at Frank and all of those who had come before him, and suddenly had an inkling of her desperation to find a place for herself in this world.

"Mother's being discharged next weekend," she said wanly, waving a letter from the Cedars.

"Just in time for the auction," taking a seat beside her. "Seems appropriate."

"No luck with the bank, then?"

"Well, you know, we hammered a few things out. They seemed quite adamant about getting their money back, though." The television was on with the sound down: Rockets fired mutely across a shaky desert. "They did say that if we could speak to our accountant he might be able to untangle this a little."

"I've *tried* to find our accountant. He's disappeared off the face of the earth. And Father's files are *impossible*. They're like code. You never come across the same name twice. I don't even know if they are the *right* files."

"Mother would know, I suppose."

"Oh *God*," Bel covered her face with her hands. "The horror of bringing Mother into this . . ."

"Well, *something*'ll turn up." I tugged gently at her hair. "Maybe we have a rich uncle we don't know about."

"That doesn't sound like much of a plan," she said dismally, picking at a patch on her cords. "This is *horrible*, Charles. Ever since this morning I've been feeling like a trespasser, like I'm sleeping in someone else's bed, and eating with someone else's cutlery. Every time I close a door it seems to *echo* almost forever. And now Mother's going to come back and make it look like it's all our fault, and go on about how we've let Father down and we've thrown away our birthright and all that—"

"Oh, you always take her too seriously . . ."

"She will, that's what she *thinks*, Charles, no one's good enough to live here, we're all just flailing about since Father died." She worked loose a thread and left it and sipped her brandy. "I wish it would all just—just *end*. I'm so *sick* of living my life at the behest of this stupid *house*, it sucks the *soul* out of you, makes you its slave, that's how it stays alive . . ."

"Well, of course it'll end, Bel, we'll find a way out, you'll see."

"I don't mean this mortgage stuff. I mean, *everything*." She kicked her feet out in front of her. "I can't keep living here, Charles. I can't keep living like this. It's too weird. It's not *life*, can't you see that?"

"Life," I said bitterly.

"Because even if we'd sold some of our antiques—that ridiculous car, for instance, all it does is gather dust, I find myself feeling *sorry* for it locked up out there—I mean if we'd gone about it correctly, I'm sure we *could* have paid them off. But . . . but the way everything's turned out, don't you think that maybe this is *supposed* to happen? Because places like Amaurot aren't supposed to exist anymore—" She paused suddenly, bowing her head to gaze down into the brandy glass swirling in her left hand, as though daunted in spite of herself by the magnitude of what she'd just said; then with an impetuous sweep of her hand she went on: "It's like some story that's gone wrong and refuses to end, and it's been like this for so *long*—it's so long since things made sense, and all we do is try and pretend it's the same as when we were little children. That's not the way life should feel, Charles, not when you're young. Father dies, Mother goes loolah, now this—it's like the world is trying to tell us something. Do something, it's saying, get out of there while you still can . . ." Her gaze lifted, wandered, alit on the glass frieze of Actaeon, beyond which Frank paraded up and down the hallway. "And it's right.

Maybe you can live in this dreamworld, Charles, without anything in it, but I can't, not anymore."

For a long, desolate moment I could think of nothing to say to her. Outside Frank bayed and ululated his battle plans; she sat bunched at the end of the divan, staring disconsolately into the cold fireplace.

"Must have taken the wind out of your sails," I ventured gently, "the company turning you down like that . . ."

She wheeled round sharply. "How do you know about that?" she demanded.

I shrugged; I wasn't about to divulge how I came to be talking to MacGillycuddy, or that this was all he had told me. "I found out. You can tell me what happened, if you like."

She crossed her arms on her knees and leaned forward, frowning slightly; I knew she wanted to tell *someone*, though she wasn't entirely happy that it was me. "Well, I had an audition and they really liked me," she said, drawing her arms high up around her as if she were cold, "and I got a callback. It was only a couple of days ago—the day we went greyhound racing, that morning. I thought I'd got it, I really did. I thought this would be my big break. Not that it was much of a part or anything, but just to *start, finally*—and it was *Chekhov*, Charles, I knew that play inside out. But then today I got this letter . . ." She broke off; she'd turned her head, but I could see a tear shimmer and tremble against the orb of her eye. "They were quite frank, it was very helpful of them, really . . ."

"So what did they say?"

"They said that while they thought that *technically* my reading was very good, they were concerned"—she took a deep, shivery breath—"that it wasn't sufficiently alive to contemporary social realities. They said I didn't have enough of a grasp on . . . on the *world*. You mightn't think that'd be important for an actress, Charles, but you have to; they want to bring out all the elements in the play that are like life today, you see, and they didn't think I could do it. I mean, they were right, there's only so many parts for *fake princesses*"—twisting up these last words bitterly as the tear detached at last to course exuberantly down her cheek, leaving me to sit and watch her, wishing that I weren't so useless and that the few inches of divan separating us didn't feel like a thousand miles, so that maybe I could say something to comfort her instead of getting up and going over to the mantelpiece to examine the dried flowers: Other people's dreams always embarrassed me, especially when they didn't come true.

An audition: that was what MacGillycuddy meant, that explained what she'd been doing locked up with Frank every morning when I thought she was giving him reading lessons. It probably explained Frank himself, in fact; things didn't get much more real than him, and Bel wasn't one to do things by halves. She wanted so much from the world, there was so much she wanted to make it *see*; if she had to, she would turn away from her own life to do it—she would explode her past, she would take a bed with a criminal, lie back and think of *realism* . . .

And this Chekhov she had always been crazy about, ever since school when they had put on one of his plays. For weeks beforehand she had wandered around the house in her silver kimono with the enormous cerise flowers, incessantly mumbling her lines like some sort of itinerant monk (with the end result that on the night she had gone totally blank). Even now, if you made the mistake of asking her what was so great about him, she would go on long harangues about how not only had he written the defining plays of the twentieth century but he had also been a doctor and treated thousands of peasants for tuberculosis, and he had founded a theater, and he had supported his horrendous drunken family, and he had loved his wife even though she'd had an affair, and actually managed in spite of everything to *like* people and listen to their stories and try to be true to them . . .

"It's this house," she said now in a slow monotone, like Mother on one of her bad days. "It makes me feel like I'm already obsolete, like as long as I'm here I'll never be able to belong anywhere else . . ." She looked up at me suddenly with a streaked face and an expression that was a mixture of accusation and appeal. "Don't you see, Charles? Maybe it's better for both of us if things *don't* work out with the bank. Maybe then we can get free of this place."

I looked at her dumbly. Get *free* of this place? Didn't she understand that Amaurot was special, that what we had here was special? Didn't she know that outside everything was *less*, that it was smaller, meaner, indifferent? But she was serious, and she was still waiting for a reply, pinning me to the wall with that funny look, as if evaluating the very essence of what I was. Then, mercifully, Frank lumbered in, and I seized the opportunity to break away. I went to the drinks cabinet and made myself a Scotch and soda, which I drank with a deliberating air, pretending to turn what she'd said over in my mind. After a moment I was feeling more composed. I lowered the glass from my lips and began to tell her sagely, evenhandedly, that although this audition was a disappointment all right, she shouldn't let it cloud her judgment—that instead of rushing into anything, we should try and sort out the bank first and see how we felt after that. But she had turned around in her seat to devote her whole attention to Frank, who through a combination of grunts and hand flapping was giving her details of his revenge plans. I didn't care to interrupt, and I didn't need her to translate either. Frank's bestial jabberings were curiously eloquent: I could see all too clearly the breaking windows, the hurtling knuckles, the burning. In my already shaken state, I found the atmosphere was getting a little too apocalyptic; I topped up my drink and told Bel I would talk to her later. I couldn't tell if she'd heard me.

Ascending the staircase, I pondered again over what she'd said. I told myself she was upset; I tried to convince myself that this was just an awkward phase—Bel's life, after all, was a more or less continuous series of awkward phases. But I knew that in her eyes this audition business was more than just a temporary setback. She dreamed on a vast scale, and she placed her whole self within those dreams; minor things, setbacks, became great waves that spilled over her, threatening to swamp her. If by some elliptical process of reasoning she had arrived at the conclusion that it was the house that had come between her and the part—between her and the bright future she envisioned for herself—then it would be next to impossible to persuade her to stay.

My task was clear. I had to find some way to save Amaurot. I had to show Bel that it worked; that unlike the shifting, unstable world outside, Amaurot would always be a haven, where we could live completely, where the years moved forward or backward or stood still as we pleased. I told myself I was doing it for her, but in my heart I knew that if she left, the jig was up for me too. What would Amaurot be without her? Nothing more than an abandoned film set, and I the thin shade of an actor, left behind after the director and soundmen and cameras were gone, reciting his lines to no one . . . Lying on my bed with the whiskey glass rested on my belly, I drew up strategy after strategy on the ceiling. But each idea that came to me had some insuperable flaw; until finally I was left with only one, the horror of which made me tremble so the ice cubes jingled in the glass . . .

"Charles!"

I opened my eyes. Outside it had got dark. How long had I been up here?

"Charles!" Bel called again from the hallway. "Phone!"

I hurried down the stairs. "It's the All-Seeing Something," Bel said, handing me the telephone.

"Oh yes," I said nonchalantly, "we're playing tennis tomorrow morning." Carrying the phone to the recital room, I whispered, "M?"

"C?"

"The situation has changed. We have to move fast. Let's get down to business."

The All-Seeing Eye's Gold-Seal Guarantee was no lie; in the few hours since I'd left him he had gathered all manner of information on my foe. Frank, as I had conjectured, came from a bad area, had gone to a terrible school that got burned down at least once a year, left with a pass grade in shadowy circumstances, had never been married although was suspected of fathering one or more children in said area, had attended a technical college where he studied Panel Beating (one year) and Advanced Panel Beating (one year), before a stint abroad with the UN Peacekeeping Force.

"After the Peacekeepers," MacGillycuddy told me, "he started work in a scrap dealership in Dublin, and then got into architectural salvage. Last year he went into business for himself. He does quite well out of it."

"Architectural salvage? What's that?" I had an absurd image of Frank scuba diving to the bottom of the sea and pulling up old libraries and Palladian casinos.

"Essentially it's about digging up old junk, cleaning it off, and selling it on at an enormous profit," MacGillycuddy explained.

"Like antiques?"

"No . . ." MacGillycuddy seemed reluctant to expand. "More like . . . put it this way, antiques are to architectural salvage what museums are to, em, grave robbing."

I blanched.

The hunting ground of the architectural salveur, he went on, was the dilapidated mansion, the bankrupted family grocer's, the outdated factory or hospital or train station: anywhere fallen on hard times, that the changing economy had rendered unviable and marked for death. To these the salveurs would flock like crows: to the auctions, the derelict rooms, the still-smoldering embers, where they would pick up for a song or for nothing at all the skeleton and innards of these institutions, anything that could conceivably be polished up and resold as an antiquity, a charming foible of the past, for installation in modern apartments, pubs, and hotels. Mercilessly MacGillycuddy described how they uprooted floor tiles, pulled out banisters and columns, removed lamp fittings, doorknobs, shop signs, lanterns, teakettles, sawed off piano legs and marble table tops, dismembered cornices and plasterwork, rifled through boxes for old picture frames, photographs, advertisements, concert programs, wardrobes for hats and wedding dresses and old-fashioned shoe racks—

"Stop!" I cried. "No more!"

This was far, far worse than anything I had imagined. Good God, could such people really exist? And was he doing a salvage job on us? Could it be that we were nothing more than carrion to him, that he had caught the smell of death on us before we even guessed, picked out Bel as his personal treasure . . . Fury boiled in my veins. But at the same time, a tremulous voice inside me was whimpering: Who is there to steal *me* away? Where is the mantelpiece out there for me?

"Is everything all right?" MacGillycuddy inquired.

What could I say? Everything was crashing down around me; suddenly, our destruction seemed not only inexorable but perfectly logical. There was only one option remaining.

"What were you saying earlier about faking your own death?" I said.

CHAPTER FOUR

"I t just seems so *drastic* . . ."

"Not at all. You'd be surprised how many people are doing it these days." MacGillycuddy was sitting on the bench opposite, a sack of post resting at his heel. "People from all walks of life, from the mighty barrister to the humble greengrocer. It's a lot more common than you'd think."

A blackbird hopped about in the moldering eaves above us. MacGillycuddy's voice seemed to come from far away. "It's the *death* part, that's what's bothering you. It's a natural reaction, you hear that word and you start worrying. But the whole point is, you're *not* dying. You're *pretending* to die. Oh, it's a big step, I'm not denying that. But really it's not that much bigger than, say, getting a kitchen fitted, or buying a new car."

"Mmm . . ." A thick fall of ivy hung down over the gazebo door, filtering damp light from the rambling orchard outside. Ivy was probably all that was holding it together, I thought morosely. No one came to this corner of the garden anymore.

"Another thing that people tend to worry about," he was saying, "is the loss of identity. There's no getting round it, a man's identity is something very special. Nothing tells you who you are like your identity, and losing it is something that each customer has to come to terms with in his or her own way." He shifted about on his seat and raised a finger philosophically. "The important thing is to have a positive attitude. There's no point faking your death if you're not going to make the best of it. So what I say is, look at it as an opportunity. Don't think of it as losing your real identity; think of it as trading in an old identity for a new one. How many people get to have two identities?" He looked at me inquiringly.

"Not many," I conceded.

"Exactly. So have fun with it. Think of someone you've always wanted to be and— Well, I'm sure you have plenty of ideas of your own. My point is, it needn't be a negative thing. I've done a good few of these now, and I can tell you honestly that in many ways I envy you, abandoning your life and your loved ones. It's like a big holiday. But what do you think, does that sound any more attractive?"

I thought about it. Sales pitch aside, MacGillycuddy really did seem to have a good understanding of insurance fraud, and though there was still something gnawing at the pit of my stomach, I was beginning to feel less apprehensive. "And you're sure the policy'll pay out?"

"Sound as a bell." He thwacked the paper against his thigh. "Accidental death, can't fail." A weak rumble came from outside as Mrs. P. hauled the garbage down the driveway to the gate. Seeing me still wavering, he continued: "Look. We've gone through the figures. You're not the first person to be in this position. You care about your family. The bank wants to take their house away from them. You have a problem, this is the solution. It's as simple as that." He paused Socratically, straightened his back, took a long draft from his glass of milk.

I clasped my fingers and studied the warped floorboards. Once upon a time, before it all went wrong, Patsy Olé and I had spent a happy night here against the clammy wood, serenaded by creaks and rustles and distant waves. And now to take my bow and disappear . . . The magnitude of it made it difficult to think straight; but magnitude was what was required now: courage, sacrifice, the graceful noblesse of the true aristocrat—*sprezzatura*, something grand and altruistic and absurd to fling in the teeth of the Golems—

"Well?"

That line of Yeats's: *Fail, and that history turns into rubbish, All that great past to a trouble of fools—*

"I'll do it," I said.

"Good," said MacGillycuddy with a Faustian gleam, reaching into his jacket for a pencil and paper. "Now, as to the details . . ."

One might expect there to be a lot of work in bringing something as convoluted as a life to a close: so many loose ends to tie up! So many final movements to be choreographed! But to my surprise—to my dismay—after that morning it all simply fell into place, the intervening days eliding so that it seemed one minute I was there with MacGilly-cuddy in the decaying gazebo and the next standing blearily at the curtains, watching Saturday dawn waxy and white, a carpet of frost on the lawn, gulls crying over the morning ferry in the crystalline blue distance; and then downstairs to pace out the void of those endless final hours, drifting through the rooms like an afternoon ghost, or fidgeting in the kitchen annoying Mrs. P.—

"Aren't you putting any ginseng in?"

"No," taking down a jar of herbs from the cupboard. "I have told you already, Master Charles, we have no ginseng in the house—"

"All right, what about some rhino horn, do we have any of that ground rhino horn?"

"Master Charles, I do not know this recipe that you think of, but me I am very sure that osso buco he does not need ginseng or rhino horn or Spanish fly or any of these things that you say."

"Well, good, but . . . I mean there'll be oysters at least, won't there?"

"Yes, Master Charles, but please, it is difficult to work here if you are all the time watching over my shoulder . . ."

"Oh, all right."

"And you will not be able to eat dinner if you keep eating all those biscuits."

"I can't help it," I said apologetically, putting the lid back on the tin. "I don't seem able to stop, it must be nerves or something."

"Mmm." She took a pinch of coriander from a jar and stirred it into a smoking pan. "Master Charles, excuse me, but I hear you talking with Miss Bel a few days . . ."

"Oh?"

"Yes," she continued hesitantly, keeping her back to me, "when you say the banks are coming to take away the house . . ."

"I see."

She turned to face me now; lines of distress stood out around her worn eyes. "What will happen, Master Charles? Where will we go?"

I didn't feel like I ought to discuss it with her, the matter being primarily one for the family; nevertheless, she deserved some reassurance. "I shouldn't worry about the bank, Mrs. P. It's a simple crossed wire, that's all." I put a hand on her shoulder and added in a confidential tone: "Anyway, I'm taking care of it."

She didn't seem to take much comfort from this but turned without further comment back to the cooker.

"I'll go and check on the dining room," I said airily, stretching myself. "You'll be all right in here, won't you? You're not feeling, you know, mad or anything?" She rattled a saucepan by way of reply. On my way out I paused to look back at her, trying to store the image: red elbows amid steaming pots, tight bun of hair, the kindly curve of her jowl . . .

"*Ow!*"

. . . and pushed through the door right into Bel. "Sorry." I reached down to help her up. "Here, let me take that . . ."

"It's okay—hang on, are you all right?"

"Me? Yes, of course. Something in my eye, that's all." I followed her into the dining room, where she set down her casket and brushed the dust from her blouse.

"How much are you planning on bringing down? Because there's boxes of Mother's family's stuff in the attic, if you want . . ."

"Actually, I don't think we could fit much more." We cast our eyes over the room.

"It looks like Aladdin's cave . . ." From every corner treasures winked and glistened: bracelets, rings, and ankle chains, jade and lapis, garnets and sapphires, Hindu statuettes, Turkish throw rugs, antique pistols and scimitars, several inscrutable *objets* from Africa, spooky green Tahitian pearls, a Byzantine loros, amulets, orreries . . . "I don't know, Charles, it seems so *ostentatious*. I mean, if Caligula were coming to dinner, it might make sense. But it's Laura. And she's coming to talk about insurance."

"Well, there's lots of things here she can insure, don't you think she'll be happy about that?"

"You should leave out a calculator and some actuarial tables, I bet that would get her going."

"Yes, that's very helpful, now could you hold the ladder a moment . . ."

Initially, when I realized I had double-booked, as it were, I thought I would have to cancel dinner. On the face of it, there didn't seem much point in sparking off a romance with Laura if I were going to be for all intents and purposes dead next morning. But the more I thought about it—how long I had waited for this night to come, how many times I had dreamed of the moment she would walk through the door—the more I began to wonder if the two events were in some way connected. Could it be that my first meeting with Laura and my flight from Amaurot were *meant* to coincide? Was this Destiny showing her hand, telling me that our fates were to remain intertwined? If the bond between us were as strong as I felt, could it be—I hardly dared think it—could it be that we might somehow go on together, beyond the grave, so to speak? That she would come with me into my new life?

In short, though it was a little inconvenient, I decided that the dinner would go ahead after all. Given the circumstances, however, and our mutual destiny notwithstanding, I thought it would be wise to hurry things along as much as possible. This was why I had inserted as many aphrodisiacs into the menu as Mrs. P. would allow, and why I had gathered up the family valuables from their various niches around the house and transferred them en masse into the dining room for the evening (though I had an ulterior motive for the latter action which would remain secret until much later). Bel was probably right, it probably was ostentatious, but it was the last chance I would have to blind anyone with fabulous displays of wealth, and I thought I should make the most of it. Furthermore, the pragmatist in me was urging me to do my romancing while I had access to the necessary hardware, viz., a bed; one didn't want to rush these things, but at the same time I didn't know where I'd be two days from now, and Casanova himself might have been at a loss if after all his hard work he had to invite his paramours back to a nice patch of grass, or behind a skip.

"I meant to ask— *Yuck*, Charles, where did you find this?"

"That's called *shunga*, it's a very old and beautiful Japanese art form," propping it up beside a Victorian cameo brooch.

"What's he doing to her? Does he have two penises?—I meant to ask you about Mrs. P., didn't you give her the week off?"

"Yes, but—"

"Because she's been slaving in there all day."

"Yes, but I could hardly cook dinner myself, could I? Not after last time, I mean I don't want to poison the girl—"

"The thing is—the topaz would be nice beside the chryselephantine, no, the little ivory thing—I'm beginning to think you were right about her being a bit, you know . . . because you mightn't have heard, but these last few nights she's been sort of *screaming* . . ."

"*Screaming?*"

"Well, maybe not exactly screaming, but calling out for someone."

"You're sure it's not the peacocks?" Since their infestation, the peacocks had been making a horrendous racket, the noise made my blood run cold—

"No, it's definitely her. Every night at three or four A.M. It's frightening. I asked her today wasn't she sleeping well and she didn't seem to know what I was talking about."

"Her cooking doesn't seem to be affected, though."

"But she shouldn't be working, Charles. She's worn out. Have I told you my theory about her?"

"Hmmm?" descending the ladder and pacing backward to view the display from the far end of the dining table.

"I think it's what happened in Kosovo. You know she used to watch all those news reports. She was practically addicted. I think it must have upset her more than she let on."

"Mmm." I squinted at the dresser through a frame of thumbs and forefingers. "Isn't all that over now, though? Didn't NATO win?" I seemed to remember the builders giving out recently about NATO winning some war by dropping bombs on people somewhere else.

"Well, maybe it's a delayed reaction, like, now that it's over and the Kosovars are returning home, now it's hitting her. Maybe the same thing happened to her when the Serbs invaded Bosnia or Croatia or wherever she's from . . . God, Charles, can you imagine what it was *like*, all those unfortunate people in those miserable camps just *waiting* and listening to horror stories about the ones who didn't escape—no wonder she has nightmares . . ."

"After tonight, she can have a nice long rest," I said. The hoard seemed to produce a light of its own, a very old light that pulsated and whispered through it—

"After next week she'll be out of a job," Bel muttered and looked at her watch. "Are you finished? I should get going."

"Oh, okay, thanks for helping," scrambling over to take her arm, "and you'll be back for tonight, won't you?"

"Yes, probably—why are you looking at me like that?"

"No reason, I just think it would be, you know, nice to see you . . ."

She arched her eyebrows skeptically. "All right, I'll try. But I have to go." Outside the van crunched up the driveway. "Shit!" She spun off upstairs. I listened to her clatter back down and grab her coat from the closet, greeting Frank at the door and disappearing in a happy rush of conversation; and for a moment longer I stood rocking on my heels as if I'd been hit over the head. Tonight, I told myself, taking a breath, there would be time to talk tonight. Now, with an hour or two yet remaining, I returned to my lonely wandering through the house, from room to empty room, with butterflies in my stomach and the light blurring and gleaming along the edges of everything I looked upon as if calling out to me goodbye, goodbye—

The telephone was ringing downstairs. "Eh, hello, is that . . . C?"

"Oh blast it, MacGillycuddy, what is it this time?"

"I just called to make sure we had it all clear for tonight."

"We've been over it a *hundred times*, of course it's all clear."

"Right," he said. "So you're positive you want to do it this way?"

"Yes, I'm positive—look, MacGillycuddy, can't you just accept that this is how I'm doing it and stop trying to change my mind? One doesn't just wander into these things, you know—"

"Right," he said again.

"I've given it considerable thought, and symbolically speaking this seems by far the best way of tying everything up."

"Grand. And that's your final decision?"

"Yes."

There was a ruminative pause. "I mean, you're sure you don't want to drown, for instance?"

"*Drowning*—what, I'm just going to fall into the sea, am I? What's that going to make me look like?"

"Well, put it this way, it's late, you've had a few drinks—no inconsistencies there, if you'll allow me—you announce you're going for a quick stroll around the cliff tops to clear your head. Cliffs now, for the death faker they really are a godsend, you should be aware of that. Anyway you don't come back, and the next morning we discover your pocket watch on an overhanging branch—"

"M," switching the phone testily from one hand to the other, "it's my death, all right, and if you think I'm going to have everybody I know saying, Oh, poor Charles, pissed again, what a shame— It's important to get the *tone* right, do you see?" The man had simply no idea about tone. "It has to be *poignant*. This is a death that has to give people pause, to make them reflect, reconsider their *values*, realize that I was right and they were wrong. In terms of—"

"Symbolism, yes, yes," MacGillycuddy interrupted, "certainly, yes, you do have to be concerned about that. But another thing you have to be sure about is whether it's realistic, y'see the police—"

"*Realism?*" I repeated incredulously. "When will you people let up with your damnable realism? Isn't a man even allowed to *die*, without having to worry about whether it's *realistic* or not?"

"Follies don't just *explode*, though."

"Of course they do, things are always exploding."

"Yes, but usually for a reason and not just *because*—"

"There'll *be* a reason," did he take me for a fool, some limp-wristed fop with no clue as to how the world worked and why things exploded? The idea had come to me only a few days before, as the builders were explaining their latest strike—something about the government inveigling the country into NATO while the Dáil was closed for summer holidays: "The whole thing's a fuckin disgrace, Mr. H., specially after what's just been happening, we'll be keeping missiles in our back gardens and learnin how to bomb hospitals, I s'pose, Partnership for fuckin Peace me hole—"

"Yes, I, um . . ."

"Well, see you later. Oh, by the way, we haven't finished hooking up the gas yet, so don't start any fires in there or anything, ha ha! Bye."

I explained all of this to MacGillycuddy. "So you see, it's quite plausible: It's late, I go out to the Folly to have a quick look at it before going to bed, I unwittingly start a fire of some kind, and then boom! I'm blown to smithereens. As far as anyone knows it's a gas leak. It's perfectly convincing. It probably happens every day, that sort of thing. I don't see what you're so worried about."

"All right," MacGillycuddy said heavily, "all right. I'll make the preparations." And he named the time at which I, Charles, should be in the Folly should I wish to be exploded with it.

"What about the other matter?" I went on. "The Frank Trap, you know what you have to do?"

"Yes, be outside the drawing room at—"

"Not the drawing room, damn it, the dining room! Everything's in the dining room, there's nothing in the drawing room, what's the point of filming that?"

"Okay," he said slowly, "so I'm outside the *dining room* from eleven o'clock, and if he takes anything—"

"Oh, he's *bound* to take something, the man's got all the restraint of a Thessalonica streetwalker—"

"—and then I give the film to your sister, is that right?"

"Yes, *anonymously*, she can't know who made it. This way I'm simply presenting the facts, I'm not breaking the pact—we have this pact, you see."

"Ah right . . ." Outside, dusk was settling; it wouldn't be long now till Laura arrived. We went briskly over the remaining details, relatively minor matters—he'd procured some cash for me, and booked the plane ticket under an alias. "Why Chile, anyway?" he asked.

"The wine, obviously."

"Oh."

"It's not without its teething problems, a certain youthful rashness, but it shows all the signs of coming into a resplendent adulthood."

"Oh," he said again, and then, after a pause, "Look, if I don't see you, all the best, all right? Seriously."

"Thank you," I said, rather touched; and the receiver clicked dead in my ear.

Once again I felt that icy hand grip my stomach. There was no going back now; that click had sounded the end of my salad days. My exile from Amaurot had effectively begun. For an instant I panicked: Where would I go? What would I do? Did they have croissants in Chile? But it was only an instant. MacGillycuddy was right, one had to be positive; and in a way it was exhilarating, having one's life so full of machination and subterfuge. Perhaps this was how all those people felt, filing off to their offices and their jar factories every morning. To them, every day was a new adventure. And soon, of course, I would be taking my place among them; soon I would be far, far away from here, set free of all my cares, and nothing that happened would matter to me anymore . . . Although in spite of my best efforts, a part of me was already nurturing a dream of the day in the misty future when I would return: creeping across the lawn in Fidel Castro beard and combat fatigues to peep in through the curtains of the drawing room, where Bel and Mother—older, silver-haired—paused at their needlework and wistfully recalled the noble son and brother for whom a place was still kept at the fireside; and then took up their cloths again, safe and secure in the grand illusion I had bequeathed them . . .

The clock struck for seven. I mixed myself a last, calmative gimlet and hastened to my room. I attached my collars and tied my tie; I clipped my cuff links and buffed my shoes. From under the bed poked the small satchel of belongings I had allowed myself to bring away with me: a Latin American phrase book; a parsimonious sum of money in dollars and pesos; an equally spartan selection of socks and underwear; a photograph of the family; a plastic tiara that Bel had favored during her days as a princess, years and years ago, in lieu of a picture of her; Father's first edition of the collected poems of W. B. Yeats; an eight-by-ten of Gene from early in her career—when they'd called her the GET girl, for Gene Eliza Tierney, because she got what she wanted; or at least that was how it looked from the outside.

Laura's yearbook photos were laid out chronologically on the coverlet from when I had been studying them earlier in the evening. As my eye fell over them now, it struck me that, arranged like that, they almost resembled a film reel: each year inscribed in a single frame, which if you projected them in sequence would show her coming—jerkily, fuzzily—to life before your very eyes; passing from wide-eyed childhood into full matinee-idol luminescence in a matter of seconds, appearing out of the ether like a djinn of the celluloid . . . And now, unbidden, my mind began to play the missing final reel: the scene where the doorbell rings and, giving my hair one last peremptory swipe, I run for the staircase, arriving at the midpoint just as Mrs. P. ushers in a slender young woman with long, honey-colored hair, who shrugs back her winter coat to reveal bare white shoulders and a dress black and sinuous as a flame; on the staircase, unseen, I observe her breathlessly—until suddenly our eyes meet, and at that moment we are transported into another world, a world where passions run simple and deep and come out in wisecracks and bold deeds, with room sometimes for an emotional monologue at the end; where everything is in its rightful place and there are no third parties waiting in the wings to change the dialogue, or close the scene for auction.

Now outside the first stars were emerging, and beneath the orange-and-purple light everything cast strange teasing shadows. I turned my eyes to the tower and had for an instant one of my visions, of capering satyrs and the angel peeping from the top; I blinked and they disappeared and all that was left was the decidedly unhallucinatory figure of Mrs. P., returning from one of the aimless pilgrimages she had grown so fond of. Who would she cook for now, I thought, sipping at my gimlet; who would look out from this window and count stars . . .

And then the doorbell rang. Giving my hair one last peremptory swipe, I made a dash for the stairs, coming to a stop midway and waiting there for Mrs. P. to hurry in from the garden and puff over to the door, clutching the handrail as it swung open and she ushered in an unmistakable form . . .

Nothing could have prepared me for this moment, I realized that straightaway. It was overwhelming, even disquieting. She was beautiful, of course, intensely so; at the same time, seeing her moving around in three dimensions was rather a shock. To my overheated mind, the physicality of her seemed brazen, almost grotesque—less like a djinn than a statue come to life and colorized and standing in one's hallway. Also, I couldn't help noticing one or two departures from the dream version of her arrival. The lustrous hair, for instance, was tied back into a functional ponytail. Then there appeared to be some confusion as to whether Mrs. P. was to be allowed to take her coat; and when in the end she did relinquish it, she revealed not a strapless evening gown but a mannish trouser suit of anonymous high-street design. Watching from the stairs I wondered if I had made a terrible mistake: But then she lifted her eyes to me, and all the fear and dread that had enveloped me was erased.

How to describe them, those impossible planets, without lapsing into cliché? I will say only that in them I saw my own glittering afterlife, a blessed and fecund next world where milk and honey would be the order of the day; and a song awoke in my heart. "You're Charles, I bet," she said.

"Quite," I replied awkwardly, borne down the remaining stairs on a little cloud.

"Somehow I knew you'd be tall," she said, cocking her head. "I just kind of knew."

"Thank you," I said, flushing, "although I wouldn't say tall exactly, really I'm just upper-medium—"

"I suppose I thought because Bel's tall," she mused, "for a girl, you know."

"Yes, yes," I agreed without hearing—for it was clear already that words would be superfluous to us, that her true meaning was to be divined from the flutter of her hands, the glow of her skin.

"So where's these vases?" she asked.

"This way," I said, taking her by the hand and leading her eagerly into the reconfigured dining room. "There's a few other bits and pieces . . ."

"Wow . . ." Her cheeks flushed as she took in the shimmering array.

"Is it just the vases you wanted insured, or . . . ?" A delicious avarice caught in her voice.

"Oh, everything, I suppose," I said carelessly.

"Wow," she said again.

"I thought you'd like it," I began to babble. "Most of the time it's just sitting in boxes, I've been waiting so long for someone to come and make sense of it all . . ."

"Index it," she murmured.

"Index . . . ," I echoed, sighingly.

"Appraise it." Her lovely eyes drifted and lingered.

"Yes, yes . . ."

"I wonder what coverage'd be most suitable . . . it must be worth so *much*."

"Oh, well, I'll leave that up to you. To me they're just trinkets, really, playthings . . . there's more to life than money, after all."

"You shouldn't ever say that, Charles," she said sternly, turning to look at me. "No one likes to think about fire and theft, but, like, they happen every day. It's your responsibility to take care of your valuables, because if you don't, who else is going to?"

"Quite so," I said, gazing at her tenderly, "you're absolutely right." In certain modes, from certain angles, her pulchritude was positively breathtaking; looking at her I found I could almost forget about what lay ahead for me. My initial disorientation had quite passed now: I was glad I had her here, an accomplice for this last hallucinatory night, helping me turn these heavy moments, these woebegone lost riches, into a private carousel of light and gaiety and pleasure. "But that's all ahead of us. Why don't we eat first, get acquainted?" I went to the door and dimmed the lights. "It's important to have an understanding, a *rapport*, in these matters . . . Please, have a seat. Can I offer you a drink?"

"I don't know if I should . . ." Her eyes flashed wickedly. "Okay so, do you have any Le Piat d'Or?"

"I'm almost certain we've just run out—but perhaps you'll join me in a gimlet? Vodka and lime juice, really quite delicious . . . ," and I rang the bell for the entrées.

Mrs. P. had outdone herself: The food was magnificent, heady, rhapsodic. Each course was a seduction, each flavor a Salome's veil floating down to the palate. However, other than getting an oyster stuck in her throat, Laura appeared unmoved. She ate perfunctorily, without seeming to notice what was on the plate; throughout starters and main course she betrayed nothing of the graceful, photographic Laura I'd fallen in love with. Conversationally, too, she was proving an elusive quarry. Far from our two souls melting into one, I found talking to her rather like climbing a mountain, a mountain of glass.

For one thing, no matter how much I dimmed the lights, some knickknack or other kept catching her eye and she would get up to look at it. "Wow," she'd say, tossing one of those silly Fabergé eggs from palm to palm, "this must be *really* old."

"It is," I'd say. "Anyway, there's Pongo McGurks and I, policeman's helmet in my—"

"It's so *old.*"

"—hotly pursued by the local cricket team—"

"And *this*, God, this must be *really, really* old . . ."

It's difficult to steer a conversation when one's interlocutor is constantly bouncing up and leaving one's field of vision; though having said that, even when she sat still nothing I said to her appeared to have any effect. Blue-chip anecdotes, the ones I reserved for occasions such as this, met with the same implacable indifference as the food: ". . . and then the morning she passed away—I remember it quite clearly, though I couldn't have been more than five or so—Father came out with a terrible, ashen face. He didn't speak; he just handed me a little shaving mirror. Granny'd had the nurse bring it to her especially so she could give it to me, even though the doctors said she didn't recognize anyone anymore—"

"Why did your granny have a shaving mirror?"

"Well it had been Grandfather's, I think I told you that, if you'll cast your mind back to a minute or so ago—"

"Oh right," she'd respond, chewing. "So, did she get better?"

"No, as I said, that was when she died, you see . . ."

"Oh right."

And then the terrible silence until I could summon up another, anecdote after anecdote like swine driven over a cliff, tumbling down and down into the dizzying blue void!

"Well, let's talk about you," I said finally, as people are less easily diverted when talking about themselves.

This proved to be disastrous.

"Well, I went to school in Holy Child," Laura began, "which you probably know all about from Bel. It was brilliant, I had such a laugh. I wasn't into arty stuff like she was—I would have loved to've been able to, like, just sit around in cafés all day smoking and being arty—but I suppose I'm just naturally practical, like my future has always been really important to me. Like you have to think about getting a good job and stuff."

"You do," I said. "You really do."

"Anyway, after my exams I got into Business and Technology in the Smorfett Institute—"

"Isn't that where they did all those experiments on monkeys?" I interjected.

"No," she said. "It's actually one of the best IT solutions centers in Europe."

I didn't fully understand what this meant, other than it had to do with computers and entailed lots of "opportunities"; but whatever it was, upon graduating she decided to look for something more "people-oriented." "I like people," she said.

"Who doesn't?" I said.

As such, she continued, she was naturally drawn to the high-octane world of insurance.

"Excuse me a minute," I said. Suddenly feeling rather dry, I went into the kitchen and took a fresh bottle of Fetzer from the cooler. I suppose I must have remained standing there for longer than I realized, because Mrs. P. asked me if I was all right.

"Master Charles, the dinner is okay? The food it is nice?"

"What? Oh—yes, yes, Mrs. P. Bravo. A tour de force."

"You look like you are tired."

"Me? Not at all, raring to go."

"But you are rubbing the eyes . . ."

"Oh, just taking a breather, you know . . . I say, Mrs. P., have you ever heard of anyone choking on an oyster?"

"On an oyster?" She gave this some thought. "No, Master Charles, an oyster I don't think is possible."

"That's what I thought. Oh well, never mind. Once more unto the breach, I suppose . . ." I took the wine and returned to the dining room. Laura smiled as I seated myself and then began telling me about the relationship she had been in during this exciting period in her life. It was quite serious; in fact they went out for almost five years.

"Five *years*?"

His name was Declan. He was manager of a service station on the Bray Road. "He was doing really well," she said, "the money's really good in forecourt retail and he was in contention for another service station, in Deansgrange. But we just wanted different things, you know?" They had parted ways six months ago, when Declan decided to give up his job and go to Australia for a year. "It's great out there!" Laura said. "Imagine, Christmas on the beach! Wouldn't that be mad!"

"Why didn't you go, so?" I asked, beginning to wish that she had.

"Oh, it was really sad," she mooned, "like I was really sad about it for a while, cos like I really loved him, he was so nice and funny and just loads of crack to be around—"

"Loads of what?"

"But, like, it's all very well for him to just give up his job and go off and have a laugh for a year, but you know, I have responsibilities. I didn't want to let everyone in work down. And as well, I'm a woman, you know?"

There was a pause here that I wasn't quite sure what to do with; eventually I said, "Oh yes?" in a tone that I hoped conveyed interest but not surprise.

"Well yeah, so like, I felt I had a responsibility to myself too, and to all the women that have been repressed over the years, to build a stable career for myself. I wasn't going to give that up just for some *man*."

I drank my glass of wine in one swallow and poured myself another. "You felt a responsibility to all the women who hadn't been allowed to work in the insurance industry?" I said, just in case I'd missed something.

"Yeah," she nodded vigorously, "and do you know, Charles, it was completely the right decision. Like, I was really upset about Dec, but the people in the company have been so good to me. It's like a family to me now. And it's been so fulfilling to me in terms of expressing myself as a person. I got promoted nearly straightaway, I'm a Team Leader now, even though I've only been there a year. At first some of the girls were jealous and they thought it was just because I went to Holy Child, but now we're all best friends and a really good team and we just have such a laugh."

"Congratulations," I cut in. "You know, I wonder if we ought to—"

"And I get a car and a phone and if I make my bonus there's this gorgeous apartment—well, it's in sort of this bad area but there's like a security guard and electric fences, so it's fine—I'm maybe going to move into with this girl from work. It's such a good job. Like I envy Bel being, you know, an actress and having so much free time and stuff, but I love having the security and the opportunities, and there's good holiday pay too—"

"Holidays," I seized desperately. "Did you go anywhere nice for your holidays?"

"Oh yeah." Her face lit up and at last she took off her jacket and propped her elbows on the table. "Like last year me and some of the gang from work went to Greece— Oh, it was mad, we met this great bunch of lads, Irish lads, you know—oh, they were mad. One night, right, it was tequila night in this Irish pub we'd go to and we were all locked, anyway suddenly the lads came in and tore off our T-shirts—"

"How awful!" I cried, bidding for the feminist vote.

"We were breaking our shites laughing," she continued. "God, I've never drank so much in my life, practically every night we used to end up on the beach watching the sun come up, drinking vodka . . ."

"Corinth?" I gasped weakly. "Minos?"

"What?"

"What?" I said in a strangulated, despairing whisper.

There was a silence, and I looked at Laura—really *looked* at her—and had the sudden impression that I was having dinner with a simulacrum, a *knockoff*. I felt like the man who buys the box of genuine wartime memorabilia at auction and brings it home to discover, under the first layer, piles and piles of shredded newspaper.

"Well, this is all fascinating," I managed to croak, "but we should probably get started on the, ah, vases . . ."

"You're right," she said, backing her chair away from the table and taking a personal organizer from her jacket pocket. "That was lovely, by the way. It's actually a really good idea, having dinner first and getting to know each other, I must say it to my department manager." She stepped over to the dresser and on tiptoes scrutinized the top shelf. "Obviously these'll have to be valued, so I'm just going to do an inventory and give you a rough estimate, okay?"

"Fine," I said, and filling my glass once more watched as she picked things up and put them down, affixing mental price tags to each and making diligent notes in her electronic pad. Even her face looked somehow *wrong*. Close up she bore only a passing resemblance to the girl in Bel's school annuals, and adjust the lights as I might I could not get her to look any more like her. How had this come to pass? Did the Laura I had fallen in love with exist only in the yearbooks? An image imprisoned in seven grainy pages, just as I was trapped in the corporeal world?

I glanced over at the clock. My God, could it be only half past nine? Laura chattered on as she went about her vivisection; I ground my nails into my palms. My last night in Amaurot wasted, my grand love story in tatters, and nothing to show for it but some overinsured vases! Then—like a ray of hope—I perceived the sound of the key in the front door. "Pardon me one moment." I sprang to my feet and dashed out to the hall, catching the newcomers just as they were sneaking off upstairs. "Bel! Thank God! And is that Frank with you? My dear fellow, what a pleasant surprise!"

"All right?"

"Charles, we're actually quite tired, I thought we might go straight to—"

"Yes, yes, you'll stop by the dining room just for a minute, though, won't you? I know Laura is dying to see you . . . *please*, Bel . . ."

"Ow, Charles, let go . . . all right, but just for a minute."

"I'm just going to run into the jacks first and have a slash," said Frank.

"Yes, capital, you do that." He lumbered off, and Bel, with the sigh of a surgeon called back into the emergency room just as she is about to leave for home, took off her gloves and preceded me into the dining room.

"*Laura*," she said, laying her handbag on a chair, "how *wonderful* to see you!"

"Oh my God, Bel!" Laura turned from her inventory with a exclamation of delight. "How *are* you?"

"I'm fine. Charles is keeping you entertained, I see?"

"Oh yes, we've had such a laugh— Do you know, I was just talking about you to Bunty the other day, no one's even seen you in I don't know how long . . ."

"Oh, you Smorfett girls have such busy social lives," Bel countered with a smile, pouring a glass of wine. "I suppose I just sort of fell by the wayside."

"Well, you still look *gorgeous*, you look so *artistic*, did you get those secondhand?"

"Thanks, so do you—where did you get that lovely suit? It makes you look so *mature*—"

"Oh, I just grabbed it off the rail, I don't really have time to shop these days, I'm so busy at work—"

"Laura's been promoted," I informed Bel.

"But what about you, Bel, are you still acting, or . . . ?"

"Oh, you know, finding my feet," Bel said. "It takes time."

"Mmm." Laura nodded, returning her attention to the Chinese jade. "You know, I had no idea your family had so much—" She stopped herself, blushing. "Sorry—it must help, though, knowing you have all this to fall back on . . ."

Blood might well have been spilled if at that moment Frank had not wandered in with a bag of chicken balls—his favorite dish, until I met him I hadn't been aware that chicken came in balls. "All right?" he inquired of the room in general, and then, his eyes falling on Laura, "Holy *fuck*."

"I *don't* believe it." Laura brought a hand to her chest.

"How the fuck are you?" he bellowed, opening his arms wide.

She jumped into them with a happy scream. "I *don't* believe it," she said again, somewhat muffled by Frank's embrace.

"What don't you believe?" Bel asked her when finally she re-emerged.

Face flushed with serendipity, Laura launched into an interminable explanation. I sat down heavily and started drinking her glass of wine. It seemed that Frank had been one of the licentious holidaymakers in Greece; indeed, he was one of Laura's beloved T-shirt snatchers.

"I'll never forget that night," she laughed, repeatedly.

"I won't either." Frank leered, eyeing her handsome chest.

"Remember that rep . . . what was his name . . . he looked like a takeaway . . ."

"Onion Bhaji!" Frank roared with delight. "Onion Bhaji, what a bollocks!"

"Remember when my friend Liz wanted to shag him and he was in her room shagging her flatmate and she burst in and said, 'You'd better not use all your sperm up on her—' "

"And remember when we went on that hike and he drank all the sangria and we threw him off that cliff—"

They threw back their heads and guffawed.

"Did she say *sperm* . . . ?" I whispered to Bel.

Bel was watching the pair of them with a faint smile.

"Ahem, Bel—"

"Charles," she said without looking at me, "we ought to have more wine. We may be here for some time."

It was a relief to go down to the cellar, to close the warped door on their debauched reminiscence and the nonevents of their subsequent lives, and breathe in the mossy, deliquescent air. There was something about it—the bare slats, the stained concrete of the walls, the spare creak of floorboards underfoot—that always renewed me. Descending the rickety steps, I thought how glad I was that Bel had come home, and how really the dinner hadn't been all that bad; I may even have chuckled once or twice, thinking of Laura's agonizing conversation. And then I saw the racks. They were almost entirely empty.

In disbelief I glanced from one bare slat to the next. Redundant rack labels peeked sadly back at me like tiny white tombstones. At first, idiotically, I thought that the bottles might have been misplaced. I looked behind the great oak casks, under the brambles of electrical cable, among the crates of empties by the stairs. Then I simply stood there, agape. All that remained was a shelf of dubious liqueurs, gifts to the family over the years that no one, until now, had resorted to opening. Everything else had been taken. My hands trembled. First Laura, now the cellar, the inviolable cellar—it was as if the world were taunting me, bearing down with all its imbecilic might: *Your efforts are in vain*, it was saying. *We have already won.*

For some minutes I was completely at sea. Then I took a deep breath. The night wasn't over yet. I still had a chance to put an end to Frank's reign of terror. Clenching my teeth, I gathered up an armful of the uncontemplatable liqueurs and stormed back up the stairs.

Frank was recapitulating his triumphant revenge on the cunt from the pub earlier that day; Laura gazed at him adoringly, hanging on every gruesome word. Bel had moved her chair to curl a proprietary arm around him.

"—so after we let the air out we broke the windows and got the radio, and then we set it on fire, see, and then we went up to his house where he lives with his granny, and there were all these fuckin like gnomes in the garden, so we started pickin them up and throwin them at his house and shoutin, y'know, Come out, you cunt, until he came out. He had a crowbar and his brother this bollocks called Rory had one of them metal bicycle pumps, and we had a two-by-four length of plywood and—"

"Sorry to interrupt, would anyone like some, ah, Rigbert's? It's made from genuine loganberries . . ."

"Weren't you scared?" Laura gushed.

"Nah, we go straight in, *dujj*, bop—it was over in a few minutes." He sat back, sipped at his Rigbert's, and with a Napoleonic air sniffed. "I don't think we'll be hearing from that particular cunt again."

"Aren't you *amazing*," Bel teased, tickling his elbow. Frank looked annoyed.

"But what if he comes after you?" it suddenly occurred to Laura, bringing a fearful hand to her mouth.

"He wouldn't dare," Frank snorted, "cos if he did, he knows I'd just kick his head in again, only even worse."

Laura responded with a long-drawn-out "Wow . . . ," as if she were melting. It was quite erotic in spite of her, and I experienced a brief flash of jealousy.

"Livin with his granny," he remarked contemptuously, "what a cunt."

"Charles, where on earth did you get this?" Bel's face scrunched up in disgust. "It's absolutely *repulsive.*"

"It was down in the cellar. I think it was a gift from that poisonous maiden aunt of Mother's, the one who lives in a boathouse."

"Something about it tastes horribly wrong."

"I'd imagine that's the 'dash of wild rhubarb.' I thought it might be a change—anyway, these two'll hardly notice." I nodded at our guests, who were talking intently, foreheads nearly touching.

"Doesn't it bother you?"

Bel laughed scornfully. "It would be like being jealous," she said, "of a sack of polystyrene chips."

"Mmm." I folded my hands and cast a wistful glance at the sack of polystyrene chips I had so failed to bring to life. "So where were you this evening? Did you help firebomb that unfortunate's house?"

"*Charles,*" she waved her hand impatiently, "I wish you'd just stop *exaggerating* everything like that—"

"Well he *said . . .*"

"Oh, he's as bad as you, he's only trying to impress that nitwit. He makes half of it up, it's just a silly boys' game that sooner or later they'll get bored with and forget about."

"The thing about *Titanic,*" Laura said, "is that it has something for everyone."

Bel withdrew her arm from Frank and, with a woeful pretense at sisterly concern, shuffled her chair over to me. "So," she whispered, "is she everything you hoped she'd be?"

"Don't, Bel, I've suffered enough for one evening."

"Has it been that bad?" Bel asked, attempting to conceal her amusement.

"It's been catastrophic. I mean, at least *he* is colorful in a delinquent sort of way. *She's* like a Valium overdose."

"Is she what you'd call a Golem, then?"

"She's a Golem Team Leader," I said sorrowfully.

"She does seem to've gotten worse since I last saw her," Bel mused. "All the same, Charles, you did bring this on yourself. I mean this is what happens when you pick your girlfriends out of school annuals."

"She really did photograph well . . ."

"That's exactly why— Thanks, Mrs. P.," as Mrs. P. bused in, stacked up the dishes in one hand, and left again in one swift motion, "but that's exactly why you need to get out into the real world and *see* people, *do* things—"

I made an indistinct mumble, picturing myself wandering the desert scrubs of Chile with a plastic tiara and an Improving Book.

"Seriously, because, Charles, it just won't work out, falling in love with people simply because they're good-looking, or because they're named after Gene Tierney movies."

"It's as good a reason as any," I objected, suddenly feeling emotional. "Anyway, what if for some people the real world just doesn't feel right, and they know it won't ever feel right, surely it's better for everybody if those people just stay out of the way, and, and . . ."

I realized I was perspiring, and that I must have been talking loudly. Frank was drawing some kind of a map for Laura, which they seemed too engrossed in to have overheard; but Bel regarded me thoughtfully, a little like she had the night we found out about the bank. My head swam. I downed the rest of my Rigbert's, embarrassed.

". . . join a monastery?" she finished my sentence for me.

"Presumably there's some kind of Michelin guide for monasteries . . ."

"There's Baker's Corner," Frank pointed to the salt cellar, "and here's Kill Lane, this sauce bottle, right? So Ziggy's is here, up next to the Texaco. Last time we were there me and this bloke Droyd, right, he had fourteen yokes and I had eleven—"

"My boyfriend was going to run that Texaco," Laura said sadly.

The long hand of the clock inched toward twelve again. I heard Mrs. P. going up to bed. By now MacGillycuddy would be installed outside with his camera, outside where I could just make out through the room's reflection on the glass the shadowy edges of trees.

"Charles, what happened with you and that Patsy girl?" Bel drew invisible diagrams with her finger on the tabletop. "You really liked her for a while, didn't you?"

"Oh, her . . ."

"And then you stopped seeing your friends—what happened? Did something happen?"

"A fling, that's all that was. Why, you think I should be settling down, do you? Find an heir for my vanished fortune?"

"Well, you can't fling forever, can you? I mean, Charles, it won't be much fun here on your own . . ."

As she said it, I could sense a sudden discomfort. She didn't look up, but her finger moved more quickly over the wood.

I reached for a bottle with an elephant on the label. "You never did tell me where you went with Frank today."

"If you must know," she said coolly, "we spent the afternoon looking at flats."

"Flats?" The oysters performed a somersault in my stomach.

"Yes, we're going to move in together." With an aloof expression she took a sip of the new liqueur, and gagged— "What is this?"

"I don't know," I said faintly. "Possibly something to do with elephants." Inside my mind everything was whirling like a carousel spun out of control.

"It's worse than the other stuff, it's *undrinkable* . . ." She drank a little more, the fingers of her free hand quivering slightly. "Anyhow, there's no point you overreacting. It doesn't have to be permanent, it's not like we're getting married or anything. I have to get out of here and I don't have any money, so it's the logical decision."

"But . . . but what . . ." I knew there was no point saying this, but I couldn't stop myself: "Bel, what can you possibly see in him?"

She darkened. "Look, whatever I say you'll persist in seeing him as a monster. But he's *not*. He's a *person*, he's sweet and he's kind and he doesn't pretend to be anything he isn't, and furthermore he has nothing to do with this place, or with Holy Child or Trinity or with Mother or Father or any of their friends—"

Words and feeling welled up in me. I ached to tell her everything— not just about the stolen chair and the menorah and what had happened to the cellar, but about Chile and MacGillycuddy and the Folly and Patsy Olé—but I knew no matter what I said, it wouldn't change her mind. Bel's attitude to my advice was to consider it carefully in order to work out the exact opposite course of action and then do it.

"It's got a sunroof," Laura was saying, "but someday I'd love to get one of those jeeps, you know, like a Mitsubishi Pajero."

"It's just that you have your whole life, and—"

Bel beat her hand on the table. "Why are you doing this to me?" she cried. "All you're doing is trying to sound like you think Father would have sounded if he'd ever bothered to speak to me!"

I flinched. Frank looked round momentarily. "It's *different*," she said, more quietly. "It's like being in another world where you don't always know what's going to happen, what time *dinner* is served. It makes me feel like I'm *alive*."

"You couldn't possibly be romanticizing it just a little, could you?"

"I wouldn't expect you to understand," she said coldly.

I couldn't think of anything to say to that; she was right, probably. She shunted her chair back up toward Frank, and I had the curious, surprisingly painful sensation that even though I was going to Chile, still it was she who was leaving me.

We had put quite a dent in the liqueurs; Laura was gabbing away with a new pink glow in her cheek and a woozy, alcoholic sparkle in her eye. She intermingled talk with giggles and playful slaps. Bel smiled mirthlessly and wouldn't look at me.

"You see?" Laura had pulled back the collar of her blouse and was showing Frank her bra strap. "Magenta."

"Just looks red to me," Frank leered over her bone white throat.

"They have special names," Laura said. "Like cerulean, that's a kind of blue. Christabel's eyes are that color. In school I was always really jealous of your eyes—I never told you, Bel."

"Really?" The lights were low, but I could tell from the way she bowed her head that Bel was blushing.

"I didn't know what it was called, like I just thought it was blue? But then I was looking at eye shadow in Boots and there was one just that color, cerulean . . . I wondered if Charles's eyes would be that color too and they are!" She beamed at me. I may have blushed a little too.

"So do you always wear knickers the same color as your bra?" Frank inquired with an anthropological expression.

I kicked Bel under the table. She started laughing.

"I do sort of understand," I said.

"I know," she said. "Give me some more of that horrific elephant concoction, would you?"

I poured her a glass and yawned absently. "Ought to be pushing on soon, though . . ."

"What, do you two want to be *alone*?"

"I want to go to *bed*, illuminating as this underwear conversation undoubtedly is. Anyway, didn't I tell you? She's had a boyfriend for the last five years."

"Surely not!" Bel said in mock disgust. "What, instead of waiting for you, the man she's never met?"

"No, but . . . I mean all that time I spent pining over her and writing her songs and so forth—"

"You only wrote one song, Charles."

"Well, all right, but still I always thought—you know, when things went wrong with the girls one actually *knew*—that she was somehow *there*." I shook my head. "Five years. With a petrol attendant called—called Dec!"

"Because I could not stop for Dec, he kindly stopped for me—"

"Yes, very funny— Oh." Without a sound, the lights had gone out.

Laura shrieked. There was a tinkle of glass. "What happened?" she said with a quaver.

"The lights have gone out," Bel's voice came acidly.

"Prob'ly a fuse," Frank said with an air of professional indifference.

"I'll call Mrs. P.," I said, getting up and fumbling about for the bell rope. The blackness had a dizzying effect. Knickknacks tumbled to the floor around me.

"Oh, let her sleep, Charles, for heaven's sake, surely we can manage to change a fuse."

"It's *awful* dark . . ."

"Could be a power cut, o'course."

"God—you don't think they've— Charles, do you remember seeing an electricity bill in among the others? I'm pretty sure we pay direct debit, but—"

"I don't really remember, there were so many . . ."

"Oh my *God*," she said despairingly.

"Ah, don't worry . . . here . . ."

"Do the other houses still have their lights on?"

"You can't see any other houses from here," I said, quickly interposing myself between Laura and the window.

There was a scratching noise and Frank's face appeared in the flame of a cigarette lighter; Laura halted on the way back to her seat, seeing Bel had repositioned herself in his lap. "Is there any candles?" Frank said.

"Mrs. P. has some in the kitchen," Bel said, without getting up. Frank was taking advantage of the darkness to give her inappropriate squeezes.

"It's so *dark*," Laura said sadly, holding her arms tight to her body and wheeling about to moon at the window.

"Well, I'll get them, shall I," I said irritably.

"I got such a fright," Laura said almost to herself—and then froze: "Oh my God! There's someone out there!"

"What?" Bel half-rising—

"Don't be silly! Frank, give me your lighter and I'll get these—"

"There *is*, there's someone like *standing* out there—"

"Look, it's—it's probably just a tree or something," taking her firmly by the shoulder and turning her away from the window. "Why don't you come with me and find these candles?"

"Okay . . ." She followed obediently out and down the hall. "Oh—Charles, is that your hand?"

"Oh yes, sorry." Evidently she wasn't in the market for squeezes—

We went into the empty kitchen. Laura leaned herself against the table as I rifled through innumerable drawers. "So how long are Christabel and Frank going out?"

"I don't know—can you hold this lighter for me, be careful it's hot—a month or so, maybe?"

"And is it serious?"

"Well, apparently they're moving in together."

"Oh," she said thoughtfully.

I moved on my hunkers to the cupboard beneath the sink, pawing in the uneven light through Brillo pads, oddly shaped brushes, stern plastic bottles of bleach and detergent, letters postmarked France, Germany, Slovenia, maps—wait, letters? maps?—but here were the candles, no time to pursue this now: "Here, you take this one," lighting mine from her wick and hastening back out toward the dining room. I was thinking that this power cut could be a blessing in disguise. There was no way Laura could insure anything else, so surely she would go home; and the darkness would be an extra incentive for Frank to strike, which was why we needed to install these and get the room cleared ASAP. "So . . . Charles, do you have a job or . . . ?" her face bobbing politely toward me in the candlelight.

"What?"

"It must be really interesting, living in a house like this?"

"Oh . . ." Was I imagining it, or did I detect a change in her tone—an attentiveness that hadn't been there a moment ago? "Oh, yes, well, it's interesting, you know, but it can be taxing too—"

"Oh, sorry," as her swinging hand brushed mine.

"That's quite all right—I say, this is rather like that scene in *La Dolce Vita*, isn't it?"

"Mmm, yeah, I was just thinking that . . ."

As if on cue, a low moan emanated from above. Laura gripped my arm.

"Who is there?" a cracked voice called. "Who is walking down there?"

"Just us," I called back, as Laura pressed herself up to me. "That is, me and Laura."

"Who is it?" Laura whispered. I could smell her breath, fecund with wine and Rigbert's.

"It's Mrs. P. . . ." The stairs groaned slowly. Mrs. P. rounded the banisters in a long white shift dimly visible through the gloom.

"There's been a power cut," I said. "We've got some candles, there's no need for you to come down." The stairs continued to groan one by one. Laura's fingers tightened around my arm. "Tell you what," I told her, "why don't you go ahead to the dining room and I'll be in as soon as I get her to go back to bed."

After a moment's delay, staring at the white shape, Laura relinquished me and flew off into the darkness. "Now then," I addressed Mrs. P., "we happen to be entertaining, as you know, and I'm not sure it's appropriate for you to be wandering about in your nightgown—"

"What's happening?" she said. "What's happening to our house?"

"A power cut, I just told you," she was starting to unnerve me, "so if you want a candle, fine, and if you don't then I think you ought to go back to bed, because frankly you're being a little, ah, frightening." Her hair was undone and hung loosely down her back; her shift was old-fashioned, with buttons at the cuffs and the neck. She was close enough now for me to make out her glazed expression. "Now, Mrs. P.—"

She moved down the last few steps with one hand on the rail. She muttered to herself, then looked sternly at me. "They are coming, they are coming back. This is how it starts."

"How what starts? Where are you going?"

She reached the foot of the stairs and walked right past me, making a sharp right and calling, "Mirela, where are you? We must hurry . . ."

"I say," I cleared my throat officiously at her receding form. "I say, now look, Mrs. P.— Ow!" A gobbet of hot wax had rolled down the shaft of the candle onto the back of my hand. "I—blast—look, I just have to go and put this down, you wait here"—hastening to the dining room as Mrs. P. ambled away in the opposite direction, a mooching white square growing dim and small.

"What's wrong with her?" Laura asked as I searched for a candlestick.

"Nothing, just a bit— Where's Bel and Frank?" She was in the room alone, arranged languorously against a rosewood cabinet. I must say candlelight became her.

"Dunno," she said, with a sort of allusive shrug—as if to suggest that this wasn't necessarily a negative development. "Must have gone to bed."

It seemed to me that she had placed an infinitesimal stress on the last word; but I couldn't be sure. I thrust the candle into a holder. Now I could look at her properly. She was directing her gaze innocently toward the fireplace, as if reflecting; but some kind of transformation had definitely taken place. Even her stance was different. She leaned against the cabinet with her hips thrust brazenly forward, hands in her pockets; a button of her blouse had come undone, and locks of hair hung in erotic disarray across her forehead.

"It is getting late," I said ambiguously, making my way around the room installing candles in candelabra. With a barely perceptible sway she followed my movements, bestowing on me what seemed like singularly amorous smiles.

"I suppose I should call a taxi." Her voice had dropped in pitch to something smoky and dry that called to a secret part of me.

"I suppose," I said. She did not move. I continued with my candles. With each successive flame my vision blurred and my desire inched higher, until it seemed I was surrounded by a bacchanalian fire, through which Laura's face danced up and down like the needle in a compass. I felt like Nero, leading Rome through her last waltz. "Must have been fun, though, catching up with old Frank like that," I said casually.

"I wish work was always this much fun," she said absently. The Rigbert's had left a carmine sheen on her upper lip. She rolled her head back, splaying her fingers and running them over the beveled doors of the cabinet. "Though if I was this rich, I'd never do a day's work again."

My heart skipped a beat. For a long, strange moment, as she smiled at me, her form seemed to take on an extra luster from somewhere that made the candles seem dim by comparison; and I was afraid to move in case I should disturb it. Had I misjudged her, after all? Was this the real Laura, shaking off the dust of the quotidian world? I glanced at the clock. It was midnight: There was still time enough for us to find out.

"Then again," she added carelessly, "I might get bored, being rich on my own."

I brought the last wick to life and extinguished the taper.

"What do you do," she said, "when you get bored?"

"I don't know." I took a sauntering step toward her. "Have things insured."

She brought her head down and stared directly at me. "Are you insured?"

I drew back sharply. "Why do you say that?"

"I mean," she giggled, "maybe I should have a look at you . . . while I'm here, like. Just to be complete."

I took her hand. Candlelight chased back and forth across her face. "Let's go upstairs," I said. Our arms curled around each other's waists, her blouse lifting to expose a cool, silvery swatch of stomach.

Under the lintel she stopped and looked up at me. "Are you just going to leave all those candles lit?"

"Does it matter?"

"It's a fire hazard," she said indistinctly. "Forty-four percent of fires are caused by naked . . . naked . . ." She sank her head on my chest. "God, Charles, I'm so drunk."

"Nonsense," I urged her. "You're quite sober. Just all that heavy food."

We reached the stairs. I tried to balance her on one hand and a candle in the other. She was increasingly unsteady. I realized suddenly that there was a real danger she would fall asleep before we could get around to doing anything. "Tell me about *Titanic*," I suggested as we negotiated the third and fourth steps; she had seemed quite exercised about it earlier on.

"So sad," she sighed, "so sad . . . all those people . . . they're all on this boat, the Ti——, the Ti——. . . I've seen it six times at least 'n' I always cry . . ."

"Oh yes?" I gasped. She was getting heavier, too.

"Leonardo DiCaprio in his tuxedo, such a babe . . . and Kate Winslet so pretty, even if she's a tiny bit fat, so what?" Her feet clunked against the steps. "But Kate's Winslet's fiancé, right, 's a fucking, a fucking bastard . . . thinks he can control her, doesn't even care she loves someone else . . . hate people like that think they're better than you . . ." Her brow clouded. "Like Bel thinks she's so special cos she's an actress—don't get me wrong, Charles," whirling around to place a finger on my lips and nearly hurling us both down the stairs, "don't get me wrong, I love her to bits—but even in school she was thinking she's like this great actress and everyone else's too boring t' talk to . . . but she's no *fun*, he'll see that sooner or later. Never even come out for a drink with us, stuck in her own little world, made herself miserable 'n' doing all that weird stuff to herself, that's her business if she wants to go—"

She stopped abruptly and pulled back to study my face. Perspiration glistened above her lip and soaked my shirt. She had grown pale, and the candlelight had turned against her, giving her hollows, making her gaunt. "Charles, don't get me wrong," slurring the words slightly, "I mean like she's great and I love her to bits . . . and it's so nice to finally meet you, she always talked about you in school, you all sounded so grand, like kings and queens . . ."

She trailed off. We looked sadly at each other.

"I think," I said gently, "we ought to call you that taxi now."

"Charles," she said tearfully, biting her lip.

"Yes?"

"I think I'm going to be sick."

"Oh. Oh well, quick, this way . . ." I led her sniffling up the remaining stairs and down the corridor to the bathroom. I handed her the candle at the door. "Do you want me to hang on for you out here?" She was about to reply, but then her eyes bulged and she put her hand over her mouth and rushed in.

"I'll just wait in my room then," I called. "Come and get me when you're finished. Down and to the right, the second door."

A series of evacuatory noises ensued. I shrugged and walked down the dark corridor to sit on my bed and toy morbidly with my cuff links. I remembered putting them on that evening, so full of nerves and hope. It felt like a week ago. I stretched back on the mattress, staring up at the invisible ceiling. I was beginning to feel thoroughly depressed. It wasn't Laura's fault she was beautiful, or that I found her boring; it was mine. If I had got her so utterly wrong, what did that mean for the rest of my plans? Were they just as misconceived? Perhaps Bel was right—perhaps, after all, there was nothing to preserve here; perhaps Amaurot had outlived its time, and now it was better to let the world take it, pull it under the waves.

The clock ticked. I took the eight-by-ten of Gene from under the bed and held it up beside the window. There was an undeniable resemblance: the cold marble contour of her brow, the shapely swoop of her cheek, the beguiling naïveté that dallied so enticingly with her beauty. And the name, Laura: its noirish elegance. Names were important, if only one could work out what they meant. I closed my eyes, replayed the famous scene in the movie—*Laura*, I mean—where the detective spends the night in her apartment—reading her letters and diary, smelling her perfume, going through her wardrobe, drinking her Scotch, always watched by, always circling back to, the portrait of her on the wall. She's dead before the movie begins, of course, shot with both barrels right in the face; it's the portrait the detective falls in love with. Tierney was equivocal about her role in the film—"Who wants to play a painting?" she'd say—but audiences fell in love with Laura too, and it made her a star. And despite what she said, it seemed the perfect role for her: this fabulous shadow that could lift like smoke above the intrigues and obsessions of her lovers—that existed among the rafters, so to speak, the interstices between life and death; even as offscreen her marriage and sanity crumbled. The GET girl, who'd come back from boarding school in Switzerland aged sixteen to find the family home repossessed; who'd stand on a fourteenth-story window ledge in New York in 1958, realize through a fog of unreason that the apartment opposite belonged to Arthur Miller and his new wife, Marilyn Monroe, worry at the last minute about leaving an unpretty corpse . . .

At least five minutes had gone by, and of my Laura, the real-life Laura, there was still no sign. I went to the door and looked down the pitch-black corridor. I couldn't make out a single thing. Was she still in the bathroom? Had she passed out somewhere? Or—I remembered the way she'd been hanging off Frank earlier. Had she slipped off into a corner with him? I began to panic: imagining her in the back of his rusty white van, rocking back and forth on the way to his mantelpiece—

I hurried sightlessly in the direction of the stairs—but then from a doorway a hand reached out and grabbed my wrist, and before I had a chance to tell her we were in the wrong room, she was kissing me. It wasn't the sort of kiss one cared to interrupt; in fact, as soon as her lips met mine, everything—*everything*—went out of my head. It was a kiss that surrounded one, delicate and bewildering as a flurry of snowflakes; and as they fell so gaily around me, they seemed to be telling me that no matter what happened tonight, I should not despair; that there would always be old stone houses and long reverberant kisses, things that existed eternally alongside the mutable world; things in which I belonged.

"Laura," I crooned the word into her cheek, "Laura . . ."

Immediately as I said it, something palpably changed. At the same moment our hands stopped moving; we stood there frozen in a tense silence that seemed to go on for far too long . . .

"*Charles?*"

"Great Scott!"

"Get *off* me!" Bel cried, pushing my hand from her thigh and recoiling with such vigor that I stumbled backward and whacked my head on the doorjamb. "Oh my God, are you all right?" She stretched a hand toward me before being overcome with horror and recoiling again. "Oh my God, oh my God . . ."

"Ow." I picked myself up off the floor, massaging my bump, and tried to get my bearings. "Ow."

"Oh my God— Charles, this is . . . this is extremely bad—"

"I think I'm having an aneurysm," I gasped. "Bel, call an ambulance—"

"Charles, get *out* of here!" She pulled her hair, stamped her foot. "Would you please get *out*, please?" Her voice hovered on the verge of tears. "Don't you get that this is really, really bad?"

"Well, don't blame *me*," I said, beginning to feel somewhat offended. "You were the one who dragged me in here, I mean you practically *manhandled* me—"

"It's *my room*, Charles, I thought you were Frank, obviously."

"How could you possibly mistake me for *Frank*?" I tucked in my shirttails. "Frank's wrists are like fire extinguishers. And he has that sort of characteristic smell . . ."

"Fire extinguishers?" She sounded quite agitated now. "Charles, what's the matter with you? Where *is* Frank?"

"Well, I thought he was with you." Although it was obvious where he must be: downstairs swiping the family heirlooms. Laura was probably helping him, she'd drooled over them enough—

"Don't move for a second." Bel edged cautiously past me into the hallway. "Charles, I . . . I don't want you to touch me, ever again."

"Yes, yes," I said as the indistinct outline of her backed away toward the stairs, "but look, there's no point blowing this out of proportion, you have to take it in the spirit in which it was meant, which is a simple crossed wire—"

"Just don't, don't move," she warned from farther away—and then took off at speed down the stairs, calling for Frank.

Without quite knowing how, I found myself in Father's study. I staggered over to the window, raised the sash, and collapsed onto the sill, grinding my fists in my eyes. Alcohol beat through my head like a tropical storm. My mind kept taunting me with sensory details: the taste of her lipstick, the gentle bump of her teeth—ugh, ugh, ugh! I breathed in the night air, vigorously shook my head, but a kind of hideous retroactive process had been set in motion, and now the events of the evening reappeared before me like a ghastly carnival: the hepatic glow of a bronze Buddha on the dresser, Bel's disembodied arm around Frank, glutinous oysters sitting lifelessly in their shells—my fingertips sweated on the windowsill, and I wondered if I was taking leave of my senses.

"Coo-ee!" a voice sailed up out of the night.

What now? I looked, but couldn't see anyone.

"Coo-ee!" it repeated. "Charlie! Down here!"

I leaned out. Frank was standing in the shadows directly underneath my window.

"All right?" he said.

"Ah, ha ha, yes, there you are." I revolved my hand weakly like an ailing monarch.

"You look a bit rough, Charlie, were you pukin?"

"No, no, quite all right, just a little . . . a little overtired, I imagine . . ." What was he doing out there? Shouldn't he be inside, finishing his larceny?

"I heard a noise so I came out to check it. Look who I found in the bushes!" A satellite appeared by the moon of his upturned face: Mrs. P., still looking decidedly somnambulant. I had entirely forgotten about her in the course of my doomed pursuit of Laura. "Oh yes," I said sheepishly. "She did, ah, wander off earlier on, now that I think of it."

"She was runnin around in the bushes like a mad thing, I don't think she knows what she's doin at all."

"Well, bring her in, would you, there's a good chap—"

Mrs. P. made a contribution that was not audible from the second story.

"She keeps sayin that, who's Mirela, Charlie?"

"I don't know, look, can't you just—"

"Hang on—" A door opened, and a tremble of light fell on the grass. "Hi, Frank," said a new voice.

"All right?" Frank said. "What are you doin out here?"

"I was looking for the bathroom," Laura said.

"Maybe Charles knows where it is." He pointed up to me.

"Hi, Charles!" she waved.

"Hello, yes," I replied rather curtly, wondering how long this pantomime was going to go on for. "I think you were actually in the bathroom already, if you—"

"It's quite nice out, isn't it?" She had returned her attention to Frank. "Like sort of refreshing, is that why you came out?"

"Look at all them stars . . . ," Frank reflected unconvincingly, craning his head back.

"I say, Mrs. P.'s going to catch cold if you stand there much longer," I called down. "And Bel's looking for you, by the way."

"Right you be, Charlie, right you be." He held the door open for Mrs. P. and Laura, and followed them inside. I turned from the window and sat down at Father's desk. On a sheet of paper was a row of faces, scribbled on with colored pencils; it took a moment to see that it was the same girl in each picture. Beneath it were notes on the respective effects, his zigzags and hatching expressed as fiendish bracketed equations, strings of letters and indices that represented the color, density, and reactivity of the compounds in question. To most people, it was alchemy and nothing less; I confess it didn't make much more sense to me. His portrait looked down on me from the wall. Why couldn't you have a normal mortgage? I reproached him silently. Why did you leave us alone with this mess? He gazed back at me expressionlessly.

I composed myself and considered the tattered remnants of my grand plan to save Amaurot. There was no question that the opportunity to leave behind any kind of inspirational message, or even a good impression, had by this point been lost. Death or no death, there no longer seemed much chance of Bel revising her opinion of me, coming to see me as noble, a good sport, et cetera. All I had managed to do was confirm her idea of Amaurot as some kind of South Dublin House of Usher.

It was no wonder Frank seemed like a safe, responsible alternative. I had practically driven her into his arms. The whole thing had been a debacle from start to finish, and it struck me that if one tenth of this had happened to Christ during *his* last supper, it was debatable whether he would have bothered coming back from the dead.

Still, I supposed I had better get it over with. I got to my feet. As I did so, the painting caught my eye again. On the spur of the moment I decided I wasn't going to leave it for thieves to take, or to be auctioned off. I seized the letter opener from the desk and set to work cutting the canvas where it met the frame. From outside there came a guttural, otherworldly dialogue; I imagined wolves gathering, or some inverted horror film where a mob of irate monsters takes the torch to Frankenstein's castle. The canvas came free. I rolled it up, folded it, and tucked it under the waistband of my trousers. Then, feeling marginally better, I fetched the bag of possessions from my room and made my way downstairs, planning to say good night to the others and then wait for death outside, where there was less chance of further embarrassment.

Voices were coming from the kitchen, but my first port of call was the dining room, where I picked up a candelabrum and saw to my satisfaction that the dresser, the cabinet, the nested tables had been stripped. Nodding to myself, I left the room.

"Those Budweiser ads are hilarious— Oh, hi, Charles."

"Well, well, isn't this cozy?"

Frank, Laura, Bel, and Mrs. P. were sitting around the table, illuminated by a single candle, cups of tea before them. Bel muttered something uncomplimentary as I came in.

"Nice and cozy," I repeated, circling the table with my hands behind my back and staring meaningfully at Frank.

"All right?" Frank said. I smiled benignly. Let him pretend innocence for now; by this time tomorrow, his jig would be up.

"Do you want some tea, Charles?" Laura said. "We thought we should give your housekeeper some tea, like to warm her up, and then Frank said, why don't we all have some?"

"Found some Jaffa Cakes as well," Frank said, proffering the box.

"Your hair is so shiny," Laura said to Mrs. P., who looked positively catatonic and had not touched her tea.

"As a matter of fact I was just on my way to bed," I said with a yawn. "But then I remembered I had something important I wanted to tell Bel."

Bel made no response to this, other than adjusting her chair to face away from me.

". . . em, Bel?" I ventured again, attempting to sidestep in front of her.

"Charles, please, I don't want to *talk* to you right now—"

"Yes, but just a quick— I say, can't you stop moving your chair around?"

"—or look at you. I'm sorry, but I can't."

"It's just that the thing is—" gripping the back of the chair and sort of leaning across her—

"Oh, *what* then?" she exclaimed. "What is it?"

"Um . . ." Caught on the hop, I couldn't remember what I wanted to say. I straightened up, tapped my foot, trying to think of something fitting. "Well, good night, I suppose, for a start—"

"Fine," she said. "Good night." She crossed her arms and returned to glowering into her teacup.

"Well," I said uncertainly, "that's it, then."

"Yeah, g'night, Charlie."

"Good night, Charles, thanks for a lovely dinner."

"Right." I moved numbly over to the back door, feet heavy as lead.

"Charles, where are you going, exactly?" Bel said irritably.

"Me? Oh, just popping over to the Folly for a minute."

"At this hour? What for?"

"No reason," I said vaguely, my hand resting on the handle. "Just thought I might, ah, pop over . . ."

"Fine." She turned away again, sounding exasperated.

"Well, good night everyone." I opened the door. "And if for some reason I don't see you again, then, ah . . . well, try to love one another, you know." I began to back out of the room. "Work for a better tomorrow, so forth. Though of course, I *will* see you. So it's just—just something to bear in mind, give it the old college try—" Overcome by emotion, I hurried out and closed the door.

The garden was cool and fresh. I leaned against the masonry and brushed my eyes. Frank was right; the sky was packed with stars. I stayed there a moment looking at them, candles in a grand celestial house, through which the gods bumped and argued, apologized and said goodbye.

I found MacGillycuddy behind an acacia tree, hands folded peacefully in his lap. Above him the video camera lay nestled in the fork of two branches, pointing at the dining room window. I took it down and fiddled with the buttons until it rewound to the beginning, then brought the viewfinder to my eye. I fast-forwarded through dinner with Laura. Even at high speed it looked insufferably boring. Ignominious matchsticks wolfed food and wine, heads snapped back and forth like birds. Bel and Frank arrived. The matchsticks zipped about the room. Then the power cut: After a period of darkness, Laura came back with her candle. I saw Bel and Frank leaving and me returning, lighting the other candles; Laura's and my brief moment of electricity by the cabinet, a split second of insignificance.

Shortly afterward we made our exit. I slowed the recording to normal speed. Some minutes passed, and then a ghostly white figure appeared: Mrs. P., making her somnambulant rounds. But then she was joined by others. The candlelight and the poor picture made it impossible to discern faces; all I could see were shadows—terrifying, overgrown shadows, moving slowly behind her like a witch's familiars. In their black paws things glinted and disappeared. A freezing sweat sprang up across my back. I nudged MacGillycuddy. "MacGillycuddy! I say, MacGillycuddy, wake up!"

"What, what?" he mumbled, half-opening his so-called all-seeing eyes. "I was awake already."

"No you weren't, you were fast asleep."

With a groan he heaved himself up from the ground. "Aren't you dead yet?"

"No—blast it, MacGillycuddy, couldn't you watch for one hour?"

"The video worked, didn't it?" he replied grouchily, pulling twiglets off his back.

"Well, it filmed *something*," I said. "But it doesn't make very much sense. According to this Frank is entirely innocent and it's actually Mrs. P. who's been behind everything, with the help of some sort of *be-*

ings, possibly supernatural beings." I thrust the camera into his hands. "See for yourself."

He replayed the tape. "How about that," he said when it was finished.

"Well, what am I going to do? You don't think Mrs. P.'s been associating with beings, do you?"

"It's hard to tell . . . ," MacGillycuddy scratched his head noncommittally.

"Damn it, didn't you see anything? I'm paying you to *monitor*, aren't I? Why weren't you monitoring?"

"I can't monitor in candlelight, can I? I'm not Brother Cadfael."

"What?" I said.

Anyway, he continued sourly, if supernatural beings were behind the furniture theft, I would be better off with a priest. He added that I might have some difficulty finding a priest willing to accept my bouncing checks. I replied to the effect that if lack of funds was his problem, there were bound to be some children having birthdays tomorrow whose cards he could intercept. He responded with an unsavory remark about inbreeding. I punched him on the ear. He retaliated with a dig in the kidneys, and before I knew where I was we were tussling on the twigs and dirt of the shrubbery. MacGillycuddy was one of those wiry types and had a ruthless streak; it might have gone badly for me had I not espied, from beneath his armpit, two burly shadows—the same shadows that had guest-starred on the video, I was sure of it—shuffling across the lawn with the piano. "Look!" I wheezed.

"Oh, the old 'look' trick," MacGillycuddy snarled. "I'll teach you how to look—"

"For the love of God!" I howled as MacGillycuddy's fingers delved into my eye sockets. "The thieves! They're behind you!"

MacGillycuddy by this point was winning the fight by such a margin that he could afford to snatch a glance backward. "Holy fuck!" he whispered, relinquishing my neck.

"Well, come on!" I staggered to my feet. "After them!"

The shadows were moving in the direction of the Folly, at a fair clip considering their heavy load. I was hampered by my ankle, which MacGillycuddy had stamped on, and he seemed reluctant to run on after them himself; nevertheless we were gaining ground when a third party stepped into our path. He was smaller and squatter than the others, with a knobbly, richly bruised face.

"Evenin'," he said.

"Look here," I gasped, massaging my throat, "I don't mind about the ottoman, or . . . or the ramekins, but the *piano*—I don't know if you're a musical man yourself, but there's a sort of a *bond* between a man and—"

"I don't know nuttin about ramekins," the new arrival interrupted. "I was just wantin to have a word wi' Frank."

"With *Frank* . . . ?" Suddenly my eyeballs returned to their customary location and I realized who this fellow was. It was the cunt from the pub. A look of deadly intent seared from his eyes. He was here for vengeance.

"Now if you could just go in," the cunt said quietly, "and ask Frank if he'd pop out for a minute . . ."

We were trapped in a gang war! Could things get any more down-market? I looked at MacGillycuddy. MacGillycuddy looked at me.

"Run!" said MacGillycuddy.

The door slammed behind us just as more cuntlike presences appeared out of the trees. We burst panting into the kitchen, where Laura was still prattling to Frank, and Bel was trying to coax Mrs. P. out of her chair. Bel rose, startled.

"I thought you'd gone to bed. What's going on? Who's this?"

"MacGillycuddy's the name, Ignatius MacGillycuddy."

"Aren't you the postman?"

"We haven't time for this," I cut in. "The fact is—" The doorbell began to ring and did not stop.

"Ooh, that must be my taxi." Laura swung her little bag over her shoulder and scampered over to the door, forcing me to lunge after her and grab her by the arm.

"If everyone could just *listen*. The fact is, the house is under attack, by the cunt and his friends—"

"That fella's a glutton for punishment," Frank remarked.

"Yes, well, be that as it may, I don't care for the girls to get mixed up in this, so Bel, if you take Laura and Mrs. P. down to the cellar, then

Frank and MacGillycuddy and I can try and— Where *is* MacGilly-cuddy?"

"He was here a minute ago."

"Oh, hell. . . . All right, Frank, it looks like—"

"Charles." Bel's cheeks blazed every time she looked at me. "If you think I'm going down to that horrible smelly cellar just because of an odious little man—"

"It's not *one* odious little man, there's about twenty of them."

"Well still, and anyway, what about Mrs. P.?" By her left side her fist clenched and unclenched repeatedly. "Do you really think she's in any condition to be sitting in a cold, dingy—"

"She's not really fit for a punch-up either, though, Bel—" I broke off and listened. The ringing had stopped and an ominous thudding had taken its place, beating against the front door like a jungle drum, making the cupboards and fixtures buzz in sympathy.

"Maybe they don't want a fight," Laura said. "Maybe they just want to use the phone, or like borrow something."

The candle guttered violently in the bottle, pitching our shadows this way and that.

"Blast it, Frank, they're your enemies, can't you go and reason with them?"

"I s'pose I'd better. You wouldn't happen to have a few lengths of plywood knockin around, would you, Charlie? Or one of them nail guns?"

Bel stood up. "This is ridiculous. I'm calling the police."

"No, Bel," following her into the hall, where down the stairs the front door could be seen to pulse, heartlike, with each blow, the frame beginning to splinter and the hinges to give. Outside the malevolent voices bubbled up; Bel stopped, swallowed, then, affecting not to notice, continued her progress toward the wicker table where the phone rested, a few steps up from the convulsing door. "Hello? That's odd— Hello?"

And then—just as I sprang to stand quivering between her and the door, and Frank lurched out of the kitchen bearing Mrs. P.'s heaviest waffle iron—the noise ceased, and there was a silence like a vacuum, in which we stood and blinked at each other like awakened sleepers. There came a squeal from outside, and then another, and then a groan and a painful-sounding crunch. We raced to the drawing room window. On the lawn five men in polyester tracksuits were being tossed about in the air by the same two huge shadowy forms that MacGillycuddy and I had been pursuing moments ago.

"Wow . . ."

It was mesmerizing to watch, balletic even. With perhaps fifteen feet of grass between them, they threw the cunts effortlessly from one to the other—the exchange perfectly synchronized so that at all times somebody was in midair—caught them, and set them gently on the ground. The cunts swore and yowled; in flight their faces became cartoonish, divested of threat. ("They're not really *hurtin* them," Frank said, forlornly raising his waffle iron.) Every so often one of the cunts would pick himself up and hurl himself at a shadow; every time—though we couldn't quite make out how—he would be repulsed without making so much as a dent. For five minutes the colossal figures passed the invaders back and forth, voices ringing sonorously together—"they're *singing*"—like jugglers swapping skittles in the Russian Circus.

"Who *are* they?" Bel breathed.

"Beings," I said huskily.

"What do you mean, *beings*?"

"Well, you know, supernatural beings."

"Oh for heaven's sake, Charles."

"I know it sounds crazy, but Bel, if you'd seen them earlier on, running about with the piano—running, mark you—" I was about to tell her about my visions too, how I'd glimpse them from my bedroom window at the dead of night, when Laura cried sadly, "They're going!"

Sure enough, the cunts—who to be fair had struggled pluckily, if vainly, against the two behemoths—were turning tail and scrambling down the driveway. Our rescuers, their work concluded, dusted themselves off and loped away in the opposite direction, to an enthusiastic round of applause from the contingent at the window, with the exception of Frank, who was mumbling that it wasn't that *hard* to throw someone if you just knew how to hold them.

"D'you really think they're like *supernatural*?"

"There's no question. No human being could possibly be that large."

"Don't be absurd," Bel snapped. "Don't listen to him, Laura."

"Look, have you ever tried to lift a Steinway?"

"Hey!" Laura pressed her nose to the glass. "Isn't that your house-keeper?"

Mrs. P., clearly discernible in her white shift, was bustling across the lawn to the spot to which our helpmeets had retreated. At first I thought she must be sleepwalking again, but she appeared quite awake; in fact she seemed to be scolding them, wagging her finger and addressing them sharply in words I could not quite make out.

"This is preposterous," Bel said, turning on her heel and marching out the door. "I'm going to find out what's going on."

"I see what you mean," Laura said to me.

"What?" I said.

"Like, about the house being interesting."

"Never a dull moment," Frank clapped me heartily on the shoulder, "with me and Charlie on the piss, isn't that right, Charlie?"

"Ah, yes, quite, quite right . . . ," distracted by a scuffling noise overhead and remembering that MacGillycuddy was still at large somewhere in the house, then realizing that I'd forgotten about the bomb, which would be going off shortly. I wasn't quite sure how I'd engineer my exit in the midst of all this activity. The surfeit of events was making me groggy and a little nauseous; I felt like I had eaten too much cake. But there was still more to come. Feet were clattering on the steps, and now, with a rather triumphal flush, Bel reentered the room with the two shadows behind her.

"Everyone," she announced, "I would like you to meet Vuk and . . . what did you say he was called?"

"Zoran." Mrs. P. brought up the rear, shaking her head.

"Hello," one of them said experimentally, as Bel guided him to an armchair. His cohort propped himself on the armrest. "We speak no English," he declared after a moment's deliberation.

"As you can see, there's nothing remotely supernatural about them."

It was true: Close up the new arrivals did appear to be human, and on top of that quite amiable, although they were disturbingly tall. Both were muscular with swarthy complexions and thick, arching eyebrows. One of them (Vuk?) was conspicuously handsome, with tousled hair and long, very white teeth; the other (possibly Zoran) had a round head and a mild, uncomplaining demeanor. They sat looking quite at their ease, glancing round disinterestedly at their surroundings. Mrs. P., by contrast, was staring abjectly at her feet, like a schoolgirl caught cheating on a maths test.

"Well, this is very nice," I said after a moment, "but I'm still somewhat fuzzy as to who, ah, exactly they are . . ."

"They are my sons," Mrs. P. said, fumbling despondently with the cuffs of her shift.

"Your *sons*?"

"Wow . . ."

"Yes. For three months now, they have been living hidden in the Folly."

"The *Folly*?"

"Charles, stop repeating everything she says."

"Sorry." I sat back heavily on the window ledge; I dimly heard Laura asking if anyone wanted tea. Then, for some moments, the room withdrew from me. Mrs. P.'s sons! Living in the Folly! A lot of things were suddenly making sense—the apparitions, the mysterious breakfasts, the underpants and the phenomenal grocery bills, the pilgrimages, the letters under the sink, the disappearing household items, and now several thousand pounds' worth of missing gemstones and artworks. "Mrs. P."—I returned to the fray, adopting a severe tone—"I'd like to know what you mean by having your children living in the Folly."

Mrs. P. trudged over to the fireplace, where she stirred up a couple of embers among the ashes of the fire she'd stoked that afternoon.

"Well?" I said.

"Don't bully her, Charles."

"Master Charles is right," Mrs. P. said fatalistically. "My sons are foolish, they want to help, so you find out and now I must tell you."

"Let's start with what exactly they were doing with my piano."

"Please, Master Charles. Now you find out, perhaps I lose my job and you send me away. This is your choice. Still I am happy, that the four of us are together. But please, you must listen to the story from the very beginning." She sighed, as if she had come to the end of a long and difficult journey and knew that she would never embark on another.

"When the war begins," she said, as Laura came in with a tray and made a circuit of the room, offering *"Tea?"* in a deafening stage whisper, "my family is already separated. The boys in Belgrade, we are in Krajina. Then, with the war—" She opened her hands to show something let fall to the floor. "Everything is the chaos. Friends, families, everyone is split up in a thousand different places. The men our leaders run away. It becomes very dangerous and we must run away too. My children I don't know where they are. Alive or dead, I don't know." In one motion her hands rose and then fell to her sides.

"Why didn't you tell us any of this?" Bel said, stroking her arm. "We might have been able to help you, Mother knows people . . ."

"Because it doesn't end." Mrs. P. passed an agonized hand over her eyes. "It was not over. Not to know becomes like the hard knot inside me, it is something I must hold tight to. I come here, I find a job, I wait. Only if I stay quiet do I keep the connection to that time. If I speak I think I let go, I am saying, now, that was then, that life is over. But in silence, only praying to myself so I know, something may still change. I wait, write letters, I hear things from people who were lost and then like miracles appear, but with nothing but stories, terrible stories."

She fell into a pensive silence. Vuk and Zoran grinned uncomprehendingly from their armchair. Frank swore as his Jaffa Cake fell into his tea.

"At last," she resumed, "we find each other, scattered in different countries. I send money so they can come here. Everything is secret; if they are found they will be sent back. But we are lucky. The builders are kind men, they help us with food and papers, they make the Folly warm, they don't tell you of what we do. I am not proud, to steal from you, to lie to you. But I am thinking, can they understand? Other things are not like this, they begin, they end. But when a home is gone, and they rub it from the map, then—"

"Hang on—" Obviously this was an emotional moment, and I didn't like to interrupt, but I had done the arithmetic on my fingers several times now and it still wasn't coming out right. "*How* many of you did you say there were?"

"Mirela, my daughter, is asleep. She is sick, she needs rest."

"Oh." I rose slowly to my feet. "Asleep in the, ah . . . ?"

"The Folly." Mrs. P. nodded.

"Right, right . . ."

"What were you saying, Mrs. P.?" Bel encouraged her. "About when your home is gone?"

"Yes, that there is no end, because the ground is taken away that you walk on, so you must fall and fall—"

"Excuse me a moment, would you?" No one paid any attention to me as I sidled out the door. Once out of their sight, I galloped down the steps and onto the wet grass. A livid roiling in the east signaled a storm coming in from the sea. The Folly emerged, stern and tenebrous, out of the night.

The bomb was just where MacGillycuddy had said, a deceptively homemade-looking bundle of wadding and tape wedged between two of the foundation stones. Thirteen minutes remained on the clock face: time enough if I hurried to get this blasted daughter out of the building and make myself scarce before it went up.

The doorway was a hole in the wall, braced by poles in plastic wrapping that whipped and rattled in the wind. Sweating feverishly, jabbed by iron prongs protruding from the stonework, I climbed the narrow stairs. Here and there little squares of yellow paper were pasted to the wooden skeleton, bearing inscrutable messages—builders' reminders to themselves, I imagined, of tasks that now would never be completed. Halfway up the tower I came upon the piano, jammed immovably between stairs and ceiling. I squeezed past it, pushed on the trapdoor at the top, and poked my head into the room.

A solitary flame bounced about in the wind that stole in under the tarpaulin ceiling. In this gothic light, the belongings that confronted me on every side had a displaced, almost uncanny look about them; it was like walking into a fairground tent and discovering the museum of your own life. The ottoman, the teapot, the menorah; countless things I hadn't even missed: a paperweight, beach towel, radio. Near the hatch was a foot massager that Bel and I had gone dutch on as a Christmas present for Mother years ago, which I don't think she'd ever even taken out of the box; beside it, a familiar table with familiar chairs, then familiar sleeping bags with familiar blankets and an old teddy bear that had fallen out of favor with me as I reached my teens.

On the other side of the trapdoor, which was just off center of the circular room, were the valuables, piled up indiscriminately into a great mound like a dragon's hoard. The coins, the pistols, the crystalware and silver, the gold and agate and ermine—all of it shored up in a corner with a literalism I found rather disarming: someone's idea of a fortune, and what a fortune was able to do.

I should have mentioned earlier that in the sleeping bag nearest the wall was a girl, sitting up reading a dog-eared copy of the collected plays of Tennessee Williams. She was either pretending not to have noticed me or else thoroughly absorbed in her book; either way, I found myself delivering a prefatory cough: "Ahem."

"Ah, there you are," the girl said.

"Yes," I said, feeling somewhat trumped.

"Come in, won't you?" she said politely, laying her book to one side.

"Thank you." Without moving, she watched me haul myself through the hatch. "I knew you'd come sooner or later," she said. "What happened?"

"Oh, bit of a dispute over at the house. Your, ah, your brothers were kind enough to step in . . ."

Even in the uncertain light I could appreciate that she was a striking girl, with the same fine black hair as her brothers and bold, imposing features. Her eyes were an intense, electrical blue, and didn't so much meet as violently earth themselves in one's own. It was something of a relief when she blinked.

"It's probably for the best," she pronounced lightly, in the same moderate, ambiguous tone, and then nodded, as if agreeing with herself. Her accent was softer than her mother's and gave her voice a velvety, hypnotic quality. I suddenly felt in no hurry to leave. In her sleeping bag she began to hum to herself, winding a tress around her finger; then she stopped abruptly, as if something had occurred to her. "Do you want a drink? We seem to have acquired a large selection of wine all of a sudden."

"No," I said reluctantly, scuffing one shoe against the other. "Look—this isn't entirely a social call. I came to tell you that the building's about to explode."

"*Plus ça change,*" she said, with a little smile.

"I'm serious," I said. "You have to get out of here."

"How long do we have?"

"I don't know. Not long."

She looked about the room as if seeing everything for the first time. "Such a shame," she said, with a kind of dispassionate regret. "Turn around, will you? I'll have to put on some clothes."

"Certainly." I gallantly took myself off to the far side of the room and, ignoring a curious tapping noise from behind, looked through Mrs. P.'s purloined treasure trove. A plastic miniature of the Eiffel Tower had found its way in there: a memento from a childhood trip to France, mostly spent in hotel rooms waiting for Father to return from interminable conferences. He and Mother had fought like cat and dog. I wondered who had kept it. "I must say, I admire your sangfroid," I called over my shoulder.

"I guess a girl picks things up on the road," she returned. "It's all right, you can look now." I turned in time to see a bare arm plunge itself into a burgundy sleeve. She reemerged and gave me a Lauren Bacall wink. Her skirt was pale and narrow and reached nearly to the floor. "Well? Am I presentable?"

"Eminently."

"What about . . . ?" She gestured generally, taking in the Folly and its contents.

I hesitated. There wasn't much hope for my plan now. Even if I could still carry off the death-faking part, which was looking increasingly unlikely, there was little chance of getting the insurance to cough up for all these obliterated valuables. Any gains made from my death would therefore be totally canceled out; I would be exiled to Chile for nothing. My next thought was that the best thing to do at this stage would be to abandon the plan and limit the damage by grabbing what I could of the valuables and bringing them outside to safety. But then I realized that anything I saved would only be put up for auction. None of this was mine anymore. It wasn't *anybody's:* at least not anybody with a face and a name, who might have come up here with a martini and a half bag of truffles of an evening to look out at the people walking their dogs on the strand. Perhaps it was something to do with this girl and the strange spell she cast, but it seemed to me suddenly that I would almost rather have our fortune blown up than see the bank sell it off to the highest bidder. If we were going to be destitute, we might as well do it in style. "Forget it," I shrugged. "We'll always have Paris."

She laughed and took a step toward the hatch.

Impulsively I took her arm. "This is absurd, I know," I said, "but in a few minutes this place'll go up, and after that I don't know that I'll ever see you again. So if you don't mind—won't you tell me why I feel we've met before?"

"We have to hurry," she began automatically, then stopped. "If you climb up on the bookcase"—she gestured back toward the sleeping bags—"you can unfasten the tarp and lean yourself out from the top of the Folly. It's a bit like flying, especially on a windy night."

"Why . . . you're the angel!" I exclaimed. "You used to wave to me!"

"You thought I was an angel?"

"Well . . . I mean I was never quite sure . . ."

"I think you were usually drunk."

"Well, yes . . ."

"You always looked so confused," she laughed again, and then it was her turn to take my arm. "Charles, what will happen to us? Will your mother give us over to the police?"

"Of course not," I said earnestly. "She wouldn't dream of it. We'll talk to her, don't worry. We'll work something out."

She seemed satisfied with this; she nodded and withdrew her hand. She looked me in the eye, and said gently, "Charles, what have you got in your trousers?"

I had forgotten all about Father's portrait, and I confess that I was somewhat thrown by this remark; our momentum might have been fatally compromised had a reddened, anxious face not at that instant popped up through the trapdoor.

"Well, well"—I snapped back to life—"if it isn't the rat come back for one last look at the sinking ship."

"Are you mad?" MacGillycuddy shrieked. "There's a bomb! What are you doing standing around talking?"

"All right, all right." He disappeared again, and I ushered the girl ahead of me—and there it was again, that tapping sound—

"Do you have mice up here? Very large mice?"

She paused at the edge of the hatch, as if debating a point with herself. "It's not mice," she said.

"What is it then?"

She half-turned toward me, the cobalt eyes burying themselves in mine, and hitched up her skirt. I thought at first she was going to curtsy; then I saw that while her right leg was bronzed and strong, the left ended just below the knee: strapped around the stump were rough steel bands that attached it to a clumsy-looking wooden prosthesis.

"Oh . . ."

"Something else I picked up on the road," she said. "A bomb. Or a mine. I don't remember. I woke up and this was there instead."

"I'm sorry," I said weakly—but she was already hastening down the steps. I hurried after her, clambering over the piano, for some reason passing Frank at the door—

"All right?" Frank said.

"Over here! Come on!" MacGillycuddy waved at us from behind a brake of shrubs and saplings. All the fear and urgency that until now had been dormant sprang up in us both; we dashed across the lawn, the girl clinging to my arm for balance. Above us the sky had darkened and the wind risen: It threw her hair about and grabbed at my cheeks like some huge, amorphous infant. We crashed down beside MacGillycuddy.

"You think we'll be safe here?" Her breast rose and fell steeply as she caught her breath.

"Don't worry, running away is one thing that MacGillycuddy really does well, don't you, MacGillycuddy?"

He pretended not to hear me, addressing himself instead to the girl. "Hope I didn't alarm you, shouting like that," he said in an obsequious voice. "I was a bit surprised to find you still there. I thought you'd be long gone."

"Wait"—her eyes flashed—"how long did you know about this bomb?"

"Well, I planted it, you see—didn't you get my note?"

"It was *you*? You planted a bomb in the Folly?" Her voice grew shrill, and she rounded on him with quite frightening ferocity. "Weren't you going to *tell* me?"

"I *did* tell you," MacGillycuddy protested, shrinking back as she loomed up over him. "I left Post-its everywhere, they were quite specific, 'Get out, bomb,' they said. 'Flee, explosion at 2:00 A.M.' I don't see how you could have missed them—"

"Post-its?" The blazing eyes looked to me.

"They're a sort of self-adhesive notepaper," I began— "But look here, MacGillycuddy, you *know* this girl?"

"Not intimately," MacGillycuddy blustered.

"But, I mean to say, you *knew* that Mrs. P. had her children in the Folly?"

"He brought my mother letters"—the girl looked ready to rend him limb from limb—"from us, in secret. Then when we came here he arranged false papers for my brothers, for a price—"

"So yes, in answer to your question—"

"Well, blast it"—the realization of his duplicity was building like steam between my ears—"I mean, when I came to you, and told you someone was stealing my furniture—"

MacGillycuddy had a decidedly besieged look about him. "I wonder how Frank's getting on," he said hurriedly, standing up and peering into the darkness.

"Don't change the subject—though what is Frank doing there, exactly?"

"He thinks he might be able to defuse it," he said. "I had to tell them about it, Charlie. I didn't know what'd happened to you."

"That's because you were upstairs hiding under the bed," I said. "Anyway, why aren't *you* defusing it, seeing as it was your idea to ruin my plan, and it was your blasted bomb in the first place—"

MacGillycuddy waggled a little finger in his ear. "It's one thing to make 'em," he said, scrutinizing the results, "and another thing entirely to switch 'em off." He cupped his hand to his mouth and bellowed: "Isn't that so, Francy?"

Frank, a dim smudge at the base of the Folly, stopped what he was doing. "What?" he called back.

"I say, how's that bomb going?"

Frank looked down between his knees. "Ah, there's a good two minutes left," he shouted, "though you might want to keep clear of the windows."

"He's going to be *killed*!" The girl dragged slender white fingers down over her face.

"Not at all. Sure he was in the UN. He's done this loads of times." He put his hand to his mouth again. "Am I right, Francy?"

"What?" Frank stopped again and turned his head in our direction.

"I was just telling Charles, you've done this loads of times."

"Just defuse the bomb!" I cried.

"I'd say it's like riding a bike, is it? Once you learn, you never forget."

Frank paused to consider this with what looked like a piece of wiring in his teeth.

"Actually," he said thoughtfully, "it's more like takin off a bra—like, you know how it works, and you've done it millions of times before, but still when you've got the girl there in front of you in the back of your van—"

"For— Would you stop distracting him!"

"Get *down*, Charles!" The girl grabbed my leg and pulled me down beside her.

MacGillycuddy looked at his watch. "Should be about eight seconds left," he said. "Five . . . four . . ."

We threw ourselves into the dirt.

A cloud drifted over the moon.

"There," said Frank.

"See?" said MacGillycuddy.

Slowly we got to our feet.

The Folly was intact.

The girl and I looked at each other and laughed a foolish, happy laugh. Frank was laughing too, getting up and walking over to meet us. Without a sound, the power came on in the house behind us, and the windows streamed light onto the grass, making everything, after the hours of gloom, ecstatic and Disney-bright; the four of us gathered on the lawn, laughing and clapping Frank on the shoulder.

"You did it!" MacGillycuddy said.

"You owe me a pint," Frank replied, his crooked teeth showing as he smiled; and though there seemed to be something not quite right about this exchange, I put it to the back of my mind and joined in the congratulations as, like troops returned victorious from a long and bloody war, we headed back for the house.

Through the drawing room window I saw Bel gazing out, sleepless and pale, by Mrs. P.'s side; I caught her eye, but she looked away before I could give her the thumbs-up. Never mind, I told myself; because even though not a single thing had gone according to plan tonight, it seemed nevertheless to have worked out for the best. The Folly was still standing, in spite of everything; surely this meant that we too would prevail, not only over the forces ranged against us but over our own misguided desires, our own best intentions. Whether she liked it or not, Bel was part of the family; wherever life took us, I couldn't lose her for long.

This was what I was thinking when, just in front of me, Frank stopped and pointed up into the sky. "Look at that funny bird," he said absently.

"Oh yes," I said, squinting at it as it soared by us; but before I could tell him that on second thoughts it didn't look like a bird so much as a piece of rock or something, we were enveloped in a deafening roar; and I just had time to turn and see that for some reason the Folly wasn't where we'd left it—

The first thing that struck me—the first thing after that fast-moving piece of masonry—was that my plan had come off; because for some time after the Folly went up I was under the impression that I was residing in Chile, in a charming period hacienda, with the poet and Nobel laureate W. B. Yeats. It sounds unlikely when I set it down like that, I know; but that's dreams for you, you can't tell they're dreams when you're in them; and anyway, Yeats and I were quite happy there and I didn't feel like rocking the boat. We were living in the lee of the Andes, on a slope of the Casablanca Valley. Santiago lay to the east and the Pacific Ocean to the west; I could see it from the veranda, a faint blue line beyond the vineyards.

It was coming into summer, so the days were long, and everything in the valley was vibrant with color and life. Sometimes it got so hot that I felt like I was being smothered; the air was a thick blanket held over my face, and my muscles ached as if I had been pulverized. But these periods of suffering never seemed to last for long, and when the heat had lifted, I would go out to the garden behind the house and wander happily amid the bees and blooming hibiscus. Lime trees grew in an odiferous corner; Yeats would pluck the fruit to make gimlets that were like nothing I had ever tasted before, so fresh and sharp and cold that they made me gasp, like jumping into a frosty sea.

The days slipped by peacefully, with little variation. I had begun work, at long last, on my Gene Tierney monograph, and that's how I spent most of my time. Generally I would rise midmorning and, after a light breakfast and a cup of mountain coffee, go to my desk. While Yeats did his chores, I would write, filling page after page without pause—fancying I could feel her come to life before me as I did so; I could sense her gratitude and relief at being restored after decades of ghosthood.

Toward the end of the day I'd send Yeats down to the bodega for some of the local wine and amuse myself with a crossword puzzle until I saw him, a spindly figure with a shock of white hair, returning up the dust road. I'd help him prepare dinner, and then, after we'd eaten, we'd sit out on the veranda together, talking and watching night fall. Out here the sunsets were like Italian operas, torrid, emotional affairs that went on for three hours or more, hanging in the sky like burning castles. Yeats could be curmudgeonly at times—it was the 1930s, and he was getting on—but he was an excellent cook and a conscientious housekeeper and we had quite a lot in common. We'd both had Follies, for one thing. Yeats's was called Thoor Ballylee, a stone keep in County Sligo that had been built by the Normans originally but had fallen into disrepair; like me, he'd had considerable trouble with the builders who were supposed to be restoring it.

"Did they have social consciences?" I asked. "Were they always going on strike?"

"I don't know about social consciences," he said, "but they were local men and they all had tiny, ailing farms, and any time they felt like a break they'd tell me they had to go and resuscitate them. Saving the harvest, that was the favorite excuse. In January, mind, or the middle of June. They must have thought I was a terrible fool. Mice as well, they all claimed to be terribly afraid of mice. The lead fellow, what was his name, Raftery, forever writing these interminable letters to my wife, 'Dear Mrs. Yates, Oi know Oi said last time the plastering would be done by autumn, but it is going terrible slow because of the mice, there is such a dreadful scurrying and squeaking every night that my men can't get a wink of sleep, I hope Mr. Yates has sent the mousetraps and that they will arrive soon, the roofing is also going fierce slow . . .'" He sighed. "Still, I suppose it was worth it. A man needs a Folly, after all."

"You're so right," I said, with a nostalgic pang.

He had little time for the modern world, its vapid protocols and blandishments. He didn't believe in jobs, or in material success. He said that he had always hated work; he was proud never to have been gainfully employed, and claimed the whole idea of working for a living had been made up by the Bolsheviks.

"Anyway," he said, "the way I look at it, living itself is a kind of work, isn't it? I mean to say, if you *have* to go through the effort and trouble of being alive, you might as well take the time to do the thing *right*, live with some manner of style—"

"*Sprezzatura*," I said.

"Exactly," he said.

I explained how instead of getting a job I'd tried to reintroduce the spirit of *sprezzatura* into the day-to-day running of Amaurot. Yeats wasn't surprised when it came to the part about the bank. Actually, he hated modernity even more than I did. "Men live such petty lives these days," he complained. "So small and scrabbling. In the days of the aristocracy a man had the chance to develop, to mold himself into something of permanence." He shook his head gloomily and sank his chin into his hand. "When I stand upon O'Connell Bridge in the half-light, and notice that discordant architecture, all those electric signs where modern heterogeneity has taken physical form, a vague hatred comes up out of my own dark . . ."

"Yes, yes"—he would go on like this all night if you let him—"here, written any poems lately?"

He'd always hesitate at first; but then after a moment he'd cough and mutter that he had been tinkering with a couple of things, and take a stand by the fire with the pages in one hand and the other holding his spectacles to his eyes, reading in that dreary droning voice of his: "Ahem. *I have heard that hysterical women say, They are sick of the palette and fiddle-bow*—"

"Hold on—"

"Yes?" he'd say, looking up.

"This isn't going to be one of your difficult ones, is it, one of those slouches-toward-Bethlehem-gong-tormented-sea things, that no one can understand?"

Yeats would pause with a chilly, quizzical smile.

"I mean, they're *good*, don't get me wrong," I hastened to clarify, "but how come you don't do any of the old-type ones? Like that fairy one, *Come away, O human child! To the waters and the wild*, that sort of thing." For these were the ones that Father would recite to Bel and me, standing on the cliff top.

"I'm afraid," Yeats would say with a grimace of politesse, "that these are the thoughts that afflict old men."

"Yes, but, these new ones, they're not the sort of thing that anyone's going to read and think, well, that bucked me up, you know, I'd love to meet that Yeats and maybe have a drink with him—"

"That," he'd say, "is not the goal of poetry." And he'd wheel round and go into the kitchen and start noisily rattling the dishes round the sink.

Most of the time, however, we steered clear of the divisive subject of poetry, and our conversations went on for hours, stretching far into the night. Yeats especially liked to hear about Father's work, how from rows of polymers on a whiteboard he knew how to transform a single ordinary face into a hundred different ones that when you looked at them seemed to ring out like steel hitting stone. Sometimes he would get excited and lean forward to me with his elbows on his knees and start gabbing away about masks and anti-selves and how, to live fully in the world, you needed to construct a new personality for yourself that was the exact opposite of your real one. Father used to say things like this too; I never pretended to understand what he meant either.

We spoke often of love, though it seemed that neither of us had any particular flair for it. I told him about Laura, and that whole rigmarole with Patsy and Hoyland, and the beautiful girl in the Folly I'd met minutes before leaving the country forever. Yeats, for his part, had contrived to fall for the one woman in the world who was immune to his poems. Her name was Maud Gonne; she was a famous actress of the time, and a celebrated beauty. She had dangled him on a string for literally years on end before marrying a policeman named MacBride, a drunkard whom Yeats had always abhorred.

"I never understood why you didn't just *give up*. I mean, when she was obviously a lost cause."

"It wasn't that simple," Yeats said, looking abstractedly into the roof beams. It was very late; we were sitting on hard wooden chairs by the kitchen stove.

"It was perfectly simple, the woman had a heart of pure Bakelite that you couldn't have melted with a blowtorch. And all this celebrated-beauty business. I've seen photographs. She wasn't so great."

"Oh, photographs," he scoffed, "what do they tell you . . ." But his voice faltered; he had never quite got over her. Really she reminded me quite strongly of Patsy. "All that we learn," he said, "we learn from failure. We come back to the business of the masks, Charles. The poet finds his true self in disappointment, in defeat. That's how he learns to face the world. Maud Gonne was my quest, the transcendent ideal I failed to achieve."

"The mountain you failed to mount," I quipped, which didn't go down particularly well.

"She was a remarkable woman," he said softly, studying the fob of his watch. Perhaps he was thinking of their glory days together, when they'd founded the Abbey Theater that would lead eventually to the Easter Rising; or the time he and she had pushed a coffin through Dublin and thrown it into the Liffey to protest about the King's visit.

"I don't see why you're always defending her," I said, swiping irritably at a moth that fluttered around the lantern. "It's all very well talking about masks and the triumph of failure and so forth, but the fact is that she led you on while it suited her, and then dropped you when it didn't. You have to watch out for girls like that, Yeats. Especially when they're actresses, I mean really you're asking for trouble there."

He took a handkerchief from his breast pocket, spread it out on his lap, carefully folded it again and returned it to his pocket. "Perhaps every woman is an actress when love is the stage," he mused; and before I could puzzle out what he meant, he went on, "But what about that actress you're so obsessed with? The girl with the man's name?"

Did he mean Gene? Because that was totally different: because what captured me about Gene was that—although she may have dated princes, danced with Picasso, attended lavish parties in the Hollywood of the

1940s—she only seemed to truly exist when she was up there on the screen; where she appeared, no matter what role they cast her in, only as herself, shimmering through every scene like a double exposure, like some panicky spirit-creature they had trapped between lights and glass—

"Aha!" Yeats leaned back in his chair, beaming delightedly, like the teacher whose recalcitrant pupil has blundered into iterating a truth. "So it's her *bad* acting you love her for! And your sister, she's not a *real* actor either, I take it?"

I didn't quite see what he was getting at, and I felt my cheeks crimsoning. "Well, she isn't," I said defensively. "I know she *thinks* she is. But it seems to me that Bel's far too preoccupied with her own life to actually *do* it. I mean she's always too busy fighting with Mother or haranguing me or swanning about with some oaf. That's her true calling, if you ask me. Though obviously I'd be far too frightened of her to actually say it."

"Do you know, Charles, I think all this time we've secretly been in agreement . . ." and with a dry chuckle he rose to trim the wick.

On some evenings, after we'd been talking, he'd fall into deep silences, and I'd know that he was brooding over Maud and thinking of what might have been. At times like these I would remind him of his Nobel Prize, which was usually enough to cheer him up; or else we'd go to the dog track and watch the greyhounds.

The races were nothing like the one I'd seen with Frank. The track was marked out in complicated chalk divisions, with flags at certain points around it, and the dogs had unearthly sounding, occultish names like Hecate and Isis. The sun could still be quite hot, and Yeats insisted on wearing his absurd sombrero with the enormous brim that obscured most of his face. This wasn't to say that he didn't take the whole business very seriously. He always brought along a sort of almanac, into which he scrawled feverishly for the duration of the race. He was very mysterious about it, guarding it jealously with his arm. I presumed it was some kind of racing form; but on the couple of occasions I managed to peek over his shoulder, all I could see were strange runes and astrological diagrams. He refused to explain what they meant; nor would he disclose why he seemed far more interested in the patterns made by the various dogs during the race than in who actually won it. Instead he limited himself to arcane remarks about connectedness.

"What does connectedness have to do with anything? It's a race, isn't it? I mean, the only question is will this Shiva win and we can buy that fancy samovar you liked, or won't she, in which case we'll have to stick with the regular teapot—"

"The shape of things, Charles," he replied, a hermetic smile flashing beneath the brim of the sombrero. "Isn't that rather the more interesting question? How can we know the dancer from the dance?"

"I don't know," I said. "Look, there's one of those snack vendors. Run over and buy us some hot dogs, why don't you." When he returned, as I chewed down the warm, spicy meat, I wondered what extra information he could be searching for, when we had everything anyone could possibly want right here in front of us. Tan-skinned natives cheered around me, raising their hands as the dogs approached the finish line; I looked away to the sun setting over the ocean, and wished for an instant that Father could be here to see it. He would have liked it here, up on this little corral east of the mountains with Yeats and me: old hunters, talking with gods.

Then one day, quite out of the blue, Yeats asked me to turn on my side as he had to administer something anally, and when I looked round to make sure I'd heard him correctly he had changed into a hatchet-faced nurse and Chile into a dimly lit room with green paint on the walls and perforated ceiling tiles. There was a strange tight clinging about my skull and shadowy figures standing around me. I resisted as best I could; I shut my eyes, I begged them to leave me in peace. But it was like being underwater: No matter how I wriggled, every second impelled me closer to the surface; and already Chile, our little house, the lime trees, were far, far away . . .

CHAPTER SIX

"You! You! You!" Bel pounded across the floorboards, gold bangles rattling down her forearm. "It was you what got me addicted to smack!"

"Me?" Mirela said incredulously, rising from the table. "But how could it be me?"

"Don't you see?" Bel implored. "My addiction was a cry for help. Heroin was replacing the love that you, and at a larger level society, weren't giving me."

Mirela reached for the back of the chair to support herself, her long dress brushing the floor. "What do you mean, I didn't love you?" she said haltingly. "Wasn't it me what clothed and fed you all these years? Wasn't it me who scraped together the few shillings so you'd always have your books for school?"

"Ma, you still don't understand," Bel said. "You're just like the government, in terms of not understanding the younger generation. We need more than just methadone clinics and back-to-work schemes. We need to respect ourselves as real people, just as good as anyone else. Yes, you done all them things for me. But you never got round to telling us the three little words what are the most important thing to any child."

Mirela seemed to wilt, right there in front of us; as she lowered herself frailly back down into the chair, you could have heard a pin drop in the old ballroom, scuppering my hopes of making a quick trip out to the bar for a revivative short.

"It's a vicious cycle, Ma," Bel went on. "Cos then, see, we never learned to love ourselves. That's what pushed Dougie into joyriding—the buzz he got from robbin cars, like the temporary release of taking drugs, took the place of the self-worth that society would not give him and let him escape the monotony of long-term unemployment."

"If only I'd known this earlier . . ." Mirela shook her head, sending a cloud of talc puffing from her wig. "He might not have died so senselessly."

"It's not too late"—Bel placed a hand on her shoulder—"to save the others. If we all work together, and remember the lessons we learned tonight."

"I'm proud of you for coming through this," Mirela said, "and becoming a stronger woman for it. It gives me hope for the future."

I too was given hope for the future and started reaching for my jacket, but the curtain did not fall, because Bel was saying to Mirela that speaking of the future she was pregnant; every time you thought it was over somebody got pregnant or run over by joyriders. My head was pounding. Couldn't they tell we were being pushed too far? I ground my teeth; I tore little strips off the program *Burnin Up a Play by the R.H. Workshop* and rolled them into balls and threw them at Frank in the front row; I knitted my brows and willed the plot to come to a close, which only made my head hurt more and drops of sweat collect beneath my bandages.

They had only let me out of hospital that afternoon, and if anyone had bothered to ask me, I might have told them that all things considered I'd prefer to spend my first night home without the company of a hundred gawping strangers. But no one had asked me, and well into the first act a few anxious faces were still turning around to check on me in the back row, perhaps surmising I was one of the endless string of long-lost joyriding half brothers, or worrying that I might pull some kind of a Phantom of the Opera stunt and go swinging from the gantry—which, I confess, was by that point not a million miles from my thoughts . . . But there, now, the lights went down, and up, and the audience was on its feet clapping. Bel and Mirela stepped forward, beaming, to take their bows; I paused briefly to applaud, then hurried out ahead of the crowd to the recital room, where Mrs. P. was polishing glasses behind the bar. "Soda, please," I said.

"Is finish?" she said.

"Yes," I said. "Actually, you know, maybe I'll have some Scotch in there too."

Mrs. P. reached for the bottle. I licked my lips, watching as it tipped the rim of the glass. "In fact maybe forget the soda and make it a double Scotch," I said, trying to keep my voice from quavering. Mrs. P. stopped and looked at me suspiciously. "Master Charles, I think you are not allowed to drink."

"Eh?" I said, feigning incomprehension, but all the bad acting must have rubbed off on me.

Mrs. P. put the bottle back down with a reproachful look. "Yes, the doctor has say to you, no booze."

"He said no such thing, Mrs. P., you must be thinking of someone else, Mother perhaps . . ." This got me nowhere. "Look, would I lie to you?" I squeezed her arm cajolingly. "For God's sake, woman!"

"Master Charles, you are hurting me!"

"Special occasion, eh?" I begged her feverishly. "Momentous, celebrate?"

Audience members were beginning to shuffle in from across the hall. Shaking her head, Mrs. P. poured the whiskey and pushed it across the bar; I retired gratefully with it to a secluded corner. But just as I was about to send it down the old hatch, the glass was snatched from my lips—by Bel, no less, with a gaggle of her noxious actor friends in tow.

"What are you doing?" I said. "Give that back."

"He's not allowed to drink while he's on his medication," Bel told the actors. "He's crawling up the walls. The world has lost all meaning to him."

"What happened him?" a fellow with foolish plaited hair inquired.

"Mind your own business," I offered.

"It's a long story," Bel said, sipping at my drink. She was still wearing her makeup from the play; offstage it looked gaudy and incongruous, as if she'd just wandered in from a Victorian gin palace. "Basically he tried to blow up the Folly for the insurance and got clocked on the head by one of his own specially commissioned gargoyles. He was in a coma for six weeks."

"The poor thing," clucked a not unappealing blonde, bestowing on me a Concerned Glance.

"Not to worry," I assured her. "Life in the old dog yet, what?"

"He's all right now," Bel said. "You should have seen him the night it happened, though. His head looked like a pumpkin."

"How awful," the blonde crooned, glancing at me concernedly again.

"And you are . . . ?" I pressed, but there, *again*, she had returned to Bel for further details, as if I were a chipped hatstand, or a beagle with a bandaged paw!

"It was actually sort of funny," Bel went on, "because for a couple of minutes after he was hit he was still running around the lawn, picking up bits of exploded silver and putting them into Frank's van—"

"Into the *van*?" the fellow with the hair said.

"Yes, so I went over, you know, to try and get him to lie down until the ambulance arrived, and Charles holds up his hand like this"—her face was quite pink, and she took a moment for her giggles to subside—"and tells me to please remain *calm*, that he's not sure which way South America is, but that we can probably ask *directions*—"

"Well of course the reason for that was—" I began, but they were all guffawing too much to hear me. I was starting to have some inkling of what that Phantom of the Opera must have gone through. These theatrical types could be quite unfeeling. Try as I might to give my side of the story, the conversation rolled right over me like so much motorway traffic; and as there didn't seem to be any hope of getting my drink back from Bel, I eventually gave up and stalked off.

I almost stalked straight into Mother, who was standing behind us regaling a group of dull-looking elderly people with one of her theatrical anecdotes, the one about the charity production of *A Midsummer Night's Dream* with the children from the Polio School, when she'd first met Father: "I was playing Titania and he was Oberon, *terribly* handsome I thought, and then these children were to be the fairies, and we were quite at a loss because they were so eager to take part and yet most of them couldn't *walk*, let alone dance . . ."

"There's a rum-looking fellow," a florid-faced gent beside her remarked.

"That's Charles," Mother's tone altered abruptly. "I want a word with him, as a matter of fact—Charles! Charles!"

I was already quite aware that Mother wanted a word; that was why I had been very carefully avoiding her all afternoon, and why I now pretended not to hear and disappeared into the crowd, inasmuch as one can disappear when one's entire head is wrapped in bandages. Strange eyes fell on me and slid off again like water; people made comments without even bothering to lower their voices, as though, because they couldn't really *see* me, they assumed that in some way I wasn't actually *there*; and then I caught sight of myself in the mirror, and flinched, and wished I really *was* invisible.

A few days previously, I had woken quite innocently from my coma and found my entire world turned upside down: not by the bank, as had been expected, but by Bel. In my absence she had hatched a plan of her own to save Amaurot. "We're turning it into a theater," she told me. This was in the hospital, the day I finally came to; I was groggy with painkillers, and the idea itself seemed so unhinged that although she explained at some length I wasn't quite able to believe it. Tonight, confronted with the scheme's first fruits—the house full of actors and wealthy patrons of the arts, the ballroom thrown open and fitted out with stage and lights and plastic seats—I still could not believe it. All I knew was that it was very, very important I find a drink.

Before I had got within twenty feet of the bar, however, Mrs. P. had made it clear by her expression that there was no chance of wheedling anything more out of her. I raised my hands, appealing for mercy; she merely stared, arms folded impassively. And so I had no alternative but to go about the room, lifting half-empty glasses from unsuspecting guests. I didn't like it, needless to say. No one should ever have to steal drinks in his own house. But I did find I was rather good at it. I discovered that on some subliminal level people preferred to sacrifice their drinks than have to confront the grim reality of my appearance, and I exploited this principle ruthlessly. After a martini, two cosmopolitans,

and a brandy Alexander, I was feeling a little more like myself, sufficiently so to approach Mirela.

She was standing at the bar, wincing slightly under a frontal assault
from Frank and Laura. She hadn't taken off her greasepaint either,
but it didn't have the disorientating effect on her that it did on Bel; instead she looked enhanced, the colors of her face deeper and brighter—
like a restored painting, I thought. I hadn't realized in the Folly quite
how beautiful she was; and—although it could just have been me mixing
my drinks—she seemed with every second to be gaining in radiance,
leaving the pale, spookish girl I had encountered that night further
behind.

"It was just so ... so ... ," Laura was saying, her hands making slow,
squeezing motions, as if groping at the huge, spongy mass of truth that
the play had communicated to her.

"Yeah," Frank corroborated.

"Like it was like *EastEnders* and *Coronation Street* and *Brookside* all
rolled into one?" Laura said. "Except like in Dublin with real people in
it."

"I could really relate to it," Frank said, pronouncing the words
slowly as if he were trying them out for the first time.

"Well, that's good," Mirela said.

"I cried," Laura said matter-of-factly.

"Did you?"

"Yeah, he did too."

"I did not."

"You did, you liar."

"No, I told you, my eyes were watering cos there was *talc* kept getting in them."

"That's not what you told *oh my God*—"

"It's just Charlie, relax. All right, Charlie, how's the noggin?"

"Well obviously it's been a big hit with the ladies ... ," nursing the
spot where her elbow had caught me as she soared into the air.

"Maybe we should get you a bell," Mirela laughed.

"Maybe ... here, try putting some tonic on it, Laura."

"I can do it myself," she muttered, snatching the napkin from my
hand and dabbing at the dark stain spreading across her breast. "This

was the last one Top Shop had in my size—bollocks, I'll have to take it off—"

"I'll give you a hand," Frank said, winking at me as he steered her, still rubbing fractiously at her blouse, toward the bathroom, though just as they reached the door I caught him floating an oddly yearning gaze over at Bel, who was gabbing away merrily at the center of her cadre. The chap with the annoying haircut and the peasant jacket was doing an inordinate amount of laughing. The more I saw of him, the surer I was that our paths had crossed before, but I couldn't place where . . .

"Such a crowd," Mirela said to me. "Isn't it wonderful?"

"Mother does know a lot of people," I concurred feebly.

"And all the *right* people, from newspapers and theaters and Arts Council and businesses, they are talking about giving us money." Her smile was as simple and transfixing as a butterfly alighting on one's hand.

"Mmm . . ." I noticed at that moment that, as well as all the right people, MacGillycuddy was here, sitting by the trestle table with a tall glass.

"I think this could really work out," she said. "I think this theater could become something important— Will you excuse me a moment, Charles? I have to talk to that man over there, I think he is from the Gate."

"Oh, of course . . ." I watched a distinguished gray-haired gent light up as she buttonholed him. After lingering there a moment to see if she'd come back, I picked up the remainder of her drink and followed the bar down to the end where MacGillycuddy was perched. "You've a nerve, showing your face round here," I said.

He looked up at me blankly. "I'm sorry, have we met?"

"Blast it, MacGillycuddy, don't play games with me . . ."

He frowned, mystified, and then in an awed whisper said, "C? Is it really you?"

"Oh hell"—I had forgotten what a serpentine experience a conversation with him could be—"you know perfectly well who it is."

"I thought you were after my drink," he said colorlessly and nudged the glass in my direction. "Take some if you want, Charlie. We're old friends, after all."

"You're no friend of mine," I said. "What are you doing here, anyway?"

"I was invited," MacGillycuddy said with a wounded expression. "I'm a Consultant."

"Is that so? Because I'd like to consult you about something, if you don't mind. How much of a sucker did you play me for, is what I'd like to know."

"Sucker?" MacGillycuddy said, assuming the kind of guileless expression the infant Jesus might have had in his manger.

"I mean, when I hired you to watch Frank because I thought he was stealing my furniture—"

"Which I did," MacGillycuddy said.

"Which you did, exactly my point, because the whole time not only were you personally acquainted with him—"

"I wouldn't say *acquainted*," MacGillycuddy interjected. "I'd seen him down the pub a few times, I suppose, maybe had a couple of games of darts with him . . ."

"Not only were you *acquainted* with him," I persisted, "but you *knew* about all those people in my Folly, and you went ahead and let me set up my Frank trap even though you *knew* that they must have been behind it."

"I didn't *know*," MacGillycuddy said. "I had sort of a hunch, is all."

"Well confound it, man, didn't you think of *telling* me any of this? I mean what was the point of me paying you good money to snare Frank, if you knew all along it wasn't Frank . . ."

"Look," MacGillycuddy said with a hint of reproof, "I just did what you asked me. An All-Seeing Eye sees an awful lot of things. It's important to ask it the right questions."

"Well for an All-Seeing Eye you're remarkably selective with your information, do you know that?"

"Maybe you should have hired the All-Speaking Mouth," MacGillycuddy said expressionlessly.

"Oh, hell," I said again and turned away, propping myself against the bar with my elbows. Mirela had gathered around her a little circle by now, well-manicured theater patrons and bluff old actors standing and grinning foolishly like moths that have found the perfect flame; in the center, she gesticulated and argued her case and measured out her smiles democratically among them. Over in a corner, her bearlike brothers joked noisily in Bosnian, playing some game with coins laid on a tissue paper stretched over a glass of beer. Bel meanwhile was suffering from a coughing fit which might or might not have been put on so the person with the hair and the peasant jacket could massage her back. And then there were the others, the men and women of Society: the bank directors and their lovely wives, the noted philanthropists, the coterie artists, the entrepreneurs and government bigwigs, animated Names with foggy semblances of personalities and a permanent entourage of worshipful diarists: And as their conversation rose sheer and vertiginous around me, I felt a burning desire to grab one of them by the lapels and shout: *What is happening here? Isn't this my house? Isn't that the Steinway in the corner on which, in happier times, I composed "I'm Sticking to You" and "Gosh, His Galoshes"? Am I not, beneath these bandages, still Charles Hythloday?*

But at that moment I spied Mother coming toward me with that alarmingly purposeful expression she'd acquired lately, and I realized that, whoever I was, it was time I made myself scarce.

I'D WOKEN WITH A START, like a commuter who's dozed off on the train home; Bel was at my bedside poring over a book. I coughed politely.

"Charles!" She set the book down with a cry. "Oh my goodness!" She jumped up and leaned over me, peering into my eyes. "Do you know who I am? How many fingers am I holding up? Can you understand what I'm saying? Blink if you understand."

"Of course I understand," I said. "Stop shouting, I'm all right."

This was something of an exaggeration, as with every passing second some new part of my body seemed to awake and sing with pain. As delicately as I could, I turned my head and took in my surroundings. We were in a poky room with pea green walls and an ugly check curtain pulled over the window. Various apparatuses were arranged around me, mapping my condition with inscrutable dials and screens. A tube fed into my arm from a drip by the bed. Directly opposite me was a poster of sunlight glinting through trees, with the legend *Today is the first day of the rest of your life.* For some reason it gave me a chill.

"How long have I been here?" I asked.

"Weeks," Bel said. "Weeks and weeks. The doctors said it's normal when your body gets a shock like that, but we were really starting to get worried." She pulled her chair in closer. "You woke up a few times, can you remember? You were rambling on about Yeats, reciting poems at the top of your voice." She smiled. "All the really lyrical stuff. I think a couple of the nurses are in love with you."

"Well they've got a funny way of showing it," I said, recalling the unpleasant turn my dream had taken and gingerly adjusting my posterior. "Bel, why does my head feel funny? It feels sort of itchy."

"You got hit by a gargoyle. You're still all bandaged up, you look like you've just stepped out of a pyramid." She hesitated, then bent down and rummaged in her bag.

"Here—" She opened her compact mirror.

"Oh, lord . . ."

"Don't worry, it's not going to be forever."

"Do I still have a *face* under all this?"

"Of course. It just needs time to heal. Nothing's broken, it's just badly bruised. You were very lucky. The doctor's explained it all to us. I'm sure he'll come in and see you now that you're awake." She caught my eye, then looked away, toying with her hair. Suddenly it seemed to me that she was acting rather strangely.

"What is it?" I said.

"What's what?" she said innocently.

"You're sitting there positively about to *explode*, is what."

"I'm just glad to see you, that's all."

"I wish I could believe that," I said. "Nothing's *hap*pened, has it?" A terrible thought occurred to me—"Oh hell, you haven't got married to Frank or something, have you?"

"Ugh, no," she said, flicking her hand disdainfully, then recomposing herself. "Let's talk about you, though. How are you? How do you feel?"

I squinted at her suspiciously. She puckered her brow in a passable imitation of attentiveness.

"I feel all *right*," I began, "although—"

"Oh, Charles, I've *so* much to tell you, so much has happened since you've been in here, I hardly know where to begin—"

I knew it—"Well begin *somewhere*," I said, propping myself up on my lumpy pillow and starting to feel somewhat uneasy.

She took a deep breath. "It's the house," she said. "We're turning it into a theater."

"A what?" I said. "A *theater*?"

"Isn't it wonderful?" Her eyes were lit up like Roman candles. "We're going to do *The Cherry Orchard* and—"

"Wait—a theater? What do you mean, a theater? Like when Mother and Father were in that Amateur Dramatics thing? Is that what you mean?"

"No, no, I mean like a proper theater company, we're going to build a little stage and— Charles, I don't like the noise that machine is making, maybe this ought to wait until you're feeling better . . ."

"Not at all," I said, through a miasma of little sparkling lights. "This is all very interesting."

She went to the window and lifted the sash. "Well, I should probably start at the start," she said. "What happened after you—after the Folly . . ." She turned her back to the glass. "Charles, what were you *thinking*? Were you really going to disappear off to South America?"

I sat myself up. "Look," I said, pressing my fingers to the outline of my nose. "As a matter of fact I don't really care to discuss it. All I want to say is that it seemed like a good idea at the time. And furthermore it would have worked, if it hadn't been for Mrs. P. and her wretched offspring—" I stopped, remembering my brief encounter with Mrs. P.'s youngest. "How are they?" I asked impetuously. "I mean—she wasn't hurt, was she? The girl?"

"Mirela," Bel said. "She's fine, apparently you acted as a sort of human shield for everybody else—"

"And what's going to happen to them? Are they still there? Is the *house* still there? What happened with the bank?"

"This is what I'm trying to tell you. It turns out that the girl, Mirela— she's *so* sweet, Charles, I feel so sorry for her with that dreadful artificial— Anyway, she's an actress, so that's . . . well, that bit comes later. First of all, that morning—I mean only a couple of hours after the explosion—Mother arrived back from the Cedars. They'd let her out early. The place was still in absolute chaos. None of us had slept, the lawn was covered with jewelry and ornaments and this smoldering stump of Folly, and of course the *piano* upside down in the middle of it—it had barely a scratch on it, isn't that weird? Meanwhile, the house was full of detectives and policemen asking these humiliating questions about our financial situation and the insurance on one hand, and trying to get someone to press charges against Mrs. P. on the other—well, I expected her to take one look and then turn on her heel and get back in the cab. But she was fantastic, she just brushed right past everybody and made herself this enormous gin and tonic—"

"I thought she wasn't supposed to be drinking," I said, surprised. "I mean wasn't that the whole point of her going to the Cedars?"

"I did ask her about that," Bel said. "She just muttered something about them being very progressive."

"Oh."

"But anyway, it was complete pandemonium, all these people tugging at her, and then Mrs. P. went into shock and they had to take *her* to hospital, and then bloody Laura thought she'd lost her car keys and cried and cried for about four hours straight. But Mother just calmly went and made a couple of phone calls, and a few minutes later all the policemen and so on just sort of vanished. Really, Charles, we're lucky she knows who she does. I mean strictly speaking you should be under arrest."

"I don't see what any of this has to do with a theater," I said. "Unless you're hoping to pay off the bank by putting on shows in the old barn, like in some Mickey Rooney film."

"The bank is paid," Bel said.

I felt my stomach turn over. "What?"

"The debt's paid off. It's gone. The auction, all that—it never happened."

"That's impossible," I said. "How can it be gone? The mortgage was . . . I mean you saw the figures."

"I know, I know. But Mother tracked down the accountant—Geoffrey, you remember him. He was away working on some island I'd never heard of. Anyway, he came back and they went to meet the direc-tor of the bank—the director, Charles, it turns out Mother and he go back years and years—and between the three of them they uncovered some annuity of Father's that no one had known about. They had the whole thing sorted out by lunchtime. I felt a little foolish, I can tell you."

"But . . ." My head was spinning. "You went through the accounts. There wasn't any money there. There simply wasn't. How can they sud-denly produce this—"

"I know, I don't quite understand it either. But we should just count our blessings that they—"

"And what about the irregularities, what about those? That time I went to see the bank manager in the shopping center, he told me the structure of the repayments was all wrong, he was going to have it inves-tigated . . ."

"I don't *know*, Charles." Bel shifted her weight impatiently from foot to foot. "Father's accounts are so complicated. Maybe your man-ager just wasn't used to it. Surely the main thing is that we're out of the woods, for now at least. We do still *owe* people, of course. But nobody's trying to take the house away."

I tried to return her smile. This was good news, wasn't it? Why did it feel so *wrong*?

"Still, you probably picked a good time to be unconscious. Even with everything sorted out, the atmosphere has been pretty apocalyptic. Mother's . . . well, you'll see yourself. But she was talking seriously about selling Amaurot."

"*Selling?*" I raised myself up on my forearms. "Mother wouldn't sell! What have you been saying to her? Have you been putting ideas into her head?"

"I haven't been putting anything into her head, Charles. You know she hasn't been happy there since Dad died, you know how miserable it must be for her, floating around this vast empty mansion . . . And meanwhile there's all these computer people buying up everywhere around us, every week practically someone arrives at the door and makes an offer—*crazy* offers, enough to pay off all our debts once and for all *and* get a little house down the country that Mother could retire to . . ." She sat back down at the foot of the bed, picked up her book, and began riffling back and forth through the pages. "But then one night I was talking to Mirela, and she was telling me about this theater group she was part of at home in Yugoslavia, before all the, you know, the war and everything. They did all kinds of things, workshops, street theater, political stuff. The founder had just started it from his house with a few friends, and it had taken off from there. And I thought, why couldn't we do the same thing at Amaurot? I mean there's all this *space* where you could have rehearsals and classes and so on, and then there're all those spare bedrooms we haven't used in years— It's like the more you think about it, the more *perfect* you realize it is. And when I told Mother she was just as excited as me . . ."

So the very next morning, she said, she had contacted some of her former classmates from the drama course to help her come up with a design for a theater; they had given this design to Mrs. P.'s son Vuk, who it turned out had been an architect before taking up residence in my erstwhile Folly—Vuk, Zoran, and the beguiling Mirela, I should add, had, in the climate of anarchy that seemed to be prevailing at Amaurot, been moved into guest bedrooms until their asylum claims had been looked at, while Mrs. P. was still in situ as housekeeper without Mother so much as docking her pay. As she went on, it slowly began to dawn on me that this was not just one of the regular Bel pipe dreams that she would obsess about for a week and then forget—that without my steadying influence, Mother and she had formed some sort of unholy alliance and were already putting their demented scheme into motion.

"We're going to open up the old ballroom and put the stage in there. All we're waiting for is the builders to come back from Tibet. Charles, isn't it wonderful? No more trudging round to auditions, we can put on anything we want—" She waltzed from her chair with her hands clasped to her breast, looking for all the world as if she were about to burst into song, and began to reel off a list of plays and playwrights, plans and strategies, with words like *artists* and *residence, space,* and *community* ominously juxtaposed, while I sat there, head stewing inside the bandages like an enormous pudding, *Today is the first day of the rest of your life* glinting mockingly at me from the far wall—

"But this is absurd!"

Bel halted midwaltz and looked at me. Over my left shoulder, one of the monitors bleeped shrilly. "It's absurd," I repeated. "The whole idea. Amaurot's already a residence. I reside there. I'm sorry you've made all these plans for nothing. But it's a house, that people live in. You can't just come in and turn it into something else."

"Charles, we've been through all this," she said. "You know we can't keep it going the way it is, you *know* that. We have to adapt, or else we lose it."

"I don't see how you building a theater is going to help anyone."

She hesitated a moment, then circled back carefully toward the bed. "Well you see it won't be an ordinary theater," she said. "We want it to be a place where people who normally wouldn't get anywhere near a stage can come and learn to express themselves, where people from disadvantaged backgrounds can come and stay and—"

My head thumped back onto the pillow. "Are you out of your mind? Don't you have any idea how society *works*?"

"I know it sounds strange"—she reached her arm out imploringly—"but if you'll only *lis*ten, there's a reason for it. I've talked to Geoffrey. He says that if we presented ourselves right we'd be eligible for all kinds of government grants. You know, if we're helping people, and then there's the cultural diversity element too, with Mirela being from the Balkans. If the theater was successful we might even be able to have Amaurot registered as a charity. Then think of it, Charles, we could stay there as long as we wanted, and never have to worry anymore about banks, or creditors, or how we're going to keep it running . . ." She sat back and hunched her shoulders earnestly. "And aside from the money. It's a chance to put Amaurot on the map again, for it to *mean* something. We'd finally be using it for something *good*. Isn't that what you want? And the possibilities are endless, once you start thinking about it, we can give classes, you know, drama classes, for inner-city kids, they can come out for the day and—"

"Why stop there?" I said. "Why not throw the doors open altogether? We could give guided tours: 'This is Charles's bedroom, visitors are asked to kindly not extinguish their cigarettes on his childhood stamp collection—'"

Outside in the corridor a bell began to ring. Sighing, Bel picked up her jacket from the back of the chair. "Charles," she said, "I'm asking you to understand that we're not rich anymore. We're just not. Living in Amaurot, it's like we're struggling to maintain ourselves in a—on a little island that's floating further and further away from what it means to actually *exist* . . ." She sucked in her cheeks and let them out again; then, lightly, she laid her hand on my arm. "Can't you see, this is a good thing?" she said. "We'll be able to keep the house, and we'll all be able to stay together . . ."

Even in my *distrait* condition, I realized that this hand was the first time she'd touched me since the whole accidentally kissing her farrago—that she was offering me an olive branch. But I wasn't going to be bought off so easily. Without replying, I turned my head and fixed my gaze on the shard of sky at the window, until her hand lifted and I heard the chair creak beside me as she rose to go.

The thing was, though—the thing was that deep down I knew she was right, about the way everything was changing, about the new money taking over. You would see them at the weekends, these new people: pale and crepuscular from days and nights holed up in their towers of cuboid offices, crawling down the narrow, winding roads in BMWs or hulking Jeeps, scouting for property like toothless anemic sharks. What if this really was the only way to secure the house from them? I tried to imagine Amaurot as a Residence, full of babbling strangers; I pictured myself at the breakfast table, the Disadvantaged sitting across from me. Would I be expected to make conversation? Would they want to borrow things? My razor, a tie?

The notion was too painful to contemplate. A far better solution seemed to be to pretend that none of this was happening, and that my conversation with Bel had never taken place. I was getting enough painkillers to make this quite unproblematic; they made reality fat and viscous and blurred at the edges, broken only by the comings and goings of the doctors and nurses and the mortal wheezing of the patient in the next room, like a dry wind through a petrified forest.

That night, however—my first night back on earth after my hiatus—I wasn't able to sleep. I lay awake for hours, gazing at the banks of screens and monitors arranged around me telling the ineffable story of my body

158 · *Paul Murray*

in blips and graphs and pulses. It seemed to me I could see things in the saw-toothed waves, all kinds of things: explosions, prophecies, impending disasters, all hastening on top of one another until I couldn't bear it any longer and, seized in a cold grip, I pressed the panic button and cried out, "Help, help!" until the night nurse's clipping stride came down the corridor, not the attractive buxom nurse in charge of sponge baths but the thermometer-happy one with no behind.

"Yes?" she demanded. "What's wrong?"

I cleared my throat and pointed at the spikes and troughs on the monitor and said, "I'm a little concerned about, ahem, that is . . ."

"Do you feel sick?" she stamped impatiently. "Are you in pain?"

"Well, no, not as such," feeling all of a sudden that I could possibly have blown things out of proportion. "It's just that—those sort of spikes there, don't they look a little, you know, off?"

"No," she said with an abrasive sigh, "they are perfectly normal, just like the last time, and the time before that."

"Oh. It's just that I thought they were a bit off." There was a moment of silence broken only by her tapping foot; "Busy?" I said, because even if she was hatchet-faced and anally fixated she was still someone to talk to—

"Very," she snapped as if she'd been waiting for it, turned on her heel and whipped out of the room, back to her crossword puzzle or her tray of entrails or whatever it was she did in her glass box down the hall; leaving me to the silent procession of the waves, to think of home, the blossoms on the trees, the ballroom where ghosts in tails and enormous hooped dresses whirled each other round in quadrilles and cotillions, as the walls mildewed and spiders made nests in the chandeliers.

SOMEONE PUSHED OPEN the ballroom door. "There you are. You didn't wait for me."

"Oh—I didn't think you meant actually wait . . ."

"It's *freezing.*" Mirela rubbed her hands over her bare arms. "What are you doing down here? You're missing the party."

"Oh you know . . . just thought I'd take a breather."

"Your mother's been looking for you."

"I know," I said bleakly.

She sat down on the other side of the aisle. "Are you all right? Is your head hurting?"

"No, no . . ." I crossed my legs toward her, suspected it looked effeminate, crossed them back again. "I suppose it's just the first time I've seen everything finished. Gives me an excuse to be maudlin."

"'Maudlin'?"

"Sad, you know, like when you think about the past."

"It must be strange, to come home and find everything changed like this."

I looked up at the raised stage, the flat planes of color, the exposed wooden beams that had replaced the fusty wallpaper and rococo plasterwork. "It's all right," I said nobly.

"I'm glad you were able to come back today," she said. "In time for the first performance."

"It did help to have the painkillers still in my system," I agreed.

She laughed. "Poor Charles! Didn't you like it even a little bit?"

I liked *you*, I wanted to say; even if your wig kept slipping, even if you pronounced *love* like *laugh* and made *joyriders* sound like something from a Transylvanian folktale, still whenever you were onstage the dialogue momentarily stopped grating and almost began to sound a little like music. But instead I just mumbled something about the realistic costumes.

"Mmm," she said, looking down into her clasped hands as if she were carrying a ladybird in there, out to the garden. "Charles—now that you are back—there was something I wanted to say to you."

"Oh?" I said and cleared my throat.

"It's a bit difficult."

"Well, try anyway," I said: because the truth of it was that I had been wondering . . . I mean, what happens in films when something seismic happens to a fellow, like he goes on the run or he gets blown up or his sister turns his house into a community theater, is that he then meets a beautiful woman who immediately falls in love with him and helps him along on his new path. They don't go into why she falls in love with him. It's just the way it works. Maybe it's a kind of reward from the Fates for daring to disturb the universe. I was thinking that none of this might seem quite as bad with a girl like Mirela by my side.

She exhaled preparatively and then said, "I wanted to apologize for what Mama did, for her stealing from you."

"Ah—right." I masked my disappointment with a cough. "There's no need to, really. Water under the bridge, so forth."

"You must think we're all crazy," she said in a low voice.

"No, no . . ." I hastened to set her at ease. "I've heard far worse stories. For instance, this one chap I know, Pongo McGurks, his family had a butler, name of Sanderson—had him for years, used to swear by him, best butler they'd ever had, et cetera. Then they came back early from a weekend away to find him in Pongo's mother's wedding dress, about to have the toaster marry him to the cuckoo clock."

"Oh." She seemed not quite to know what to make of this. "And this happens often?"

"No, I suppose it's pretty rare," I conceded. "I mean it's rare that you have a butler who's a perfect size ten." This wasn't coming out right at all.

Mirela frowned and hooked a strand of black hair with a finger. "I must not be explaining it right," she said. "What I want to say is that Mama's not really like that, you see. She's not a thief. I told her over and over again, why do you steal from these people, they care about you, they will help us. But you must understand that it's hard for her to trust people, after what has happened. At first she takes only small things you wouldn't miss. But when she finds out about the bank, that you might lose the house, she starts to panic, she doesn't sleep, she gets an idea she can steal enough to get us back home. As if there is anything to go back to there." She grimaced sardonically. "What I'm trying to tell you is, the reason she did these things is not because she is mad or a bad woman. She is just someone who terrible things have happened to." The sizzling cobalt eyes swiveled to confront me: I felt like I'd been skewered and lifted from my seat. "I wanted you to know that we are just a normal family that things have happened to. Do you understand me?"

"Of course," I croaked, "of course."

"I knew you would," she said quietly. She looked down at her hands again and then said: "Did you notice my leg onstage tonight?"

"Your . . . ?"

"My *leg*, Charles. You must have, everyone must have. I don't want you to be diplomatic about it. Just tell me."

"I didn't notice it," I said. "Honestly. Maybe a little at first. But I soon forgot."

"That was something else Mama wanted to do with the money," she reflected. "They can do amazing things these days, everyone says."

"It's not that bad," I said. "I mean I think it rather suits you." Possibly this wasn't the right thing to say; I wasn't sure of the etiquette on missing limbs.

But she started to laugh. "It's good to finally have someone I can talk to about being blown up!" she said.

"It's no joke," I averred.

"The world never looks the same afterward, does it?" She stopped laughing. "When you realize that things can just happen like that." She bowed her head; I let my gaze settle on her face, tried to figure out what it was about it that mesmerized me so . . .

"I really am grateful to you for taking us in, Charles," she said. "Most people don't even know what happened over there. They think we just come here to beg."

"That's quite all right," I said. *Sfumato*, that was what the painters called it; a blurring or elision of the lines, the kind Leonardo had used to give his Mona Lisa her beguiling flux.

"I knew you would understand," she repeated. A moment of silence drifted by. It seemed quite plain what she was getting at. The time had come to make my move. "That reminds me," I said, "there was something I wanted to say too. About the play, that is."

"Oh?" She looked up.

"Yes," I said, thrusting my wrists out of my cuffs. "I meant to say that one thing that I found interesting—I found *heartening* about it—was what it said about love."

"Love?" she repeated.

"Yes, the way it showed love could triumph over all the, ah, poverty and car theft and so on."

"Oh, I see," Mirela said. "Yes, though it's not really a love story, I don't think."

"But the love between Bel's character, for instance, and the—the chap with the mustache—what it said to me was, you know, that even when terrible things happen to you, and your life is uprooted, there's still hope, because that's just when you'll meet that special someone who'll sort of help you along with it all. That's what I really took from it."

"Yes," Mirela nodded vaguely while inspecting a left-behind program on the seat beside her. "That's very interesting, Charles, because it wasn't something that we were trying specifically to bring out as a theme . . ."

She wasn't following me. "That's the thing about love, though, isn't it?" I persevered. "You know, that it sort of turns up in unexpected places, even when it's not strictly speaking a—a theme . . ."

"Mmm," she said, then turned and added volubly, "Yes, you're right, of course, and also *friendship*, you know, loving friendship, that's very important in the play too. The kind that Bel had with her half brother."

"Which one," I said.

"The one that worked in the chip shop," she said.

"Yes, that's friendship all right," I agreed. "But there was love as well, such as when the heroin-addict chap and that girl who kept shoplifting from Marks & Spencer's—"

"Yes, but mostly friendship, Charles," she blurted and then paused, and then there was an awkward silence. She was obviously too preoccupied by her big night to perceive the true meaning behind my commentary. Confound it, it was impossible to handle these delicate moments without the benefit of a face!

The silence persisted awhile longer, and then she said, quite out of the blue, "Have you met Harry?"

"Who?" I said.

"Harry, he's the boy who wrote the play. Didn't you meet him earlier today?"

"I didn't meet anyone," I said dolefully. "Bel told me to stay out of the way. I think she'd have locked me in the cellar if she could."

"Oh. Well, then, you have to come and meet him now," she said. "He's so funny and clever and kind. I just know you'll like him."

Perhaps I was wrong to go immediately on the defensive, but a fellow doesn't go ten rounds with Patsy Olé without learning a thing or two about the darker workings of the female mind. Suddenly she seemed far too animated. Could it be that her Balkan upbringing had not stretched as far as the protocol of torrid love affairs? Could it be this Harry and his wretched play had so dazzled her that our tender moment together in the Folly had flown right out of her head?

"I won't," I volunteered.

"What?"

"I won't like him," I said. "This Harry person."

She laughed a sparkling laugh. "Don't be silly! I'm positive you will. Anyway, you can't hide away in here all night." She grabbed my wrist and, without looking me in the eye, pulled me to my feet. With a mounting sense of doom, I found myself being tugged down the hallway, like an old dog being dragged off to the vet.

Father's portrait had been reinstated just outside the recital room, with a plaque underneath it that read RALPH HYTHLODAY CENTRE FOR THE ARTS, as if it had all been his idea. He looked trapped; our eyes met briefly, helplessly, as Mirela led me back into the party.

Inside the company had thinned out a little. Mother was holding court to a brace of journalists with her back to us just inside the door. The red-faced gent had got even redder; he stood with his cohorts in a ragged semicircle around the piano, belting out some awful show tune. Behind them, MacGillycuddy was peering into the old dumbwaiter.

"What's he doing hanging around here anyway?" I grumbled. "What sort of theater has MacGillycuddy as a consultant?"

"Hmm? Oh, he's . . ." She stopped and frowned. "Well I don't know, exactly. He just seems to *appear*. I don't think anyone's ever asked— Oh look, Charles, there's Harry!" Gaily she waved her hand at a group of dramatic types in the corner, and my heart sank as I realized that, just as I had feared, "Harry" and the annoying fellow with the avant-garde hairstyle were one and the same person.

Bel had her arm linked to his right, and now Mirela insinuated herself into his left.

"I don't consider *Burnin Up* to be a play as such," he was saying. "It's more of a call to arms. It's a kind of an insurgency. It's about exploding the whole—"

"Harry, this is Charles that I wanted you to meet—"

He glanced around uninterestedly and gave me a vacuous smile.

"Charles, this is Harry that I was—" Mirela turning back to me.

"We've met," I said grimly.

"We have?" Harry said.

"Oh yes," I said. For the penny had finally dropped. I knew where I'd seen him before: and the mechanics of this whole sinister enterprise were now clear to me. The supposedly Disadvantaged actors clogging up the recital room were none other than the food-scrounging Marxists who had plagued my afternoons during Bel's college days; and this fellow, though he'd had pink hair then and gone under the name of Boris, had been their ringleader. How many times had I overheard him harping on about dreams or freedom or revolutions to some starry-eyed girl as he lay with his feet up on the chaise longue, or agitating Mrs. P. to rise up against her oppressors, viz. Mother and me, even as he stuffed himself with truffles or devoured the pecan plait that one had specially set aside for oneself. "Oh yes," I said again, to let him know that I was on to his game and would be keeping a very close eye on him. However, the conversation had already moved on, which is to say that the girls, gushing like twelve-year-olds who had eaten too much sherbet, were pulling his sleeve and asking him to tell them more about the insurgency, so I took a couple of canapés from a passing tray and contented myself with chewing on them in a vaguely threatening way.

"Well, the way I think of it is as a kind of 'guerrilla warfare,'" Harry said. Close up, his plaits looked like a gaggle of snakes that had been poisoned while crawling over his head. He was one of those people who make imaginary quotation marks with their fingers, which seemed another good reason to despise him. "Taking an elitist art form and using it essentially as a Trojan horse from which we can then spring out and confront bourgeois audiences with their own wrongdoing. So the play itself has to have the kind of explosive power that can so to speak 'shatter' the edifices it's being staged in, like a bomb—"

"Just a minute," I cut in here. "You're not talking about shattering *Amaurot*, I hope."

"It's a metaphor, you dope," Bel said crossly.

"We're hoping we won't have to use any actual explosives," Harry said to me.

"I should hope not," I said, returning to my canapé. "You can't fool around when it comes to blowing up edifices. I speak from experience."

"Because I suppose the legacy of postmodernism," Harry went on, "has been to deny art the power to make any kind of meaningful statement—about this, about us. So it seems to me that what we have to do is get back to the theater of Berkoff, of Artaud—"

"Charles, you've got pâté all over your bandages," Bel said.

"Have I?"

"Yes. No, don't rub it, you're just making it worse . . . Oh, now it's really disgusting."

The assembled faces groaned and assumed attitudes of repulsion. Bel lowered her eyebrows truculently at me, like a bull about to charge.

"I'll go and wash it off," I said apologetically and withdrew to the bathroom, past the florid gent, who was now weeping slumped over the closed piano lid. I did not rejoin the actors when I came back; instead I took up a position by the wall, shielded from Mother by a potted plant, and sucked dejectedly on an ice cube. It was turning into a singularly depressing evening. Wasn't there anyone who wanted to talk to me?

As if in answer, a large, malformed shadow at that moment fell across me. "All right?" it said.

I confined myself to a soundless expletive.

"What's the story with the oul head, anyway?" he said. "Have you still got one under there, or what?"

"I am reliably informed I still have a head," I said.

"Cos I was thinking, right," Frank said, scratching his belly, "you wouldn't want to turn out like your man in *Batman*, would you, like when he takes the bandages off and he's turned into this freakish Joker."

"No," I agreed, "no, I'm hoping that's not going to happen."

He nudged me conspiratorially. "I'd say there was some bangin nurses in there in hospital, was there?"

"Mmm," I said, wishing this conversation had some kind of ejector seat. What was he bothering me for, anyway? Shouldn't he be off groping Bel?

"Ah yeah—as me oul man used to say, there's only two things in life you can be sure about—death, and nurses." He followed this wisdom with a long sigh: A curious expression passed over his face, and I had another of those unsettling intimations of some deep chord of melancholy ringing through his monolithic interior. I was wondering whether I ought to get out of the way when, scratching his stomach, he asked offhandedly if Bel had said anything about him to me.

"About you?" I said. "To me?"

"It's not important," he said quickly. "It's just that, I haven't seen much of her these last few weeks, that's all."

Casting my mind back, I seemed to recall her saying something along the lines of *Frank, ugh* that time she came to visit me in the hospital; but apart from that she hadn't even mentioned him, or their apartment hunting, for that matter. I looked over at her now where she stood with the theater types, and then back at Frank. It struck me that I *hadn't* seen him groping her or trying to look down her shirt all evening.

"I was just wonderin," Frank said morosely. "Every time I call out here she's busy putting in wires, or doin her lines or havin meetins. Half the time she won't even talk to me on the phone." There was a faint sheen of perspiration on his forehead and the most forlorn look in his eyes. I had the strongest urge to toss him a dog biscuit.

"Well . . . she's busy," I said. "That's all. She's tied up with this wretched theater. I'm sure she'll be back to normal before long."

"Charlie," he whispered. "What are they doin puttin a fuckin theater in your house anyway?"

"I don't know," I said tersely. "I was away in hospital. The house was full of women. Anything could've happened, in that kind of a situation." I shifted uncomfortably from one foot to the other. He was making me uneasy; even as I spoke I was thinking that there had been a certain coolness between Bel and me tonight too. To the uninformed observer it might appear that Frank's situation and my own had distinct parallels— "Look," I said. "I'll have a word with her, all right? I'll find out what's going on. But I'm sure there's nothing to worry about. This theater shouldn't last long. You know Bel, she gets bored with everything after a few weeks—"

It was only when I had said it that I realized the statement's full implications. Frank gaped at me in horror. "That is," I began in a strangulated voice, "when it comes to—" But it was no good, I couldn't bear to stay there one second longer. With a gurgle of apology, I turned and fled. I saw that Mrs. P. had left the bar unattended; I slipped behind it and, without quite knowing why, began to fill my pockets with canapés.

As it turned out I never did get to have that word with Bel. All those unguarded bottles distracted me: I was administering myself a double Hennessy, just to get my nerves back on an even keel, when I felt an icy draft whip over my shoulders and a voice said, "Ah, Charles, there you are."

I downed my drink in one and slowly turned around.

"You know, for a man with such an uncluttered schedule, you can be awfully hard to track down."

"Ha ha," I laughed feebly, casting about for an escape route. There was none. "Well, here I am."

"Indeed," said Mother, smiling a steely smile.

I should explain that, whatever they had done to her in the Cedars, Mother had changed. She'd visited me in hospital and it was obvious from the minute she came through the door: storming in like a Valkyrie late for Rotary club, marching over and without so much as a polite inquiry after my numerous injuries launching into a wide-ranging sermon about responsibility and holistic dieting and twelve imaginary steps our souls had to go up in order to reach the top of something else. She'd made me quite nervous, and I knew beyond a shadow of a doubt that she was the reason I had woken up after weeks of unconsciousness surrounded by fruit baskets but no chocolates.

At the root of this transformation was an entity hitherto unfamiliar to me, known as Higher Power. Apparently this Higher Power was quite a big wheel over at the Cedars, in terms of persuading wealthy neurotics to give up their vices and take on their share of life's various burdens; and while the giving up drinking end of things seemed to have passed Mother by, she was extremely taken with this notion of duty and doing one's bit. Even then I had known that this did not augur at all well for me and my bid to revive the life of the country gentleman.

Perhaps it seems foolhardy to think, as I had arriving home that day, that I would be able to avoid Mother indefinitely. With the old Mother, however, the Mother who stayed in bed till two or three in the afternoon and then confined herself to an armchair in the drawing room with a bottle of gin, this would have been quite unproblematic. With the new Mother, it was almost impossible. I had been back only since lunchtime and it had taken all of my wits to steer clear of her. She appeared to have new and boundless reserves of energy. She was ubiquitous; she was immanent. Wherever one went she seemed to be there first, with a can of furniture polish or a book of carpet swatches or the sinister red ring binder she'd taken to carrying around, labeled "Projects." By teatime I was quite exhausted. And now she had me in her grasp.

"It's been quite an evening, hasn't it?" she said, reaching behind me for the sherry. "I'm *terribly* proud of the girls. Aren't you *terribly* proud?"

"It was nice to see Bel onstage again," I said. "She hasn't acted in a while."

"Oh *yes*, surrounded by all those *awful, awful* hoodlums, I was quite on the edge of my seat—it was like a voyage to the Underworld, in a way, wasn't it?"

"Mmm," I agreed morosely.

"And Mirela—what a find, Charles! Such presence! She'll go places, that girl— At least"—her reason catching up with her—"if she can do something about that awful— She does move so terribly slowly."

"I suppose she'll never dance the Kirov . . ."

"Still, one could hardly hear it, could one? And so pretty and exotic—" She filled up her glass. "Bel'll find herself with some competition if she has her sights set on Harry, at any rate. Quite a charming young man."

I threw back my drink and wiped my mouth with the back of my hand. "Didn't seem so charming to me," I mumbled mutinously. "Didn't seem too Disadvantaged either. None of them did."

"*Charles*," Mother said sharply and looked over her shoulder in case anyone had heard. "All of that will be taken care of in good time. The important thing now is to get everything up and running. When that is done, then we can investigate the finer points of who's disadvantaged and who isn't. And thus far it's been a remarkable success. A re*mark*-able success." She twisted a ring around her finger as she looked out over the crowd. "Which leaves us with the question of you."

"Me?"

"Yes, what are we going to do with you, Charles?"

I began to itch forebodingly about the nose. "Oh, I shouldn't worry about me," I blustered, fumbling out another dram of brandy from the bottle. "You know me, quite happy just to potter along, watch the odd film, drink the occasional glass of wine—"

"Shush," she said. "There has been a sea change in the affairs of this house since you took your little leave of absence, Charles. And it is a change that was long overdue. We in this family have been living in Cloud Cuckooland for far too long, living beyond our means, shirking our responsibilities. You children have been let run to seed. As your mother, I must take my share of the blame."

"Well, I think you're being a little hard on yourself—"

"Thankfully, with this new project Bel seems finally to be using her energies to some positive purpose. I have to acknowledge that this is largely due to Mirela, who has been a better influence on her than, perhaps, her father or myself in recent years. You, however, seem quite intractable." She shook her head. "When I look at how that girl has triumphed in the face of adversity to slot into the household in a way that is a credit to her dear mother, and then I look at you—"

"I slot into the household, Mother, don't be callous—"

"Lying around on the couch all day is not slotting, Charles."

"I'm *sick*," I protested. "Lying around is what you *do* when you're sick—"

She silenced me with a finger. "The devil makes work for idle hands. Ever since you dropped out of Trinity you have been living devoid of dreams or ambition and without so much as a pretense at concern for the future. And while lethargy is one thing, your antics lately have become quite deranged. Lord knows I'm happy to see the back of the preposterous Folly of yours, but it has come to the point where your chronic laziness is putting innocent lives at risk."

The tingling spread up my forehead and over my scalp. "What are you getting at," I said faintly.

"You've been living off the fat of the land for too long now," Mother said. "It's high time that you got a job."

A job!

There it was: This was the thanks I got for trying to save a few shreds of the family dignity. My fate had been decided, even as I lay comatose in my sickbed. A job! The walls of the recital room bore down on me. A job!

I argued, of course. I highlighted the rich irony of pushing me, her own flesh and blood, out to work in some jar factory even as she invited a bunch of layabout actors to stay here for nothing; I pointed out that Bel wasn't being made to look for a job, when she was the one who was always going on about how much she hated this place and how she longed to rub shoulders with the hoi polloi; I closed with a stirring speech to the effect that Mother was sending me on a wild goose chase, seeing as even she had conceded that I simply didn't have any dreams or ambitions, and so installing me in the working world was just going to be a waste of everyone's valuable time.

Mother listened to it all with a grim expression, as if this were exactly what she'd expected me to say.

"Tough Love," she said. "That's what we in the Cedars called this sort of thing. Helping you to help yourself. You'll thank me for it someday."

"I won't," I said.

"You will. Life is a precious commodity, Charles. It's time you achieved your full potential and learned the true value of things."

"You're talking like a Stalinist!" I cried. "People don't get jobs to *achieve* things and learn *values*! They do it because they *have* to, and then they use whatever's left over to buy themselves nice things that make them feel less bad about having jobs! Can't you see, it's just a terrible vicious circle!" I broke off to claw at my bandages. The itch had seized control of my entire head; it was getting worse and worse, and scratching didn't do any good. Mother coolly turned her attention back on the room, where the florid-faced drunk had been ousted from his residency on the piano lid and someone had humorously struck up a funeral march.

"Damn it," I declared in anguish, "damn it, you wouldn't think it was such a barrel of laughs if you'd worked a single day in your life"—halting abruptly as Mother turned stiff and white as alabaster—"Your charity work, of course," I said quickly, and then seeing a lifeline, "I say, maybe *I* could do charity work." It didn't look too hard, gala luncheons, wine tastings, celebrity auctions, none of these would be beyond me— The glass in Mother's hand began to tremble. "Or—how about a vineyard? What about, I could start making my own wine, in the, you know, in the garden, and then sell it—"

"I'm glad we had this discussion, Charles," Mother said glacially. "I only wish we'd had it sooner. Your allowance will be discontinued as of next week. That seems to be the best way of going about this. I shall speak to Geoffrey tomorrow."

"Fine then!" I threw my hands in the air. "I mean it seems to me that *I'm* the only one who cares about this place. It seems to me that *I'm* the one who's been keeping it going all the time you were away, I'm the one who's been telling Mrs. P. what to do, and feeding the peacocks, and burying them when they die. But if all anyone thinks is that I'm some sort of a *moocher*..."

"There's no need to raise your voice, Charles."

"I'm not raising my voice!" I shouted. The architecture of the room was contorting itself into the strangest shapes. Over Mother's shoulder I caught sight of Harry, the light falling in such a way as to appear to be emanating from him—a plaited, peasant-jacketed sun, with Bel and Mirela on either side of him like pretty, laughing moons. What did that make me, I wondered feverishly. A splinter? An asteroid, left to languish alone in the cold dark outer reaches of space? Then over her other shoulder my eyes fell on Frank, who saluted me with his can of beer—

"Damn it, if that's all anyone thinks, why not go the whole hog and fling me out on my ear while you're at it! In fact, why don't I save you the trouble, and fling my*self* out on my ear! Because—because I didn't come here to be insulted!"

"No one's insulting you, Charles. If you're not even capable of having a calm, rational discussion—"

"I'm perfectly calm, now if you'll excuse me, I'd like to calmly go upstairs and—and rationally pack my suitcases—"

Mother stepped wordlessly out of my way. Heart pounding madly, I marched for the door. In the hallway the staircase loomed up, crowned with spires and shadows like something from a German Expressionist film. "A moocher!" I whispered as I climbed the steps. "A moocher!" It was simply too monstrous. After everything I had done for the house, to be charged with lethargy, with "chronic laziness"—with *not caring*, when all I did was care!

I had been wounded terribly; it appeared furthermore that all those drinks had finally caught up with the painkillers and mounted some sort of campaign on my brain. Yet even as I packed my suitcase, even as I made my way back down the stairs, even as I removed my coat from the closet and spent more minutes than were strictly necessary standing there brushing imaginary dust from the lapels, if *one person* had come after me to remonstrate—to say, *Charles, can't we talk about this?* or *Don't be a duffer, old chap, come and have a drink*—I'm sure I would have thrown down my bag and laughed the whole thing off. I even went back into the recital room, just in case someone had meant to come but been delayed. I stood by the door and I watched them, talking and laughing and swirling about the room like colored smoke, and no one came.

Once, many years ago—I must have been about ten or so—I gate-crashed one of my parents' parties. Putting me to bed, Mother had hinted, as she always did, at the dreadful things that would befall me if I strayed from my room. But I couldn't bear any longer not to know what went on down there; so shortly after eleven, I stole down the stairs. As luck would have it I walked straight into Father. I thought he would be angry, but he was in a jovial mood and said that if I was that curious I could stay up for a very short while, provided I sat quietly in the corner and didn't let Mother see me.

At first it was so exciting I was quite overcome. The ballroom was a jungle of expensive fabrics, heavy with the steam of a dozen mingled perfumes that promised all sorts of things I didn't understand. Though it was dark, there was light everywhere you looked—catching on the platters of mysterious foodstuffs, refracting through dancing glasses of Shiraz and Sauvignon, glinting off chokers, rings, tiaras—so that if you half-closed your eyes it seemed like the air was alive with fireflies. And the noise: Who would have thought that a roomful of grown-ups talking about nothing could produce such a roar?

But most remarkable of all were the thin girls that stood dotted here and there among the circling guests. They rose above the heads of the others like statues in a garden; they looked very bored, and they never spoke. These were Father's models, here to showcase whatever new suite of cosmetics was being launched; they weren't supposed to talk, in case it lessened the effect. Father called them his canvases; the idea was that guests could pause and study them as they moved on to the next conversation.

When I would see them in the days leading up to these parties, skipping down the staircase from Father's study, these girls didn't look so much older than me. Some of them were nice; they were from all kinds of places, though they mostly lived in Paris, where they'd been working with the lab. But tonight they had been changed into something not quite human. There was an apocalyptic quality about them that was almost frightening, as if they were outside of time, or as if they were the same all the way through, without blood or guts. Their eyes looked at you and passed right through you. They stood with their limbs bent in motionless arabesques, blazing silently like priceless, preternaturally beautiful Anglepoise lamps.

Now and then people found themselves in my corner by mistake—gaunt couturiers with shaven heads, or creepy sensuous-looking men with crushed velvet suits and brilliantined hair, who smoked spicy cigarettes and who may, in retrospect, have been women. "Oh," they'd say, confronted by my nine-year-old stare, "hello"; then tugging at their ivory cigarette holders or making anxious goldfish mouths, they'd hurry back the way they came.

But where were they going, I began to wonder, what were they making their way *to*, when, in short, was the thing going to *start*? It took a long time before it dawned on me that this walking around talking was the whole point of the evening. I was bitterly disappointed. Now when the jewel-strewn old ladies came over to pat my head, I no longer bothered to give them my best Cub Scout smile, because I knew that none of them was going to say, "Charles, now it is time for the trampoline, and we would like you to have the first bounce," or "Charles, we have set up this boring party to try and trap a spy, now we need someone inconspicuous, for example a small boy, to discover him, or her."

And the things I overheard people talking about weren't even interesting. The men just went on about percentiles, or how so-and-so wouldn't do, or about rugby games they had seen recently. The women meanwhile were all of a flutter about Yves Saint Laurent's new concealer pen, a miraculous trompe l'oeil affair that reflected light away from wrinkles, or something—"Your father's a genius," they told me. "How is Yves anyway?"

"Usual. Moping," Father said with a little sigh; and then from the French windows at the far end a voice cried, "The Beaujolais's arrived!" and everyone bubbled forward, leaving Father and me standing there watching their backs.

"Well?" he said to me. "Learned your lesson?"

"What?" I said. "I mean, pardon?"

"You don't look like you're having much fun."

"Well,"—I didn't want to hurt his feelings, so I tried to pick my words—"it doesn't seem like a very good party."

"It doesn't, does it."

"There's no cake," I observed. "There's no *chairs*, even. *And* no one brought presents."

"Better off in bed, if you ask me."

"Dad . . . what do they all *want*?"

Father laughed his big braying laugh that Mother was always complaining about. "That's a good question, old chap. Very good question. What *do* they want." He took a swig of his wine. "What you have here, see, is a room full of very important people. And what very important people like more than anything else in the world is being made to feel important. So what they do is, they come to parties like this one where they can meet other important people and have important conversations about important things and they can all feel important together, see? Are they having fun? I don't know. I don't think *they* know anymore, either. They get a bit like those peacocks out on the lawn, do you think *they're* having fun?"

"I don't know," I mumbled.

"Course they aren't, parading around, showing each other their feathers, what kind of fun is that?" Father tilted his head back and drained his glass, then stood and frowned, collecting his thoughts. "See, the thing is, Charles, the thing is, old sport, that although they tell you in school—and it's very important to pay attention in school, and apply yourself, and learn as much as you can, do you hear me?"

"Yes, Dad. Except it's the holidays now."

"Well of course, yes, good fellow . . . where was I? Oh yes—the thing is that the world isn't like a—a swimming pool, you know, where everybody's splashing around in the same water, you know, in their togs. It might look that way, but in fact, in *fact*,"—he brought up his finger for emphasis, the abruptness of the motion almost unbalancing him—"there's *another* swimming pool, a tiny little one, and the people in *it* are the ones who make the—the . . ." He blinked deliberately. "It's like—what's the name of that fellow in *Flash Gordon*, the baddie?"

"Ming the Merciless?"

"Yes, him . . . Well, take the folks in this room. They mightn't look like much more than a bunch of old fogies, but if you add them together, they run the show just like Ming does in . . . whatever his place is called."

"Mongo."

"Right, Mongo. So as I say, although this might *look* like a party, where you might have a bit of fun, it's actually more like work, because this is where all the people from the small swimming pool make their deals and decisions. So it's very important that we're nice to them, nice and polite and we let them eat all our food. Second nature to a woman like your mother, of course. Grew up in a place like this, all the great and good, all splashing around . . ."

I had never heard Father speak this way before. It was a bit like when the babysitter lets you stay up and watch a horror film—too strange and scary to actually enjoy, but at the same time unquestionably a unique opportunity, so you stayed quiet and didn't draw attention to yourself. His voice was loud and puffing, but his speech was somehow becoming dimmer now, and his face was starting to sag: "splashing around . . . pluck ideas from a dreamland of Beaujolais and that revolting cheese and dump it on the unsuspecting . . . Wives at me for free cosmetics, should call the next line bloody Lazarus, ha ha . . ."

"Dad?" pulling on his hand.

He looked down, the white collar of his shirt too tight beneath his surprised red face.

"How's that brioche?" he said.

"It's all right," I said, quickly chewing off a piece because I was discovering at that very moment that I wanted to cry.

"Caterers ought to be shot . . ." He laughed again, and his brow unfurrowed. "See the tennis today? That Lendl? He's something, isn't he?"

"Yes, but Boris Becker's going to beat him."

"Boris Becker, listen, my boy, the day a red-haired German—a red-haired German, that's all wrong for a start—the day a red-haired German teenager wins Wimbledon, I will personally eat my hat. Germans can't play grass court. They're too analytical. For grass you need an artist. Pancho Gonzalez, ever see him play? Now there was a man. Beautiful to watch. That's what it's all about. Or take cricket. Who's the greatest bowler of all time?"

"I don't know. Underwood?"

"To the untrained eye, perhaps, but if you want a true craftsman you need to go right back to Rhodes, bowled over four thousand wickets, he had this funny sort of a spin, he— Well, I'll show you, come on." Taking me by the hand, he led me out of the room and down the hall. *The wrong of unshapely things is a wrong too great to be told,* know who said that?"

"Yeats?"

"Good lad,"—he was impressed, opening the front door—"bugger, it's raining—well, we'll just go out for a minute, you're wearing shoes, aren't you?"

I followed him disorientated down the steps to the front lawn and stood shivering in a late-night drizzle while he ran about assembling a wicket from two wine bottles and a Frisbee. Then he bounded back into the house to fetch the bat and ball, the first of which he handed to me. "Here's the line, all right?" He dug his heel into the grass and scraped out a muddy mark. "You bat first. Now here's how they say old Rhodes used to do it—"

He hung his jacket on somebody's wing mirror and began a long, lolloping run. His shirtsleeve shuttled up his arm as his arm came round in an arc and the ball flew from his hand; I shook the tiredness and the strangeness of it from my eyes and drew the bat protectively to my shins as the ball materialized before me—

"Bravo!" Father clapped, jogging up to me. "Not bad at all. Now you have a turn."

I'd rescued the ball from the undergrowth and was just about to start my run-up when a silhouette appeared in the doorway and inquired as to what, exactly, we thought we were doing?

"We're having a very important philosophical debate," Father said, touching his bat on the ground. "We're righting wrongs."

"Would it be too much to ask for you to do it inside?" Mother said icily.

"In a minute."

Mother's arm dropped from the lintel to fold tightly across her chest. "People are wondering where you are," she said, and then, "your *guest* will be getting lonely."

"Come on, Charles, let's see what you have." He motioned me to deliver the ball; obediently I started to run.

"We wouldn't want her to start *frowning*, and jeopardize her lucrative career," Mother said from the doorway in a wicked singsong voice. "What would your insurance think of that?"

"*Christ*"—he turned and roared, his bow tie askew—"I said in a minute, didn't I, can't you see I'm with the bloody boy—"

Mother brought her right foot down onto the next step and screamed, "You can't even get that right, can you, you don't speak to him for weeks on end and then you keep him up half the night because you suddenly feel *paternal*—" She flinched back as he hurled the bat in her direction. It clattered onto the gravel and slid under a car. Mother spun on her heel and stamped back inside, slamming the door behind her.

I retrieved the bat and waited. Father was standing under a tree, rubbing his temples.

"Dad, do you want me to bowl?"

"Sorry, what?"

"Are you ready, or—?"

"Tell you what, let's call it a night, old chap. Your mother's right, it's time you were in bed." He sighed as he trudged over toward the door, and me. "Ah—mm," he said, patting my head and turning to look out over the bay. He jingled the keys in his pocket and cleared his throat, and after we had looked at the bay some more he said, "The thing is, Charles, that life is a lot like cricket. The wicket is—is . . . No, well, listen, anyway, it's, life's a nasty business, can be a nasty business." His breath nearly knocked me down. "What I want is for you and your sister, for you and Christabel . . . I don't want you to have to claw through the—the *shit*, do you understand?"

He never swore in front of us; my heart pounded with alarm. "Yes, Dad."

"*Unshapely things*, remember that. World's full of unshapely things. Some of 'em'll look shapely enough, though. Some'll be quite alluring. So you can't listen to anybody. And what you've got to do is . . . what you've got to do . . ." He stopped, seeming to lose his thread; turned away from me and shambled back toward the house, pulling at his jaw, lost in his own thoughts. So I never found out what it was I had to do; I could only take my best guess. And closing the door of the recital room gently behind me twenty-odd years later, I had to admit to myself that it was quite conceivable I had got it wrong.

One of Bel's actor-friends had taken the piano and was tinkling out a melancholy "Over the Rainbow" as, with my suitcase in my hand, I proceeded down the hall. Voices fell in for the parts they knew: *there's a land that I dreamed of* . . . I walked by the glass frieze of Actaeon down to the door and surveyed my lost kingdom through a fine, sifting rain: the forlorn trees the birds had deserted, the twisted iron lattice where the Folly had been.

Would the Twister that had seized our lives never set us down in Kansas again, in good old black and white? Or couldn't you ever go back: Was that only for fairy tales, was the real world everybody got so excitable about precisely this gaudy Technicolor, this relentless, senseless impulsion forward?

Birds fly over the rainbow, the voices filtered out from inside, *why then, oh why can't I* . . .

Numbly I descended from the porch. I passed Frank's van there among the Saabs and Jaguars, and wondered briefly if I'd ever see him again. Then, retrieving a squashed canapé from my pocket, I took the first dark, rain-laden steps of my life away from Amaurot.

CHAPTER SEVEN

"This really is awfully good of you."

"No bother, Charlie, no bother."

"I mean, it'll only be for a week or so, until I get myself sorted out . . ."

"This is us here, Charlie."

"Aha, yes." We stopped outside a plain white wooden door. I hummed nervously to myself as Frank rummaged for the key.

"Go ahead," he said. "Age before beauty."

"Ha ha, thank you," edging into the gloom. "Oh. Well. Isn't this . . . ?"

"It's a bit of a mess. I didn't get much chance to tidy up."

"Not at all, not at all, it's quite— Oh dear, I seem to have stepped in someone's, ah, someone's dinner."

"Don't worry about it, Charlie, I wasn't goin to eat any more of it."

"Oh good, good. More of an *atelier*, really, isn't it? I say, is it always this dim?"

"Hang on, I'll turn on the box." He pushed past me and pressed a button on an ancient television that squatted in a corner. After a moment two women in bikinis appeared, taking swipes at each other with large foam clubs. "Don't worry, your eyes get used to it after a while."

"Yes, yes, of course . . ."

"Fancy a cup of tea?"

"Thanks." I lowered myself gingerly onto the edge of an armchair. Its guts spilled out of a rent in its side. I sat with my legs pressed tight together and tried not to touch anything. The floor was conspicuously sticky and, when you looked at it out of the corner of your eye, appeared to be moving.

"How do you like it?" Frank's voice called from somewhere within a teetering wilderness of junk.

"Just milk, please," I replied faintly. There was an overpowering smell in the air, a kind of vastly amplified version of the one that followed Frank around. A magazine entitled *Tit Parade* rested on the coffee table, the young lady on the cover entirely naked save for some carefully positioned citrus fruits. "Grocer Greta's Grabulous Melons," it said.

Frank reemerged with a couple of mugs. "There you go," he said, handing one to me and depositing himself upon a dysmorphic sofa opposite. "So," holding his arms outstretched, like Kubla Khan welcoming Marco Polo to Xanadu, "what do you think?"

"Nice," I croaked. "Very nice."

"Home sweet home," he said fondly, and slurped his tea.

"Although . . . ," I began.

"Yeah?"

"Well, I have to say," I said, in a careless, jokey sort of way to show there were no hard feelings, "I don't think much of your doorman."

"Doorman?" Frank repeated.

"Yes, the doorman," I said, trying to maintain my smile. "You know, he was really quite slovenly."

"That wasn't a doorman, Charlie, he's homeless."

"Homeless?"

"Yeah, he lives in that cardboard box on the steps."

"Oh," I said in a small voice. "I wondered why he wasn't wearing a cap."

There was a pause. "Doorman," Frank chuckled to himself.

Light struggled in through the ungenerous window, weak gray light that was more like the residue of light. I looked down thoughtfully into my tea, which had bits in it. After a time I said judiciously, "I imagine that's why it's taking him so long to bring up my cases."

Frank put his cup down, wincing. "Ah, Charlie . . ."

"You don't suppose," I ventured, "he might have forgotten which room—"

But Frank had already leapt from his seat and was hurtling back down the stairs. I got up and hurried after him, catching up outside the front door, where he stood studying the cardboard box and blanket until a short while ago occupied by the homeless person–doorman. "Fuck," he said, stroking his chin.

"He's gone," I said superfluously. The street was empty save for two moonfaced children watching us from the curb opposite. One was standing in a supermarket trolley, the other gripped the handle; both were entirely motionless.

"Come on." Frank poked me in the ribs and took off down the street. We reached a crossroads dominated by two huge breeze blocks of flats, where we took a left past a vacant lot overgrown with weeds and burned-out cars, and came to a long concrete bunker with metal shutters. I padded after Frank to the door, where he stopped.

"What? Is he in here?"

"Charlie," he said gravely. "You must never, ever, ever go in here, all right?"

"Fine," I squeaked. He went inside, and I waited there, whistling tunelessly with my hands in my pockets, attempting to blend in with my surroundings. It was hard to tell which buildings had people in them. The shop windows were covered with heavy grilles. In some of the blocks clothes were hanging out on balcony washing lines, but the doors were boarded up and covered in graffiti. Others seemed in such a state of disrepair as to be uninhabitable by man or beast—and then one would hear a radio from an upper level, or a child would pop its head out to spit down onto the pavement.

After what seemed a long time, Frank reemerged. In his hand he held a single suitcase, which he said the patrons of the pub had kindly agreed to sell back to him for only a small profit after he'd told them how I'd mistaken a homeless drug addict for a doorman.

"Oh," I said, and to hide my despair, "That place is a pub?"

It was called the Coachman; there had been a sign, but someone had stolen it. "You prob'ly seen it on telly," Frank said, as we trudged back up the hill. "It's on the news a good bit."

"Did anyone say anything about the rest of my things?" I asked sadly, shaking the lighter-than-it-had-been suitcase.

"No."

"I wonder where they are."

"Dunno," Frank said equably. "Gone."

It started to rain again.

"I don't suppose there's any point contacting the authorities . . ."

"They don't really come out here anymore, Charlie."

"Oh." The water was soaking into my bandages, making my head feel tight and cold.

"Well," I reflected—I was trying to keep a stiff upper lip about this as long as he was watching—"I daresay that homeless chap needs the money a lot more than I do."

"I'd say he's just goin to buy smack with it."

"Oh, right."

"He's not a bad bloke, like, once you don't ask him to mind stuff for you."

"Right." We turned back down his street. The moonfaced children were standing where we had left them. Frank unlocked the door, and I looked ruefully down at the box and grubby blanket. On the door jamb someone had written in small defiant letters, ARM THE HOMELESS.

"Home sweet home," he said, and went inside.

Something struck me on the back of the head. I turned to see a small gray pebble at my feet. The moonfaced children grinned at me mockingly from their trolley. I followed Frank inside.

And so it was that I arrived at Apt. C, Sands Villas, Bonetown.

MY FIRST PORT OF CALL after walking out of Amaurot that night had been the Radisson in Mount Merrion, where I had taken a suite. The hotel boasted a sauna and a pool and did an excellent Dover sole, all of which went some way to comforting me in those traumatic first days away from home. I found out that an old pal of mine, Boyd Snooks, happened to have a room going in his house as of next week; I called him up, and he promised to reserve it for me. Boyd was a jovial, freewheeling sort of fellow, who in school had been famous for his ability to turn his eyelids inside out; and now, although I was under a cloud rather about leaving Amaurot, he persuaded me there were high times to be had *chez lui*. The lower floor of his house was shared by three young air hostesses, also jovial and freewheeling and, according to Boyd, partial to the odd game of strip poker in their free time.

"I don't know," I'd said. "It's just that I hate leaving Bel . . ."

"Air hostesses, Charles," he said huskily. "Svenska Air. Know what that is? It's the Swedish national airline. They're Swedish, Charles. And they're all terrible poker players, they get drunk and forget the rules . . ."

In short, everything had seemed to be going terribly well, and I even began to wonder if I had been mistaken about the rigors of life in the real world. That said, I still spent the best part of my stay sitting in my room in case Mother should call wanting to apologize and begging me, her only son, to forget all that nonsense about getting a job and come back home. But she didn't, and by the end of the week I was looking forward to the move just so I could be shed of the hotel. Pool and Dover sole notwithstanding, it was deathly dull there; also I was getting rather concerned about the inroads it must be making on my finances. I hadn't bothered to ask how much the suite cost when I checked in, but I suspected it was a lot, especially for a man with a discontinued allowance. I hadn't seen my bank balance in quite a while, but every time I thought about it I got a queer, cold feeling, as if someone had walked over my grave.

I ought to mention as well that there had been a minor unpleasantness with some of the other guests after I frightened a small girl one evening in the bar, and I was beginning to feel my presence was no longer quite so welcome. It had all been perfectly innocent—I'd had a drink or two and, momentarily forgetting my hideous disfigurement, thought it might be funny to surprise her by popping out from behind a pillar. But she hadn't seen the funny side, in fact the hotel doctor had had to give her a sedative, and then on top of everything she turned out to belong to Americans, who are always so dreary when it comes to a chap frightening their children. The long and the short of it was that they'd complained to the concierge, and he'd decided I was a Bad Element and wanted me out ASAP. I got this from the chambermaid, after I cornered her one morning to find out why she'd stopped leaving those little complimentary mints on my pillow.

The upshot of all this was that by eight o'clock the evening before I was due to depart, I had my suitcases, which Mrs. P. had sent over from Amaurot, packed and Frank enlisted to pick me up in his van next day at ten and help me with the move. I was lying on the bed drinking a miniature bottle of crème de menthe when the telephone rang. "Mr. Snooks for you," the receptionist said.

There was a problem with the room. "The chap leaving's come down with a cold," Boyd said. "He's had to postpone his move."

"Oh damnation," I said.

"Beastly thing," he said adenoidally. "We've all got it. Still, he should be better and buggered off in a week or two. Hope it doesn't put you out too much."

"I suppose it can't be helped," I said; and as he didn't sound too well himself, I told him not to worry and that I would make other arrangements.

"That's the spirit," Boyd said, stifling a sneeze. "Think of the air hostesses."

I set down the receiver and bit my lip. The denuded minibar gazed at me accusatorily from the other side of the room. This was a blow, all right. I went and retrieved my address book and spent the next half hour calling up acquaintances to see if they could help me out. I had no success. Those that hadn't, like Pongo, decamped to London, were living in Dublin in mortal terror of their landlords—tyrannical, Victorian fiends who wouldn't let them so much as hang a picture frame, let alone entertain houseguests. "Sorry, Charles," they'd mutter down the line, then, urgently, "I have to go."

Finally it appeared there was no alternative but to swallow my pride and call home. Mother answered the phone, needless to say. "*Charles, how sweet* of you to call, I was just saying this very second to Mrs. P. how must you be doing. You know I still can't quite believe you've flown the nest, we all miss you *terribly*—"

"Really?" I said. Perhaps this wouldn't be so humiliating after all. "Because actually . . ." And I explained about Boyd and my predicament.

There was an uneasy silence when I had finished. When she spoke again Mother's voice had taken on the quasi-tragic, overcompensatory tone she used when someone had thoughtlessly left her in a difficult position. "Oh dear . . . that is a pickle," she said. "But don't you know we're rather swamped at the moment, darling. You know the play starts in town tonight and then . . . Well, we thought that seeing as you're not here—"

"You haven't put the Disadvantaged in my room, I hope," I cut in abrasively. "I don't want my bed infested with nits and what have you."

"Why, no, not the Disadvantaged," she said silkily. "We thought we'd give your room to Harry, actually."

She waited a moment, and then when I hadn't said anything added brightly, "There's the couch, of course, you can always sleep there, if you're stuck . . . Or perhaps one of your friends has a spare bed?"

"Oh yes," I said through clenched teeth, as if it had just occurred to me. "That's a good idea. I'll ring around."

"Do call, darling, if you're still stuck."

"Yes, yes."

"This is your time, Charles. You've spread your wings, and now you must fly high, you know we're all terribly proud—"

I put the phone down. Harry! I felt my blood bubble with rage. That jackanapes, with his Trojan horses and his offbeat hairstyle, he was the golden boy now, was he? I picked the phone up again and dialed reception to tell them I wanted to extend my stay.

"Certainly, sir," the girl said. "Room number, please."

I gave her my room number. She put me on hold.

"Mr. Hythloday?" she said, returning.

"Yes?"

"I'm sorry, sir, but we're booked up."

"Just a single? For one night even?"

"I'm sorry, sir."

The concierge had got there first! I was beginning to get the unpleasant sense of being caught up in some sort of mechanism over which I had no control: as if, in leaving Amaurot, I had submitted myself entirely to the whims of Fate, and I could do nothing but follow on docilely until it had brought me where it wanted. I took the last Baileys from the refrigerator under the mirror, poured it into a plastic glass, and went to the window. The Radisson had a couple of acres of park around it; the land had used to belong to a convent. Perhaps this was where the nuns would play rounders and tip-the-can on sunny days.

There was nothing for it: I would have to find another hotel, preferably a cheap one. I still had a couple of credit cards left I could use. I returned to the locker side of the bed, picked up the phone again, and dialed Frank's number to tell him the move was off.

"What's the story?" Frank said. His mouth was full of something.

"It doesn't matter," I said irritably. "The point is I'll have to stay somewhere else for a few weeks first."

"Must be costin you," the voice said. "I'd say them places set you back a good bit."

"I'll survive," I replied curtly.

"Yeah, but," he continued, then paused to swallow his—*chicken balls*, suddenly I found I knew it with the unshakable certainty of an epiphany—"but here, why don't you just kip in my gaff for a while?"

I was caught off guard. "What?" I stammered. "What?"

He repeated his offer. I cast about for an excuse not to take it, but after all the twists and turns the evening had taken I found I was unable to think straight. "I wouldn't want to put you out," I said feebly.

"I don't give a monkey's," he assured me.

In the distance I seemed to hear singing, as of ghostly nuns.

"Well, that's very kind," I tried to sound grateful, "that's really very kind."

"Nice one," Frank said.

And so the next morning I left my room and took my suitcases down in the elevator to the lobby, where I handed in the key. Every movement, every tiny social transaction seemed backlit, consecrated somehow, like the footsteps a prisoner counts off in his head as he is marched to the scaffold. Frank was waiting outside, leaning with his arms crossed against his rusty white van. Someone had drawn a penis in the dust on its side. "All right?" he said.

"Capital," I said. "Capital."

—

FRANK'S APARTMENT WAS part of a tall redbrick building—Georgian, by the looks of the fanlight over the door—that must once have been a respectable, even a dignified town house. Here and there were traces of a more illustrious past: delicate flourishes to the moldings, fragments of the original plasterwork. But they were no more than traces, like shards of pottery in the dirt. The facade had been blackened and corroded by decades of grime and most of the original fixtures torn out in the course of splitting the interior into ever-shrinking tenements. The present landlord was a former Garda who owned several properties in the area and was, Frank said, "a gobshite even for a Garda."

Apt. C was composed almost entirely of corners, as if whoever built the house had cobbled together an extra room from the nooks and recesses that were left over at the end. The rooms wobbled in a way that one was not accustomed to in architecture, and certain walls could not be leaned on because they were, I quote, "holding the ceiling up." Even the daylight seemed to have trouble negotiating the flat's eccentricities; it came through the window and then stopped short, with its finger on its lip, so to speak. Consequently it was always rather dark—or *dank*, perhaps *dank* was a better word. It was easily the dankest apartment I had ever stayed in.

I slept on a mattress of uncertain lineage in a room about the size of one of the smaller broom closets at Amaurot, with those possessions that the patrons of the Coachman had been kind enough not to steal—Improving Book, shaving kit, second-best dinner jacket, socks, Gene Tierney memorabilia, journal of thoughts largely as yet unthought—arranged in a little heap beside me. The bulk of the apartment was taken up by Frank's junk. Every day he'd come home with more, carrying it in from his van in crates and dumping it where he could. Cigarette cases, ballet slippers, window sashes, hymnals, cornerstones, cash registers, rocking horses, picture rails, things with parts missing, parts separated from their things—everywhere you looked you were confronted with uprooted elements of other people's lives.

"I don't get it," I said, examining a stringless Dunlop tennis racket that had just arrived. "How do you tell what's valuable and what's, you know, garbage?"

He thought for a moment. "The stuff people won't buy is garbage," he said.

"Oh," I said.

Most of the stuff they bought; evidently it was a good time to be in architectural salvage. Half the city was being demolished and built over; things could be picked up for a song and then sold on at a premium to all the people with new pubs and new hotels and new houses who wanted to give their property a touch of authenticity. "All this old shit"—Frank waved his hand over the latest plunder spread over the floor—"like horseshoes, signposts, firemen's helmets, and that—pubs go mad for it. They're gaggin for old gear to put on the walls to make it look more old-lookin, like. Same with the new flats. People don't like things just bein new. They want to be reminded of bygone days and that."

"Why don't they just stop knocking down the old buildings, then?" I said. "If everyone's so wild about bygone days."

"Cos then we'd all be out of a job."

Piled up like that, in no particular order, the junk seemed to take on a kind of generic identity—a musty, melancholy pastness that filled the room like an old perfume. During the day, when Frank was out, it made me feel a little like a relic myself. I had nothing to do, other than fidget with the tassels of my dressing gown—which may not sound unusual in itself, but this was a different kind of nothing than before, a fluttery, restive, unsatisfying nothing. I rarely went outside, other than brief forays to the petrol station, where one could buy the essentials at trumped-up prices; most of my time was passed at the window, gazing down at the grim slums below.

The streets of Bonetown were gray and dismal, without trees or decoration, and the grayness, the dismalness, had etched themselves into the faces of the inhabitants. I discerned two distinct strata to Bonetown society. Firstly, the natives. These, to speak plainly, were as villainous a bunch of ruffians as one would find anywhere in the world. They were uncouth and badly dressed, and they spent their days lurching from the pub to the bookies to the petrol station, toting seemingly infinite numbers of children—many of whom, I noticed, bore a strong physical resemblance to Frank. I mentioned this to him, but he only smacked his lips and made some arcane remark about how looking like someone didn't actually prove anything in a court-type situation.

The second grouping, which had little interaction with the first, was the foreigners. These came in all shapes and sizes and, the way Frank told it at least, had appeared more or less overnight; though no one seemed to know where from, or how exactly they had ended up here. "Maybe they came out of that hoo-ha in Bosnia," I surmised. "Like Mrs. P. and her lot."

"That one or another one," Frank said with a shrug. "Never any shortage of wars."

None of them seemed to be employed, and it struck me that this situation could work to our advantage in terms of getting someone in to do the cleaning at relatively little expense. Frank, however, put the ki-bosh on this straightaway. "Me ma was a cleanin lady, Charlie," he said. "It'd be weird, like."

At night the estate was taken over by the local Youth, and everybody who didn't have an interest in marauding or terrorizing the elderly was expected to go indoors or suffer the consequences.

The Youth amused themselves in a variety of ways. Sometimes they'd set fire to things, or spray-paint swastikas on the doors of asylum seekers; occasionally someone would arrive in a stolen car, providing a few hours of merriment as they raced it up and down. Mostly, however, they simply stood in bristling gangs on street corners, selling each other heroin. The buildings rang out with cries; inevitably a baby would start wailing, and through the wall I would hear the neighbors argue. A couple of times gunshots echoed from the direction of the Coachman: Frank told me how men from the flats would go down with shotguns and balaclavas to rob it, and then return the next day to buy drinks with the takings.

Sometimes, as I languished at the windows, I would see a pair of eyes peeping back at me from the tower block opposite, and I would think of Mirela waving angellike at me from the Folly; and then I would see the moonfaced children with their supermarket trolley, always the one pushing and the other standing up looking over the side, little fingers wrapped around the metal rim—rumbling by like dusty pilgrims who had forgotten their purpose and their destination and now made only endless circles around these same dead-end streets.

It hardly needs to be said that I was far from comfortable cohabiting with Frank. In the early days especially, I felt much as Jack must have, living at the top of the Beanstalk with that Englishman-eating giant. One effect of the Hobbesian nightmare around me, however, was to make Frank, by comparison, seem that bit less frightening; and I had so many other things to brood over that before long I had almost grown accustomed to his small acts of kindness, his microwaved dinners, his bad jokes—

"Here, Charlie, d'you hear about the midget that walked into the ladies' jacks?"

"Can't say I have, old man."

"Yeah, he got a box in the face!"

"Ha ha, yes, very good, well, better turn in, I suppose—"

"It's only eight o'clock, Charlie."

"Yes, busy day tomorrow, though," hauling myself up from the couch.

"Busy?"

"Well, not really *busy*, I mean I thought I might watch a film or two . . . I say, old chap, that reminds me—lend me another fifty pounds, would you? We have to get some decent wine in. I can't drink any more of that wretched petrol-station Riesling, it's giving me an ulcer."

"Eh, yeah, Charlie, no problem," and he'd peel the notes from the fat wad in his pocket.

"Thanks. Well, good night then."

"Night, Charlie."

Most evenings he went out drinking with his mates, regaling me next day with the stories of their exploits—how such-and-such a fellow "Ste" had bought "whizz" from such-and-such a fellow "Mick the Bollocks," except when he inhaled it, it turned out it wasn't "whizz," it was stuff for killing ants, and Ste had gone berserk and started eating plates and trying to pull out his eyeballs. "You should come out with us some night, Charlie," he'd say from time to time. "They're great crack, the lads are."

"That's all right," I'd say, as the stories alone were enough to make me feel quite unwell.

I suppose I was too caught up in my brooding ever to ask myself what Frank might have hoped to gain from having me stay. I didn't know how things stood between him and Bel. Whatever had happened, her name was never spoken in the apartment; but sometimes I would catch him looking at me in a peculiar, wishful sort of a way, for all the world as if he expected me to pull her out of a hat; and I would wonder shudderingly if he planned to use me to take revenge on her, or keep me as some manner of Love Hostage.

By and large, though, he came and went without disturbing me; I could sit and watch television uninterrupted. Having been abandoned by the world, I'd decided that now was the perfect time to complete my Gene Tierney project, or, if one wanted to split hairs, to begin my Gene Tierney project. Every afternoon after breakfast, when Frank was at work, I would close the curtains (a formality, given the permanent darkness of the room), sit in the armchair with a notepad and a glass of the gruesome Riesling, and watch a film, beginning at the very start with *The Return of Frank James*—a diabolical performance for which *The Harvard Lampoon* named Tierney Worst Female Discovery of 1940 and more than one critic compared her unfavorably to Minnie Mouse. To me in my woebegone state, however, her films were like dispatches from some kinder upper realm—flashes of a faraway lighthouse to a becalmed and fogbound ship. I *needed* them; I watched compulsively, and soon I had got all the way to *The Razor's Edge* (1946).

This was one of my favorites. The hero, played by Tyrone Power, is a pilot who has returned from World War I totally disaffected by the horrors he has seen there and unwilling to take any part in the postwar boom, even though Gene, his fiancée, refuses to marry him unless he gets a job. The movie opens at a fabulous country club ball under the stars, where in a little moonlit arbor she takes him aside and tries to convince him of the merits of the soaring economy. She tells him America will soon be so rich that it will dwarf anything in history; she tells him that it's a unique opportunity for a young man like him and he ought to leap at the chance to be a part of it. But Tyrone Power, gazing lugubriously into the middle distance, tells her that it is, in his eyes, utterly meaningless. He then informs her that he is removing to Paris, to be a bum.

She follows him to France, and there's a famous scene later on when she brings him back to her apartment and, in a remarkable black dress that resembles the tenebrous sheath of a dagger, makes one last effort to seduce him into the mercantile world. The dress was designed by Oleg Cassini, the brilliant Russian exile whom Tierney had married in 1941, and in it she proves too much for even the saintly former pilot to resist, at least for the duration of a kiss.

I confess to feeling a certain affinity with Tyrone Power in this movie, in terms of our defiant stands against the emptiness of modern society; and I might have considered following his lead and relocating my stand from Bonetown to the more sympathetic environs of Paris, had I thought there was even the slightest chance of a beautiful woman in a black or any other color dress pursuing me there. As time went by, however, it became increasingly clear that this would not be the case.

Since I had come here no one from Amaurot had so much as called me, not even Mirela, in spite of our promising conversation in the ballroom that time. *Burnin Up* had opened in a small theater behind Tara Street station the same night I'd been excluded from the Radisson. There was a short review of it in the newspaper I'd lifted from the hotel lobby, not wildly enthusiastic but certainly approving of what it called the "unflinching debut" of the Amaurot Players. It might have been on another planet for all I heard from them. So much for Mirela's gratitude, I thought miserably; now I was no longer lord of the manor—now that I was homeless, just as she had been!—it seemed everything was forgotten.

As for Bel, I was quite sure she had thrown herself into her belle époque, no pun intended, without so much as a thought for the purgatory to which her bleeding heart had inadvertently condemned me. Though that didn't mean I didn't think about her, didn't wonder at any given moment what she might be doing as I sat counting dust motes in the eviscerated armchair; it didn't mean I wasn't dreaming every night of home, the squeaking trolley wheels outside my window becoming

Old Man Thompson's rusty weather vane, the susurration of faraway traffic the sound of waves on Killiney beach, the fraught, cheerless urban night becoming a July evening where Bel and I threw a party on the lawn, with Manhattans and lobster bisque laid out under an advancing sunset that stretched flamingo pink across the whole sky; until "Come on," she'd whisper, and we'd steal away hand in hand, through the trees, to that spot on the cliff top where Father had looked out and recited his poems; where the sky had turned that eternal-seeming blue of twilight and we watched the sea fetched up and dashed again by a teasing moon, and the lights on the far-off shore like tiny blazing shipwrecks . . .

And then one night I was roused from my sleep by a calamitous thumping. The noise reverberated through ceiling, walls, and floor alike; the whole apartment was juddering unmercifully, as if we were having a minor, very localized earthquake.

My first thought was that someone was trying to demolish the building. This had happened before, Frank had told me; apparently when the developers couldn't shift someone from a house they wanted to knock down, they would arrive in the middle of the night and accidentally-on-purpose drive a lorry into it. I rubbed my eyes and put on my dressing gown, intending to go out and tell them that they had the wrong house. But as I stepped into the living room I realized that the noise was coming from right here. An enormous stereo machine had materialized atop the television; and beside it, wagging its head in time to the noise, was what appeared to be a large, shiny ferret that had learned to walk on two legs. Or that was the impression I got in the split second before the ferret launched itself at me; then, to my infinite surprise, I found myself on the floor being throttled.

This fellow had obviously throttled before; he cleverly defused my resistance by banging my head on the ground as he was strangling me. After a minute he was clearly getting the best of it, and it's fair to say that had I not managed to cry out before he got a good grip on my windpipe things might have come to a sticky end then and there. But just as I was about to black out, a hand appeared at his shoulder and pulled him away, and the din stopped abruptly. After I'd rolled around coughing for a while, I was recovered enough to drag myself halfway up the armchair—and see Frank, not beating my assailant to a bloody pulp but shaking his hand and clapping him on the back!

"All right, Droyd!" he was saying. "How's your fanny?"

"Not three bad, Frankie," the ferret thing chuckled, "not three bad." He was small and wore a sort of two-piece tracksuit with a satin finish, the same kind the actors had worn in *Burnin Up*. Around his neck there was a heavy gold chain, and on his hands clunky gold rings as well as clumsy tattoos in blue ink that looked like he had done them himself.

"Would someone mind explaining to me what is going on?" I rasped. "Who is this fellow? What the devil does he think he's doing, coming in here unannounced in the middle of the night?"

"This is Droyd, Charlie," Frank said, then turned to him. "What *are* you doin here?"

"I just got out," the ferret said.

"Out of where?" I pursued.

"Out of prison. Frankie, who's this shirtlifter anyway?"

"That's Charlie. Are you all right, Charlie?"

I waved an arm stoically from my position on the floor, onto which I had collapsed again to hyperventilate.

"You shouldn't've strangled him like that, he's a bit sensitive like."

"Wasn't my fuckin fault," the other voice returned somewhere over my head. "I wasn't expectin some fuckin Egyptian mummy burstin in like that."

"Ha!" I rejoined hoarsely. "That's funny, because, you know, I wasn't expecting some total stranger to break into my home and wake me up at an ungodly hour—"

"It's not ungodly, Charlie, I haven't even had me dinner yet."

"That's funny, neither have I," I heard the ferrety chap say, where-upon Frank of course invited him to dine with us. I tried to sneak away, back to my room, but Frank grabbed my arm. "Come on, Charlie," he said. "Come and have a bite to eat with us. Soon we'll all be the best of friends." And so, only half an hour after being dragged from my bed and beaten, I found myself sitting at the table with the two of them, listening to Frank inquire of the interloper how he'd enjoyed his time "away"—as if he'd been off taking the waters at Carlsbad!—and numbly wondering how I had managed to bring my life to this terrible pass.

"It wasn't that bad," Droyd was saying. "It was like anythin, there were good days and bad days. And you'd meet some right characters in there. Like you know that bit in *Lethal Weapon* where Riggs is in the straitjacket and he like fuckin pops out his shoulder so he can escape?"

"That bit's fuckin disgustin," Frank recalled pleasurably.

"Well, I had a mate in the Joy could do that. Well, he could pop it out but he couldn't pop it back in. Actually it wasn't him what popped it out so much as this other bloke done it to him called Johnny No-Fingers. Now he was a real character . . ."

It seemed that Droyd had been imprisoned for his activities as henchman to a local drug peddler called Cousin Benny. This Cousin Benny lived in a tower block over to the west, and he wasn't anyone's actual cousin: I would hear his name again during my sojourn in Bonetown, always accompanied by a lowering of the voice and a furtive glance over the shoulder. Even Frank appeared somewhat daunted by him.

"For fuck's sake," he said. "How'd you get mixed up with that scumbag?"

"I was on the gear," Droyd said matter-of-factly. "You know how it is. You never have enough money. I started off just robbin old ladies. But soon that wasn't enough, so I started robbin cars. But then that wasn't enough either. So I started workin for Benny. It makes sense if you think about it. He used to give me an employee discount." He chewed and swallowed and laid down his fork. "Ah yeah, it's all a laugh in the beginnin," he said with a sigh. "But it's a mug's game, a mug's game. Anyway, that's all behind me now. I'm a changed man, yes sir."

He leaned forward, elbows on his knees, and cracked his knuckles, the subterranean light of the television playing over his bony face; for a moment I almost felt sorry for him, and I was about to ask whether he'd taken heroin to replace the self-worth that society hadn't given him when, turning his attention to the plate in front of him, he said, "Here, d'you ever notice how pasta when it's wet sounds just like when you're givin a bird the finger?"

"What?" Frank said.

"Listen." Droyd had taken his fork and was prodding the pasta with it to produce a series of slaps and slurps and squelches. "See? It sounds exactly like when you've got your fingers up a bird's growler."

I set down my plate and inhaled deeply. "I say," I appealed.

"You're right," Frank said. "That's fuckin amazin."

"Look, stop that, will you?"

But now Frank had joined in with *his* pasta, and the air was filled with lubricious noises. "Give it a go, Charlie. It's fuckin amazin."

I could bear no more. Holding my handkerchief to my mouth, I staggered away from the table, grabbing the telephone when they weren't looking and bringing it into my room. There, kneeling in the darkness, I brushed a tear from my eye and dialed Boyd's number. The phone seemed to ring for a long time before it was answered; then all there was at the other end was a sort of a low croaking noise.

"Boyd?" I whispered. "Is that you?"

"Charles . . . ," the pitiful croak responded.

He was unrecognizable—indeed, he barely sounded human. A chill wave of dread surged up through me. "What's happened to you?" I said. "Is it that awful cold?"

"Not a cold," he whispered.

"It's not? Well what on earth is it?"

"Lassa fever," he said.

"Lassa *fever*?"

"Looks like it," he said, breaking off for an extended fit of coughing.

"But that's absurd," I said querulously, picking up the phone and carrying it across the room. "How could it be? Where would you possibly get Lassa fever?"

"Air hostesses," he said bitterly.

"Oh," I said, feeling my knees give way and lowering myself onto the mattress. "Oh, hell."

One of them had brought it back from Africa, and now the whole house had come down with it; they were all in quarantine, Boyd said. "There's a policeman at the door, even," he said glumly. "In case we try to break out and rub ourselves up against the local shopkeepers. No one's allowed in except doctors."

I slumped back against the wall. I was getting that hideous sensation of inevitability I'd had before in the hotel: as if I was not master of my own destiny, as if someone or something were out to teach me a lesson. Bawdy laughter rang out from the kitchen.

"Sorry, old man," Boyd mumbled.

I rubbed my jaw bluely. There was nothing to be done, and Boyd sounded like he was getting worse by the minute; I told him to go to bed before he keeled over.

"Yes," the voice slurred at the other end of the line. "Better do that. The rhinoceros'll be coming in soon, y'know."

"That's right, so go to bed."

" 'S a damn . . . a damn pest, Charles . . . keeps waking me up . . . wanting to play strip poker . . ."

"Yes, yes. Look, be a good fellow and—"

"I tell it, how c'n you play strip poker? M'n t' say, y're a bloody rh'nos'rus, so (a) in the first instance you've no hands, and (b) you've no . . . bloody . . . clothes, thing's a foregone, a foregone c'nclusion . . ."

Droyd did not go home that night, or the next morning, and for most of the following afternoon I was subjected to what he referred to, seemingly without irony, as his "music." Sometimes it sounded like a huge metal something—a tank, maybe, or an enormous set of cutlery—falling down an infinite staircase; sometimes it sounded like a hundred thousand Nazis, goose-stepping through the Place de la République; the general idea seemed to be to capture the sound of civilization collapsing, so loudly that while it was on one could do little more than lie on one's mattress and vibrate.

Obviously one didn't want to be inhospitable, but the next day when he was still there I began to feel that our good nature was being taken advantage of. During an especially loud passage in his racket making, I took Frank to one side in the kitchen for a quick word.

"What's that, Charlie?" he shouted, taking a can of beer from the fridge.

"I said, obviously one doesn't want to be inhospitable," I bellowed back with my fingers in my ears, "but I mean, isn't he planning to go home at some stage?"

"Dunno, Charlie. Why don't you ask him?"

"I don't want to ask—" I broke off. This was hopeless. With every thump the mugs on the draining board danced a little closer to the edge, a tendency with which I could thoroughly identify.

"Y'see, the thing about Droyd is— Here, want a can?"

"No," I said, but he didn't hear and handed me an opened can of Hobson's Choice, the cheapest beer on offer at the petrol station.

"The thing about Droyd is he doesn't really have a home. So he's prob'ly better off stayin here for a bit, till he sorts himself out. I mean we don't want him goin back to that fuckin Cousin Benny, like."

"No," I said, "no, ideally we—"

"Anyway, there's plenty of room for the three of us. And it's nice to have a bit of music, it sort of cheers the place up a bit, doesn't it?"

I was about to make a sarcastic reply but realized at that moment that the music had dislodged a filling, so instead I returned to my room and cocooned myself as best I could in my threadbare duvet.

In a way, I suppose I am indebted to Droyd. Left to my own devices, I might have drifted along forever in my post-Amaurot fugue. Thanks to him, the situation became untenable almost immediately.

The simple fact of it was that sharing a room with him was totally unbearable. He made Frank look like Noël Coward. He thoroughly spoiled the test match I was trying to watch by shouting "Howzat!" at inappropriate times, even after I'd explained at length to him precisely what the term meant. He insisted on referring to the Pakistani team as "the wogs" and to England as "the shirtlifters." The air was constantly choked with the fumes from his cannabis cigarettes, which he smoked more or less nonstop, with the result that I kept nodding off; then every five minutes or so, out of the blue, as it were, his stereo would produce an almighty thump that made me jump out of my seat. When I asked if he wouldn't like to switch it off for a while and perhaps catch up on his reading, he told me he'd "rather iron his sack." It was after this last exchange, as I recall, that I went to fetch the newspaper I'd stolen from the Radisson to see if I could find somewhere else to live.

There were several classifieds regarding apartments for rent; I circled half a dozen, taking note of the viewing times. They were all rather on the pricey side, as Droyd pointed out when he came to see what I was doing.

"Fuck's sake!" he exclaimed, reading over my shoulder. "Where are you going to get that kind of money?"

"That's my business," I said unkindly, pulling the newspaper away from him.

"You need to be a fuckin millionaire to live in this city these days," he reflected.

"Yes, well," I grunted. But there, after all, was the rub. I didn't need to open the credit card statements that Mother had very kindly forwarded to me to know that my days of being a millionaire were long gone. And yet I simply couldn't go on living like this. It looked like there was nothing for it but to borrow more money from Frank. However, when I took him to one side for a quick word about it that night, he told me he didn't have that kind of money.

"What are you talking about?" I said. "I thought business was booming."

"It's not booming that much," he said. "And there's rent to pay, and food and stuff for you lads . . ."

"All right, all right," I snapped. Was it that he enjoyed seeing me brought low? Was that it? I wiped my brow with the back of my hand.

"You could always get a job, Charlie. I've a mate's got a warehouse, if you want I could give him a call. He's a good bloke, and the money's—"

"A job, oh yes," I ejaculated. "Why don't I just get a job, and sell off my soul to the highest bidder, and then everybody's happy. If you ask me it's a damned poor reflection on so-called society that in this day and age the only way a man can survive is to sacrifice his *ideals* and his *dreams* and his whole *identity*—"

"That's it," Frank agreed. "As me oul lad used to say, there's nothin comes easy in this life . . ."

"Wait a second." Suddenly something in the newspaper on the table caught my eye. "Look at this—" I folded the page over and raised it up. "'Sick of the employment rat race? Still waiting for your slice of the pie?'"

"Where is it?"

"Here, see? With the picture of the pie, and the rat looking sad?"

"Oh right."

"'Tired of watching your friends get ahead while you're stuck doing the same old thing? Dublin is booming, and there's enough to go around for everybody. If you want your slice of the pie, contact Sirius Recruitment, Ireland's leading premium specialist in IT, multimedia, and e-business solutions NOW. Why waste any more time? Call now and

JOIN THE PARTY!' " I laid the paper back down with an air of vindica-
tion. "Well, there it is, old man. There's your answer. Give my regards to
Broadway, if you get a chance."

"Eh, isn't that all computer stuff, though, Charlie?"

"What is?"

"Like, IT and multimedia and that."

"Well, what if it is? I'm not an idiot, am I? I went to college, I can
learn how to multimedia-ize and so forth. Anyway, that's just industry
jargon. All it means is that they want people with a can-do spirit, such as
myself. I'm going to go and see them."

"Yeah, and I s'pose if it doesn't pan out I can always ring me mate . . ."

"Yes, well, thanks, but much as I'd like to be stuck in some dingy old
rat race of a warehouse while, you know, my friends get ahead and Bel
swans around in her fancy theatrical space"—I reached into the fridge
for a can—"I have to start thinking of myself. I'm not spending the best
years of my life sleeping on people's floors."

"You need your own place all right," Frank agreed.

"Well of course I'd like to move into my old place." I plunked the
can emphatically on the table. "Obviously in an ideal world there wouldn't
be any question about it. But this preposterous theater is what Bel wanted,
and I can't be expected to put my life on hold just in case it all goes
wrong. I have to put the house behind me and, you know, claim my slice
of the pie. I'm my own man now. Give my regards to Broadway."

"Yeah, you said that already, Charlie."

"Well, I mean it."

CHAPTER EIGHT

Trinity College, where I'd crossed swords briefly with higher education, was located right at the heart of Dublin, and as most of my time there had been spent bunking off lectures to play croquet with Hoyland, or flaneuring with him about the streets, I had come to know the city quite well. It was a comfortable, scuffed sort of a place, rather like an old shoe, consisting for the most part of greasy spoons, third-rate department stores, and dingy pubs patronized by scrofulous old men. The talk among my peers then had been of where one would emigrate to after one had graduated—Dublin in those days wasn't the type of place one contemplated sticking around in, not if one had any kind of pep or ambition. I say "in those days," though it was only a handful of years ago. It was evident as soon as I stepped off the bus that everything had changed.

Frank was right: Everywhere you looked something was being dug up or remodeled or demolished. The dilapidated shops and hostelries were gone, and in their place stood extravagant cafés, bijou stores full of minimalist chrome furniture, couturiers announcing the very latest fashions from Paris and London. The air crackled with money and potential. Help Wanted signs hung in every window; the streets teemed with people and beeping cars. It

202 · *Paul Murray*

was like being backstage at a musical—everyone hurrying to get to their positions, scenery being carted on and off—or one of those old Ealing comedies where a ship is wrecked and its cargo of whiskey washes up on the shore of some wee Scottish island, except here instead of whiskey the crates were full of Italian suits and mobile phones, and instead of getting drunk the natives were running up and down trying on pants and ringing each other up.

The sky had brightened, tipping impasto clouds white-gold; the slanting October sun gave everything a new-minted look. As I stood on O'Connell Bridge consulting my street map, with the river flowing beneath me, heterogeneous lights and sounds all around, jostled by umbrellas, schoolbags, newspapers, personal organizers, it all felt quite miraculous; and now someone bumped me, and the map fell out of my hands, and I let myself be carried off by the crowd. We surged up College Green, joined at every interstice by further tributaries of people, and it would have been easy to convince oneself that here was not just a random collection of bodies coincidentally going in the same direction but a mass, a *movement*, on its way to doing something profound. I was so taken by the whole thing that I nearly walked right past Vuk, who was slouched against some railings in a line of nondescript foreigners. He hailed me, and I stopped and said hello and asked what he was doing. "Waiting," Vuk said—I say Vuk, though I couldn't swear that it wasn't actually Zoran—"for papers."

"Really?" There were about a million people ahead of him and the queue didn't seem to be moving at all. I told him that the newsagent's up the road wasn't half so busy, if he wanted to go there instead, but he didn't appear to understand me. Maybe it reminded him of home and the bread lines and so forth. I should have asked after Mirela, but I didn't want to delay, and if she was kissing that Harry I preferred not to know about it; I quickly made my excuses and continued on my way to Merrion Square.

Sirius Recruitment was housed in a graceful gray building with tinted glass doors, in which I conducted a quick inspection of myself before going inside. It had to be said that my attire was not ideal for the occasion—the dinner jacket slightly foxed, the waistcoat a trifle gaudy.

However, the rest of my suits having been redistributed among the patrons of the Coachman, I didn't have an alternative; and secretly I thought it gave me a rather dashing *The Mummy Takes Manhattan* sort of a look, even if Frank had said I looked more like Frankenstein's butler and Droyd had called me a shirtlifter. But they would soon see that what I lacked in style was more than made up for in can-do spirit.

I entered a spacious chamber filled with cool, silvery light. The distant sound of twinkling chimes permeated the air, and fresh-cut lilacs adorned the reception desk. One wall of the chamber was covered with photographs, showing the Sirius Recruitment team with satisfied customers, or enjoying themselves after a hard day's work. Everyone was smiling and hugging each other.

After the horrors of my recent life, all the serenity and welcome rather took me aback. In fact, for a moment I simply stood and gaped, like the man who has stumbled on the back door to Heaven; and then a voice addressed me, a voice of indescribable musicality.

"Hello," it said.

I looked round. There behind the desk sat a beautiful receptionist. "H-Hello," I stammered back. She was exquisite, tawny and elfin, wearing a telephone headset so tiny and golden it looked positively genteel.

"You look lost," she said playfully.

"No," I began, then stopped—realizing in that moment, for the first time since the Folly exploded, that lost was what I undeniably was. "That is, yes," I said. "What I mean is, I'm looking for a job."

"Then you're in the right place to start," she laughed. "Fill in this form, and Gemma will see you shortly. She's the boss," she added. "But don't worry, she's an absolute sweetheart."

I took a seat on a long plush couch and set to work. The form didn't present me with much difficulty, there being several pages (Previous Experience; Languages; Other Skills and Abilities; Long-Term Plans and Ambitions) that I was able to skip right over. I was soon finished and could turn my attention back to the photographs, mentally inserting myself beside the beautiful receptionist at the staff outing to the go-kart track, covering her with Silly String at somebody's thirtieth birthday party . . .

"Charles?"

I snapped awake. A woman was standing at the end of the curving reception—a tall, regal woman with fine crow's-feet. "Gemma!" I bounded up to take her hand.

"Follow me to my cubicle," she laughed.

We threaded through a kind of open-plan maze of potted plants, watercoolers, and cappuccino machines. Everywhere workers talked on the phone or tapped at their computers with an air of quiet satisfaction. Gemma's cubicle was at the back, by a long window giving onto a well-manicured Victorian spice garden.

"First of all, Charles," she said, motioning me to sit, "I want to thank you for coming in to see me today."

"That's all right," I said. Her cubicle walls were crowded with more pictures: the Sirius gang at a rodeo, on top of the Empire State Building, at a performance of *Cats*.

"Before we start talking about you," Gemma said, "I'd like to tell you a little bit about our agency, and hopefully convince you that you made the right decision coming here." She didn't seem at all perturbed by my bandages, I noticed; it was as if she were able to see past them, to the man underneath. "Why Sirius? Well, as we both know, Ireland is experiencing growth like never before in its history. In fact our economy is the envy of all of Europe."

Unless she actually *liked* the bandages, it struck me suddenly, that wouldn't be beyond the bounds of possibility—

"Where has this growth come from? The answer is simple: you."

"Me?" I said.

"Yes," she nodded. "You, and other young graduates like you. You see, it's Ireland's highly educated, highly motivated young workforce that's made it such an attractive prospect for foreign companies seeking to invest. The information-technology revolution is making things happen that a couple of years ago seemed like science fiction, and here in Ireland we've been able to put ourselves at the forefront of that cutting-edge technology. Charles, would you like a mochaccino?"

"Yes, please, Gemma."

"At Sirius," she continued, stepping over to a gleaming chrome machine in the corner, "we're aware that our employees—our partners, we like to call them—are among the very best in the world. That's why when Bryan and I founded this company, back in the mid-nineties"— she gestured back to a photograph of Bryan sitting on the bonnet of a gold Saab with his arm curled around Gemma, outside the graceful gray building—"we were determined that we weren't going to be one of those stodgy places that sends its temps off to Timbuktu for the day to lick envelopes." Expertly she worked the machine's levers and knobs, releasing bursts of steam into the milk. "We think of our employees not as automatons to be ordered about but as creative, talented individuals with flair." She handed me a cup and sat down opposite me. "We have all kinds of clients. As a Sirius partner, you could find yourself designing the web site for an indigenous start-up, or working on e-solutions for the Irish branch of a huge multinational. You could be creating a 3-D simulator for an oil-drilling concern—or customizing the software for a top recruitment agency!"

We both laughed, although I wasn't sure what she was talking about. "The one thing I can promise you is that you will never be bored here, Charles. We want you to develop your talents to the fullest—because that's when you make us look good, and we all make more money!"

We laughed again. "But seriously"—she uncrossed her legs and sat forward—"what I'm saying is that without you there is no Sirius Recruitment. So, although I'm the head of the company, I like to say that *I'm* working for *you*." Gemma sipped her mochaccino and licked away the foam. I pictured myself having an affair with her, Bryan weeping desolately in his Saab. "Some people might think that that's no way to run a business. They might call us naïve, or utopian. But we say to them, the future *is* utopian. And we're in the business of making the future. The changes we see around us in the city now—the new cars, the new hotels, the restaurants and sushi bars—owe their existence to the technology revolution—to people like you and me. Soon, we predict that everyone will be doing things our way."

She tossed back her sleek, dark hair and folded her hands. "But that's enough self-promotion. Tell me, Charles, what was it that attracted you to us?"

"Hmm? Sorry?"

"Why did you choose Sirius Recruitment?"

"Oh . . ." I had been busy wondering what I would do when the beautiful receptionist found out about Gemma and me; it was a hell of a bind. "Well, mainly because of the things you said in your ad. The whole rat race, you know, I was getting pretty fed up of it."

She nodded encouragingly, motioning me to continue.

"Well, I mean, the fact is . . . ," I began. "The fact is . . ."

The fact was, I wasn't sure how much I should tell her; but then I looked into those cool gray eyes and everything just came spilling out: Mrs. P.'s stowaways, Bel's theater group, Mother giving away my room, Boyd and the air hostesses, moving into Frank's. "But I mean Frank is one thing," I told her. "This fellow Droyd is another matter entirely. Yesterday, for example, he dried his washing in the oven even when I quite bluntly asked him not to. Now the whole apartment smells like socks. It's utterly intolerable. If I don't find somewhere of my own I don't know what I'll do. I mean I'm already getting hives. So you see it really is important that I get my slice of the pie right away."

Gemma considered this in silence. Then she said slowly, "Charles, those are all good reasons. Because you can't separate your work from your life, can you? How can you be expected to do justice to your individual talent and flair if you're sleeping on somebody's floor?"

"This is what I ask myself," I said.

"Okay," Gemma said. "Well, the important thing is not to panic. We have literally thousands of companies begging us for bright young computer-literate people like you. It's simply a matter of matching your history with the business profile that best suits you. So let's not waste any more time, and we'll . . ." She flicked open the application form, then flicked it back again with a concerned expression. "Charles, you did know that there were actually four pages to this booklet, didn't you?"

"Yes," I said.

"Because I'm noticing that a lot of the sections have been left blank here."

"I didn't need to bother with most of it," I explained.

"Oh," Gemma said. "Okay. Really there's no reason why you should have to fill out some boring form, is there, we can just . . . Okay, so it says here that in college your primary degree was in Theology." She looked up. "That must have been fascinating!"

"Yes," I said vaguely. "Actually, it was Father's idea, you see it was the only course in Trinity I was able to get into, so the plan was to take it until junior soph and then hopefully transfer into Law."

"Law, ah, I see. And then . . . ?"

"Well, then Father died."

"Oh . . ." Gemma shrank back minutely. "Oh, I'm so sorry . . ."

"It's perfectly all right," I assured her. "But that put paid to law for the time being."

"Yes," Gemma nodded gravely, "so instead you . . ."

"I left college at that point," I said. "I felt I needed time to think."

"Okay, good, and then you . . . ?"

"Actually, that takes us right up to the present day," I told her.

"Oh," Gemma said. "Oh." She lowered her eyes, as if to scrutinize the blank pages of the application form. "So since then you've been . . . thinking?"

"Oh, you know, knocking about, doing this and that." I sipped thoughtfully at my mochaccino. "Funny how the time just sort of *goes,* isn't it?"

"It is," Gemma agreed heavily, making a steeple of her fingers and pressing it to either side of her nose. "Obviously what I'm wondering here, Charles, is how all this ties up to your career in information technology."

"Mmm," I said simply, stroking my chin.

"Perhaps you could tell me just exactly what it is that interests you in this field . . . ?"

I thought I detected a hint of something in her voice. I couldn't say what it was, exactly, but I began to have the inexplicable feeling that I had dropped the ball in some important respect. Suddenly I found myself thinking of the bank manager and how I'd shaken his faith in the system with my baccarat losses and wayward mortgage; I didn't want to do the same thing to Gemma.

"Well," I said slowly, "the fact is that information technology is indispensable these days. It's inescapable. Because I mean everyone needs information, don't they, or else, you know, how would we know anything? So now everywhere you go there's—there's information." I glanced furtively at Gemma. She was chewing the end of a ballpoint pen; I couldn't tell if this was a good or a bad sign. "And technology," I went on, "much the same story, all over the place, making things faster and . . . and . . ." For a moment I faltered, but then I had a burst of inspiration—"and when you think about it, really what better way to find out your information, than with technology? And vice versa, what better way to learn about technology, than with, you know, information?"

"Good," Gemma said opaquely when I'd finished. "Good." She picked up the application form again. "Charles, for my own records there's something I just need to make sure of, so if you wouldn't mind, what I'm going to do is read out this list of computer languages and applications, and if you've worked with them or are familiar with them or have encountered them before in any way at all I want you to say 'yes,' okay?"

"Okay," I agreed.

"Quark," she said.

"What?" I said.

"Word," she said. I realized she had begun to read out the list. "Excel. PowerPoint . . ."

It was a long list; every so often she would glance up to see if I was still there. As she went on I felt shame creep up my cheeks. So many languages, so many applications! How was it possible I had failed to master even one? On and on she went—"VOID. Basic Basic. Advanced Basic Basic"—and I could do nothing more than sit and listen as she recited the string of meaningless words like some awful futurist poem!

Finally it ended. Gemma stared at me keenly. I cleared my throat and made an invisible adjustment to my tie. "Charles," she said, "this may be premature of me, but I'm guessing that your multimedia skills are at a more or less equivalent level to your IT?"

I nodded dumbly. I was wondering if now was the time to bring up my can-do spirit.

"So in short, Charles"—Gemma stood up rather abruptly to look out at the spice garden—"it's fair to say you've *never* worked for a living, is that right?"

"Not as such," I admitted. It struck me that I had tended to Father's peacocks for a number of years, but I wasn't sure how relevant this experience would be, and given that most of the peacocks had actually died in my care, I decided it might be better not to mention them at all.

"Interests?" Gemma said. "Hobbies?"

"I like watching old films," I said. "There's usually something good on in the afternoon, around lunchtime."

"Yes." Gemma rattled her nails against the slate gray veneer of the desk. "I need something more proactive than that, Charles. You have to help me out a little bit here. What is it, tell me what it is that you want to *be*."

"Be . . . ?" I had never really wanted to *be* anything specific—not like Bel, say, who had wanted to be an actress since she was twelve, and before that put considerable preparation toward the day she became czarina.

"Put it this way, where do you see yourself in five years' time?"

I rested my finger on my bottom lip. It was a compelling question. Five years! I imagined my future self, who had mastered the intricacies of this complex world, and the trappings of my successful life there. I pictured myself in a sumptuous suite, with Art Deco prints and mirrored ceilings and automated windows overlooking the city, where I would sit at my computer effortlessly typing Solutions. I envisioned the fashionable bars where I would drink gimlets with my new friends, and how at the weekend we would go go-karting, or to see *Cats*. I looked rested and content. Everything was provided for; life was good. But then I thought, *five years*, and I wondered, just out of curiosity, what Amaurot might look like then—and instantly the parallel universe of my successful career dissolved, and I was back walking through the orchard in a smoking jacket, beating away at nettles with a good stick, while on the lawn Bel paced back and forth with a sheaf of papers, murmuring the lines of the play she was auditioning for, and Mrs. P. appeared on the doorstep with a jug of lemonade, and so did Mother, and Mirela, and anyone else who wanted to be there, all of us just there and not worrying about how, or why—

"Charles?"

"Oh, yes," I said, disorientated. "That's right. Five years. Well, anywhere, really. That is to say, I'm not particular."

Gemma sighed. "Charles, you see, that's just no good. How can I place you if you don't even know where you want to be placed? Today's employer wants commitment. He wants to know that you share his dreams and ambitions. Because that's how this boom came about, Charles. It's not just about U.S. venture capital and drastic cuts in Irish corporate tax. It's about a group of gifted young people brought together by a dream. A dream, Charles, do you see? It isn't enough for someone to just wander in off the street looking for their slice of the pie, if they don't understand what the pie even *is*, Charles. I mean, do you even *want* the pie?"

"Well, I want to eat," I said agitatedly, "you know, and I'd quite like to sleep in a bed again—"

"Of course you do!" Gemma said. "Of course you want to live in a nice place and drive a big car. Who doesn't? But the prospective employer needs *more* than that. And my concern is that when I fax him *this*,"—she lifted the application form—"what he's going to *see* is not the individual of flair and imagination that I know you are but someone whose life just *stopped*, three years ago."

I blanched. *Stopped?* How could she say that, when so much had happened? Bel's passage through college, her string of unbroachable men, my efforts to reprise the courtly life of the Renaissance, Mother's collapse, Mrs. P.'s collapse, Father's death and all the screaming at that horrendous funeral—

"Okay," Gemma said brightly, clapping her hands to her thighs. "Charles, I want to thank you again for coming in today. And I'm not going to say goodbye, because I know that you're going to come back in here as soon as you've figured out what you want to do." On her noticeboard, the photos seemed now to have taken on a melancholy tint, as if somehow they'd turned their backs to me. "Because there's a place out there waiting for you. It's only a matter of wanting it enough."

"What?" I said dazedly. "Oh . . . ," realizing she'd stretched out her hand. I shook it limply and got to my feet.

"So see you soon," she said, pointing me toward the exit.

"See you soon," I said.

"See you soon," the beautiful receptionist said as I passed back through the lobby; and the fragrance of lilacs accompanied me a little way down the street.

The city seemed quite different now. The sun had gone in, and a lowering gunmetal sky hung over the streets. All around huge cranes labored, drills snored, jackhammers juddered. The noise was earsplitting, and with every step it became more unbearable—the din, the hustle, this endless parade of unfamiliar faces, each presenting its own split-second interrogation before merging back into the amorphous throng.

Coming down Clare Street, I saw that a coachload of elderly Americans in space-age rainwear had become snarled up with a mass of pasty-faced native schoolchildren, and thinking to avoid them, I ducked through the Lincoln Place gate into my alma mater. Immediately I wished I hadn't, because I saw at once that not even Trinity had been spared the ravages of the new era. Sanding machines assailed the Museum building; a veritable Golgotha of a library was being raised to the west. With a sudden fretful pang I sought out the little grove of trees in a secluded corner of the cricket pitch where, one woozy outrageous night, Patsy and I had come closest to consummating our love, or my love anyway. But it had been railed off, and from behind the palings a bulldozer could be heard, devouring. It was depressing. I wondered at these glossy people who didn't seem to care, who walked blithely through the destruction as if they had been born yesterday.

I was walking through New Square wrapped in somber thoughts when somebody called my name. I turned to see a flabby office type in a cheap blue suit. He was standing with his hands in his pockets on the ramp leading up to the Arts building, where Trinity's high society traditionally gathered to snipe and flirt and smoke countless cigarettes: I thought at first he must be a ghost, or a shade stepped out of my memory.

"It *is* you," he said. "I thought I recognized the, ah . . ." He tapped at his breast. I looked down and saw that the monogrammed corner of my handkerchief was protruding from my jacket pocket.

"Hoyland Maffey," I said. "Well, well."

"Been a while," Hoyland said.

"Yes," I said. After that, I didn't know quite what to say; neither did he, obviously, and for a moment we stood there awkwardly, unsure that we wanted to take the conversation any further.

"Funny I should run into you here," he said, gesturing at the trees, the architecture. "What are you doing, reminiscing?"

"Yes, I suppose." His spare tire had inflated noticeably—yet at the same time he looked lessened somehow, not so Hoylandy as he had been. No doubt he was thinking the same thing about me; I could see him glance covertly over my bandaged head, debating whether or not to ask me about it. He didn't; the silence reached an embarrassing level.

"Well!" he said peremptorily.

"Yes!" I followed with an uncomfortable laugh, and was making to take my leave when he said again sharply: "Charles—"

"What is it?"

His blue eyes flickered over the rococo structure of the Campanile. "I just wondered," he said in a tight, strained voice, "if you still had those peacocks."

I flushed and did not reply right away. And then the old response came into my head, and with it the croquet games, the flaneuring, all the warmth of our past lives. "As a matter of fact I do," I said. "And you—you had seabirds, as I recall? I believe you kept several egrets?"

Hoyland stood a moment, looking off into the distance. "Egrets?" he said. "I've had a few. But, then again, too few to mention . . ."

Students glanced disdainfully at us as we exploded into guffaws and then performed the secret handshake; then Hoyland pointed out that it was lunchtime, and having nothing to look forward to but an afternoon in my slum, I agreed to let him buy me a sandwich.

"BLASTED NEW ERA," Hoyland said through a mouthful of crab salad, gazing dyspeptically down the long, ornate hall at the swarming financial types eating gourmet luncheons. We were in one of the new cafés, an airy, wooden-beamed chamber plastered with posters from the 1920s; I had just asked Hoyland why he was wearing that lamentable suit.

"I shouldn't be here at all, you know," he said. "I'd retired from

public life. Moved back to the Kingdom, thought I'd work on my fly-
fishing for a few months before embarking on any more disastrous—
Well, you know. Best-laid plans of mice and men, Hythers. Arrived back
in Kerry to find a full-scale war going on between the old man and the
town council."

"A war? I say, you were right about this sandwich . . ."

"It's the mozzarella. They import it directly from the Tyrol, by helicopter." He dabbed his mouth with a napkin. "Anyway, it seems the
council passed some sneaky law when no one was looking allowing them
to build holiday homes all over the headland. Place is covered with 'em.
Horrific things, sort of like upmarket sardine tins. Idea is they lie
empty ten months a year, then in July you're invaded by a horde of ancient Germans Heil Hitlering each other in the village grocery. Now
they want to turn the park into a golf course— Ah, thank you, dear," as
the waitress dropped down our coffees. "Well, naturally the old man's
had kittens. He's retained about every solicitor in Munster, spends the
whole day storming around the house muttering about Dunkirk. 'We
will fight them on the beaches, Hoyland,' he says. I've lost count of how
many actions he's taken. They're suing us back, of course." He picked
gloomily at the cheap fabric of his cuffs. "In the meantime, no one has
two pennies to rub together. And instead of having a little time off to
think about, you know, one's life, one's direction, the old man's sent
me back up here, to earn money for the War Effort—he calls it the War
Effort, Charles. I tell him I can barely make enough up here to keep
body and soul together. He doesn't listen." He heaved his shoulders
jadedly. "Hence this regrettable downturn in my fortunes. What about
you?"

Taking a deep breath, I gave him a summarized account of the story,
from my selfless bid to save Amaurot to my current state of exile and my
ignominious attempts at finding a job.

Hoyland was shocked. "A job? You?"

" 'Fraid so."

"But what about that Italian thing you were always busy with—what
was it, spirulina?"

"*Sprezzatura.*"

"That's it, what about that?"

I shrugged. "Needs must, old man."

"I never thought I'd see the day when you had to get a job," he said, shaking his head. "What kind of a bally world is it, anyway?" He looked thoroughly despondent.

I was surprised: I didn't recall him ever being quite this downbeat before. "It could be worse," I suggested. "At least a man can make a decent living nowadays, I mean I gather they're having some sort of a boom . . ."

"Ha!" Hoyland said.

"Ha?"

"It's a sham," he said. "It's nothing but a blasted sham."

"Oh."

"I'm not denying people are getting rich. But I'll tell you one thing, Hythers, it's not the chaps on the ground like you and me. Rudimentary knowledge of theology doesn't get you far these days. It's all computers now. We're just drones, as far as these technology people are concerned. We're bottom of the heap. Yesterday's news."

"It can't be that bad," I said.

"It is," he said, mopping his plate with a hunk of bread. "It's worse. Look at me, Hythloday. Look at these *wrists*. I used to have the wrists of one of those twelve-year-old Russian piano prodigies. Now they're worn away to nothing. I sprained one playing Ping-Pong the other week, *Ping-Pong*, Charles!"

"I say, you're spitting, old man . . ."

"I don't care!" Hoyland cried, pounding the table. "You'll spit too, when you see what it's like! Spending all day long typing blasted VOID and PowerPoint, going home to your shoe box of an apartment block with electric fences to keep out the locals, never seeing a soul from one day to the next—that's no way for a man to live! I've lived before, I know that that's not living!"

The office types at the table next to ours had fallen silent and were shooting us wary glances.

Hoyland took a deep breath. "Sorry," he said. He fiddled out a cigarette from the pack in front of him and lit it. I studied his tortured brow wonderingly. I felt a bit like Dante, chancing upon one of his old acquaintances in the nth circle of hell.

"So this is the boom, eh?" I said. "Not exactly Scott Fitzgerald, is it?"

"I'll tell you what it's like," he said glumly. "It's like being in Caligula's Rome, and everyone around you's having an orgy, and you're the mug stuck looking after the horse." He pulled heavily on his cigarette. "The whole thing'll come crashing down," he said bleakly, "and all anyone'll have done is eaten a lot of expensive cheese."

Rain had begun to fall outside. Beside us the office types were jawing noisily about some takeover or other. Hoyland smoked the rest of his cigarette in silence.

"Seen any of the old crowd?" he said eventually. "Pongo, that lot?"

"From time to time," I replied. "Pongo's in London now."

"Lucky blighter," he said. He stared a moment into the middle distance, then in a casual voice said, "I hear Patsy's back."

I made a little horseman of the salt cellar and marched him along the table. "Oh yes?"

"Yes, someone met her working in a café."

"Oh," I said colorlessly.

"Christ, Hythloday," Hoyland said flatly, "we've been dopes, do you know that?"

"What do you mean?" I said.

"You know what I mean. Not patching things up. Letting the whole gang drift apart for the sake of a girl."

I puffed up my cheeks and blew.

"Well, damn it, what do you think?"

"Oh hell," I said irritably, "I don't know. It didn't come out of nowhere, did it? Maybe it was meant to happen. Maybe that whole gang was past its sell-by date, and that was just the, you know, the catalyst. I mean, good God, if Patsy Olé was the only thing holding us together, Patsy Olé who has all the loyalty of the ball in a roulette wheel—"

"So what?" Hoyland said bitterly. "So now for the rest of our lives we just dwindle off into our own little private solitary worlds, is that it?"

"I don't know," I said. "We can't pretend it didn't happen, can we? How should I know?"

We fell into a fractious silence.

"Sure, the public got burned in the buyout," one of the business types declaimed energetically next to us. "But that's what *happens* in a revolution. You've got to understand that this is a *whole new paradigm of management.*"

Hoyland fumbled out another cigarette but didn't light it; then, catching sight of his watch, he swore and started to his feet. "I have to get back," he said. "My masters don't look kindly on tardiness. But look here, Hythers—I'm glad we met. We should go for a brandy sometime. I'm free most evenings."

I nodded mechanically. Suddenly everyone was leaving: massing round the door, unfurling their umbrellas. Hoyland reached into his wallet and handed me a card. "Do call," he said. "Silly to let everything just go to the wall." He hovered there a moment, blankly watching the exiting hordes, the unlit cigarette hanging from his lips. "I still think about her, you know," he said abstractedly; then he turned up his collar and passed with the others back onto the boulevard. In a few minutes, the café was almost empty.

Damn it, I had forgotten how a fellow couldn't go twenty yards in this city without running into someone he used to know, wanting to dig up the past. Maybe that was why they were knocking the whole place down. As the waitress moved from table to table with her tray, piling up the dishes, the old faces appeared in front of me out of the rain, like the cast of a play taking its curtain call . . .

We had all been wild about Patsy, of course; though none of us would ever have claimed he truly knew her, or understood her. She was like the moon moving through the houses of the zodiac—favoring each of us in turn, yet remaining always remote, her love a mysterious influence you couldn't quite put your finger on but didn't dare disbelieve. In retrospect it's obvious she was quite happy in this orbit of her own, from which she could enjoy the chaotic effect she had, the squalls and storms and other aberrant weather patterns caused by her peculiar magnetism. But each of us had hoped that he would be the one who finally brought her to earth.

My chance had come that spring. She appeared by my side one day, more or less literally, amid a pageant of bluebells and forget-me-nots. I didn't know how she had got there, exactly, but I didn't ask questions. I fell instantly under her spell, just like everybody did.

I don't remember exactly what we did together, or what we said to each other. It's possible we didn't do or say anything at all. It was the time itself that seemed enchanted: becoming a single evening that didn't begin or end, through which we drifted along hand in hand as if plunged into a wonderful dream. And if she never quite yielded, if some part of her always seemed to be elsewhere, still I—spending my solitary hours frantically learning off Yeats, searching for the insight, the single line that would deliver her to me—still I assumed that this would only be a matter of time.

The problem was that the part of her that I felt was always somehow elsewhere was usually, more specifically, with Hoyland Maffey. Indeed, Hoyland was frequently there with us, helping us to witness the spectacular spring. It seemed to me rather unorthodox for two people who were falling in love to have a third party present for so much of the falling. At last I put this to Patsy.

"What do you mean?" she said.

"I mean, usually it's just the two people on their own."

"But Hoyland's our friend, Charles. Our *bosom* friend. It's not fair leaving him out just because we're so terribly, terribly in love."

The way she said *bosom* would probably have been enough; but when she went on, completely unprompted, to deny that there had ever been anything between her and Hoyland, any doubts I had left were extinguished. At that moment I knew that she was telling Hoyland exactly the same story about me; I knew she knew I knew, and I knew that Hoyland knew it too.

The enchanted spring was quickly poisoned. Every moment was shadowed by mistrust and deception. Time and time again Patsy and I would be alone together in the library—a candle burning low on the ledge as we approached, seemingly inexorably, a moment of ecstatic union—when the doorbell would ring and Patsy would spring up from the billiard table saying, "Oh good, that'll be Hoyland," as casually as if we'd just been playing an uninspired round of Scrabble; and there he would be, his mirthless grimace and darting eyes the mirror image of my own:

"Hello, Hythers, just thought I'd stop by . . ."

"Ha ha, always a pleasure, old man, get you a glass of something?"

Before long my love for Patsy had been totally superseded by my hatred for Hoyland. Every hour apart from her I spent in torment, imagining the two of them together. When I was with her I oscillated between desperate bids to impress her and equally desperate attempts to find out her true feelings. Every dainty sniff, every equivocal cough, every half-raised eyebrow I would pore over for hours seeking to decode. Patsy, of course, had no true feelings; or if she did they had nothing to do with us. But even if I had known this it would have made little difference. What mattered now above all was that I thwart my former friend.

Finally, toward the end of April, things came to a head. Patsy was traveling to Rome for a couple of weeks to do some work for her thesis, something to do with Raphael and his courtesans. I had thrown together a send-off party and had managed to pip Hoyland's rival party by hiring Patsy's favorite local jazz trio for the occasion. It was quite a soirée, or so I am told. The night was sweltering, presided over by a full silver moon; all kinds of carousing took place out on the lawn, including (allegedly) a striptease by Bel's old schoolmate Bunty Chopin, right down to a couple of peacock feathers.

But Hoyland and I cared nothing for the celebrations. For the entire night we sat staring balefully at each other from armchairs in opposite corners of the recital room, rising only to top up our whiskeys. From time to time Patsy would breeze in from the garden where the trio had set up and drape herself over one of us, with the express intention of infuriating the undraped party in the opposing armchair, which it invariably did.

At four o'clock, both Hoyland and I arrived at the sideboard to find that only a single measure of whiskey remained in the decanter. We looked at each other, and the rest of the party—the conversations, the bragging trumpet, the hoots from the lawn—seemed to fall away. There were only the two of us: deadlocked.

"Help yourself," I said.

"No no, please," he returned.

"My dear fellow, you're the guest."

"It's fine, really, I've had quite enough."

"Oh, you have, have you?"

"Yes, as a matter of fact I have."

"Well, so have I, in that case."

"Well, 'in that case' I'd be interested to hear what you intend to do about it."

"I—ah . . . that is . . ." The ball was in my court, but I had gone completely blank. The whiskey had turned my brain into a furnace of dry heat. All around me I could hear whispers like the crackle of kindling, and Patsy whistling "Sophisticated Lady" as she drew up the hall—when I saw that as luck would have it someone had left her gloves on the piano. I seized one of them and threw it down at Hoyland's feet. A gasp went around the room. "I'm challenging you to a duel, that's what," I said.

Hoyland looked surprised. "Really?" he said.

"Well . . . ," I said uncertainly. Just then Patsy came in and asked a girl on the periphery what was going on. "Charles wanted Hoyland to finish the whiskey, but Hoyland thought Charles ought to have it, so Charles challenged Hoyland to a duel," the girl said.

"Oh," Patsy said. She sounded impressed.

"Yes," I said to Hoyland.

"Good," said Hoyland, who had had time to regain his composure and was superciliously buffing his cuff links. "Swords or pistols?"

"Pistols, obviously," I said, adding contemptuously, "Swords."

The arrangements were quickly made. The antique pistols were brought down from the study, where Father had kept them loaded in his desk—a secret Bel and I weren't supposed to know about. Solemnly, we chose our seconds: Boyd Snooks was mine and Fluffy Elgin, Hoyland's. After trying vainly to talk us out of it, Pongo agreed to adjudicate. Other than these parties, everybody, including Patsy, was asked to remain inside. At five, we left the house by the back door.

We strode over the long grass to the gazebo, recently vacated by the jazz trio. Above us the sky was tinged with pink and a few early birds chirruped in the branches. Fluffy Elgin couldn't stop giggling. Hoyland blinked at me from under the apple tree on which he'd hung his blazer. Pongo's voice, when he spoke, was high and taut and cut into the quiet of the morning. "Gentlemen," he said, summoning us together before the gazebo and requesting that we shake hands before holding up the mahogany box: "Choose your weapons."

The pistol was heavy and dull with a long barrel. Pongo ushered me into place, standing with my back to Hoyland's. I realized how cold it was. Every detail of the garden blazed at me.

"When I give the word, you must take ten paces. Then, at my signal, turn and face one another. When I throw my hat in the air, you may shoot. Understood? Right. Commence pacing. One . . ."

As I took my paces, stretching out my leg stiff at the knee, dew soaking the cuffs of my trousers, I did wonder what exactly I was doing. But it all made a kind of sense: in fact, a singular kind of sense.

"Two . . . three . . ."

Every element of my life had, at this moment, cohered. If the worst came to the worst, and I died here, it would be in my own garden, surrounded by friends, for the honor of the woman I knew beyond a doubt to be my true and eternal love. As deaths went, this didn't seem a bad one.

"Five . . . six . . ."

Bother, I realized I hadn't said goodbye to Bel. She was away putting up lights for a show. It was probably just as well—she tended to be a wet blanket when it came to parties and I daresay would have frowned on duels too; furthermore she disapproved strongly of Patsy Olé, whom she referred to as the Dalkey Chameleon. I made a mental note to mention her in my dying words.

"Eight . . . ," Pongo called. "Nine . . ."

Fluffy Elgin's giggles had turned into hiccups, and she had to sit down.

"Ten . . . Oh hell, hang on a second . . ."

There was a padding sound and then silence. Moments passed. I stood trembling with the muzzle cold against my cheek. I stared into a clump of peonies, emptily taking in the form of the leaf, the gleaming stem, the petals. Fluffy hiccuped dolefully.

"I say, Boyd," I called out, after a little more time had passed.

"Yes?" Boyd replied from the log where he was trying to get Fluffy to hold her breath.

"What's going on?"

"I'm not sure," Boyd said. "Pongo suddenly ran off somewhere."

"What?" Hoyland's voice wafted over from his position under the larches.

"I think he had to get something from inside," Boyd said. "I shouldn't think he'll be long." He started humming to himself.

"It's deuced cold," I observed.

"Can't we sit down?" Hoyland wanted to know. "Or turn around, at least?"

"I don't know," Boyd said. "You'd have to ask Pongo, he's the adjudicator."

We remained where we were. More birds joined in the tweeting. "The sun's shining directly into my eyes," Hoyland complained. Somewhere a car raced down the road.

My teeth began to chatter.

"Raaaaaah!" Boyd exclaimed suddenly, making us all jump.

"What on earth—"

"I was trying to scare Fluffy," Boyd apologized.

"Hiccup—hiccup—hiccup," Fluffy hiccuped miserably, twisting a peacock feather limply between her fingers.

"This is ridiculous," I said and turned around, whereupon Hoyland immediately began jumping about shouting that I had forfeited the duel and that he was the winner by default.

"Don't be absurd," I said. "I'm going to find Pongo. This is no way to run a duel." I tossed my pistol under the apple trees and set off back toward the house, Hoyland scrambling after me.

Pongo wasn't in the kitchen, nor was he in the dining room. Hoyland checked the library while I looked in the drawing room, but he wasn't there either. He wasn't one of the slumbering bodies in the recital room, nor was he among the mésalliances that had unfolded in the bedrooms.

"It's as if he's disappeared," Hoyland said.

"Very peculiar," I said.

"I thought he'd been doing a very good job up until then," Hoyland said.

And then—just as we were about to abandon our search and call it a night—we found him. He was in the cloakroom, standing almost submerged in the layers of coats that hung on the back wall. His face was frozen in a remarkable expression, somewhere between astonishment and rapture. In his hand he held a triumphal-looking brandy. We asked him just what the blazes was going on; and he informed us, in a halting, wispy voice, that he had just been fellated by Patsy Olé.

Behind me, I heard Hoyland's pistol clatter to the floor.

"What?" I whispered.

"I only came in here to get my hat," Pongo reflected.

"But—but—" spluttered Hoyland, "but where is she now?"

"Gone," Pongo said.

"Gone?"

"She flies to Italy in half an hour," he said dreamily. "Her taxi was waiting outside."

"But this is incredible," I said, ignoring the toxic contents performing a *danse macabre* in my stomach. "You mean to tell me that—that you were in here simply minding your own business, when she burst in, and—" I broke off; it was too hideous to contemplate.

"Yes," Pongo said. "That's the long and the short of it. Then she took her coat and she left." He took a thoughtful sip from his brandy. "That's some lady," he said.

A low moan emerged from Hoyland. The pair of us were hunched up like old men.

"What about us?" he managed to croak. "Didn't she say anything about us?"

Pongo considered this. "She said," he recalled at last, *"Salute,"*—and he raised his glass to both of us.

aking my chance meeting with Hoyland to be nothing less than a warning from the gods, I did not attempt any other agencies that day. The rain had become a deluge, and by the time I got back to Bonetown I was in a foul mood. It didn't help that from the bus stop I had to run a gauntlet of local youths, who appeared to have gone on some sort of rampage. The sky was lit up by explosions, and the streets were filled with urchins calling to each other as they hauled timber, car tires, and any other flammable business to the pyre that had materialized before the block of flats.

"Halloween," Droyd explained, when I pointed this out.

"It's weeks to Halloween," I said sourly, taking off my scarf as, outside, a series of metallic creaks and groans was succeeded by cheers and an expensive-sounding crash. "They're not going to keep this up all night, are they? I mean presumably *some* of them have parents, who might eventually begin to wonder—"

"Ah yeah," Droyd said happily, looking down at the mayhem. "There's always a bit of crack round here on Halloween, am I right, Frankie?"

"Ah yeah," Frank concurred lugubriously.

"Look out, neighborhood cats," Droyd said.

"I don't mind crack," I said. "I like crack as much as the next man. But it's not doing a thing for my nerves, and I already have a splitting headache— I say, I don't suppose those heroin dealers carry Anadin or acetaminophen or anything like that, do they?"

"I think they just have heroin, Charlie."

"Here, Frankie, remember that time the fire engine came out and we all threw rocks at them and I hit this one bollocks with a plank, remember that?"

"Yeah."

"You assaulted the fire brigade?" I said incredulously.

"We were just tryin to have a laugh," Droyd's face crossing swiftly silver then pink as a brace of rockets went up. "Is that too much to ask? If they'd just let us enjoy ourselves one fuckin day a year then no one'd have to get hurt, would they?"

"A laugh," I repeated sardonically. "It looks like *Bosnia* out there." As I said it I felt a pang of homesickness for Mrs. P. and the cups of cocoa she made for one on rainy days like this . . .

"I wonder if they'll come out this year," Droyd said, rubbing his hands.

With a heavy sigh, Frank got up, went to the refrigerator, took out a six-pack of Hobson's, and left the room.

"What's eating him?" I asked.

"That bird was here," Droyd said disapprovingly.

"What bird?"

"That bird with no tits," he elaborated. "Your sister."

"She was? Well, damn it, why didn't he— I say!" I stormed out into the living room just in time to see Frank vanish into the bathroom and slide the lock shut. I went up and hammered indignantly on the door. "I say!"

"Occupied," came the small voice from inside.

"You didn't tell me that Bel was here."

"Oh yeah," the voice said, with an air of cloudy recollection. "That's right, she asked if you'd give her a ring."

"Why didn't you tell me before? What was she doing here?"

"Eh . . . I don't know," the voice said meekly. "Just droppin off a few things I gave her a loan of for the play. Oh yeah, and she wanted to make sure I knew we were broken up."

"She . . . oh." I thought he'd seemed a little quiet.

"I already had a fair idea. But it was nice of her all the same, just so I know where I stand, like."

"Ah," I said. A few moments elapsed; I stared somewhat helplessly at the flaky white paint of the door. "And you're not . . . that is, you're not . . ."

"Me, Charlie? Ah, no. Right as rain." I heard the sound of a can being opened on the other side of the door, followed by a distinctive glugging. Reluctant to press him further, I stole away.

Bel came to the phone in a state of such agitation that I was sure something had happened, and when she said she was just excited because I had finally called, I was downright alarmed. "Are you sure you're all right?" I said. "You haven't had a blow to the head or anything?"

"Of course not, I wanted to talk to you, that's all. Oh, Charles, something wonderful has happened, I've been dying to tell you—"

"Oh?" I had learned to be on my guard whenever Bel announced something wonderful.

"Yes, it's about Harry. You remember Harry, don't you?"

"Of course. How could I forget old Harry? Hasn't fallen off a cliff, I hope, or been snatched away by an eagle—"

"Don't be silly, no, he's"—she took a deep breath—"he's giving me the lead in his new play."

"Is he now? Well, well. Congratulations."

"I only found out last night, isn't it amazing?"

"Definitely," I said, although I wasn't sure it merited actual *paroxysms*, such as were filtering down now from the other end of the line. "Though didn't you have the lead in the last one too?"

"That was different, that was an ensemble piece. This is— I mean he's been working on it for ages, obviously, but last night we had this amazing conversation and afterwards he told me he'd just realized that he'd written it *for* me, like it was *about* me almost and he'd only just realized—"

"Well, bravo," I said, trying to get in the spirit a little. "And what about old Mirela, is she going to be in this thing too?"

"Oh, Mirela," Bel said impatiently. "Let's not talk about Mirela."

"She is going to be in it, though?" I persisted hopefully.

"Yes, but that's not the *point*, the point is I'm trying to tell you about this amazing conversation I had with Harry last night . . ."

A chain of squibs spat fractiously outside, and somewhere a curtain of glass tinkled to the ground. I lowered myself to a sitting position. "Go on, then," I said reluctantly.

"You know that last night the play finished its run—well it did, anyway, and we were having the wrap party in the theater in town, except I didn't really feel like being there, because it was sort of sad, you know, the end of our first play and the first thing we had done together. Anyway I said it to Harry and he said it was weird because he'd just been thinking the same thing, so he said, why don't we just leave? So we left. He knew how to get up to the theater roof from the fire escape. It was so lovely, Charles, you could see the whole city spread out, it was so peaceful, and all these stars were out, and I just *knew* that something was going to happen—"

"What sort of thing?" I interjected warily.

"Well that's when we had the amazing conversation."

"Oh," I said.

"It was just . . . ," she said dreamily. "It was so . . . Have you ever had one of those conversations where you're so connected with the other person that you stop being sure which of you is talking, because when they speak it's like they're articulating all these thoughts you've had that you've never been able to put into words before? He was telling me these *things*, like—like for instance about *The Cherry Orchard* when I didn't get the part that time, Harry was saying you know Stanislavsky's thing you can't act Chekhov you have to live him, well that in Amaurot I've basically been living Chekhov for three years only I didn't realize, and I was trying to be someone else when I was already exactly what they needed—God, he's so insightful, it was like—like hearing my own *heart* speak up and tell me exactly what it was thinking, and you know it's so weird because he and I have known each other for years, and now suddenly we find out we're so *alike*, little things even like we both like Doris Day and Mozart and Hart Crane, and the way the wind when it blows through the pylons it sounds like it's singing—" She stopped and repeated to herself, as if in disbelief, "*God.*"

"At the same time, it's not as if your heart's been especially *quiet* up until now," I felt compelled to point out.

"Yes, but, Charles, you know what it's been like since college ended," she said, "stuck out here in the house, feeling like I wasn't *alive*, even, like I was in this little closed-off area that was *contiguous* to life, and sort of along the same lines as life, but not actually life—and now suddenly in a single moment everything just opens up—I mean it's so exciting, don't you think it's exciting?"

"What about Frank?"

"What?" She broke off midgush. "What do you mean, what about Frank?"

I hesitated. I didn't know what I meant. It had just come out.

"Since when do you care what happens to Frank?" she said.

Suddenly I felt very confused. "I don't know," I said. "It just seems like an offhand way to treat somebody, that's all."

She groaned. "Charles, you're not going to *start*, are you?"

"I'm not starting anything," I said. "But a few weeks ago I seem to recall you being all set to move in with *him*. And while we're on the subject, you don't even like Doris Day."

"What?"

"Doris Day, as long as I can remember any time 'Qué Será Será' has come on the radio you've made juvenile vomiting noises, and then last year when I was watching *Pillow Talk* you said she looked like an Aryan sex doll—"

"Well, so what? What's that got to do with anything?"

"Yes, but Mozart too, I distinctly remember you telling me that people who liked Mozart ought to be made to ride around in elevators for the rest of their lives. And those ghastly pylons, in fact all of those things you just said you have in common—"

"People *change*, don't they?" she broke in. "Why are you being like this? Can't you for once just be happy for me, instead of trying to pick holes? I mean, for months you did nothing but complain about Frank, and I *know* you've developed one of your stupid crushes on Mirela. So isn't this what you wanted? I mean, what is it exactly that you want?"

Once again I found myself stuck for an answer. A Roman candle came to my rescue: It detonated right outside the window, throwing a hellish red up on the bedroom wall; the rumble took several seconds to die away. "What's going *on* there anyway?" her voice crackled from far away. "It sounds like the peasants are storming the battlements."

"They've stormed the battlements," I said glumly. "They're having their wrap party."

She laughed. "Poor old Charles," she said. "And here's me shouting at you on top of everything. You know I promised myself that I wasn't going to shout at you this time. I haven't even asked you how you are. How are you?"

"Well—" I began.

"Charles"—her voice cut across me—"sorry to interrupt, but I have to go to a meeting now, so before I forget the reason I wanted to see you—I wanted to tell you that I know everything's going to work out, for both of us. I mean that's what all this stuff I've been going on about has made me realize, that things do change, and . . . and just when it seems everything's against you, that's exactly when something'll appear out of nowhere and suddenly it'll all be different. I just wanted you to know."

"Thank you," I said stiffly.

"And the other thing was, will you tell Frank we need a wheelchair for the play, if he comes across one?"

"All right."

"I'd better go. Remember what I said."

Deep in thought, I mooched back into the living room. Frank had emerged from the bathroom and was silently watching television with Droyd. On the street, fireworks continued to crack like enemy artillery; huddled in the shifting light, the two of them had the look of soldiers caught in a foxhole.

"Bel wants a wheelchair," I said.

"Right," Frank said, without looking round.

I sat down on the sofa. I felt like I'd been walking through a hurricane. I wasn't used to hearing Bel so *happy*. It made me nervous. It was like a car driving in a gear that it didn't actually have. I wondered what that bounder had said to her, up on the roof.

"—forces allege that this is just one of dozens of similar sites scattered across the region," the television said, showing a soldier kicking dirt away from the ground to reveal what looked like a pile of washed-out rags.

She was right about one thing, though. For months I had prayed for the day when Frank would be given the heave-ho. There was nothing I wanted more than for her to be rid of him, his rusty white van, his mutilated gerunds. Now that the day had come, surely I was due a moment of jubilation or triumph or at least a cold sense of closure and the transience of all things. Yet as I sat on the dysmorphic sofa, waiting for the flush of victory to sweep through me, all there seemed to be was an annoying hollow feeling.

This was absurd! Hadn't I been paying attention? Had my life really grown so complicated that its most fundamental notions of right and wrong no longer held? Good God, now that one tiny success had presented itself, was my *own soul* going to step in and turn it to defeat?

"Good God," I uttered involuntarily.

"What's that, Charlie?"

"Nothing, nothing, bit of a twinge is all," patting my bandages; he returned to the television and I to grapple with the mounting evidence of inner mutiny.

I tried to counter it. I pointed to the facts. I recalled his odious groping sessions with Bel. I remembered how he'd blown up my Folly. I took in the mournful cherubim on the shelves around me, the lonesome garden ornaments, the inconsolable tallboy, all torn from people's houses. From the corner of my eye, I considered Frank himself, staring at the television, the can of Hobson's propped on his exposed belly moving, with a noxious quiver, slowly up and down. None of it made any difference. The hollow feeling refused to go away.

The next days were very hard. I found myself in the grip of a crippling ennui. I was back at square one, but I couldn't bring myself to resume my job hunt; it was all I could do to drag myself from the bedroom floor to the sofa. With every passing day my financial affairs grew more ruinous, and it became harder and harder even to conceive of how I might dig myself out of the hole I was in—which only compounded my ennui, and my disinclination to do anything about it. Instead I threw myself into my Gene Tierney project: I wrapped myself in her movies, lost myself in them, just as she had tried to lose herself years before. I

watched each one avidly, meticulously cross-referencing it with her biography, charting the trajectory that emerged.

If you looked at her life from start to finish, it seemed clear that her
marriage to Oleg Cassini was the event that set loose all the other catas-
trophes that befell her—the initial transgression that woke the Furies
until then lying dormant at the edges of her life. Marrying him, in fact,
was about the only rebellious thing she ever did. She had been reared to
be a nice girl, and she had always done exactly what she was told: living
frugally with her mother in Hollywood, sending her paychecks back to
the company her father had set up, catching hell from him for any extravagance. And then Cassini came along.

Oleg Cassini was Russian, the son of a countess who had fled to
America after the defeat of the White Army; he was also a designer and
a playboy and had not been to Yale, and as such could not have been
further away from what Gene's parents thought of as a suitable match if
they had sat down and planned it. They would not countenance the romance. Gene's father said that if she married Cassini he would have her
declared mentally instable. The studios concurred; and whatever about
her parents, in those days no one defied the studios. They had made
you, and they could destroy you just as easily. But Gene was in love.

She thought that once they were married, and there was no longer
anything anyone could do about it, things might die down; so, traveling
in disguise, she and Cassini eloped to Las Vegas. On the night of their
wedding Gene came back to Los Angeles—having agreed with Oleg, in
the interests of diplomacy, to spend it apart—only to find that her
mother had already fired the servants and flown home to New York
City. And worse was to come.

Parents and studio now joined forces. Paramount fired Cassini,
and Gene's studio, Fox, refused to take him on. Her parents, meanwhile, complained to the press that Cassini had taken advantage of
their daughter, and tried to have the marriage annulled. Suddenly the
newlyweds found themselves blacklisted by Hollywood society, deserted
by their friends. Cassini was still out of work; Gene, by contrast, was
working constantly, and they saw each other increasingly rarely. As the
pressure began to tell, her father and mother started calling her up at
all hours, trying to persuade her to leave him. In the midst of all this,

during the shooting of *Heaven Can Wait*, Gene discovered she was pregnant, and America entered the Second World War.

After so much personal turmoil, the war must have seemed something of a reprieve. Old differences were set aside; the nation busied itself "pitching in." Gallant Cassini joined the cavalry; Gene, like most of the stars, took part in bond drives to raise money for the war effort. She toured around the country, speaking at factories and outdoor rallies. A week before she went down to Kansas, where Cassini's division was stationed, she appeared at the Hollywood Canteen to entertain the marines. A few days later she was diagnosed with German measles.

She had kept quiet about her condition—the studio would suspend an actress's salary if she became pregnant on their time. In 1943 the connection had not yet been made between German measles in early pregnancy and brain damage in very young children. Gene gave birth prematurely in October to a baby girl, weighing two and a half pounds. She named her child Daria.

It was a year later that the newspapers picked up on the story of the rubella epidemic in Australia that had apparently produced a generation of severely retarded infants, and Gene began to admit that her baby might not be just a late developer but was having serious problems. Specialists were called out at great expense (paid for by Gene's old flame Howard Hughes, then beginning his own retreat from the world after his disfiguring plane crash). They all said the same thing. The damage had already been done, while the baby was still in the womb, and it could not be undone. The best thing for everyone now would be for the child to be put in an institution.

Gene was tormented by guilt and confusion. Hadn't she always tried to be good? Hadn't she always done what people asked? What had she done to bring this catastrophe down on top of her and those she loved? She resisted as long as she could; but she was twenty-four years old, and after everything that had happened the pressure was too much. Daria was put in a home, where she would remain for the rest of her life with the mind of a nineteen-month-old infant.

One quiet Sunday years later, at a tennis party in L.A., Gene happened to be approached by a fan. This young woman was an ex-marine;

she said she had met Gene before, at a show in the Hollywood Canteen during the war. "Did you happen to catch German measles that night?" the woman asked. Gene said that she did, as a matter of fact. The woman laughed and said the whole camp had come down with German measles, but she had broken quarantine, to sneak out and meet her favorite star.

Anyone else would have screamed, or punched her; but Gene, who had been reared to be nice, merely smiled and turned away.

It seemed to me that after that her films became a kind of refuge for her. Not the work, or the scripts, but the movies themselves: As the betrayals mounted up, as the birth of their child achieved what the combined forces of parents and studio could not and her marriage to Cassini slowly fell apart, it seemed to me that the movies became places where she could hide herself, where she could disappear. Take, for example, *The Ghost and Mrs. Muir*, in which she plays a widow who falls for the ghost that haunts the cottage she has moved into. The ghost, played by Rex Harrison, first catches her eye in the form of a portrait in the living room—which seems a neat flip of what happens in *Laura*, where the cop falls in love with the painting of Gene, who has been murdered. People falling for ghosts, people falling for paintings, in more and more of her movies I found this secret tendency elaborated: a tendency for the movies to create spaces for her within them, interstitial spaces of one kind or another—as if, although she couldn't make the movies hers, she had elicited a secret pact whereby she could escape into them and exist away from life, untouchably, as an image; as if in here, after all, she found her true domain: the illusory, the shadowy, the in-between—

"Charlie, this is like the fuckin most borin film I've ever seen in me life."

—although much of this was lost on others—

"Yeah, Charlie, and it's time for *Hollyoaks*."

"Charlie, can you not just let us watch *Hollyoaks* and then you can watch the rest of this thing?"

"Charlie, we know you can hear us so like why aren't you sayin anything? Charlie?"

"Blast it—because I know that once *Hollyoaks* is over you'll want to watch *Streetmate*, and then *Robot Wars* and then that unconscionable *Dawson's Creek* . . ."

"I don't watch *Dawson's Creek*, Charlie."

"Well, you were certainly doing a good impression of it the other night. Confound it, can't you just sit still for half an hour and then I'll quite happily—"

"I'd give her one, wouldn't you, Frankie? Charlie, would you give her—"

"Look, you scoundrels," rising apoplectically to my feet with the rolled-up television guide as though shooing a pack of mangy street dogs, "hang it, can't you just leave me in peace for a few minutes more, and then I swear to you I will return your deuced television!"

"All right, all right . . . fuck's *sake* . . ." The pair of them slunk away to the kitchen, only to strike up from there a few moments later:

"Hang it, Droyd, I wish to the devil you'd roll up an oul joint there."

"Confound it, Frankie, where's me deuced Rizlas?"

And then five minutes after that:

"Frankie?"

"Yeah?"

"D'you ever see your reflection in a spoon, like, and just for a second you think, Ah fuck, I'm upside down?"

"Yeah, o'course."

"Fuckin scary, isn't it?"

There was only so much insulation any film could give one, and tonight was the night I reached the end of my tether; I almost heard the snap. As if in a trance, I rose from the couch and headed for the kitchen, and it's quite possible that something terrible might have happened if I hadn't been diverted by the telephone.

"Yes, what? *Oh* . . ."

It was Gemma Coffey from Sirius Recruitment. She had called to offer me a job.

For a moment I was paralyzed. Could it really be true? Out of the blue like this? Had the time come at last for me to step up to bat, to play my part in—

"Charles?" she said.

"I'm here," I said faintly.

"Well, can you do it?"

I assured her that I could; I added how grateful I was to her for remembering me out of the millions that came to her door, and that I wanted her to know I *believed* in this job, whatever it was, and I would do my level best to help make the dream come true—

She said Good, but all that wasn't so important with this particular job. "It's only a temporary position, and it's not quite as glamorous as the ones we discussed. It's factory work, basically. You don't have a problem with factory work, do you, Charles?"

"It's not a *jar* factory, is it?" I said, there being only so many ironical twists I was willing to put up with in my life.

Gemma said that it wasn't, it was a bread factory in Cherry Orchard. I said that, in that case, I didn't have a problem, and I was just happy to be a part of the Sirius Recruitment team. Gemma sounded pleased, though she pointed out that technically I would be employed not by Sirius Recruitment but by its sister company, Pobolny Arbitwo Recruitment. "But that's not important," she said. "The important thing is that I'm not going to forget about you out there, Charles. Come through for me and I'm going to find something really special for you."

I told her she could count on me. She said she knew. She asked if by any chance I spoke Latvian. I said I didn't. She said it didn't matter. She gave me an address, the bus route to take, and a name to report to— Mr. Appleseed—then we thanked each other and said goodbye.

To think that only a moment ago I had been close to throwing in the towel! Now, as if someone had waved a magic wand, my problems had disappeared; I had been lifted out of the doldrums and my sails filled with wind again.

I forgot all about having it out with Frank and Droyd. Instead, I stood in the living room, stroking my chin and smiling to myself as the good news sank in. *Well, I'll be,* I thought, *the system works;* and Gene's eye twinkled at me from across the room where she waited, frozen mid-scold, with the ghost.

The following morning, while it was still dark, I set off for my first day of work. I traveled on a bus full of surly men who looked disdainfully at my pristine blue dungarees—a gift from Mother's poisonous maiden aunt—to Cherry Orchard, a dismal slum which did a passable impression of the middle of nowhere. At first I thought it rather a lark that an industrial park should share the name of Bel's favorite Chekhov play; however, as with most aspects of my job at Mr. Dough, it stopped being funny almost immediately.

When Gemma had told me that I would be working in a bread factory, I had taken it for a slip of the tongue, for everyone knew that bread was made not in factories but in bakeries, by red-cheeked men in tall hats. But I quickly learned that the mistake was mine, because a factory it undeniably was. Everywhere one looked men toiled like pygmies in the mighty shadows of the choppers and slicers, or stood on stepladders, as in some industrialized Hieronymus Bosch painting, stirring with oversized ladles at huge smoking vats. Machinery clanked and moaned; the air churned with bread dust that mixed with sweat to form a sticky film on one's skin and collected about the eye sockets in prickling crescents. From the unseen ovens, the heat rolled in unrelenting waves, turning the floor into a furnace.

I worked in Processing Zone B, as a lowly Bread Straightener in the Yule Log Division. Yule Log was a Christmas delicacy made from marzipan with a shelf life something like plutonium's; they enjoyed it on the Continent, or so we were told. There were five of us working in the room, not including Mr. Appleseed, and except for Mr. Appleseed's abusive comments no one spoke; we labored in silence like so many flour-covered Golems, performing the same mechanical motions over and over and over again. My role was to monitor the Yule Logs as they came in from the ovens through the hatch in the wall, removing any defective ones and ensuring that each loaf was sitting correctly on the belt, in a perpendicular relation to the rim, as it entered the sugarfrosting machine. Mr. Appleseed had warned of the catastrophic consequences of a loaf entering the sugar-frosting machine in any position other than this one, and Mr. Appleseed wasn't the type of man you liked to cross.

As talking was discouraged in Processing Zone B, it wasn't for a couple of days that I discovered why Gemma had asked about my Latvian—namely that, apart from Mr. Appleseed and myself, the entire complement of Yule Log Division hailed from the town of Liepaja, having been rounded up at a recruitment fair held there by Pobolny Arbitwo, Sirius's sister company, some months ago. It sounded like a rum sort of arrangement to me, but the Latvians said that many of their kinsmen had come to Ireland to work digging potatoes or cleaning hotel swimming pools, explaining that the pitiful wage they earned here was worth many times more when you sent it back to Latvia, and that as such they were coming out the real winners from the deal. Certainly they were homesick, they said; and their wives wrote letters to say how strange it was in their sorely missed city of Liepaja, with so few men to be seen. But the money they made at Mr. Dough was enough to provide for their loved ones, and even set aside a little for their future; and for a modest sum Pobolny Arbitwo rented them barracks-style accommodations with a microwave oven and comfortable bunk beds.

"And you don't mind it? You don't mind the boredom, or this ungodly heat?" We were in the canteen, a small, cramped room with a table and vending machine and walls painted bilious green to discourage procrastination.

"Not heat compared to some places," Bobo, who operated the bagging machine, said soberly. "For instance, last summer we worked in a marmalade factory in Aachen. Very, very hot. Many wasps." This provoked rueful murmurs of assent from the men around the table. "We are very lucky, to be here at Mr. Dough," Bobo added.

"Huh," I said. Frankly I didn't know how lucky I would call myself to be dragged halfway round the world in order to spend all day processing Yule Logs. That said, compared to box making, packing, or stacking the pallet, I suppose I had it relatively easy up here in Straightening. For the most part, the logs behaved themselves, and most of the adjustments I made were more or less cosmetic—although every half an hour or so, one bold specimen would appear, sneaking along the belt in a perilous diagonal position. It was then that I would swoop in, with one hand deftly twisting it a little to the left or a little to the right as the situation required, before sending it safely on its way to the frosting machine, having averted disaster.

The rest of the time I merely supervised the hundreds of identical logs going by, the hundreds and hundreds of identical logs . . . I was quite alarmed the first time I began to hallucinate, but the Latvians told me that it was quite a common phenomenon at conveyor belts, and something not to be feared but to be enjoyed. Soon much of the day came to be frolicked away in happy illusions, plucking multicolored apples from Old Man Thompson's orchard, sporting with my imaginary dog on the lawn, sipping a gimlet with Mirela as we looked out from the pristine Folly, as she caressed my cheek and whispered sweet nothings . . .

Mr. Appleseed kept watch on us at all times, patrolling tirelessly through the unbearable heat of Processing Zone B, or peering down from his Perspex foreman's box like a monstrous dungareed spider. Standing up straight, he would have been about nine feet tall, but he never stood up straight; he stooped with his shoulders gathered around his neck, muttering constantly in a gravelly, maledictive rasp. He was impossibly thin, with thick glasses and a downturned mouth, and we were all afraid of him. In the early days, when I still held hopes of somehow rebelling or escaping or breaking free, it was always the thought of Mr. Appleseed that stopped me.

I suppose it was because I spoke the best English that he singled me out as his confidant. It wasn't that he cared anything for me personally; he told me so in as many words.

"I hate bastards like you, know that, Fuckface?" he'd say.

"Yes, Mr. Appleseed."

"I've seen your file. I know your type, all right. Think the world owes you a living, and Yule Log just drops out of the skies."

"Yes, Mr. Appleseed."

"Yes, Mr. Appleseed," he mimicked, his malign yellow stare boring into me through a mask of congealing sugar.

I had never met anyone who was quite so enthusiastically devoted to hatred. He hated everyone working at Mr. Dough. He hated the countries they came from. He kept a sort of league table of his most hated races, on which they could move up or down.

"Did you ever see anyone as bone stupid as those Latvians?" He'd lurch over, munching on a dry cracker, and lean against the rim of my conveyor belt. "No wonder their country's such a shitheap. They must have driven poor Stalin to drink. If you'd said to me ten years ago, Fuckface, high up in your ivory tower, that someday I'd be in charge of a team of Latvians, I'd have told you where to go. But there it is. These days it seems that working in an international bread concern isn't good enough for the Irish." He'd gaze mistily over Processing Zone B a moment, perhaps thinking of better times. "In fairness, though, I suppose these Latvians have their advantages. Cheap. No fuss with unions or anything like that. Hit them over the head enough and they usually understand what I tell them. And they work hard." He chuckled. "Bastards have their hearts set on winning that Productivity Hamper of Luxury Goods. Think they get many hampers where they come from, Fuckface? In Latvia? Think they're already overrun with luxury goods over there?"

"No, Mr. Appleseed."

"No, sir," chortled Mr. Appleseed. And then he'd catch sight of me, staring glumly at the logs going by and wishing he would let me go back to my hallucination, and his countenance would blacken. "Oh, you can call me a racist, Fuckface. You can think you're better than me. But let me tell you one thing, Mr. Theology Course, Mr. Trinity College, all it takes is one phone call from me and they'll be flying your replacement in from Latvia faster than you can say Abner Applese—— Actually, two things, the second being that I went to university too, except it was a university called the University of Life. And I may not have a lot of airs and graces, but there's a blue Lexus out there in the car park with my name on it that's fully paid up and no one can take away from me. Remind me again, Fuckface, how many Lexuses was it you said you had out in the car park? How many was that again?"

"None," I'd mumble.

"That's right, Fuckface, because for all your fancy ways you own precisely—what was it exactly?"

"Nothing," I'd confirm, and he'd slap me on the back and say that I had a sense of humor at least, which was an important quality in a worker, and that he saw good things happening for me at the company, or rather he would have were I not on a temporary contract, which meant I would remain a Straightener for the rest of my days, which by the way were numbered.

It quickly became apparent that I would not be learning values or realizing my potential or anything of that nature while at Mr. Dough. It seemed clear as well that I would not be getting out of the rat race and joining the party for the time being. No sooner did I lodge a check than Frank would be after me, hounding me for his due. If it wasn't groceries, it was central heating, and if it wasn't central heating, it was rent—

"Rent? What do you mean, rent? I gave you money for the rent last week, what have you done with it?"

"Yeah, but see there's more rent this week, and anyway you only gave me twenty quid and then the next day you borrowed fifty so you could buy that big fish . . ."

"That 'big fish' happens to be a wild salmon from County Donegal, and if you knew anything at all you'd know that fifty pounds is practically giving it away. I'm trying to make some sort of stab at civilized living here, I mean my God, man, we're not wild beasts, are we?"

"Yeah, but see we're a bit behind, though, Charlie . . ."

"Huh," I said. To anyone who had witnessed Frank's attempts at a household budget, this hardly came as a surprise. Every few weeks he would sit down at the kitchen table with a six-pack of Hobson's Choice and a plastic bag full of bills, receipts, scraps of paper, and beer mats with numbers doodled on them, which he would empty out into a pile at the center of the table. Then, slowly and carefully, he would drink the cans. Then, when all the cans were gone, some hours after he had originally sat down, he would with a little sigh sweep the pile of bills back into the plastic bag, which he then placed carefully in the dustbin.

Rarely had I seen someone in such dire need of an accountant, but Frank didn't have so much as a bank account. "They're only robbers, Charlie," he'd say. "If I wanted to give me money to robbers, I'd give it to robbers I knew, not some bunch of prats." Instead he kept it in his "secret hiding place," namely a Celtic F.C. sock under his bed.

It seemed to me that he had plenty of it, too, and he was only haranguing me out of spite. Ever since Bel's visit, the two of us seemed to be bickering constantly—usually about money, though anything could set it off. It was plainly obvious that, although he pretended otherwise, Frank was also deep in ennui. Oh, he larked about with Droyd as if nothing was wrong; he drank countless cans and smoked countless joints; but he left his chicken balls untouched on his plate, and on more than one occasion I found architecturally salvaged items hidden behind the couch, crushed and twisted beyond recognition. He was oafish and unbearable even by his standards, and I was grateful that he was going out even more than he had before, and not returning until late.

With winter coming in, and me and now Frank both plunged in ennui, it was small wonder that Droyd too was down in the dumps. Frank never invited him along on his sprees, and apart from trips to the methadone clinic and to see his parole officer, he didn't leave the house. He'd taken to spending whole evenings just sitting at the window, gazing out at the rain-swept street. He didn't play his music as much as he used to, either, though I can't pretend this troubled me overly. One night, however, he asked me if I could check something he'd written for spelling, and he handed me a grubby serviette on which, I saw, wedgelike forms had been inscribed.

"What is it?" I asked.

"Press release," Droyd said. "For me music."

"Oh."

"Have to get word to my people that the Droyd is back," he clarified.

"I didn't know you composed," I said.

"Wha?"

"Music, I mean."

"Ah yeah." He scrutinized one of his chunky gold rings. "Well like I haven't done any yet, cos I was banged up in the nick and that. But I'm goin to, as soon as I get meself sorted out. Play all the big clubs. Rotterdam. Ibiza. You ever been to Ibiza?"

"No," I said.

"It's deadly there," he sniffed. "There's these foam clubs where they pour in all this foam onto the dance floor and birds just come up to you and start ridin you. It's magic."

"Yes, that does sound jolly . . ." I had been examining the serviette from different angles, but the wedges were stubbornly holding on to their secret. "This looks all right to me," I said. "Why don't you read it out, and we can hear what it sounds like."

"Right." He took back the serviette and, tracing his finger along it, read in a halting monotone: "For DJ Droyd it is all about the music. He is like a machine cos like nothing can stop him. Also cos nothing matters to him except the beats, which they are the only hope for the future. He is known as the Droyd to represent what he is sayin like in his music. He is sayin that we are livin in a future war zone and it is goin to get worse. When the war comes against the robots and the computers they will easily win probably because they don't get tired or hungry like humans and they never give up not like humans. The only hope is to be more like a robot yourself and not go mopin around havin feelins and that like a sap. This is what he is sayin." He looked up. "That's all I done so far."

"Very interesting," I said. "Thought it possibly strayed off the point a little toward the end, that whole part about the war against the robots. Over all, though, very impressive."

"It's the truth," Droyd said in a low voice, pulling down the peak of his cap.

"What is?"

"All this stuff, right," waving his hand at the prevailing clutter, "it's all an illusion. We seen a film about it in the Joy. It's just created by the computers so we won't realize what's really happenin, which is we're in these energy pods and they're harvestin our energy."

"Cripes," I said.

"Yeah," he said.

In spite of his occasionally erratic metaphysics, we did reach a kind of détente over those weeks. He told me how Frank and he had first met, when Frank had gone to salvage a bathtub from a condemned building and found Droyd sleeping in it. He'd taken him back to the flat in his van with the rest of the junk, and then let him stay on the couch until he sorted himself out, which turned out to be the best part of a year.

"Then what happened?" I inquired.

"That's when I started taking the gear," he said, wiping his nose matter-of-factly. "You know yourself, you start off just smokin a bit to come down after you've had a few yokes, next thing you know you're knockin off the chip shop."

"And working for Cousin Benny?"

"Yeah, but that's all behind me now," he said. "Here, what's the most yokes you've ever had?"

"Hmm, let me see . . ."

"Once I had seventeen, right, me and Frankie were at this rave in this car park down the country. It was fuckin mad, me heart stopped for five minutes. They had to take me to hospital in a helicopter and then I was in a wheelchair for two weeks and this doctor told me if I ever took a yoke again I'd die." His eyes misted over nostalgically. "I just told him to fuck off."

As far as I could work out, these "yokes" were some manner of energy-boosting pill, with similar effects to those of a multivitamin supplement. According to Droyd, malcontents and dropouts gathered to consume them at "raves," open-air dances staged in the middle of the night under motorways or in muddy fields.

"Fields!" I said. "But what if it's raining?"

Droyd shrugged. "You have to have a laugh, don't you?" Jogging his knee, he turned back to the empty black square of the window. "Cos otherwise, y'know, what's the bleedin point?"

As the days went by at Mr. Dough, each one identical to the one before, this was a question I frequently put to myself. Far from stepping up to bat, and fulfilling my long-cherished dreams of becoming a productive member of society, I felt I was embarked on a vast and inconsequential digression from my own life; and just as the logs on their way to the sugar-frosting machine merged, under my gaze, into one, so the hours and days blended into a single unbounded expanse, and life itself took on the trappings of the conveyor belt. There didn't seem any reason why it shouldn't go on in the same way forever.

Then one night Frank happened to stay home.

We were all sitting together watching the television. Frank liked to watch the twenty-four-hour news channel, which usually had footage of things exploding from one war or another. My theory was that this enthusiasm harked back to his days in the Lebanon with the Peace

Corps, though to hear him speak about it you would think that all they had done out there was lie around and play practical jokes on the U.S. Marines, sneaking up behind them and bursting balloons in their ears, shouting "Incoming! Incoming!"

Footage of a tank rolling over the rubble of a woman's house gave way to a commercial break. A cartoon sun with spirally, psychedelic eyes rose to repetitive thumping music over what appeared to be some sort of skinhead prison island.

"Ibiza," Droyd said authoritatively. "One of these days Frankie and me are goin to Ibiza, aren't we Frankie?"

"Ah yeah," Frank said.

"One of these days"—Droyd yawned, stretching his arms wide—"we're just goin to say fuck this, we're off, see yiz later, yiz bollockses . . . On the beach all day drinkin cans, down the clubs at night ridin all the birds, am I right, Frankie?"

"Ah yeah," Frank repeated plaintively, scrunching his can and dropping it to the floor.

Droyd turned around and gave him a long, withering look. "For fuck's sake," he said.

"What?" Frank said.

"She's only a bird, Frank."

Frank maintained his expression of witless innocence.

"You know what I'm talkin about," Droyd said, getting exercised. "Mopin around the place like a muppet." He rose to his feet. "The Three Fs, Frankie, who was it told me about them? Find 'em, fuck 'em, forget 'em, who told me that?"

"I say!" I protested. "That's my sister you're talking about!"

"I don't give a monkey's!" Droyd responded hotly. "Look what she's done to this cunt! He won't come out with me for a fight. He won't go out to Ziggy's and take yokes. Do you know what he's been *doin* every night? Do you?"

Frank froze.

"Yeah," Droyd rounded on him, voice trembling, "you didn't think I knew, did you, you bollocks. Lyin to me, your own mate. Sayin to me you was goin out drinkin with Niallser and Micker and Ste and Bignose Rogan. They said they haven't seen you in months." He turned back to me, his acne livid on his pasty white face. "So last night I hide in his van to find out where he's really been goin, which is he drives out to Killiney, and he *sits* there, *lookin* at the *sea*."

Frank cast his eyes shamefully at the ground.

Droyd was now stamping around the room waving his arms in the air. "The *sea*!" he shouted. "The *fuckin sea*!"

Frank did not reply: He made a pitiful sight, shriveled up in his armchair. Droyd grabbed his jacket from the floor and pulled on his cap, then came back round to stand between Frank and the television. "I can't *take* it!" he bellowed. "I don't know who ye *are* anymore!" And with that he blazed out of the apartment, slamming the door after him, and leaving Frank and me to a long and uncomfortable silence. " . . . legations of financial and political misdealing that quote boggled the mind," the television said, depicting a corpulent man in a gray suit battling his way through reporters outside Dublin Castle.

Frank made a minute burbling noise and pretended to wipe something out of his eye.

Let me take a moment here to concede that I am not, in the general run of things, a man noted for his sensitivity to others. Bel was forever reminding me of this—indeed, when we were younger she had turned it into a kind of party piece; whenever she had school friends over, at some stage of the evening she would turn to me and ask, in a loud voice, "Charles, what's empathy?" and I, who was always meaning to look it up in the dictionary but had never quite got round to it, yet felt pressed to give some sort of reply, would say that wasn't it when somebody yawned and it made everyone else yawn too; and her friends would all cackle maliciously, and Bel would say to them, "You see? It's like living with some kind of sentient beanbag."

So it was with intense surprise and discomfort—of the sort one experiences when, for example, one accidentally sits on a pudding—that I discovered I had, at that moment, a very good inkling of what was going through Frank's mind; because I realized that for the last few weeks it had been going through my mind too. And so I turned to him and asked him if he was all right.

"Ah, Charlie . . . ," he said brokenly, his piggy eyes shining. "Ah, Charlie . . ."

"There, there," I said, patting his wrist. "I know."

Smacking himself on the head, he exclaimed, "I'm such a thick bollocks! Thinkin we'd get back together, when I never—I never even knew why she went out with me in the first place . . ."

"Don't be silly," I said. "She had lots of reasons. You're, you know, you're Frank. You've got a van. And a successful business. And you beat up those other people, the cunt and that lot."

He shook his head mournfully. "If you'd seen her that last time, Charlie, the way she looked at me—like she was ashamed of me, like I was just some fuckin scumbag . . ." A large, gloopy tear trickled down his nose.

"Oh, Bel's ashamed of everybody," I said. "She used to tell people I'd been put in the house as a government experiment— Here, take this . . ." I handed him a tissue, which I realized only too late was Droyd's press release. "I know everything seems, you know, kiboshed. But you can't let yourself get downhearted. Plenty of fish in the sea, and all that."

He nodded unconvincingly, and we fell into a troubled silence, one of us now covered in inscrutable wedgelike forms. Plenty of fish in the sea: It wasn't much consolation. But what else could I tell him? He wasn't the first to come bumbling along and have his unthinking heart snagged on her spare angles and complexities; he wasn't the first to imagine he had found his grand love story, only to discover that all this time he had just been reading for the part—that this was merely an audition, that he was just something she had encountered on the way to wherever it was that Bel was going.

Blast it, I thought with a sudden rush of feeling, why couldn't she ever do things properly? It wasn't supposed to end like this, the triangle we had built so carefully, with its delicate tensions, its vertices and oppositions. There were supposed to have been trembling lips, tears, recriminations; there were to have been stern words, dashed hopes, dramatic sweepings out of rooms. And then, as it slowly dawned on her who she was, and what grand tradition she came out of, and she understood at last that this love simply could not be—then she was supposed to be sad, and mope about the house for months on end, until the day when her kindly if frequently misunderstood brother succeeded in coaxing a smile, and she realized that the skies were still blue, and she was restored to us. She wasn't supposed just to get bored and walk away from the triangle altogether; she wasn't supposed then to throw in her lot with the blighter who'd usurped the kindly brother's room and basically seen him thrown out in the cold.

But that was exactly what she had done; and I found myself, after everything, in the same boat as the smudged figure sobbing beside me. Now, I reflected gloomily, I would have to begin all over again. I would have to find a place for myself in the life of this new character—this new Bel who remembered her lines and sang Doris Day songs and who wished in her heart of hearts to be away on a stage in London! Broadway! Already, impossible seas rolled up between us, as night lengthened and darkness percolated through the nooks and crannies of the misshapen apartment.

CHAPTER TEN

Halloween in Bonetown went on well into November. With every night the destruction seemed to intensify, and scurrying back from my bus stop after work I genuinely feared for my life—although because of my outlandish appearance the revelers tended to view me as a kind of seasonal mascot and generally received me with cheers and thumbs up.

Finally, around the middle of the month, the violence reached its peak. I remember I had double-locked the doors and was sitting with Frank trying to watch the news. But it was nearly impossible to make anything out, what with the rioting going on outside our window. Glass was being broken like it was going out of fashion; flats were pelted with eggs, toilet rolls, homemade fertilizer bombs; theoretically unstealable things—telephone poles, skips, a suite of leatherette furniture—were duly stolen and added to the pyre that climbed and blazed ever higher like a beacon marking the end of the world.

It was the morning after that we found the wheelchair for Bel's play. It was just sitting there on the curb, with no one in sight who might have been able to explain where it had come from, or who had been occupying it previous to last night—as though it had been left there especially for us. Although it was surrounded by debris, torn metal, bits of cat, the wheelchair was quite intact, pristine, in fact, in a way that seemed somehow wrong and un-settling even before we realized what was missing from the scene. The box and blankets were no longer on the doorstep. Homeless Kenny, who had remained camped outside the house through the worst of the hostilities, was gone—vanished as mysteriously as the wheelchair had appeared, as if in someone's idea of a fair swap; with no clue as to what had happened, except that to his small, defiant graffito had been added a deathly black *H*.

"Harm the Homeless," Droyd read out.

"I wonder where he went," I said, affecting a nonchalance I did not feel.

"Maybe he went to the park for the night," Frank said.

"Maybe he went to a hotel," Droyd said, "or he found somewhere proper to live."

But we knew that he hadn't, or why would we have stopped talking, and why would everything have seemed so mortally still as we hoisted the wheelchair on our shoulders and carried it up the stairs.

For days to follow it sat in the corner, gleaming at me in a way I didn't care for. Finally I asked Frank when he was going to get rid of it. He mumbled something about how he'd been meaning to deliver it only he'd had a very busy week. This was an untruth, as for most of the week he'd been sitting around the apartment snuffling, and I told him so. He squirmed about unhappily. "I don't want to go out there on me own, Charlie."

"Out where? Out to Amaurot? Why not?"

"I don't know," he said, hanging his head. "I just don't."

"That's absurd," I told him.

"Yeah," he agreed pathetically, and then, lighting up, "Here, you could come out with me."

"Me?"

"Yeah, you could give me a hand, like."

Now it was my turn to prevaricate. My plan for some time had been not to return to Amaurot until I had made a success of my life. I didn't want to go back now, in my current straitened circumstances, and have

Mother going I-told-you-so and those hateful actors gloating at me—and I didn't think I could bear to witness Bel embarked on yet another ill-conceived romance, with all that oleaginous stroking and canoodling. But there really was something sinister about that wheelchair, and in the end I gave in.

Frank barely said a word the whole way out. His knuckles bulged whitely on the wheel, and I confess that I too felt a certain frisson as we left the city for the coast road. Wind ruffled in through the broad slat of the open window; buildings gave way to trees, flicking past match pale; to our left the sea surged introspectively in and out, like a gray ghost pacing its corridor. And now here was the iron gate, and the old horse chestnut with the scar where Father had hit it late one night, from which a covey of pigeons broke as Frank took us up the bumpy driveway.

"Looks well, the old place," he said woodenly, as the roof and upper floors of Amaurot began to peep over the trees.

"Mmm . . ." It seemed bigger than I remembered, I suppose because of having spent so much time in Bonetown, in that cramped apartment. The closer we got, the higher the walls seemed to tower, the heavier the house's shadow bore down on us and the rusty white van . . . And then, from behind us, came a cheery *Parp! Parp!*

"What the blazes . . . ?"

"Looks like someone's drivin round that old banger of your dad's, Charlie."

"Thank you, I can see that." The bottle green Mercedes was out on the lawn, white-blue smoke pouring merrily from the exhaust pipe as it trundled round in low-speed circles. "What does he think he's doing?"

"Hello there! Hi there! Hythloday!" We were being saluted by a figure in a tweed cap and old-fashioned leather motoring goggles.

"It's that ponce Harry," Frank said darkly.

"Just ignore him," I said. "That oik—no one's taken that car out in twenty years. If it explodes under him, it'll be too good for him." Balefully I sat back in my seat. "Taking liberties like that. And who does he think he is in those ridiculous goggles, Toad of Toad Hall?"

Lapsing into a bad-tempered silence, we drove on and pulled up outside the portico, where we got out, took the wheelchair from the back of the van, and set it down by the steps. I had lost my house keys some weeks ago down the back of Frank's sofa, which was the Bermuda Triangle of the apartment; however, if memory served, Mrs. P. kept a spare set down here under the laburnum . . . I was casting about on my hands and knees when I heard the engine restart behind me. "What are you doing?" I said. Frank had climbed back behind the wheel of the van. "Aren't you coming in?"

"Ah no, Charlie," bobbing his head evasively, "no, better get back to the old work—"

"But it's Sunday," I protested. "Don't you want a cup of tea, even?"

"No, I just remembered this thing I have to do . . ."

"Well, can't it wait a minute? We can't just leave the damned wheel-chair sitting there, help me carry it inside." He gunned the motor, drowning me out, and with a fugitive expression began to reverse the van and turn back down the driveway. "For heaven's sake, she's not go-ing to bite you!" I called after him, to no avail. "How am I supposed to get home?" Too late: the indicator blinked and the van nosed out onto the road. For a moment I wished that I had gone back with him.

Cursing him, I went back to my search for the keys. I was still searching when the elderly Mercedes came chugging up a moment later.

"Hey there, Charles," Harry said, dismounting. "Long time no see."

"There's a reason for that, you oik," I muttered under my breath.

"What's that?"

I straightened up and shot him a cold, reproving look. His hair was more annoying than ever, but he seemed to have traded in his revolu-tionary attire; instead of combat trousers he was wearing pantaloons of a robust tweed, and the tedious peasant jacket had been replaced by a waistcoat with an appalling Aztec motif. "What do you think you're do-ing, driving that car around?" I said.

"Just thought I'd take it for a spin," he said mildly. "Seems a shame to keep a beautiful machine like that cooped up in a stuffy old garage."

"That car is a museum piece," I said. "It is not meant to be driven."

"Oh, come on!" he laughed. "Of course it is. That's what cars are for, not sitting around under a tarpaulin." He ran a gloved hand affectionately over the bottle green flank. "It still runs like a dream. All it needed was a little tinkering."

"Be that as it may," I said in a tight voice. "I'm telling you now that that car is a priceless antique, and I would prefer if it were left alone."

"Suit yourself," he shrugged.

I turned my back on him and resumed my search beneath the flowerpot.

"You know, if you're looking for the keys, we don't keep them there anymore," he said.

Slowly, I rose again to my feet, clenching my teeth.

"Don't worry, though, I can let you in. But hey—you haven't met the new inmates, have you?"

"What, more Disadvantaged?" I said witheringly.

"Stay there a second." He jogged over to the undergrowth by the garage and started making a clucking noise.

"Look here," I said, "I'm in rather a hurry—" That is, I began to say it; but then, out of the bushes, strutted the peacocks, and my jaw dropped.

They were barely recognizable as the vermin-infested creatures I had left behind; in fact, I don't think they had ever looked so handsome. Every vein of their nacreous feathers shone, every eye on their fanned tails glistered; and running about and cheeping in front of them were what appeared to be small, very mobile balls of dust.

"What," I said incredulously, "you got new ones?"

"In a manner of speaking," he said. "Rosa had them last week—we call the taller one Rosa, after Rosa Luxemburg?"

"She never did that before," I said, scrutinizing the peacock in question.

"Well, I thought when I got here they looked a bit down, so I changed their diet a little, fixed up their coop—I used to work with birds when I lived in Guatemala. I guess I must have put them in the mood for love, because next thing you know Rosa has these two little bundles of joy, little Che and Chavez."

What was he doing to my house?

"Yes, well, you must be very proud," I said. "Look, if you wouldn't mind letting me in now—"

"Oh, sorry," he said. He bounded up the steps and turned his key in the lock, then bounded down again to help me carry in the wheelchair. We set it down inside the door. I looked at him. He smiled at me gormlessly.

"I can manage from here," I told him.

"Oh, right," he said. "See you later, then."

He ambled back down to the lawn; for a moment I stood there in the threshold, contemplating the hallway. Everything appeared to be just as I had left it: there was the poinsettia, there was the Brancusi, there the glass frieze of Actaeon threw its queer curlicues of light onto the floor. And yet in some unaccountable way it felt different—unconvincing, almost, that curious sense of dissonance one gets when one finally visits a place seen many times in photographs. Then, as though specifically to allay these misgivings, Mrs. P. bustled out of the kitchen with a tray of butterfly cakes and a carafe of orange juice.

"Master Charles!" she cried. "Is it really you? Please, you will take a butterfly cake?"

"Thanks," I said. This was a bit more like it.

"How long you have waited to come to see me?" she scolded. "Why have you waited so long?"

"Oh, you know how it is," I said carelessly. "How's things? How is the old place?"

"Ay, Master Charles, we miss you very much," she sighed, moving behind me to take my coat. "Now everyone is working, everything is rush rush, nobody has time to sit, enjoy a nice meal . . . But you too, Master Charles, you are important too, eh? Now that you work, make money . . ."

"Not *that* important," I assured her, as she folded the coat over her forearm and brought it away to the cloakroom. There was a creak on the stairs behind me. I looked around—and with a little kick of exhilaration saw Bel coming into view.

"Charles!" she exclaimed.

No, wait, it wasn't Bel, it was Mirela wearing Bel's silver kimono. I felt my heart back up, as if it had taken a wrong turn down a one-way street—

"My goodness, how are you?"

"What?" I said distractedly, trying not to look at the shapely half-moon of flesh disclosed by the aperture of her kimono as she leaned out over the banister. "Oh—tolerably well, tolerably well . . ."

"I wish I knew you were coming," she said, sashaying down the intervening steps. "You catch me looking like this. Why haven't you come to visit before? Did you forget about us?"

"Oh," I croaked, "you know . . ."

"I suppose your new life is much more exciting. But couldn't you have called me, at least?"

I should explain that I had given considerable thought before coming out here as to what strategy to adopt if, as was likely, I ran into Mirela. In the end I'd decided against making any direct accusations as regarded her negligence or general heartlessness, in favor of a tone of polite but implacable *froideur*. However, everything already seemed to be getting confused; for she—paused just above me with her hand resting on the stair rail like the flower of some exquisite vine—seemed adamant that it was *I* who had neglected *her*. "I thought we had such a good talk that night after the play," she said. "But then you were just gone. You didn't even say goodbye."

I could only gape. Had I got everything back to front? Had she been pining for me all this time?

"You look well, Charles," she said softly, coming down onto the second-to-last step.

"They changed my bandages," I whispered.

Who knows what might have happened had she been allowed to reach the bottom of the stairs. But without warning, our idyll was shattered—by Mrs. P., who arrived back from the cloakroom and took up a stance behind me, from which she launched into a wordy and by the sounds of it highly critical speech in Bosnian.

"Oh Mama, speak English, can't you?" Mirela shouted. This served only to increase the volume of the harangue. "Why can't one of the boys do it? They're just sitting in there playing *backgammon*—"

Mrs. P. folded her arms and eyed her daughter squarely; and after a

254 · *Paul Murray*

moment's token resistance, Mirela buckled. "All right, all right, in case anyone should forget my mother is the *maid*." She turned to me entreatingly. "Sorry, Charles. But maybe we'll have a chance later to catch up," and I felt her hand slide coolly over mine to squeeze my fingers before she hoisted her head and marched down the hallway, her prosthesis clattering defiance on the parquet as she went.

"See what I mean?" Mrs. P. expostulated beside me. "Everybody so important!"

"Yes," I said faintly, caressing the fingers of the lucky hand. "Yes . . ."

Mrs. P. went to pick up her tray of cakes. "I must go and bring these to the others. Master Charles, you have eaten lunch?"

"Hmm? What's that? Lunch?"

"Perhaps I make you a sandwich?"

"Oh, no, Mrs. P., I'm perfectly all right, I'm sure you have enough to do without—"

"Or we have some cheese, if you like?"

"Cheese, eh . . ." It had been a long time since I'd had a decent piece of cheese. "Well, tell you what. Why don't you get the cheese and I'll deliver these for you, wherever they're going."

"Ah, you are always so kind, Master Charles." She told me they were for the actors in the rehearsal room, patted my arm, and waddled away into the kitchen, from which Vuk and Zoran emerged a moment later, rushing past me like scalded cats in the direction of the garden shed.

Now that she mentioned it I *was* feeling rather peckish, so I ate the rest of the buns and drank the orange juice. Then I went into the recital room, where I found practically the whole menagerie had gathered to rehearse their lines. In one corner, a tubby fellow and a girl with barrettes were arguing over a hat and whether it looked *legal* enough; here and there along the wall, people sat in the lotus position with their eyes closed and lips moving. The majority, however, were pacing the floor, frowning at the scripts in their hands and murmuring to themselves. Some kind of sixth sense seemed to keep them from bumping into one another; the effect was rather uncanny, like being at a sleepwalkers' convention.

"Darling!" Mother's voice came from behind me. "Oh, how good of you to come and see me! But how *pale* you look, my dear. Please, sit and tell me what's the matter—"

"Oh, hello, Mother, nothing really, just a little overtired I suspect..."

"What?" She looked up distractedly from the pages in her hand. "Oh, hello, Charles, what are you doing here?"

"What?" I blinked. "Oh... I just came over with the wheelchair."

"The wheelchair, bravo! We must tell Bel, it's for her part— Charles, why are you carrying around a tray of dirty dishes?"

"Mrs. P. gave them to me," I said.

"Tsk, tsk," Mother said, shaking her head. "Is there no end to that woman's corner cutting? Well, put them down, dear, we're rather busy, but you might as well have a glass of something while you're here."

I left the tray on the sideboard and followed her into the hallway. "You look well, Charles," she declared, nodding at various passing Residents. "There's a bit of color in your cheeks."

"They changed my bandages, if that's what you—"

"A *fortitude*, that's what it is. I knew it would do you good, getting out there into the rough-and-tumble of the real world."

"Yes, Mother," trailing after her into the dining room.

"There's something *bracing* about an honest day's work," she reflected, pouring a glass of sherry for me, then one for herself, "doing one's bit, getting one's due, going home on the tram with the satisfaction of knowing that the part one plays, small as it may be, is indispensable to the whole. One can't put a price on that kind of satisfaction, can one, dear?"

"No," I said, "although in terms of actual *pay*, they've managed to put a—"

"Good, because that's what keeps the whole world turning, Charles, isn't it? What are you doing, exactly? Wasn't it something about the Civil Service? Is it terribly bracing?"

"Well, I suppose it's moderately br——"

"You know that we're all *terribly* proud of you..." Glass in hand she clipped back out. "Though as I say we're very busy here ourselves,

Harry's new play is going up in three weeks and we're all working like blacks. Not that any of *us* is making any money from it—perhaps we could enlist you as one of our patrons, Charles?"

"Ha ha," I rejoined dully, shying away from the Pandora's box of Oedipal and economic problems inherent in that particular idea.

"A remarkable piece of work, remarkable. That boy has such a touch for the stories of everyday life, the stories of the Common Man, you might say. Because it's all very well for us in our ivory towers and our cozy Civil Service positions, Charles, but what about the less fortunate? It's no picnic for them, you know."

"Yes, I can imagine—"

"Which is why they are so lucky to have a writer like young Harry to give them a voice. Although I can't claim to be entirely impartial, seeing as I myself have a small part, as the ailing mother." She laughed and tossed back her sherry. I took advantage of the interval to inquire after Bel's whereabouts so I could tell her about the wheelchair.

"Oh, heaven knows," Mother said. "Wafting about somewhere upstairs, I think. Do tread softly with her, she's been a perfect Antichrist lately."

"Really?" I said. "She sounded all right when I spoke to her."

"Well take my word for it," Mother said grimly. "And it is not very helpful, Charles, when one is trying to rehearse a play, and one needs everyone rowing in together." She sighed one of her martyr's sighs. "I just hope she's not slipping into her old ways, just when at long *last* she was seeming halfway socialized . . ."

I recoiled. "Well, don't say *that*," I said. "She's probably just over-excited, you know how she gets . . ."

"Mmm," Mother said skeptically, fingering her sherry glass. I excused myself and, with a touch of trepidation, mounted the stairs.

Bel was in her dressing gown at the end of the corridor outside her bedroom, shuffling up and down with her head bowed over her script, making odd thrusting gestures down her side with her free hand.

"I don't want your charity, Ann," she was saying. "In fact I'm sick of your whole saintly act. Maybe you're right. Maybe I am a bitter and self-involved person. But I could have been just as good a model as you—better even, if it hadn't been for that car that knocked me down at an early age." She paused here, as if allowing for a reply, then, angrily: "Help me? How can you help me? Are you going to wave a magic wand and make the fashion industry sit up and take notice of the disabled community? Are you going to make it so when society looks at me, they won't see only this chair, and push me into this narrow stereotype of an *oh my God*"—as I tapped her on the shoulder and she spun round with the script clutched to her breast—"What are you *doing*, sneaking around like that?"

"Hello, Charles. Delighted to see you, Charles. Charles, how kind of you to come over here in your spare time and bring out our stupid wheelchair for our tiresome play—"

"You brought the wheelchair?" she said, sitting down on one of several dusty cardboard boxes that cluttered the landing. "Where is it?"

"In the hall," I said. "Mother said you'd want to know. What are you doing up here all on your own? Why are there boxes everywhere?"

"They're from the attic. We're going through them to see if there's anything we can use. I *had* come up here in the hope of getting a minute's peace to go over my lines. But obviously I was deluding myself."

"Was that Harry's thing you were reading there? The new thing?"

"See for yourself," she said, thrusting the script at me and repairing to her room.

RAMP, said the first page, with Harry's name in big letters under the title. On the next was

DRAMATIS PERSONAE:
MARY—an embittered young woman in a wheelchair;
ANN—her loving and beautiful younger sister, a model;
MOTHER—their mother;
JACK REYNOLDS Q.C.—a dashing socially
concerned young lawyer.

"What's it about?" I asked, following her into the bedroom.

"It's about," Bel recited, taking some pins from her hair and putting them down on the dressing table, "a girl in a wheelchair, which is me, and my mother's dying of cancer in hospital, but I can't get in to see her because I can't get up the steps, so I go to court to try and get this ramp installed and it turns into a huge legal battle and a cause célèbre."

"Oh," I said.

"I mean it's all allegorical, obviously."

"Yes, yes," I said; although inside, my mind was shouting things like *Good grief!* and *How does he keep getting away with this?* I sat down on the bed and leafed through the pages. "So this is the part he wrote for you? This is your tailor-made part?"

Bel nodded, taking a brush from a drawer and beginning to work the tangles out of her hair.

"Seems to do a lot of shouting, to judge by all these italics," I commented, though I supposed this wasn't too far off the mark.

"It happens to be a very good part," she said to the mirror, brushing vigorously. "She's complicated. You don't often get to play women who are complicated." She reached up to undo a snarl. "Most of the time you're just there to look pretty and weep occasionally."

"And who's the beautiful sister? Mirela?"

"Mmm," Bel said unenthusiastically. "And Harry's the lawyer, and Mother, in spite of all my pleading with her, is the ailing mother."

"Sort of funny that you're the girl in the wheelchair, and Mirela's playing the model," I joked. "I mean, when you think that she's the one that only has one leg."

Bel did not reply, but her brushing increased in intensity and there was the crackling sound of hairs snapping.

"I mean when you think about it, it's sort of funny," I repeated, in case she hadn't got it.

"Charles, I'm actually quite busy," she declared to the mirror.

"That's all right," I said genially. "You carry on doing what you're doing. Don't mind me."

She rolled her eyes and began to dab at her face with a swab of cotton wool.

I stood up and went to the window. The heat in the room was stifling; I wondered that she didn't notice it. "I say, you don't mind if I open this, do you? Getting a bit of a prickly neck . . ." She shrugged. I raised the sash and looked out.

It was winter: you could see it better out here where there were things that lived and died, and not just a cramped square of sky to be filled with clouds or fireworks. In the garden, trees clasped the last of their leaves to them, blushing deeply like thin girls caught skinny dipping. Old Man Thompson, looking every one of his million or so years, was braving the cold out on his veranda. A silvery fog had started to roll in from the sea, like miles and miles of cobwebs floating over the waves.

"Frank sends his regards," I said, tickling the lily on the window-sill. "Wanted to come in but he had to rush off somewhere. Man about a dog or something."

"Good," muttered Bel, more categorically than was strictly neces-sary. I turned and from the corner of my eye watched her frown at her-self in the mirror. She didn't look at all as she had sounded that time on the phone, so full of energy. Mother was right: There was a dark cloud in her brow that didn't mean any good. Around her neck she was wear-ing a sort of a pendant—a blank metal disk on a cord, that for some rea-son seemed faintly familiar.

"So how are you?" I asked innocently. "Everything going all right?"

She dropped the cotton wool into the wastebasket. "Everything's fine," she mumbled, unscrewing the lid from a jar of aromatic cream, one of a small army of bath oils, cleansers, and face balms amassed on the dressing table.

"Just you look a bit, ah, under the weather . . ."

"Everything's *fine*," she repeated. "I'm a bit tired, that's all. It's a lot of work getting a play up."

"It is?"

"You have no idea." Leaning into the mirror, she made two quick Red Indian dabs under her eyes and smeared them into her cheeks. "Everything's so much work that sometimes I could swear the damn *house* was resisting me, as if it didn't want us to have a theater. I mean I know it sounds ridiculous . . ." She caught up with herself and stopped; then, after a moment of deliberation, she turned around and said, "But I don't *mind* the work, like the rehearsals, and staying up all night pro-gramming the lights, and trying to get the posters designed and doing twenty different things at once, I don't mind that. It's the *money*, that's what gets me. The endless harping on about money, you'd think there was nothing else in the world . . ."

"Money?" I said.

"We don't have any," she said. "I mean we *should*, we should have enough to keep afloat, at least. But any time I ask Mother about it she's busy, and when I look at the house's accounts they're like a *labyrinth*, or—or modern *art* or something. And without it we can't do anything, we can't afford publicity, so we can't get audiences, so we can't get a grant, it's like a vicious circle." It struck me that the only way they could have got better audiences for *Burnin Up* would have been to go down to the docks and shanghai drunken sailors, but I kept this to myself. "So the drama classes and the outreach program, all that's been put on hold while we have these endless meetings, and meetings about meetings, and meetings about meetings about meetings, and everybody just talks and nobody ever *does* anything . . ." The cloud in her brow darkened ominously. "Mirela wants to have a *fund-raiser* for the next one. Put on an invitation-only event where we can woo corporate sponsors."

"Well, I suppose Mirela knows what she's talking about," I put in. Apparently it was the wrong thing to say, because Bel immediately went pink and started lecturing me about how banks and e-businesses and phone companies and the rest of them were exactly what the theater was supposed to be working against, and how she'd rather the whole thing failed than sell out like that, and so on and so forth.

"I only meant that, you know, hasn't she done this sort of thing before, with her group in Slovenia or wherever it was?" I said. "So she probably knows how the whole thing works, that's all."

"She likes to give that impression," Bel said icily.

"What's that supposed to mean?"

Bel opened her mouth and closed it and opened it again, and said in a rush, "It means that she comes on like this great actress who's seen it all before, but all she is really is a big *void* with no emotions of her own, I mean all she does is go around telling people what they want to hear so she can get her own way, and if you ask me the whole routine is getting pretty tired."

I compared the Mirela that Bel was presenting here with the tender, hand-squeezing, maybe-we-can-catch-up-later-Charles one I had encountered on the stairs. It was painfully obvious that Bel's version didn't hold up. "That's nonsense," I said.

"It's not," Bel said petulantly.

"What does she do, then, that's so bad? Give me one example of her being a void and getting everything her own way."

From the corner into which she and her cloud had retreated, Bel mumbled something about borrowing her clothes without asking.

"Borrowing your clothes!" I repeated scornfully. I looked her up and down; she scowled and twitched and pulled compulsively at her pendant. "You know, you're acting awfully strangely."

Bel sniffed and stared at the ground.

"There's nothing *wrong*, is there? This thing with Harry hasn't blown up in your face, has it?"

"Oh *Lord*," she exclaimed, stamping over to the bed and retrieving her script. "Charles, has it ever occurred to you that I might occasionally have problems that aren't related to men?"

"I'm just asking," I said. "I'm just making sure that everyone's thought everything through, and no one's taking liberties—"

"I mean is it so hard for you to believe that someone could actually want to be with me without having some ulterior motive, like—like wanting to steal the furniture, or having their eye on your bedroom—"

"No, of course not," I said. "Although now that we're on the subject I might as well mention that we do actually still have a pact. I mean it's probably slipped your mind, but you did agree that when you and Frank broke up, as you tragically have, that you wouldn't—"

"Charles, what's that smell?"

"What smell?" I said. "Don't change the subject."

"There's an overpowering smell of *marzipan*," she said, sniffing the air.

"I don't smell anything."

"It seems to be coming from *you*."

"Oh that," I said. "It's Yule Log."

"*Yule* Log?"

"It doesn't seem to come off," I said sorrowfully. "Even in the shower."

Abruptly her gloom was eclipsed by a peal of unladylike laughter. If

I had been paying more attention, I might have found this transition too swift; I might have detected an uncomfortable treble note to her habitual Schadenfreude. But I was too busy being annoyed. Smelling of marzipan was a matter taken very seriously among the staff of Processing Zone B, several of whom had been attacked by roaming packs of hungry dogs. I told her this, but it only made her worse. She was practically doubled over with laughter.

"It's not funny," I insisted. "It's all very well for you people with your plays and your ivory towers. This is the sort of thing we poor mugs down in the trenches have to put up with every day. Frankly, the roaming packs of dogs are just the tip of the iceberg."

"I never thought I'd see the day when you tell me I'm living in an ivory tower," Bel chuckled, massaging her midriff.

"Well, it's true," I said sanctimoniously, forgetting about the pact as I realized that here was a chance to take revenge for all the preachy speeches she had made to me over the years. "You people have it pretty easy. It's no picnic for the working man, let me tell you. Especially when the first thing he hears when he comes in the door is Mother telling him how *bracing* it all is, honestly, to hear her talk you'd think the blasted world was some kind of exclusive *tennis camp*, where you go to learn which fork to use and work on your *backhand*—"

"Maybe you should write a play," Bel taunted, going through her drawer of unmentionables.

"I should take her out to Bonetown," I said. "See what she thinks of that, when the Common Man runs off with her damned handbag—"

"Oh, for God's sake—I've *been* in Bonetown, it's not that bad . . ." She stopped in front of me, a pair of briefs balled up in her hand. "Charles, why is it that every time I want to get changed I seem to find you in my room, even when you don't live here anymore?"

"All right, all right." Taking her point, I withdrew to a discreet spot in the corridor outside. The door closed behind me. I gazed vacantly at the boxes a moment. Then I went back to the door and reopened it a chink. "Anyway, it is that bad. All of that stuff in Harry's plays about the poor being jolly, or the salt of the earth, it's a total fabrication. You've never seen such a crowd of malingering, dissolute layabouts. All anybody does is break things and drink and be sick on our doorstep—"

"Well you should feel right at home then," came the reply, with the snick of a clasp.

"Maybe I *should* write a play," I grumbled. "Shake up you people in your ivory tower a little." Raising my voice, I added, "And I'd show that charlatan a thing or two!"

There was a pregnant sort of a silence, and then the sound of bare feet stamping across the floor, and Bel appeared at the door. "Charles, I shouldn't even bother, but for your information the reason why Harry is twice the man you are is because he *has* opened his eyes, he's lived in places and worked all kinds of jobs and actually tried to *like* people, instead of covering his ears and clicking his ruby slippers and wishing he was back in Amaurot—"

"Well, you wouldn't know it to look at him today," I said, shielding my eyes from the sight of her bare legs, "hurtling about in Father's Mercedes, gotten up like a country squire as if he owned the place—"

"That's his *costume*, you fool, we have a scene later on—and for another thing, I *told* him he could drive that wretched car if he wanted to. I mean no one else has so much as looked at it in two years—" She broke off and for a moment sagged limp against the doorjamb, rubbing her eye with the heel of a hand. "This is absurd. Charles, I'm *not* going to get in an argument with you over who's more alienated, you or Harry—"

"No, because I would win," I said.

With a gurgle of rage she stormed back inside, slamming the door. Seconds later it reopened. "You know what your problem is?" she said, having thrust herself into a pair of jeans and fastening the button. "You expect life to be like some kind of continuous *Déjeuner sur l'Herbe*, with—with wine and *amuse-gueules* and women lounging around with no clothes on, and then when it's not—"

"Are you referring to Manet's *Déjeuner sur l'Herbe*?"

"Yes, Manet's, obviously Manet's— But then when it's not like that you just throw your hands in the air and you think that's good enough—"

"Well, I mean to say," I said mildly—actually I was rather taken with the idea of a continuous *Déjeuner sur l'Herbe*—"it has to be something, doesn't it? I mean I'm the one who has to live in the damned thing."

"That's just it, Charles," she said, furiously waving her sandal, "you think you live in there all on your own, you tell me I'm in an ivory tower when you carry the ivory tower, you carry around this fucking *house*, inside yourself, and you never let anyone in, and you have no inkling what life is like for the people outside—like you complain about having to work, but at least you *can* work, do you ever think of what it's like for Vuk and Zoran, who aren't even *allowed* to? Do you ever think what it's like for them, sitting around here day in, day out, what that does for their dignity?"

"Of course I—" I began, then stopped, sidetracked by the memory of my own happy days sitting or indeed lying around the house, and how dignity had never seemed to enter into it.

"And all those people in Bonetown, what about them, all those people who came to this country to try and make their lives better, because this for them is *hope*? This for them is over the rainbow?"

"I'd say they need to have a word with their travel agent," I said. "I say, wait!" as with a gasp she pushed free of me and headed down the stairs. "Wait! I was only joking—"

I caught up with her midsweep and grabbed her elbow; she turned unwillingly around, and to my astonishment I saw that her eyes had filled up with tears.

"I was only joking," I repeated.

"It isn't funny," she said, her voice slipping down into a whisper. "You can't do this anymore, Charles. You can't come over here and run everything down. You're just like Father, all you want to do is lock yourself away in your study with your lovely fantasies. That's no *use* to me anymore, don't you see? Because . . . because, God, Charles, something has to be good, doesn't it? Something has to be worth doing? You're my brother, can't you just support me? Can't you just tell me I'm not a fool for trying? Even if you didn't believe it, couldn't you just *say*?"

Her eyes gazed, overbright and condemning, into mine; the mysterious pendant ran glittering through her fingers as if it were trying to tell me something, and I realized that this wasn't just one of her regular harangues, that there was more at issue here than my laziness, or Harry's plays. I recalled what Mother had said earlier on. Was something really amiss? Was she asking me now to do something about it?

"Master Charles!"

But these questions would have to wait, for here was Mrs. P. at the foot of the stairs, bearing a plate of delicious-looking nibbles.

"Ah, bravo, Mrs. P.!"

"Oh, for God's sake—" Bel followed me down.

"What have we got here?" I examined the platter. "Brie . . . Gorgonzola . . . Edam . . . a real international selection."

"Mrs. P., you're not supposed to be waiting on *him*," Bel remonstrated.

"Oho, what's this?"

"I find a little Roquefort too, Master Charles," Mrs. P. said, chortling bashfully.

"Yes, indeed!" I held up a tender little *morceau* like a prospector with a nugget of gold.

"Mrs. P.!" Bel stamped her foot authoritatively. "He doesn't *live* here anymore, do you understand?"

"Yes, but, Miss Bel, if Master Charles is hungry . . ."

"Yes, Bel, if Master Charles is hungry . . ."

Bel clenched her teeth. "And another thing, I thought we'd agreed we weren't going to have any more of this Master Charles, Miss Bel business."

"Comrade Bel," I chuckled through a mouthful of Roquefort.

Bel exhaled sharply. "That's it—Charles, I think you should go now."

I looked up. "Eh?" I said.

"Get out, Charles. Go."

"You can't be serious."

"I'm quite serious," she said. She was. Just as in the bedroom earlier, her mood had changed quickly as a cloud passing over the sun; the tremulous, solicitous Bel of a moment before had given way to a steely, unflinching Bel, who with a thunderous countenance pointed to the door. "If you're just going to come round and try to ruin everything we've done, then I think you should just *leave*."

"Can't I at least finish my cheese?" I said.

"*No*," she said, snatching the platter out of my hand. "Just go."

I looked to Mrs. P. for a measure of sanity or reason, but her eyes were set discreetly on the ground. "Very well, then," I said, drawing myself up to my full height. "Mrs. P., my coat, please."

Mrs. P. went to fetch my coat. Bel continued to glower blackly at me like something out of *Der Ring des Nibelungen*. I knew better than to argue. Instead, I waited for the coat to return, and then—without fuss, without so much as a backward glance—I proceeded in a dignified manner down the hall, past the malevolently winking wheelchair, and out of the front door.

But there I stopped and, closing the door behind me, stood for a time at the top of the steps. The sea shushed invisibly to the east, the fog whirled up over the grass; I stood there, sucking my cheeks and staring into nothingness.

After her daughter Daria was put away, Gene went into a long, long tailspin. Her marriage to Cassini had now completely foundered; she was wooed and conquered by a series of notable men. John F. Kennedy visited her on the set of *Dragonwyck*. He had just returned from the South Pacific, still thin from the Navy hospitals after PT-109. He was about to run for Congress; Gene promptly fell in love with him. They were both part Irish, and their first date was on St. Patrick's Day, when he took her for lunch in New York. JFK was wearing a new hat, which later that night he left in a bar; he never wore one again, no matter how the nation's hatters pleaded with him, and thus began the slow disappearance of the hat from American life.

She saw him on and off for nearly a year before he told her— casually, waiting for friends to join them for lunch—that he could never marry her. She should have seen it coming; he had his political career to think of, and his mother would never approve of him marrying a divorcée—an actress, and Episcopalian to boot! But she hadn't seen it coming. She rebounded into a long-drawn-out, absurd affair with Aly Khan, the son of the Aga Khan, whom she met in Argentina while shooting *Way of a Gaucho*. He was just divorced from Rita Hayworth; with him, her life entered the tawdry whirlwind of the jet set—polo matches, ocean cruises, meetings on the Riviera with Picasso, a life of leisure conducted in the full glare of the media spotlight and the gossip columns.

It was hard to say exactly when Gene's crack-up began. The day she arrived in Hollywood she had got stomach cramps and they didn't go away until she left for good, fourteen years later. On her fourth picture, *Belle Starr*, she had come down with an eye complaint that no one was able to explain: Her eyes would swell up and itch, and shooting would have to be suspended for days on end. (Cassini used to visit her in the trailer and kiss her hideously inflamed eyelids and assure her she was still beautiful to him; she would say that that was when she first knew he really loved her.) But people who knew her well saw that this was different—that the relationship with Aly Khan was a symptom of a spiraling mental state.

She began to have difficulty remembering her lines. This had never happened before. She was under no illusions as to her gifts as an actress, but she had always been able to memorize her parts; in fact she used to say that she felt best when she was playing someone else, and that it was when she was herself that her troubles began. Now she became aggressive and bossy on set. Her moods fluctuated wildly, from stretches of total lethargy to flashes of hyperreal awareness when she said she could see God in a lightbulb.

The last picture before her breakdown was *The Left Hand of God*, with Humphrey Bogart. Bogey's sister had been mentally ill; he knew the signs. He went to the studios and told them that Gene needed help. They assured him that Gene Tierney was a trouper and wouldn't let them down, not on a movie as expensive as this one.

It was Bogey's kindness that carried her through the picture; he was dying of cancer then, though nobody knew it. Afterward, she remembered the time of the shoot as being itself like a silent movie. There were no sounds or words—but she told her doctors she could see herself the whole time, as if she were floating outside her own body, watching herself from afar.

CHAPTER ELEVEN

I t wasn't the haranguing that worried me; one didn't live with Bel for twenty-odd years without getting used to being harangued every once in a while. As for being banished from Amaurot, I was getting used to that too.

"But she asked me for support. Bel never asks me for support. In all the years I've known her she's never once asked me for support or advice or so much as a hand assembling her Barbie's Dream Kitchen . . ." I swirled my glass and frowned into the vortex. "Something's up, I can tell. And it's something to do with that blighter Harry."

"He's a balloon, right enough," Frank commented from the sofa.

"It's not just that he's a balloon," I said. "He's an *actor*. They're bad news. Personally I wouldn't trust an actor as far as I could throw one. Because look at the facts. The facts are that she's known him for four years without a hint of romance, and then the moment this theater idea manifests itself he reappears with a script in his hand and suddenly everything's Doris Day and pylons singing in the wind, with Mother eating out of his hand and the run of the whole house." I paced over to the kitchen door. "I mean, talk about your tailor-made parts."

"Someday," Frank said, staring at the ceiling, "he's going to get what's coming to him."

"If only she weren't so infernally *naïve*," I said vexedly. "The fundamental problem with Bel is that she's *so* naïve that she's under the impression she's *streetwise*. She shouldn't be let within a thousand miles of a blackguard like Harry—blast it, what was I *thinking*, leaving her there on her own? How could I just let her fall into the hands of that snake in the grass?"

"Snakes don't have hands, Charlie."

"Be quiet, Frank, there's a good fellow." I crossed back over to the tallboy. Frank had found it in a skip; dilapidated as it was, I'd taken rather a shine to it, and persuaded him not to sell it. Things never seemed quite as grim with a tallboy in the house.

I refilled my glass, drumming my fingers on the wood. It *had* to be Harry; what other reason could there possibly be for that bizarre performance? She had her wretched theater, she had her leading role, she had filled the house with Marxists; the only conceivable explanation was that this latest dalliance had somehow gone awry.

This, if it were the case, would not be without precedent. She had always played her romances out this way—back to front, I mean: chancing upon these chumps and falling in love with them purely because they fit whatever impracticable ideal she was laboring under at the time, diving in headfirst without a moment's thought, and when it went wrong, as it inevitably did, blaming it on me and my interfering. The fact was, though, that Bel *needed* somebody to interfere. She might get away with that kind of recklessness with a character like Frank, who couldn't think two things at the same time without having to sit down. This Harry was another kettle of fish entirely. He was a schemer, a dissembler, one of these sneaky types that spend their evenings in a basement, cobbling together new personalities for themselves. But what could I do about it, stuck miles away in my slum? How could I help her from here?

A few days after the visit Mother called to tell me that Old Man Thompson was dead. Apparently Olivier had accidentally left him on the veranda while he went out for groceries; he came home to find the old man stiff in his bath chair, "frozen like a fish stick," as Mother picturesquely put it. Olivier was hysterical. It had taken three paramedics to prize him away from the old man's body; they wouldn't allow him to ride in the ambulance, and Mother said he'd stayed out on the lawn for hours after they'd left, bawling and running around and practically howling at the moon.

The real reason she called was to ask me if I was available to help out at the premiere of *Ramp* in two weeks' time. They were going ahead with Mirela's idea and staging a special one-off performance in the house, to which potential investors would be invited. It seemed to me rather paradoxical to have a fund-raiser in such lavish surroundings, but Mother explained it was common knowledge that the best way to get money out of the better off was to look like you didn't need it. There would be complimentary tickets, she said, for everyone who lent a hand.

I told her that, enticing as that offer was, given the direction our last meeting had taken, it might be better if I stayed out of Bel's way for a while. "She seems a little highly strung," I said.

Mother would not hear of this. "There is nothing remotely the matter with that girl," she said, "other than resentment because she is no longer the center of attention."

"You don't think she might be . . . ?"

"Not in the slightest," Mother said firmly.

I wished I could be so sure. After what had happened at the house, I wondered if Thompson's death might not be some sort of portent. I began to feel, in the days that followed, a nameless darkness pressing down on me; and now at night it seemed I could hear Olivier's banshee cry, borne in on the wind.

Even the news of that time seemed to take on an antic slant: the bodies waiting under the clay in the Balkans; the steady stream of gray-suited politicians declaring their corruption to the tribunals; once, during a live report from some kind of fracas at an accountants' convention in Seattle, I could have sworn I saw one of the builders, hurtling around with what looked like a large yellow plastic W taped to his head, mooing noisily as four policemen in gas masks chased him with their batons.

The solution came to me one evening from a quite unexpected

source; though really, like the best solutions, it had been right under my nose all along. Frank was in the kitchen throwing pots around; Droyd had gone off to sign in with his parole officer; I was sitting there in the armchair as I always did after work, smoking a pipe that Frank had brought home in one of his boxes and thinking what bad luck it was that of all the rotters in the world Bel had hitched her wagon to Harry. In short, it was an evening like any other, except that someone must have rearranged the rubbish, or else Frank had found a more credulous than usual buyer in the last day or two, because there was an unusual air of spaciousness in the room, and several areas of carpet I was sure I hadn't seen before. Fresh flowers, furthermore, had materialized in a vase on the table; the television had been switched off and the apartment lit instead by an old-fashioned storm lantern, hung from the fixture in the ceiling. And now Frank came in and began skirting the room, picking things up and glancing meaninglessly at the bottoms of them. After a while he started making me nervous, so I asked him what he was doing.

"Not going out tonight, Charlie?" he said.

"What?" I said. "Your tie's a little crooked there, old man." He was wearing one of those clip-on ties that I think had come free with something.

"Oh right," he said, turning a deep puce color. "No, I just thought you might be goin out, like with them Latvian lads or somethin."

There had been some talk in Processing Zone B earlier in the week of possibly going over to Bobo's to play cards; but in the end I had decided I was too depressed and would prefer to have a night in. I told this to Frank, adding that I was thinking of varnishing the tallboy later on if that interested him at all.

"Oh right," he said again. He lingered purposelessly a moment longer, then lumbered back to the kitchen. I thought nothing more of it and began to flick through the listings of insipid TV movies:

HE GOT GOYIM (1992): *True story of an uptight New York rabbi whose life is turned upside down when he is transferred from his synagogue to coaching an inner-city basketball team.*

At that moment the doorbell rang. I wasn't expecting anyone. I called out to Frank, but there was no answer. I imagined he was occupied with whatever was producing that noxious burning smell in the kitchen. Grumbling, I got up and opened the door, to be greeted by a familiar ear-piercing scream.

"Laura!" I said. "What a pleasant surprise."

"Sorry, Charles," she gasped. "I just keep forgetting you have all that . . . ," waving her hands illustratively in front of her face.

"That's perfectly all right." I helped her to her feet and held her bag while she sucked on her asthma inhaler. "As a matter of fact, Frank and I were about to have some tuck, perhaps you'd like to . . ."

She wheezed gratefully and ducked under my arm into the many-cornered apartment. "Wow, it's really . . ."

"Kafkaesque?" I suggested.

"Yeah, like in a Laura Ashley type way?"

I took her coat and asked what she was doing out in this neck of the woods.

"Oh, it's funny," she said, with a silvery laugh. "Like, just the other day I was coming over to have a look at— well, Frank, why don't you tell him?"

Frank had appeared in the doorway, adorned with a fixed smile of uncertain meaning. His apron was gone, and so was his blush; in its stead was an ashen gray color possibly induced by smoke inhalation, as the kitchen was, by the looks of it, very close to impassable. After it became clear that for the present Frank would be confining himself to that perplexing smile, Laura giggled and explained that she had run into Frank a couple of days ago when she was over here to look at her new apartment, and he'd said to drop by. "So here I am!" she squealed, shaking out her hair.

"Here you are," I said. Smiling, Frank turned and was swallowed up by the billowing smoke.

"Sorry, he's not really much of a host. You will have a drink, won't you?"

I went into the kitchen and told Frank I'd invited Laura to stay for dinner if he didn't mind, and that she could have some of my food if

274 · Paul Murray

there wasn't enough. I wasn't sure if he'd heard me, as fires had started
in several of the saucepans and he was busily trying to put them out. I
decided I'd better leave him to it.

There didn't seem to be any wine, but as luck would have it an un-
opened bottle of Rigbert's had materialized as if from nowhere on the
counter. I took it and a couple of glasses and told Frank to pop out and
say hello when he had a chance.

"Oh my God," Laura laughed when she saw the bottle. "I totally
shouldn't drink that stuff, the last time I had a total *blackout* . . ."

"Nonsense, just a light aperitif," I said. "I didn't hear you say you
were getting an apartment in Bonetown, did I?"

"They're very competitively priced," she said. "And they're going
to be gorgeous, I've seen the plans."

"Going to be?"

"Well, they're not built yet, they still have to knock down those horrible old tower blocks. Like at the moment there's nothing to see except
lots of people waving placards about."

"Oh yes, I wondered what that was about."

"There are some very rude people living round here, Charles," she
said. "Some of them threw stones at my estate agent, even."

"You don't know the half of it," I said.

"You'd think they'd be glad. I mean, they're going to be moved off
to somewhere way nicer, like out near the country? Like it's not like
they're just going to be left at the side of the road."

"Indeed," I said. "Well, here's to somewhere nicer—chin-chin."

I hadn't seen Laura since that disastrous dinner party when I
kissed Bel instead of her, and to tell the truth I hadn't been in any great
hurry to see her again. However, we ended up having rather a jolly time.
It was quite a novelty having a woman in the apartment, particularly a
woman of Laura's spectacular beauty. She had a litany of bawdy jokes
that she had received by electronic mail at work; each was more outrageous than the last, and I was positively gasping for breath by the
time Frank finally emerged in a flurry of smoke, bearing three smoldering plates.

"Bravo!" I called, clapping and whistling. "Author! Author!"

"That looks gorgeous," Laura said.

"Eh, Charlie, do you want to sit in the armchair?"

"No, no, old fellow, that's quite all right." I was tucked up cozily on the couch next to Laura, who was sitting in a sideways position so that her legs arched over my lap and her toes—she had kicked off her shoes two drinks earlier—wiggled over the armrest.

Frank muttered something and lowered himself into the armchair. Laura and I attempted to compose ourselves and concentrate on the old burnt offering. There was a lull as we chewed silently on the unidentified meal, then Frank struck up thoughtfully, "You know, sometimes it's nice, isn't it, when it's just you an' your mates, and there's not all noise and stuff—"

"'Put it in my Volvo!'" I exploded, interrupting him. "Sorry old man—just thinking of that poor, that poor valet!"

Laura hooted and kicked her legs in the air. Frank—who seemed somewhat out of sorts this evening—looked at me with a questioning, almost a disapproving mien.

"But I mean, like," he reattempted, "how in life, sometimes you think what you want are these real big things—"

"I said, 'Put it in my *Volvo!*' Oh my word! No tip for him, I shouldn't think!"

Laura squealed and stood up and declared that if she didn't go to the bathroom this minute she was going to *burst*. I brushed a tear from my eye and slapped Frank on the knee. "Very tasty, I must say. Compliments to the fire brigade. I say, what about dessert?"

Frank stared petulantly at his feet and did not reply.

"Cheer up, old chap. You look like a wet weekend."

He looked up at me with an expression of such scruffy downheartedness that I immediately felt like a heel. "Oh hell," I said. "I'm sorry—"

"What's wrong with Frank?" Laura said, returning. "You're out of Rigbert's, Frank. Charles, give him some Rigbert's."

"Oh, he's been like this since Bel gave him the old heave-ho," I said.

"*Has* he?" Laura said. "Oh, the poor thing."

Frank coughed and started saying something about not keeping a good man down.

"It's true," I said. "He's been positively maudlin. Weeping all the time, that sort of carry-on. Driving out to look at the sea."

"The *sea*?" Laura repeated, pityingly.

Frank sat up quickly and said why didn't we watch the video now; but the Rigbert's had made me garrulous. I started telling Laura about how Bel had humiliatingly tossed Frank aside after her romantic epiphany with Harry up on the theater roof.

"Although it's completely obvious he's nothing but a con man," I said. "I mean, those plays of his are a total sham. You saw that last one. It was diabolical. You could hardly understand what those wretched people were supposed to be saying. It was like some kind of troglodyte ballet. But she's fallen for him hook, line, and sinker. It's a disaster waiting to happen."

"I wouldn't worry about Bel," Laura said. "She can take care of herself. Half of our school were like completely afraid of her."

"I'd like to believe that," I said dolefully. "Honestly, though, if you'd seen some of the *goons* she's brought home over the last year— I say, no offense, Frank, old fellow—" clapping him on the shoulder.

"Maybe you should write a play," Laura said.

"Ha ha," I said scowlingly.

"No, but think about it. You want to get back into your house, okay? Well, like who lives there now? Disadvantaged Artists, right?"

"I'm not following," I said.

"Well, I mean you already *look* totally Disadvantaged, like with those scuzzy dungarees . . ."

"That's true," I mused. "And I do live *here*, with a reformed drug addict and Frank."

Frank butted in rather pointedly to ask if we could please watch the video now.

"Jeepers!" Laura said. "I totally forgot."

"What video?" I said.

"*Titanic*," she said, taking a plastic box from her handbag. "Frank's never seen it, can you believe it?"

"I haven't either," I said.

"You *haven't*?" Laura's jaw dropped. "I can't *believe* it!"

"I don't know if it's your type of thing, Charlie," Frank put in.

"If you like films, you can't *not* like *Titanic*," Laura told him.

"I'm just not sure it's Charlie's type of thing," Frank said.

"Well, we don't have to watch it now. I'm having loads of fun."

"Maybe we could play a game," I proposed. "Like charades."

"Let's watch it now," Frank said heavily.

I dimmed the lantern and squeezed back in beside Laura. Frank was sitting in his armchair with an inordinately put-out expression. Perhaps he was wishing we had been left alone to varnish the tallboy as had been planned originally; I suppose Laura was something of an acquired taste, although as she snuggled against me, heat seeping from her thigh, I did wonder fleetingly if perhaps I hadn't been overhasty in my dismissal of her before . . . but then I remembered Mirela's hand on mine, and I caught ahold of myself.

At first I wasn't sure what Frank had meant by this not being my sort of thing, as I had found myself quite moved by *A Night to Remember*, the 1958 depiction of the fatal voyage—a sort of floating paean to the stiff upper lip, in which passengers and crew, all apparently drawn from the British upper classes, sink very politely and with as little as possible fuss to the bottom of the ocean. *Titanic*'s early stages bore scant resemblance to *A Night to Remember*, however. There was a ship, all right; but instead of it sinking, we seemed to be spending all our time trailing around after a couple of dull teenagers: an English Rose type, played by one Kate Winslet, and a slow-witted painter she meets onboard, played by a fellow who looked remarkably like one of those dogs with the squashed-up noses beloved of wealthy dowagers. They went to a ball, then capered around in steerage with a bunch of Irish people. After a while the Rigbert's ran out, so I started drinking Hobson's from the refrigerator.

I DOUBTED THAT Honor Blackman would have let anyone paint her nude only a few hours after meeting him; and she certainly wouldn't have let him have his way with her in the backseat of a car—the backseat of a *car*, I ask you, on the most expensive ship in history—

—

"ISN'T THERE SUPPOSED to be an iceberg in this?" I said.

Laura was weeping quietly. Frank coughed uncomfortably and wouldn't meet my eye.

THE ACCURSED SHIP didn't sink for a full three hours. By the time it did, I was feeling so traumatized that even watching Dogface die offered little consolation. The dialogue, the acting, the vast emptiness of the whole endeavor! Was that what passed for cinema these days? I felt like I had been violated; violated by a team of accountants.

Laura, prostrated by grief, lay weeping on my lap. Frank stared stolidly at the credits, over which, as a coup de grâce, a cat or cats were being strangled to the effect that "My Heart Will Go On," which at this moment in time was not a sentiment I could endorse.

It was several minutes before I could summon the energy to speak. "Frank," I said palely, "I'm going to go to bed now."

"Fair enough," Frank said.

"I'm sorry," I said. "I just don't think I can bear to even have my eyes open anymore tonight."

"That's all right, Charlie," Frank said kindly. "I understand."

"What about . . . ?" I nodded down at the desolate figure crying into my trousers.

"Don't worry, Charlie, I'll take care of her."

"Thanks, old man," wanly gripping his arm. "Thanks."

Extricating myself, I went to my room and lay down in the blackness. But there was little hope of sleeping. The deathliness of the awful film had whipped my present fears into a frenzy, and reawoken old fears that had hitherto lain dormant; and now they joined forces with the phantasmagoric powers of the Rigbert's to assail me, flapping down like bats from the spinning walls. I covered my head; I shrunk to the top of the mattress, tormented by visions of disaster and decay—of Harry fingering the shiny buttons of his waistcoat, of great crows perched on the chimneys of the house, of Bel adrift on that Golem ship, surrounded by cardboard people who recited dead words and would fall to pieces as soon as the iceberg appeared . . . I couldn't bear it; I couldn't bear to think of her there alone, alone!

And so—even though I knew I would regret it in the morning— I found myself reaching for what, in my desperation, seemed the only lifeline left to me. I went to the telephone and dialed MacGillycuddy's number.

It was well after midnight, and the voice on the other end, when it finally picked up, was far from happy at being disturbed. "Who is this? C, is that you?"

"Damn it, MacGillycuddy, I'm not in the mood for your games. I have a job for you, if you have a gap in your snaky portfolio."

"Have you been drinking?" MacGillycuddy asked reproachfully.

"Yes I have. Now do you want to hear about this or don't you?"

He yawned. "It's not Frank again, is it?"

"Of course it's not Frank. If it were Frank, I— Look, it's different to last time, it's this fellow Harry—"

"Banging your sister, is he?" MacGillycuddy chuckled. "Stealing your furniture too?"

I swore silently and wrapped the phone flex tight around my hand. "It's different to last time," I said again, struggling to keep the rage from my voice. "Bel's— I'm worried Bel's not well. I think this Harry might have something to do with it. I want you to keep an eye on her. On him too. Find out who he is, what he wants. No fiddling around this time. Keep an eye on both of them and make sure no one's . . . taking advantage."

From the receiver came the sound of MacGillycuddy sucking his teeth. Finally he spoke. "Can't do it," he said.

"Can't do it? What do you mean? Why can't you do it?"

"Confidential," MacGillycuddy said.

I reeled back. I had expected contrariness; I had expected some gloating, even; but I hadn't foreseen a flat refusal. *Confidential:* Who would have thought the word could strike such dread into a heart? *Confidential:* It meant that whatever dark game was unfolding at Amaurot, MacGillycuddy was already in it up to his neck—MacGillycuddy, whose appearance in the recent history of the house was an omen more ill-starred than any black cat or screeching peacock or cracked mirror . . . I argued with him, needless to say; I threatened and cajoled him; I begged him to at least let me know who it was he was working for. He wouldn't budge. All he would say was that it was nothing for me to be worrying about, nothing for me to be worrying about at all.

"Qué será, será," he said, "as the song goes."

"What?" I whispered. "What do you mean?"

"What will be will be, Mr. H. What will be, will be." And he laughed; and then with a click the line went dead.

Maybe he was right; maybe they were all right, and I was blowing things out of proportion, and there was nothing really wrong; I did try to console myself with this thought. But then there had been nothing really the matter the time of the Episodes either, that's what the doctors had told us; it was just a phase she would grow out of, that's what they'd said as they bandaged her up and increased her dosage; cold comfort for those who had sat at her bedside and held her hand while she convulsed, or flailed at imaginary terrors, or lay for hours staring at us without recognition from the far side of wherever it was she had gone.

For a long time I sat with my hand over my mouth and my feet under the covers like two blocks of ice. And then—just when everything seemed at its most hopeless—Laura's words came back to me. *Maybe you should write a play.* She was the second person to say it, although Bel had been being sarcastic, and Laura was Laura, so I'd more or less dismissed it straightaway. But now, as I thought about it, it seemed to make a kind of sense . . .

I stumbled into the living room. It was empty: Frank must have called Laura a taxi. I sat on the vacated sofa and stared interrogatively at the darkness. Of course! Write a play! How had I never thought of it before? If I was a Disadvantaged Artist, they would *have* to let me back into the house!

And suddenly it struck me that perhaps Bel *hadn't* been being sarcastic when she'd suggested it—that maybe on some unconscious level she'd *meant* it, was asking me to do it, in order to return to Amaurot and set things to rights. Maybe—feverishly, I half-stood, feeling the fabric of the sofa still damp with tears beneath my hand—maybe I was *destined* to write this play; maybe I had been cast out of the house precisely so I *would* write this play. A play that would set the record straight, a play that would see off Harry's tepid little pantomimes of bourgeois guilt—an apologia for everything I had ever thought or done, a paean to a lost way of living, a rage against the dying of the light! To speak out at last, to show the world! I snatched up a pen and a sheet of paper from the sheaf set aside for my monograph. The apartment was utterly silent: a silence taut and quivering as the surface of a lake, as if the universe herself were saying to me, *Now, now is the time, we cannot wait any longer*—I took up the pen and, with a daunting sense that history was being made, wrote in the upper right-hand corner: *Charles*.

I sat back and surveyed my efforts. *Charles*. Good. I tapped the pen lid against the back of my teeth and pictured myself back in my parlor, festooned with garlands and surrounded by worshipful ingenues eager to learn from the author of *Charles*. This page was very white, I noticed. Was it this particular brand, or was paper always this white? Someone else might find it disconcerting. *Now! Now! Without delay!* the universe pressed. Sinking the nib once more, I wrote *by* in front of *Charles*. Then, after *Charles*, I wrote *Hythloday*. After that I thought I might take a break, so I went to get a can from the refrigerator and switched on the television for a little while. Then, as the clock tolled for three, I was seized by inspiration. In one mad dash I wrote five entirely new words beside the three I had already written: the title, my title. It was a great title, a momentous title, holding within it all the joys and the sorrows, the mysteries and commonplaces of a life. I found myself brushing a tear from my eye.

With a title like that, most of the work was already done; but I was not letting up now. My mind raged with possibilities, witty characters, wise insights into the human condition. They could all be in it: Laura as a kind of ironical Greek chorus; Frank as basically an unfettered Id running around; then there was Mother (Fickleness of Women), Mirela (Desire, Impossibility of); Bel would feature as a one big Tragic Flaw, representing a society that had lost its way . . . Champing my pipe, I took a fresh page and wrote at the top in capital letters:

PLOT

nitially, the idea had been to have the play finished and presented to Bel before Harry's new one opened, in the hope that they might scrap his and do mine instead. However, it takes longer than you might think, writing a play—if you want to do it right, I mean—and before we knew where we were, the opening night of *Ramp* was upon us.

They were still short of hands, so I had agreed to being temporarily unbanished in order to work as Hatcheck Girl for the evening. With some effort, I'd managed to persuade Frank to come along as moral support; Mother gave us a little table in the hallway from which to take coats and greet arriving personages. Outside, the night was cold and tingling, but here there were candles and sprays of autumnal wildflowers and warm smells enticing the guests down to the recital room, where they were received with claret, mulled wine, and music courtesy of Vuk and Zoran and some friends of theirs from the queue at the Registration Center.

Whatever spell she had cast, no one seemed to have been able to resist Mirela's invitation. An hour before the performance the house was bursting at the seams with heavyweights of the business world, each of whom Laura identified to Frank and me as they went by. (Laura had also volunteered to help out, even after

I'd told her pointedly that it wouldn't be necessary. Ever since *Titanic* she'd been around at the apartment practically every night—supposedly assisting Frank putting up bookshelves, though judging by the amount of giggling coming from his room it didn't sound like she was being much help.)

"There's the French cultural attaché," she said, appearing in a puff of taffeta with her tray of vol-au-vents. "That's Roly Guilfoyle, that chef? And there's that guy from the beans company— Oh, excuse me . . . ," as another personage arrived to check in her coat with the by now customary double take, looking in alarm from my mummified face to Frank's sadly unmummified one.

"Thank you, madam, you're number 105, straight through on the right . . ."

"*Oh* my God, the head of StoneWall Friends and Mutual is here. He is like *the* insurance guy in Ireland. He was in *VIP* last month, his bathroom has this kind of Etruscan design . . . ?"

"Well, go and give him a vol-au-vent, why don't you? We're busy here— Yes, sir, number 106, thank you. Yes, sir, quite safe. Yes, sir, I'm aware that they don't grow on trees. You're most welcome, sir— damn it, Frank, stop lowering, can't you? You're *scaring* people."

"I'm not lowering, Charlie, this is me regular face."

"Guys"—Laura tiptoed over, muttering clandestinely from the corner of her mouth—"you are not going to believe who's here. Niall O'Boyle." She pointed to a nondescript man in a blue suit whose face appeared to have been sat on at some crucial stage of its development.

"Who?"

"Niall O'Boyle? He's like CEO of Telsinor Ireland? You must remember, last year when the phone company went public and he leveraged that buyout with those Danish guys? And he owns that radio station and that magazine, he must be worth *stacks*— Oh my God, look at his watch, he has like the biggest watch I've ever seen."

"Look." I rapped my stapler assertively on the table. "I don't mean to be rude, but Frank and I have been placed in charge of some very valuable coats, and we can't afford to be distracted."

"All right, all right." She turned up her nose and returned to her mingling.

"Some serious heads at this thing, isn't there, Charlie?"

"I'll say, it's like an Illuminati mixer." And I wondered what exactly Bel thought of that.

Various members of the *Ramp* cast had been in evidence earlier on, working the room, explaining to anyone who would listen the Meaning and Significance of the theater. Bel was there too, wearing a long champagne-colored dress and an expression of such naked hostility that only the more senescent or kamikaze of the visitors had dared approach her. Up until now, I had contrived to stay out of her way; however, after the fuss she'd made last time, I knew I'd better say something. As the first bell rang for the guests to take their seats, I decided to make a quick foray up to the dressing room and pay my respects. This way, even if I met with a frosty reception, there was at least a chance of seeing Mirela au naturel. I left Frank with strict instructions not to ruin anything or attack anybody, and going round by the scullery I climbed the back stairs to the dressing room.

The air in the room was tense and hot and so thick with talcum powder that it was hard to breathe. Heat glared from bare bulbs over a long mirror with a counter, at which cast members sat in deck chairs. I spotted Bel at the far end, holding a cup of undrunk black coffee to her frumpy costume as Harry kneaded her shoulders. I tried to make my way down to her, but it was like swimming against the tide: After being rebuffed a number of times, I gave up and retreated to a relatively quiet spot by the door to wait for an opportunity to present itself. In the meantime, I engaged myself gazing wistfully at Mirela, who was sitting near me (*hélas!* already dressed) with not one but three girls clustered round her, applying makeup and brushing out her shining black hair.

From somewhere in the scrum I could hear Mother piping, "Well, what did he *say*?"

"We probably shouldn't talk about it till afterwards," Harry said with a coy half smile.

"Oh, nonsense," Mother persisted.

"Well, he's interested," Harry allowed, his smile expanding as the room caught hold of this and a hubbub spread through it. "Apparently his wife came to see *Burnin Up*, so if he likes what he sees tonight . . ."

"*What?*" pressed the girl with barrettes, thwacking him with her script.

"He did say that if something were to go ahead—*if*—it would have to be on the basis that Telsinor was sole backer of the theater, which'd mean a total sponsorship package." He shrugged modestly as whoops and whistles greeted this news, then lifted his hands for calm. "I should remind everybody that we do have a play to put on first."

Everybody laughed, except Bel, who was looking up at Harry with a wounded expression. "But I thought we didn't *want* a single backer," she said.

"That was because we didn't think we'd *get* a single backer," replied Harry.

"No, I thought we'd agreed that if all the money was coming from one place then—"

"Oh, darling, we've been through all this," Mother cut in. "We can't wait forever while the government hems and haws. Talk about compromise, you wait till the bank comes looking for its loan back, then you'll see what it means to be— Charles, what are you doing lurking over there?"

"I'm not lurking, I'm standing here quite conspicuously."

"You're supposed to be down minding the cloakroom. You haven't left that poor idiot boy on his own, have you?"

"I just wanted to come and say good luck—"

Everybody groaned in unison.

"Oh, I mean break a leg, sorry—"

"Charles"—Mother grabbed me firmly by the elbow and propelled me doorward—"we happen to have important visitors watching tonight. For once try to keep your dissolute antics to a minimum."

"Five minutes!" called the tubby fellow, appearing behind me at the door; and everyone gasped and started rushing around even more hurriedly than before. Through the tumult of bodies I could see Harry's hands still absently kneading her shoulders as Bel turned to the mirror and, with a hand pressed to her bare clavicle, stared into it, as if searching its depths for something she had lost.

I ducked back down the stairs. The hallway and recital room were clear; the cloakroom had been locked. Closing the double doors behind me, I took my seat in the darkened auditorium.

"Everythin all right, Charlie?" Frank said.

I found myself quite out of breath: I merely coughed and pointed to the stage, as the curtain rose and a single spotlight came up, and a girl in a wheelchair trundled out.

BEL HAD LOOKED awfully nervous up in the dressing room, and given her checkered onstage history one might have been justified in fearing the worst. But in the opening scene she turned it quite cleverly to her advantage. As she shunted herself, grousing, around the suburban kitchen, the wheelchair became a kind of carapace, shielding her from her surroundings; the nerves became the restive, uncathected energy of someone who is sure she has been cheated by life. And then Mirela entered, and as before, everything fell into place around her.

The makeup girls had done their job well. She looked at once perfectly simple and perfectly captivating; she was like a magnet, pulling you in, so that suddenly you no longer noticed the threadbare dialogue or that the model limped and the paraplegic kept tapping her foot. The lights themselves didn't seem to want to leave her and sparkled around her constantly like colored butterflies.

And you couldn't help but sympathize with her, trapped between an ailing mother and this vampiric sister. Nothing was good enough for Bel. She needled her sister incessantly; she made endless demands on her store of goodness and affection; she seemed determined to stifle Mirela's promising modeling career purely out of spite, even when Mirela wanted the money only so that Bel could go and see this doctor everyone was talking about, the one with the revolutionary though potentially fatal new technique.

"You indulge your sister too much, Ann," Mother said from her hospital bed, stroking Mirela's cheek (she was pretty good, too—though only a churl would suggest that she made a far more convincing mother onstage than she ever had with Bel and me). "We all have. She wants to see me, she says—but if she were a true daughter to me, and a true sister to you, then she would know that my love goes with her everywhere. She doesn't see that love, Ann, is the important thing; she doesn't see that the ramp she must install is not on the hospital steps but in her own heart. It is a ramp she must erect over the steps of her own selfishness and bitterness at having been run over at an early age and confined to a wheelchair."

"Oh, Mother," Mirela turning diffidently from Mother's bed and exclaiming quietly with prayerful hands, "Mary is your daughter too! We can't stop caring about her just because there is no room for the un-lucky ones in our fast-paced modern world. To me, there is no greater joy than looking after her, in the hope that she will one day walk again."

"She's so nice." Frank turned to me with tearful eyes, squeezing my hand in his. "Why doesn't Bel just—just leave off?"

"I don't know— Ow, you're hurting me," tugging my hand free and nursing it in my lap. The thing is, I was inclined to agree with him and wish that Bel *would* leave off, and when Harry came on as the crusading lawyer, I did find myself hoping that Mirela would run away with him and leave this workhouse behind. But then from the lousy seats Mother had given us in the back corner of the auditorium, I caught a glimpse of Bel waiting in the wings for the next scene—looking so cold and crabbed in the wheelchair, so disengaged and alone, that immediately I felt sorry.

This last scene, in which Bel seduces Harry with a tray of biscuits that had actually been baked for him by Mirela, was the subject of much debate in the cloakroom during the interval.

"I'm not saying it's not *good*," Laura said. "I just don't get why the lawyer doesn't go for the model. Like she's so beautiful, and he's so dashing, they're just so *right* for each other . . ."

"I don't know about dashing," I observed grouchily. "I think he'd be hard-pressed to actually *dash* anywhere, to judge by the way he's filling out that waistcoat these days. Anyway, what's wrong with Bel?"

"Hello? She's in a wheelchair?"

"Yeah, Charlie, and she's always schemin and stuff."

"She's not that bad," I said stoutly.

"Charlie," Frank said solemnly, "you know it was Mirela what cooked them biscuits."

"I just find it a bit hard to swallow." Laura frowned, and then for no reason the two of them started giggling. It was tiresome, so I told them that they knew nothing about drama and stomped off to get a drink.

In the recital room, Vuk and Zoran had struck up "Some Enchanted Evening," with a Chinese pal helping out on the erhu and a chap from Mozambique keeping time on djembe. The bar was crowded by paunchy business types. The straw-haired telephone fellow O'Boyle was ahead of me, talking to another suit about property in the Algarve. "Must get some nice golf out there," the other suit was saying.

"Sumptuous," agreed Niall O'Boyle. "Sumptuous."

By the time I finally ordered, the bell had rung for the resumption of the play, and I had to go and find Frank and start herding the punters back into the auditorium. I had just settled into my seat when there was a *psst* from somewhere below me. I looked down to see a hooded figure crouched at my ankles in the darkness. *"Psst!"* it said again. At first I thought someone had overindulged in the claret and become confused; but then it said, "Charles!" and I realized it wasn't someone, it was Bel.

"What are you doing?" I whispered. "Aren't you supposed to be on-stage?"

"Quiet," Bel hissed. "I can't let anyone see me here."

"Ah yes," I said comprehendingly. Suspension of disbelief: This was very important in a play.

"I need you to find MacGillycuddy for me," Bel whispered.

Instantly my blood ran cold. "What? He's here?"

"I saw him from the stage," Bel said, "over there somewhere."

"But . . . what's he doing here? You didn't *invite* him, did you?"

"I don't have time to explain, Charles, just—just find him, and send him backstage."

"Can't it wait till after the show?"

"No," she said. "It can't."

"Wait, how am I supposed to—" But she was gone.

I turned to Frank. "You didn't let MacGillycuddy in, did you?"

"What, Charlie?"

"Never mind . . ."

Onstage, the action had restarted. Harry was in a courtroom, re-monstrating with a fellow in a wig. "You're out of order, sir!" the wig was saying. "Never have I seen such insubordination!"

"M?" I called softly, making my way down the dark aisle. "M?"

"Shut *up*," audience members hissed; someone tried to punch me in the leg as I went by.

This was absurd. It was far too dim to see anybody's face. Bel must have imagined it. Just to be sure, though, I went back to the recital room to ask Mrs. P. if she'd seen anything unusual—and there, on a stool I was sure had been unoccupied when I left a few minutes earlier, he was, propped at the bar, drinking a glass of milk.

"You," I said.

"Ah, it's yourself," he said, and he flashed me a disingenuous grin, no doubt in the hope of distracting me from whatever it was he was slipping back into that long brown envelope, which in turn went under his pullover.

"Bel wants to see you," I said curtly.

"Thought she might," MacGillycuddy said with a sigh. "Thought she might." He speared an olive from the dish at his elbow and heaved himself to his feet.

I shot out a hand to grab his arm. "Not so fast," I said.

MacGillycuddy looked at me with a faint air of amusement.

"I want to know what's happening to my sister," I said. He smiled gently and then, one by one, began to prize away the fingers fastened around his wrist.

"Tell me, damn it!" I gasped, wincing with pain. "And don't give me any of that hooey about confidentiality, MacGillycuddy, you wouldn't know confidentiality if it sidled up to you and whispered confidentially in your ear—"

"You know, I never could understand the appeal of all this theater stuff," MacGillycuddy mused, delicately bending back my index finger, my middle finger. "Everybody pretending they're somebody else, mixing things up till you can't even remember who they started out as. Give me a nice documentary any day. A nice history program. The facts, ma'am. Jes' the facts."

"What the hell are you talking about?" I said through clenched teeth and eyes full of tears.

"Ah yeah." He stepped away, absently rubbing his freed hand. "Must be a lot of history in an old place like this." Turning his back, he dawdled over the burnished floorboards out to the hallway. "You know what history does, don't you, C?" pausing to examine the portrait of Father. "It repeats itself."

"What do you *mean*?" I responded distractedly, coming away from the bar. "What's happening?"

But, sucking his teeth, MacGillycuddy had passed out of sight. From the doorway Father's painted face looked down, thin lips buckled inscrutably shut, as though reserving judgment to himself for all eternity. Somnambulantly I wheeled round and stumbled back into the theater.

"Where were you, Charlie?" Frank leaned over to me when I returned. "You missed a deadly bit, the judge didn't want to put in the ramp cos he said that the hospital was this like special historic building you can't put new bits on, and Harry went on this big speech about how if someone wasn't able to walk up the steps of the law, then the law had to come down and carry them . . ."

"Oh," I said, looking at the figures on the stage with a gnawing in the pit of my stomach.

"By Jove, sir!" The judge was pounding his gavel for all he was worth. "You can't just waltz in here and turn two centuries of the law upside down! We have procedures for dealing with cases like this, formal channels—"

"My client doesn't give two pins about your formal channels!" Jack Reynolds Q.C. exclaimed, rolling up his shirtsleeves. "You know why? Because it's the same bunk she's been hearing her whole life!" A buzz ran around the courtroom set. "That's right, bunk!" he repeated. "Her whole life, she's been pushed down the 'formal channels' other people have chosen for her. And she should be happy to go where she's pushed, that's what you're thinking! She should be glad to have someone to push her! She's in a wheelchair, isn't she? She's a *cripple*, isn't she?"

This time the ripple of noise ran right out into the audience and for a moment drowned out even the judge, who thrashed his gavel, roaring, "Order! Order! By God, sir, if I don't see some respect for this court, I'm going to come down and teach it to you myself!"

"Well, it's what you're thinking, isn't it?" Harry bellowed back. "It's what you're all thinking, so why don't you say it! A cripple!"

He swung his finger round to Bel, sitting pallidly in her corner looking over to the cavernous darkness of the wings, where MacGillycuddy would be waiting with that long brown envelope . . . "Because that's what you do with people, put them in neat little boxes with neat little labels, so you don't have to think about them anymore! That's your system! That's your 'procedure'! Well by golly, those wheels are going to turn, whether you like it or not, the wheels of Justice, the wheels of Destiny—"

"You've got to give him respect, Charlie," Frank whispered. "He may be a ponce, but he's a deadly lawyer, that Harry. Like you can see why your one Mirela fancies him."

I didn't reply: I was struggling with these colored dots that were floating before my eyes, and this horrible sensation that the words the actors were speaking onstage belonged no longer to the play but to a darker something beneath it, that stretched to take in not only us but the walls and ceilings and foundations . . .

And now Harry and Mirela were alone, back in Harry's chambers. "No, no, no!" she was crying. "We can't tell her, we can never tell her! Last night was a mistake—a wonderful, an exhilarating mistake, but one we cannot allow to happen again!"

"Oh, Ann," Harry said desperately, "don't you see? It wasn't Mary that I loved but her court case. The chance to strike a blow for our differently abled friends, the opportunity to further the cause of freedom—that's what I fell in love with. But my love for you is for you alone—not just for your beauty, and your promising career as a model, but because you're real—because of your soul and heart, the soul and heart that Mary still has to find within herself—"

"What's wrong, Charlie?" Frank whispered. "Do you need to go to the jacks?"

"But she loves you," Mirela said tearfully, gripping onto his lapels.

"No," Harry said. "Mary never learned to love, curled up in the shell of that wheelchair. But these last few weeks, the court case, have changed her. We have led her up the ramp of self-knowledge; perhaps this will be what pushes her over the brink, into redemption." He reached out a hand and ran it down her hair; she laid her teary cheek against his cravat. I leapt from my seat and hurtled out the door.

MacGillycuddy sat at the base of the maids' stairs, shaping his toothpick into some sort of animal; I was past him before he had a chance to speak.

The dressing room was empty and the floor covered from end to end with photographs: glossy black-and-white shots, blown up to about the size of a sheet of typing paper; quite professional looking. I picked one up. It was my room—you could see the old poster that Harry had left up, Jimmy Stewart kissing Donna Reed in *It's a Wonderful Life;* the wee hours of the morning, according to the digitized numbers in the bottom right-hand corner. Blurred by motion and the scant light, the lustrous black hair caught midswing, the body on the bed appeared no more substantial than smoke: a genie billowing from the lamp, curling up to the lucky chump that freed her . . . I let it slip back down to join the others. There must have been thirty or forty of them. Strewn across the floor like that, they resembled a kind of mosaic, the limbs interlocking anonymously toward some larger, indeterminate meaning; with here and there a motif from the waistcoat, hung on a chair in the background, or the prosthesis, gleaming dully like a bad joke. Little was left to the imagination; they'd put on quite a show, between themselves and MacGillycuddy.

Sounds of distress emanated from the little water closet in the corner. I picked my way over and knocked on the door. "Bel?"

There was a retching noise, quickly covered by the flush of the toilet. "Go away," the small voice came back.

"Are you all right?"

"Of course I'm not all right," the voice said.

"Well—are you coming out?"

She took a moment to consider this. "No," she said. "I'm never coming out."

More choking noises ensued. I went back to the long counter, the bare bulbs blazing for no one, and stared into the mirror at my own unreadable visage. Then I turned one of the deck chairs round and sat down on it. A few moments later, Mother appeared at the door in her hospital shift. "Where's your sister?" she demanded.

I gestured lethargically at the locked door. Mother marched over to it without appearing to notice the photographs under her feet. She rapped once and, in a voice that could have cut metal, ordered Bel to come out. There was only a short delay; then the key turned in the lock and Bel emerged, shamefaced and grubby with tears.

"What were you thinking?" Mother grabbed her by the arm and tugged her toward the door. "You're on in the next scene, come *on*!"

But she resisted, pulling her arm free and shying back to the corner.

"What," Mother said very quietly.

Bel tried to speak, but it just came out as nonsense: She turned crimson and hung her head.

"Bel," Mother said, "whatever issues you may have, they can wait till afterwards. I will not allow you to ruin this night. I will not allow it, do you understand?"

"But didn't you see?" Bel managed now, pointing to the floor. "Didn't you *see*?"

"What I see," Mother said, raising her voice, "is a vain, troubled girl letting a temper tantrum jeopardize everything we have all worked so hard to achieve—"

"A *temper* tantrum?" Two high pink spots appeared in Bel's cheeks.

"That's exactly what it is," Mother sailed on. "It may offend your *principles*, but what we have been offered here tonight is a lifeline—not only for the company but for this house, this *family*, to pick itself up and dust itself off, to make Amaurot known and important again, as your father would have wanted—"

"This *family*," Bel broke in. "What *family*? Why do you go on even pretending to care about these things, when everybody knows all you want is to get back on the society pages, so people will invite you to gallery openings again—"

"Christabel," Mother said in a measured, sibilant voice, "I understand that you are having problems. But there are ways we can address them. There are doctors—"

"—and you'll turn a blind eye to everything that's going on as long as you get it, and *that's* what Father would have wanted, isn't it?"

Mother slapped her across the face in a single, precise motion.

"I say!" I cried, springing out of the deck chair.

Mother's livid countenance was enough to stop me in my tracks;

she looked like something that had just floated up out of a tomb. "The play," I pleaded, backpedaling slightly. "We have to finish the play, don't we?"

This seemed to bring her to her senses. She cleared her throat and smoothed down her shift. She turned once more to Bel—who was staring into space with an expression not so much of shock as of *revelation*— and said in a tone cool and rational as water, "Charles is right. We can continue this discussion later. Are we agreed?"

Bel, whose cheek still bore the crimson imprint of her hand, nodded mutely.

"Good," Mother said, straightening up. "Now, you are on in the next scene. Charles, you will follow us, please."

She led Bel by the elbow over the sea of glossy black-and-white flesh and out the door. MacGillycuddy was still sitting where we had left him, at the foot of the maids' stairs; the two women passed him without a word and went on in the direction of the wings. But I stopped and looked at him. Before I had a chance to say anything, however, he launched into a long self-exculpatory speech to the effect that he was merely a tool of the client, and that he just did what they told him to, and that all he offered was a little peace of mind—

"Peace of mind? You call selling pornographic photos to a wretched, addled girl peace of mind?"

"This is the way she wanted to do it," MacGillycuddy said querulously. "This was her idea, not mine. She asks me to do a little job for her, ring up a few of that muppet's old girlfriends, find out what makes him tick—I do it. Everybody's happy. She comes back to me two weeks later, she's not sure, she thinks he's banging the refugee, she's distraught, she can't sleep— What am I supposed to do? I'm in a position to deliver the facts. You're saying I should have turned her away?"

Suddenly I was too exhausted even to be properly angry at him. I closed my eyes and held my head. "Get out of here, MacGillycuddy."

"It's not my fault if she's like you," he said, raising his hands defensively, "with a head like fuckin cement. I just gave her the facts. There's no right or wrong about a fact. I can't be held responsible if—"

I feinted at him. He sprang sideways, like a cat from a hurled stone, and then slunk away toward the back door. "And don't come back!" I called after him, then joined the others crowded anxiously around the wings.

The lawyer and the beautiful model were back in the kitchen. They had decided to come clean about their affair; now they were waiting for Bel to return from visiting Mother and the new ramp so that they could tell her. In the script this leads Bel to an epiphany, wherein she realizes what a horrible person she's been and in a spirit of setting things to rights decides to undergo the revolutionary but potentially fatal new procedure—which goes tragically awry, killing her and leaving Harry and Mirela free to get married. But of Bel there was no sign: Mirela had given her cue three times now, and the two of them were beginning to look a little edgy.

"I hope nothing's happened to her," she said from the table, looking to the crevasse on the far side of the stage.

"Who knows?" Harry, at the edge of the stage, improvised, fiddling with the buttons of his waistcoat. "Possibly the thought of taking her destiny into her own hands, instead of moving her to reevaluate her role in society, will cause her to shrink back into moral cowardice." He lifted a pedagogical finger. "In which case, Ann, it will be up to you and me to convince her—"

But no convincing was necessary, because at that moment Bel walked out onto the stage.

The audience gasped.

"Ah, Mary," Harry stammered. "Where's your wheelchair?"

Without replying, Bel crossed the floor to come in behind Mirela, who sat stock-still, staring at the table. Bending down, she whispered, quite audibly, in her ear: "Cuckoo."

One or two of the spectators laughed nervously. Beside me, Mother murmured something I could not make out. Bel rounded the table and came upstage to where Harry was standing with his shoulders raised slightly, as if girding himself for a blow; and for a long, tense moment, everything around them seemed to fade into darkness. She gazed at him with the same dissecting gaze I had been subjected to on a couple of occasions. "Golem," she said; then she turned and walked gracefully offstage, breezing right by us in the wings as if we weren't there.

The audience rustled uncomfortably. Mirela fell back limp in her chair. For a moment the house, the world, seemed to list in utter disarray. Then Harry snapped back to life. With an opportunism one could not help but admire, he went to Mirela, drew her to her feet, and said, "Don't you see what's happened? We've saved her. Oh, darling—we've saved her." And with that, he pulled her to him and kissed her.

"The curtain," Mother gurgled in my ear. "The curtain, for the love of God—"

I bounced over to the panel, where the tubby stage manager stood dumbstruck, and pulled a likely looking lever. The curtain fell to absolute silence.

"We're ruined!" Mother wailed. The cast and crew gathered wretchedly around, looking to one another in bewilderment. One of the actors proposed quite earnestly that we take advantage of the curtain to flee and begin a better life elsewhere; this was vociferously seconded by the others, but before I could suggest Chile as having much to recommend it, a great noise rose up from the other side. It was huge and amorphous—like an avalanche, I thought, or an entire forest falling down—and then the whoops and hurrahs began, and the curtain was winched back up for us to be confronted by a standing ovation.

A TRIUMPH, the reviews would say next day: Harry Little's amiable melodrama lulling the audience into a false sense of security, then delivering from nowhere a knockout punch, when the growing love between her sister (a luminescent Mirela Pribicevic) and the dashing young lawyer (Little) prompts wheelchair-bound Mary (sympathetically played by Belle Hithloday) to literally find her feet and take her first faltering steps into solitary but redemptive freedom. What seems at first a slight though generous work examining the difficulties of the mobility-impaired in getting in and out of buildings reveals itself in a shocking and conflicted resolution almost Lacanian in its prematurity— the latter half of the play is only seventeen minutes long—to be an explosive commentary on the nature of freedom and the compromised but still cathartic power of love and also the theater in the modern world—et cetera, et cetera.

"Ironic, isn't it," I said. "I mean, it looks like your little *épater les bourgeois* may actually have saved the day."

"It hadn't escaped me," she said dully, as the doctor-cum-joyrider conga'd by with a drink with a little umbrella in it. Around us the party was in full swing: Bel was watching it from between her knees, her expression with every passing second becoming more remote, like a Cinderella who has outstayed her time to see not only her carriage change back to a pumpkin but Prince Charming's suitcase fall open and a whole horde of glass slippers spill across the floor . . . I leaned forward, resting my elbows on my thighs, and massaged my bandaged scalp. "Damn it, Bel, what on earth were you thinking?"

"I was angry," she said.

"I know you were angry—that's not what I mean. I mean the pictures. Mac*Gilly*cuddy. What possessed you?"

"*I* don't know," she said miserably. "He gave me a Gold-Seal Guarantee of Success."

"MacGillycuddy's Gold-Seal Guarantee isn't worth the paper it's written on," I snapped. "You know perfectly well everything that man touches turns to disaster. How could you have been so . . . I mean, I just don't understand it."

"I just wanted to make it work," Bel mumbled through the cleft of her knees. "That's what you do when you like somebody, isn't it? You find out what things they like, you pretend you like the same things, you laugh at their jokes . . ."

"But don't you *see*?" pulling at my ear in frustration. "Don't you see there's a difference, between laughing at someone's jokes, and—and having them investigated by MacGillycuddy? I mean it's just not *like* you . . ."

"I couldn't *help* it," she said. "I had to do something, didn't I? You don't know what it's been like here, with her crowding me out all the time, trying to control everything, practically *undressing* in front of him at rehearsals, even though she didn't even want him, it was just so—just because she *could* . . ." Her brow puckered sorrowfully. "God, they must have rehearsed that kissing scene a hundred times . . ."

"That's no reason to try and *fabricate* an entire romance like that. I mean how did you expect it to turn out? How could anything good come of that kind of . . . ?"

"It worked, didn't it," she said quietly.

"That," I said, "is what they call a moot point."

"It *did* work," she insisted, as if to herself. "That night up on the roof, everything was perfect."

"Well, if it was all so perfect," I said sourly, "why did you have him trailed with a camera?"

Bel dipped her head, fiddled with the pendant that had been restored to her neck. I didn't mean to be so harsh. I suppose I was just feeling a touch misused myself. I sighed. "What are you going to do now?"

"I'm going," she said slowly, "to have another drink." She held out her empty glass.

"All right." I took it from her and patted her on the knee. "Don't go anywhere," although by the looks of her there was little danger of that.

"She has a shock," Mrs. P. said, preparing a samovar of tea and placing it beside the glasses on a silver tray. "She should be drinking this, not the double brandies."

"Try telling her that."

Mrs. P. paused and looked me in the eye. "What happen, Master Charles?"

"Oh, nothing, really," I blustered. "Just the gals letting off a little steam. You know what they're like."

"Mmm," Mrs. P. said equivocally, performing one of her half-shrug-half-grimaces.

"You should be happy though. Mirela's gone down a storm."

Mrs. P. frowned over at the middle ground, where her daughter and Harry stood deep in conversation with the telephone fellow. "I will be happier when it is over," she said. "I am old, I have seen enough fight. Excuse me, Master Charles, I must bring this man his drink."

The party raged on. Not far away, Laura, who was already tipsy, pestered Mrs. P.'s sons to play her requests; Frank came in and out, carrying off entire sections of the buffet to the cloakroom, which he had kindly agreed to man while I stayed with Bel. The cast and crew, meanwhile, were full of themselves. The telephone fellow, after asking a newspaperman what *he* thought of the play, had pronounced himself delighted, and the air was alive with rumors: that he had commissioned Harry to write a new play with a vast budget; that Mirela was going to appear on a billboard for Telsinor, that everybody was getting a free phone in exchange for a phone mast being installed in the back garden at Amaurot.

Everyone acted as if the sabotaged ending had been planned all along. As for the pictures, when we went back up to the dressing room after the curtain call, they had disappeared; no one mentioned them now, no one seemed to find it odd that it was Mirela, and not Bel, who cruised the room on Harry's arm. It was as though here, too, the lines had simply been rewritten, with only the presence of Bel, sitting despondently in the wide berth the others had given her, to hint at the existence of an earlier draft.

On my way back to her I paused to eavesdrop on Niall O'Boyle and Harry, who had been buttonholed by a journalist. "And what do you see Telsinor getting from such an investment?" the journalist was saying.

"It's not about us getting something *out* of it," Niall O'Boyle said. "What we're talking about here is a— What did you say it was?"

"Synergy," Harry said. He was still wearing his fusty costume from the play.

"Exactly, a synergy. We're both on the same team. This is the new Ireland, and it's all about *communicating*. It's about youth and young people talking to each other and turning over the old ways of doing things. And at Telsinor Ireland, we see ourselves as providing the equipment for creating that vision."

"The medium is the message," Harry put in.

"And what about you?" The journalist turned to him. "How do you feel about getting into bed with big business?"

"Well," Harry said slowly, "I don't think we'd say we were quote-unquote getting into bed with anybody . . ."

"Exactly," Niall O'Boyle came in. "That's a very old-fashioned way of looking at it. Because art, so-called big business, at the end of the day what they're both about is *people*. For example, take Marla here"— he reached over to take Mirela by the arm and presented her to the journalist. "Someone like Marla is exactly what this center, the Ralph

Hythloday Centre, and Telsinor Ireland are about. It's about creating a space for people where they can be who they want to be and say what they want to say. It's about inclusivity and diversity. It's east meets west, coming together in peace and harmony, young people forgetting about the past, turning their backs on war and politics and saying, It's our turn now, and we just want to have a good time. For me, that's really what the play was saying tonight."

"Was that what it was saying?" the journalist said to Harry.

"Well yes, in a way," said Harry, "because to communicate . . ."

I returned to Bel, still slumped dejectedly in her chair. "I don't know what you ever saw in that charlatan," I said. "By golly, I've a good mind to go over there and clean his clock for him."

The tea seemed to rouse her a little; she lifted her head and watched the ceiling flash white as the newspaper photographer went around the room taking pictures of cast members and guests.

"It isn't his fault," she said, after a long time.

"I see," I said tartly. "I suppose Mirela put a gun to his head and made him do it. Or maybe it wasn't her idea either, maybe they just tripped and fell into bed together—"

"It's the house," Bel said.

I turned around. "What?"

"The house," she repeated. She was staring straight ahead of her, frowning slightly, as if trying to work out a complicated maths problem in her head; her voice was soporific, faraway seeming. "It's like it's changing them," she said. "Like it's making them do what it wants, so it can keep itself alive."

I sat up with a jerk and pulled her head round so I could peer into her eyes. "Are you all right? Do you want me to get someone?" Mrs. P. had just come in with a fresh tray of canapés. I waved my arm at her, but she didn't see me.

"Just look," Bel said simply, twisting the pendant in her fingers.

I looked, not knowing what I was supposed to be seeing. To the right there was a flash and a laugh, and a group of people broke apart in front of the camera. "Why not get one of just you and the kids," I heard Niall O'Boyle say. "Take one of Georgie and the kids, why don't you? Theatrical family, sort of thing."

Bodies shuffled around. Harry linked his arm with Mother's, Mirela doing the same on the opposite side, all three of them with their backs to us. "Ready?" the photographer said.

"Shouldn't we have Bel in it too?" someone—Mirela—asked; I heard Mother explain cursorily how Bel, for reasons of her own, preferred not to have her picture taken.

"Perfect," the photographer said. "One more—"

"Don't you get it?" Bel said. "They're us."

"What?"

"Everybody smile . . ."

"They're us," she said: and at that moment the flash went off, and, though I was sure I was going to say something, the light caught me right in the eye, so that whatever it was I forgot it; instead I reeled back, blinking and waving my hands—"Though in that case," she murmured invisibly beside me, "who are we?"

I took a deep breath and placed my hands over my eyes, waiting for my vision to compose itself before I told Bel that what she was saying didn't make one iota of sense and perhaps it was time to get Mrs. P. and go for a lie-down somewhere quiet. But then her voice broke in my ear—"I'm going to get a drink"—and I looked up through a glaze to see her move away across the floor, the long dress, the still-settling light, the roomful of strangers combining to give her the appearance of floating . . .

CHAPTER THIRTEEN

She didn't come back. I knew she wouldn't; still I waited an hour or so, there on the outskirts of the party, drinking gimlets and drifting along the peripheries of other people's conversations: the men in suits discussing offshore investment, property, golf; their wives discussing property, holidays, surgery, good causes.

On my way out I encountered an argument in progress at the cloakroom. "I'm not sure you understand the severity of the situation," a lady was telling Frank in a chandelier-shattering falsetto. "It's not just a question of expense. That fox fur is irre-placeable. It is a piece of history, can you comprehend that?"

"Well, it's not there," Frank said with an air of finality.

"But where else could it be?" The woman's voice rose another couple of octaves. "Where else could it be?"

"Maybe it ran off," Frank suggested. "Maybe it didn't want to live in a house anymore."

"It's *dead*!" the woman wailed, bringing a jewel-laden hand down on the table; then, as though horrified at what she had just said, she staggered backward with the same hand clutched to her throat. I got the impression that this discussion had been in train for some time; I felt a little sorry for her, but I turned my collar up and kept my eyes on the front door.

Outside the night was clear and cold and bit at my lips and nostrils. One of the company's underlings was standing at the top of the drive-way in an old-fashioned bellhop's uniform (discovered among the seemingly endless store of antiquities Harry was having excavated from the attic), directing cars out with blue fingers and a stoical expression. As they left, their swinging lights created crazy shadows, conjuring knotty, elfish faces from the boles and branches of the sleeping trees. Through the hedge another light could be made out, burning in Old Man Thompson's den. Mother had sent Olivier an invitation to the play, though I don't think she'd really expected him to come. No one had seen him since the old man's funeral; he wouldn't even answer the door. There were all kinds of stories flying around: that the will, which left everything to Olivier, was being contested by an obscure nephew living in Australia; that this nephew was planning to knock the old place down and build new houses to sell on; that Olivier, out of whatever perversity, was refusing to speak to Thompson's solicitors, or for that matter anyone else.

I descended the steps, making for the line of taxis waiting at the gate, in the hope that one of them could be persuaded to take me back to Bonetown. But as I passed the laburnum, a figure stepped out in front of me. I rocked back on my heels. For a moment neither of us moved; we stood there, eyeing each other up.

"I thought you'd gone to bed," I said eventually.

"No," she said, shaking out her wrists. Her entire body was trembling; I wondered how long she'd been waiting, out here in the trees.

"Well—" Having exchanged our pleasantries, I made to move on, but she anticipated me and blocked my way again.

"Take me with you," she said.

I looked at her.

"I need," she said falteringly, "I need to get out of here for a little while."

I paused and then said, without warmth, "Where is it you want to go?"

"Anywhere," Mirela said.

I should have walked right past her, I suppose. What could we possibly have left to say to each other, after tonight? But there was something in her disorientation—the panicked eyes, the gestures that had come unmoored from their meaning—that was hypnotic, in the same way that a car crash is hypnotic; it struck a chord in me, in spite of everything, or because of it. And life isn't like the movies: There's no ominous swell to the sound track, no fatalistic overhead shot, nothing to tell you that this moment is the one your life will turn on; instead it's like a train silently switching tracks, sheering off midjourney into a whole other part of the night. She looked at me again with that strange uncloaked expression. "Please, Charles," she said, and I remembered her hand moving to cover mine on the banister that time, her eyes falling on me with the weightless insistence of a petal on water.

The taxi ride took the best part of an hour, and we spent it in silence. She sat at the far window with her head resting against the glass and the dark city passing through her reflection. When we came closer to Bonetown, however, she seemed to rouse: She sat up and looked around her, taking in her environs with a little nod, as if the dismal towers, the crumbling roads, were the answer to some unframed question in her mind.

I directed the taxi to stop outside Frank's building. Without a word to me she got out and waited shivering in her ball gown on the curb while I paid the cabbie. At the end of the street a shopping trolley rattled and was silent, like an animal bolting for the undergrowth.

Frank hadn't come home yet, and there was no sign of Droyd. The room was full of smoke and a chemical odor. I took a match to the lantern and, not knowing what else to do with her, offered Mirela a drink. I came out of the kitchen with the glasses and a bottle of Bulgarian Cabernet to find her making her way slowly about the back of the room, gazing at the galleries of salvage, which in the ungiving light looked more forlorn than ever. "What is all this stuff?"

"It's Frank's. It's his work. Things he gets out of houses. He sells it on to dealers, decorators, so forth."

"Mmm-hmm . . ." She picked up a moth-eaten cloth head that must once have belonged to a child's hobbyhorse and turned it over in her hands.

"That particular lot he picked up at an auction. Belonged to a recluse. Junk, mostly. Went in for stuffed animals in a big way. They don't really sell, Frank says, not these days."

She nodded absently, replacing the horse. Heavy swathes of smoke were still descending from the ceiling, slipping like so many diaphanous stoles over her bare shoulders. "We used to see this kind of thing in some of the towns we came through," she said, running her fingers over the bricolage. "When the people had run away, and the soldiers would go in and take whatever they had left behind. Washing machines, video recorders, picture frames, rugs, heaters, you would see it all sitting out on the street, waiting to be put in lorries and driven away and sold. When the houses were empty they burned them."

I had never heard her speak about what had happened over there; I waited, not moving, in case she might say more. But instead she turned away with her drink and took a chair opposite where I sat on the windowsill. She smiled artificially and drew her hands into her lap. "So this is where you live now," she said.

"Yes," I said.

"Hard to imagine, you in the middle of all the pots and pans."

"It's not that bad," I said defensively.

"I suppose not."

I tapped my foot. What did she want from me? Did she really expect me to sit here and make small talk while she took in the derelict ambience? I looked her over biliously, willing her to leave; then following her line of vision down to her clasped hands, I said suddenly, "Aren't those Bel's?"

"What?"

"The gloves."

"These?" Somewhat bewildered, she held them in the air in a hands-up position, as if I had pulled a gun on her. "Yes, they are. She gave them to me."

They had been another gift of Father's, I remembered; he was always buying Bel expensive things she never wore. Bel didn't like new clothes—she preferred her clothes to have lives, she'd say, that was the whole idea of clothes, wasn't it?

"It was a while ago," Mirela said. "When you were in hospital, probably. I didn't have any clothes of my own." She splayed her fingers and wiggled them experimentally. "We were getting on better then." She gave me a rueful smile, which I did not return. She sighed and with her right hand began bending back the fingers of her left, one by one. "I didn't want this to happen, Charles. I never intended to hurt anybody. These are just the things you have to do when you're a girl. This is what you have to do. For your sister it's the same. She would have done exactly the same thing, even though she won't admit it."

"If you're referring to what happened with Harry—" I began.

"Oh, let's not talk about Harry!" she cried, hair flying across her face. "I don't want to talk about him, you can understand that, can't you?"

I withdrew back into the window frame. She took a hasty gulp from her glass and looked down at her lap. "I'm saying that this is what's it's like, when every man you kiss thinks he's unearthed you, and everyone has a role for you to play, the brave little refugee, the obedient daughter, the foreign girl with loose morals . . ." Her hand made a quick mechanical gesture. "You do what you can with that. You can't stop life from happening, can you? You don't get to choose what parts you get. So you take your opportunities. You use the means available to you. Your life becomes something that takes you further and further away from yourself. It sounds cynical, I know. It is cynical."

She got up and went back over to the array of salvage, standing at it with her head bowed, touching its surface. "But what you have to remember is," she continued, keeping her back to me, her voice dipping and fragmenting as if unwilling to go on, "I've done all this before. I've had a whole life that no one here even knows. I had friends. I had someone I loved. How come no one ever asks me about that, Charles? How come if everybody's so concerned about me they never ask about that? Because I loved him and he loved me, we took walks by the river and put daisies in our hair and all the things that people do when they're in love, except that we were in a war, except that meanwhile everyone else was trying to kill each other for things that happened before any of them were even born . . . Still, what did any of that have to do with us? We didn't want to kill anybody. We thought they'd leave us alone. We thought being in love made us different. We told each other how we'd run away from it and start everything again." The fingers of her left hand passed again one by one through those of her right.

"How can a person, how can *your* person, just disappear, Charles? How can someone go for food one night and just never come back? It's ridiculous. It doesn't make any sense. But everyone had stopped caring about making sense. And then it was time to run away again, and when I tried to go back to look for him I found out about the mines—they put mines down in our street in case we tried to come back. Where is he now? A grave somewhere in Krajina? The same one as my father? Nobody knows. How can nobody know? I don't understand it. But that's what our love amounted to. That's what my love could do for him." A faint wobble ran through her chin; the hobbyhorse head looked at me mournfully from the mausoleum darkness at the back of the room.

"And so I come here, where no one knows or cares what happened over there, no one's even sure what language I speak, and I forget. I forget my father, who went back to the village because his friends had left their dog in the basement. I forget that my mother came here hidden in trucks full of meat and computer parts. I forget the brothers I grew up with so it doesn't hurt to see the boredom on their faces. I pretend I don't see the news when it shows the same thing happening all over again. I forget, like everyone wants me to forget. I make myself think only of my new life—the plays, the boys, the opportunities. Every night when she says good night to me Mama asks when we will go back. She doesn't understand that everything is gone now. All the people we knew are gone. Different people live in our houses, strangers. I explain it to her every night and then the next night she comes in again and looks the way she thinks is east and asks the same question. She doesn't understand. But I understand. And I'm never going back, whatever I have to do."

There was a long, subdued silence. I frowned at my glass, which needed a top-up. Mirela wrapped an arm around her waist and gently swayed her dark cowl of hair. "I don't expect you to forgive me," she said more quietly. "I just don't want you to think of me as a thief, who came in and stole your life away without even thinking. I didn't want it to be like this. I would have made it different, if I could. I would have made us friends. You with your face and me with my leg. Maybe if they added us together we might make a whole person."

She laughed: In the penitent atmosphere the sound was startling, like the report of a gun. Perhaps because I started, I laughed too. The tension dissipated somewhat and she turned away from the wall; and as she did I caught her perfume for the first time, and I was put in mind suddenly of home: the smells on Father's hands when he came back from the lab, the fragrances the models trailed after them as they skipped down the staircase that would stay behind long after they had gone, haunting the house like warm, sweet ghosts, slinking up to you unexpectedly in a corridor, or springing out—*Boo!*—from the corner of a hardly used room, then with a wink disappearing as if they had never been there at all . . .

"Sorry," she said. "I didn't think I'd be making any more speeches tonight."

"That's perfectly all right."

She had come back toward the center of the room, but under the lantern she stopped, and her smile receded into something more pensive; reaching up, she made a *tink* with her fingernail against the glass. "We had one of these in the Folly," she said.

"I know," I said. "It was ours."

"It seems like so long ago," she said. The lantern canted away from her fingertips, sending light swirling in the hollows of her collarbone like the dregs of some opalescent drink. "You know I never told you . . ."

"Told me what?"

"Nothing." She lowered her head, coming back up to the table and leaning her hip on its edge. "Just something stupid I used to do."

I moved out to the table and filled up our glasses. "Tell me," I said, glad to be on to a less morbid line of conversation.

"Well . . . it was when we were hiding in the Folly, my brothers and me. Every day they used to go into the city, trying to register. But I wasn't allowed outside. They said it was too dangerous, because of my leg. I can't move very quickly on it, obviously. And anyway I was ashamed of it. When I got to Ireland, and I saw all these people who weren't running away from anybody, who were living normal lives, I felt ashamed. I felt—what's the word?—absurd. So every day and every night I stayed up there in that tiny little room. Eventually of course I started going crazy. I had to get out. I didn't care who saw me. So at night when the boys were asleep I started sneaking out. Not going anywhere, just around the garden, just to taste the air." Absently she peeled off her gloves and laid them neatly on the back of the armchair. "Then one night I saw a light in the drawing room window, and that night I must have been particularly bored and particularly lonely, because I went up and peeped through the crack in the curtains. And it was you."

"Was it?" I said cautiously, it having been my occasional habit to watch television in the drawing room without the encumbrance of trousers.

"You were watching an old film, I could tell by the light on the walls. And it reminded me of when I was a little girl, and they would put on old films late at night, and Mama would let me stay up because I told her it was to help me learn English. But really I liked them because everything looked so beautiful in black and white." She smiled bashfully. "I even used to get angry when Dorothy went to Oz, because I didn't like the world being colored in, and I just wanted her to go home to Kansas."

I said nothing to this, but inside my heart was clapping its hands, exclaiming, "Me too! Me too!"

"Anyway, there I was in the flower bed looking at you, and it was—it was like I could tell exactly what was happening just by looking at your face. Like when you frowned, I knew the murderer was comforting the widow, and when you put your hands over your face, I knew the pistol had been kicked across the floor, and when you smiled, I knew the hero had kissed the girl—" She laughed again, and drew breath. "Or that's what it looked like to me. After that I used to check through the TV guide and mark out all the movies you might watch, and at night when I would steal out of the Folly I would always go to the window, just for a few minutes, and imagine I was in there beside you, and it was my home, with the fire in the fireplace and a glass of red wine."

She rocked herself still and pulled in a little closer to the table. "What do you think, Charles?" she said softly. "Do you think that's *de trop*?"

"Not at all," I said. "Not at all."

She stood up and came around to my side of the table. She brushed her hair back with one hand and looked at me seriously; and the universe seemed to pull up, like a horse at a high fence. "What would it take for you to kiss me, Charles?" she said.

I gave it some thought. I thought about everything that had happened tonight. By rights I oughtn't even to be in the same room as her; and yet, although it made little sense, it felt as if the girl in front of me *now* had nothing to do with those other things. It was as if somehow she predated the awful events of this evening—as if she were a different Mirela, an essential Mirela: the girl I had found that night in the Folly, and unreeled in my mind's eye every night since.

"I think you would have to put down your drink," I said.

In one smooth unhurried motion she set down her glass and snuffed out the lantern; then taking my hand, she led me away into the darkness.

Imagine a fade-out here, if you please, or one of those discreet rows of asterisks, to indicate the passage of time—not very much time, admittedly, as one of us was out of practice and perhaps a little overexcited—anyway, we return to the scene with the two participants lying back on their pillows, bedsheets now chastely drawn up to their chins, watched silently through the doorway by a stuffed otter and the head of a china basset hound, half-hidden under a frayed gingham tablecloth. Everything was perfectly still; it felt like no one in the whole wide world was awake but us—like we had stolen a march on time, and although our problems waited for us on the other side, these moments were ours to let float by as we pleased. How sweet it was, after so much turbulence, not even to have to talk, or think.

In between long drifts of nothingness I was wondering idly what I could give her for breakfast next morning—I had brought home a cheesecake the day before yesterday and I thought there was some left in the fridge—when her bare arm stretched over me to retrieve the brassiere adorning the lampshade. "What are you doing?" I murmured, through a mouthful of sleep.

"I have to go," she whispered.

"You have to *go*?" I sat up, blinking. Sure enough, she was hooking herself up. "But it's the middle of the night."

"Exactly. Harry's going to be wondering what's happened to me."

Even hearing his name was like a taking a shiv between the ribs: I gasped slightly and clutched at my chest. But this was no time for theatrics. Suddenly she was all brisk efficiency, arranging her hair, searching the bedclothes for a stocking, making it impossible even to remonstrate properly.

"But how will you possibly get home, there's no—"

"Sorry, Charles, could you just pass me that—"

"I mean, there's no way you'll get a taxi round here, and anyway you can't go out dressed like that—"

"I'm resourceful—zip me up, will you?"

"No," I said. This at least had the effect of stalling her temporarily. She turned and looked at me.

"Stay," I pleaded. "I mean it's practically tomorrow anyway. Why don't you stay?"

"I can't, Charles," she said, with just a trace of exasperation. "We're meeting the Telsinor people at nine to start working out our strategy. It's a big day and I need to be ready." She cocked her head, scrutinizing me almost playfully. Then she sat down at the end of the bed and placed a hand on my forearm. Frostily I shook it away. She seemed genuinely surprised. "I thought we'd been through all this," she said. "I thought we understood each other."

I pursed my lips. "Well maybe I didn't," I said. I felt horribly like a hoodwinked schoolgirl. "Understand, I mean."

Mirela sighed and stroked her hand and looked down at the cold shaft of the prosthesis. "We had a nice time, didn't we? But now we have to go back to our lives. You know that."

I got up and began storming about the room. "But you don't—" I said agitatedly. "I mean to say you don't *love* him—"

She could not have turned cooler if I had poured iced water over her; I could feel the temperature in the room drop. "I never said it had anything to do with love," she said impersonally, like a piano teacher correcting a child who keeps fudging his scales. "Who or what I love is my business. I said I needed him. Charles, sit down for a minute."

"*Needed* him, there's a word for that sort of thing, you know . . . ," as now outside, as if to complement our little scene, as if to make it so that everything was finally and perfectly hellish, a drunken battering set up at the front door, Droyd must have forgotten his keys again . . .

Mirela reached behind her and pulled up the zip of her dress, then got up and drew me over onto the mattress beside her. "I thought I explained it to you," she said. "I had a life before. But it's gone. My memories are of things that don't exist anymore. The world stood by and let it happen and now all that I have left of home is this— Look, Charles," lifting her dress over the rough splint of metal and bitten, singed wood. I gazed at it dumbly, and then back up at her. Outwardly at least she appeared quite composed. "Don't you understand, Charles?" she said softly. "Do I have to spell it out for you? None of this matters to me. Not you, not your sister, not the house you grew up in. I'll act in the theater. I'll go on the billboards if they want me to. I'll try hard to be a success. But none of it means anything to me. I look at the people around me and all I see are the little cardboard counters in a board game."

She patted my hand; I stared paralytically into the mild gaze of those alien blue eyes. Somewhere far, far away, the pounding recommenced. "Aren't you going to answer that?" she said.

I rose numbly, threw on a dressing gown, and went out to the living room, where the door juddered on its hinges. "All right, all right, for God's sake . . ." Cursing, I pulled it open. "Oh," I said.

"Can I come in?" Bel said.

"Hmm," I said with a finger to my lip, "you know now might not actually be the best time . . ."

But she had already tottered past me, pulling a suitcase behind her. "It's pitch dark in here," she declared. "I mean how are you supposed to see anything?"

Surely this couldn't be happening—I swallowed and wiped my hands on the dressing gown. "Yes, that's because do you know what time it is?"—rushing in to redirect her as she veered dangerously toward a promontory of junk, then with trembling fingers taking a match to the lantern—"What are you doing here anyway— Good God . . ."

She looked an absolute state. Her makeup had run all over the place, giving her smudgy black rings around the eyes and a luridly Cubist appearance. Beneath her red coat, the lovely champagne-colored dress hung bedraggled around her, like the wings of an affluent moth that had been caught out in the rain: except that it wasn't raining. She swayed beneath me in the glow of the lamp, emanating not so much a smell as an aura of alcohol so toxic it made my eyes water just standing next to her.

"You're all pink," she said, squinting at me. "What've you been doing?"

"Doing?" I squeaked, glancing back reflexively at the sliver of darkness at my bedroom door. "Nothing at all. Probably just that it's warm tonight, haven't you found it unseasonably warm?" But she had already forgotten her question and continued on her dizzy tour to the couch, where she deposited her suitcase. "Now, Bel." I skipped past her, hurriedly removing the lipsticked wineglass and secreting it in the pocket of my dressing gown. "Now, Bel, I—"

"There's a nice *smell*, I don't remember there being a nice smell—"

"Oh yes," opening the window and vigorously shooing in fresh air, "yes, Laura came by with about half a ton of potpourri. Now, Bel—"

"Do you have anything to drink?"

"I think you've probably had enough," I said, then reluctantly added, "I'll make you some tea, if you want."

"You're prob'ly right," she said, crashing onto the sofa. "I had to stop the taxi three times on the way over because I thought I was going to be . . ." She pored over her purse as though it might contain the key to the whole business, then turned it upside down and shook it, to no avail. "I think he overcharged me," she concluded mournfully.

I went into the kitchen and put on the kettle, then stood over the sink racking my brains. What was she doing here? How was I going to get her out? Of all the nights she could possibly have chosen to visit me . . .

The kettle clicked off. At least Mirela had had the good sense to stay in the bedroom, that was something. And it was just possible that Bel was too drunk to notice anything amiss.

"Oh my God . . . What's *this*?"

Heart pounding, I sprinted out into the living room to see her gazing at a sheaf of dog-eared pages.

"Put that down," I ordered her.

"*There's Bosnians in My Attic!* A Tragedy in Three Acts by Charles Hythloday—"

"Give that to me, please." I held out my hand. She dodged it and turned over the page.

"Plot." She flipped it over, then back, then through the other pages. "Is that all you've written?"

"It takes time," I said haughtily. "If one is going about it properly."

"*There's Bosnians in My Attic!*" She rolled over onto her stomach. "Please tell me you're not writing your autobiography."

"There are autobiographical elements, yes," I informed her. "Though as you can see I changed the Folly to an attic. I thought people might be able to relate to it better."

"Re*late* to it . . ." She rolled back, groaning, and folded the pages over her face. "Wealthy mother's boy moons about house, twiddles thumbs, conducts imaginary conversations with his late father . . . God, Charles, only you could possibly find our stupid lives in any way interesting or—or edifying."

"Just because a fellow's life isn't set in a kitchen *sink* doesn't mean it's not interesting," I said stiffly. "That's a prejudice that belongs to you alone. Anyway, sounds a bit like *Hamlet*, when you put it like that."

Bel mumbled something about a tale told by an idiot and didn't offer any resistance as I bent down and gathered the pages scattered over her face, drifting off instead into dark babblings half-lost to the couch about how someday she'd tell me a thing or two about Father and we'd see how instructive it was. She was fond of making ominous pronouncements at times like this; I didn't pursue it. I crossed over to my bedroom and, without looking in, thrust the pages through the door. I brought it to and, hearing the *snick* of the latch, felt my heart begin to slow its pounding. I returned to the kitchen and poured the tea. "May I ask to what we owe this very great pleasure?"

She didn't reply; she was lying with her hands folded limply over her midriff, staring at the ceiling as if picking out constellations. I set a cup down in front of her. "Bel, what are you doing here?"

There was a pause, and then she said slowly, "I've left Amaurot."

I felt my heart sink again. "You've *left*?"

"I couldn't stay there another second," she said. She held her head still a moment, then pronounced, "Not another second."

"But you'd gone to *bed*," I beseeched her, clasping my hands. "When I left you'd gone to bed. I mean what happened, did someone spike your hot-water bottle?"

"I couldn't sleep," she said. "They were making such a racket, singing songs and . . . So I came downstairs for a nightcap. And it made me feel better, so I stayed there. I was drinking White Russians but then I used up all the cream so I thought the logical thing to do would be to move on to Black Russians and I was looking in the kitchen for the Coke when he came in."

"When who came in? Harry?"

"Don't even *say* it." She turned over on her side. "I don't even want to hear his name. He came in and instead of just leaving me alone he started talking to me. He just started going on and *on*. Apologizing for not saying anything earlier but there were all these people round and he didn't want to make a scene, and then about how if we cared we shouldn't want to possess each other, and then about how the theater was bigger than both of us. And I was standing there *listening* to this, when all I wanted was the Coke, and I started thinking, This is unreal, this has got to be some kind of sign, this is like the universe saying once and for all would you please get out of there—"

My shoulders slumped. "You're not going to start all that business about the house again, are you?" I said wanly. "Because I have enough on my plate without being told I don't even exist anymore."

"No, but—well, *yes*," pulling herself upright and gazing at me earnestly through her mask of streaked colors. "I mean it made me realize that nothing there is ever going to *change*. Harry is one thing. I mean, you were totally right about him. But he's probably better off with her, if you think about it. They probably deserve each other. But the truth is it doesn't *matter* whether there's a theater there or not. That's what

I realized while he was making his speech. All the reasons I've ever wanted to leave—they're still there. They'll *always* be there. They're like a part of the house. And suddenly it was like this fog had been lifted and I could see that everything I'd been doing was basically *wrong*, that it's no good just waiting around for things to change. So I listened politely, and then as soon as he was finished I went upstairs and packed my suitcase and called a cab. I should have done it years ago. I don't know why I didn't. I was afraid, I suppose."

Bel and her signs! Everything had to be a sign, nothing could simply be the result of lack of foresight or bad planning— "You can't just *leave*, though," I said weakly. "I mean, where would you go?"

Her eyes widened, as if in surprise that I hadn't guessed. "Well, I thought I'd stay here with you."

"Here?" I repeated. "With me? Now?"

"With you and Frank," she said. "What's wrong with that? I thought it might be sort of fun."

I passed around behind the sofa and paced about, distractedly wringing my hands and glancing back at the shut door. "Wouldn't that be rather awkward? What with your and Frank's, shall we say, *history*?"

"It's not a history," Bel said. "And he wouldn't mind, I'm sure of it."

"Yes, but—well, where would you sleep, for a start?"

"I thought I could sleep on the couch, please don't get all moral guardianish . . ."

"It's not that, it's just a little awkward, you see Droyd normally sleeps on the couch—"

"Well, the armchair then, or the floor, I don't care— Charles, why won't you sit down? Why do you keep skulking around like that?"

"I'm not skulking."

"You are, you're making me nervous," she said.

I sat down in the armchair opposite her as unfurtively as I could manage.

"Is it that you don't want me to stay? Because if it is, just say."

"No, no," leaning forward to reassure her, "it's not that at all. I'm just worried that you're being overhasty."

"I'm not being overhasty," she said. "I mean I've been talking about it for *years.*"

"Yes, but"—unconsciously bounding up from my chair and returning to my pacing—"do you see, it's just that in this situation the *danger* would be— I mean quite often the best thing to do in these matters is to—to go home and sleep on it, and then in the morning when you wake up and you can consider it in the cold light of day—"

"I've had all the time I need to consider it. I'm totally sure about this, Charles. That's why I had to leave the house right away, before it caught me up in it again and everything got confused. Because maybe I'm not meant to be an actress, even. Maybe I'm supposed to be something else and I don't even know what it is yet." She rubbed her eye excitedly, spreading a streak of kohl out to her hairline. "So what I was thinking was that I could stay here with you until I've worked out what I should do with my life, and then maybe we could look for a place together—"

I stopped in my tracks. "Together?"

"I don't have much money, so you'd have to tide me over for a little while. But I could get a job, and then in a few months I'll have my trust—"

"Wait," I said. "Together?"

"It's easier to find a place for two," she said. "And you want to get out of here, don't you?"

I flopped into the armchair, running a hand over my jaw. "Are you being serious?" I said. "This isn't some sort of White-Russian-pink-elephantish whim?"

"I can't go back there, Charles," she said quietly. "I can't go back there, to him, and her, and Mother, and that awful phone company with their marketing strategy. It feels like—it feels like Vichy *France.* And just the thought of getting up there and reciting those lines, his lines, it makes me feel physically sick."

"But what about—what about old Chekhov? What about that play you wanted to put on, what about that?"

"They've decided they're not doing Chekhov," she said.

"They're not? Why not?"

"There aren't any phones in it," she said darkly, then shrugged at me through the dimness. "So you see, you're the only person I have left, Charles. Sad as it sounds, you seem to be the one person left in my life that I can actually trust." She put down her cup and knocked her knees together. "But what do you think? Wouldn't it be amazing, a totally fresh start?"

I didn't know what to think. I wasn't able to think. Everything suddenly seemed terribly unreal. Could we really just start again? Forget about the house, abandon it to those unbearable people, when all of our lives, everything we were was bound up in it? When even here, exiled in Frank's rattrap, I had always assumed that I would someday be going back, that Amaurot's fortunes and my own would go forever hand in hand . . . But maybe she was right: maybe the house really did have interests of its own to protect. Maybe it really had found replacements, and forged them into the son and daughter we had never quite managed to be, and it was this new pair that would map out its strategies from here on in, would fill its halls with gaiety and laughter and the best brocade, and live the lives of the scions of the great . . .

Well, if it had: We had done our best for it, hadn't we? Wasn't this the best course now? The two of us united at last, on a Grand Digression through the world . . . As the idea took wing in my mind, and the city unfolded in front of me with all the places we could go, a gust of wind came blowing through the window: billowing through the dusty crannies, through the gingham tablecloth, the stringless tennis racket, and the yellowed Chantilly lace, through all the dingy evidence of a hundred used-up lives. I felt a foolish, astonished smile spreading over my face; and for an instant, superimposed over the benighted Bonetown skyline, I had a vision of sunlight glinting through branches, and the words *Today is the first day of the rest of your life* . . .

"Charles, don't move." Bel's dilated pupils were fixed on a point just above my right shoulder.

"Eh?"

"There's an enormous spider sitting on the back of your chair."

"Ugh!"

"Don't *move*," she said again, squinting through the shadows. "God, it's the biggest spider I've ever *seen* . . ."

"Help, quick, kill it!" I moaned.

"It's bad luck to kill a spider," Bel recollected.

"Well, do *something*—ugh, I can feel it *eyeing* me . . ."

"All right, hold still . . ." I clenched my teeth, sitting there entirely immobilized as she reached her hand slowly for the TV guide, rolled it up, and then—with an agility quite unexpected, considering all those White Russians—leapt over and dealt a lightning blow to the back of the armchair, and then another and another, until with a soft thud the unfortunate spider hit the ground. I sank back in a pool of sweat while Bel lurched behind the chair to examine the remains.

"Is it dead?" I said, patting my brow.

She didn't reply.

"I say," I said.

But the curious silence continued. And then I heard her say, "Wait a second. That's not a spider."

As soon as she said it, I realized what had happened and in an instant was out of my seat. But it was too late. Bel was already getting to her feet, holding in her hand a long black glove.

She recognized it, naturally; not to labor the point, but it fitted her like a glove. There was no way I was going to be able to lie my way out of this. I backpedaled to the threshold of the kitchen, watching her stare in bafflement at the glove, struggle to comprehend its appearance in my apartment. As the blood drained from her face, I knew she had figured it out; as she sank back down onto the sofa, gazing into space, I knew she was recalling everything she had just said about trust, and fresh starts, but especially trust. The glinting sunlight, the trees, retreated into the ether.

"I can explain," I said, but only as a matter of course.

"Is she here?" she said, swallowing. "Has she been here the whole time?"

"Don't ask me that," I pleaded. "I mean it's not what it looks like."

"That's just what Harry said," she remarked desolately, behind her smudge of colors. "That's exactly what he said."

"Yes, but." I strained. "Yes, but, that is to say . . ."

"Oh, Charles," she murmured, shaking her head.

She didn't say it damningly, or vindictively; I might not have felt so bad if she'd said it like that. Instead it was more that tone of tired, un-judging sadness one hears in people's voices after something terrible has happened on the news, when humanity has let itself down in some significant way; it was a tone Bel had reserved since childhood for my more spectacular blunders. And standing there in the gloom, I found myself transported back to an afternoon many years ago: the afternoon when, having spirited it away from the drawer in his study, I had suc-cessfully sold Father's fob watch via a newspaper classified to a private buyer, in order to raise money to buy a digital alarm clock for his birth-day. I didn't often come up with plans—that was more Bel's forte—and this one I had kept secret even from her until I'd come back from Dun Laoghaire with the alarm clock carefully hidden in my lunch box and could present it to her as a fait accompli. But she didn't take it with the level of unbounded admiration I felt a plan of this order deserved. Quite the opposite: She'd opened her eyes very wide and shaken her head very slowly and said, "Oh, Charles," in this awestruck way, as if like a character in those Tales from the Greek Myths she was always reading I had broken something big, very big, and beyond anybody's power to fix, such as the World—

That time, however, I had been sure I was in the right. "I don't see why you're getting so worked up," I'd said. "Of course he's not going to be angry. Why would he be angry?"

"Don't you know anything?" she'd said, taking her finger out of her mouth. "That watch was grandfather's."

"Well, so what? It was *old*. I don't think it worked, even. This one is *new*. It has a radio and you can see the numbers in the dark. He needs an alarm clock. He always stays in bed too late, that's why Mother shouts at him all the time. Come on, it can be from you as well. I don't mind."

But instead of leaping to accept this kind and unselfish offer, Bel covered her face with her hands, as if hoping to make the situation dis-appear.

"Maybe we could get another watch, just to be on the safe side," I mused. "One exactly the same as the old one. Or maybe he won't notice it's gone. Or maybe he will, but he just won't be angry."

But Bel just stood there, shaking her head, swaying to and fro, repeating, "Oh, Charles," in a way that after a while got under your skin and then really started to *nag* at you—

"Well, what are we going to *do*, then?" I shouted at last.

"You'll have to run away," Bel said automatically, and a trifle glibly for my liking. "Fine," I retorted, "so will you, then." "Why will I have to?" she said. "I don't know," I said irritably. "Because they'll punish you too." "Why would they punish me? I didn't do anything." "They just *will*, that's all, you know what they're like— Well, so long, I don't suppose I'll ever see you again—"

"Charles, *wait*," running after me out of her bedroom and down the stairs and out the door to begin our new life in the gazebo, which continued happily enough until nightfall, when Bel—who was at that time deeply afraid of the dark, indeed unhappy about the entire concept of darkness, having developed grave doubts as to the likelihood of the sun, once it had been allowed to set, ever rising again, even when one told her that in one's own experience, which remember was eight years compared to her five, it had always risen in the past: "But what if it *doesn't*?" she'd say, whispering in case it might hear, "what do we do *then*?"—when Bel began to cry, and continued to cry, and would not be comforted even when I switched on the radio part of the radio alarm clock, till at last, worried that she was going to stop breathing, I took her hand again and led her back across the lawn, the house rising forbiddingly out of the twilight, ice bolts of terror plunging through me, but still fair was fair, she'd been a good sport about the whole running-away business in the first place, she was good about that sort of thing, Bel was, even if she was a girl, if only she wouldn't cry so much, and we went round to the back door to knock to be let in by whatever maid was there at the time, to troop in to Father in the drawing room and take our punishment . . .

Only this time, of course, there was no gazebo to run to, no higher power to arbitrate or condemn; there were only the facts, lying there inert as the glove on the table. Neither of us was sure of the protocol; so we merely stood, wilted slightly, as though the room were short on oxygen. It must have looked rather comical, the two of us with our hands in our pockets, staring at nothing, searching for the words to resolve or express or at least reanimate the scene, to carry it out of this awful moment. Then Bel got up and walked out. I tried to follow her, but I got my foot caught in the stringless Dunlop tennis racket, and by the time I'd pulled it free and gone down to the street she was nowhere in sight. And so, like a man in a hall of mirrors, or in an endless Chinese box of dreams, I stumbled back upstairs and thrust open my bedroom door— only to find the room empty: emptier than a magician's cabinet, emptier than anything ought possibly to be.

CHAPTER FOURTEEN

THERE'S BOSNIANS IN MY ATTIC!
A Tragedy in Three Acts

—

by Charles Hythloday

SETTING: A crumbling château on the banks of the Marne.

DRAMATIS PERSONAE

COUNT FREDERICK: A Count, the young master of the house. Battling with the past and with the dog-eat-dog world of the French wine industry to restore his Father's vineyard to its former glory.

BABS: His sister, a beautiful if judgmental would-be actress.

LOPAKHIN: A Machiavellian bank manager–theater impresario, who is staying at the château but secretly plotting to destroy it and build a railway through it and steal Babs away from Frederick.

[Note. Why has Frederick let Lopakhin stay in the house in the first place?]

MAM'SELLE: A comically inept French maid

HORST AND WERNER: Some Bosnians

INSPECTOR DICK ROBINSON, SCOTLAND YARD

ACT ONE · SCENE ONE

(The drawing room. COUNT FREDERICK *is gazing pensively out the window when* BABS *bursts in in a state of agitation, followed insidiously by* LOPAKHIN.*)*

BABS *(agitatedly)*: Frederick! Oh Frederick! The peasants are revolting!

FREDERICK: I know! Don't they ever wash?

(Pause for laughter.)

BABS: How can you joke at a time like this? The harvest is next week! How are we supposed to reap it with no peasants?

FREDERICK *(grimly)*: I know. Just when it seemed that the vineyard was finally getting back on its feet. *(Turns pensively.)* I can't understand it. They're normally such a jolly bunch. It's as if someone had been stirring them up by circulating false data about the EU's new agricultural policy. But who would do such a thing?

LOPAKHIN: Why don't you just give up, Frederick? That's what I don't understand about you. You're an intelligent man. Why do you persist in trying to revive this old dump? When you could have a railway station right here where we're standing, or a multiplex cinema.

FREDERICK *(coldly)*: There's another thing you don't understand, Lopakhin, and that's a thing called tradition. My father worked this vineyard, and his father before him, and his father before him. It's not about money. It's about producing a half-decent bottle of Burgundy. It's about giving employment to generations of local peasants, although frankly they don't deserve it. We will never sell this château! They will have to wrest it from our very hands!

BABS *(sadly)*: That reminds me. The bank manager called again this morning. He wants to speak to you urgently. And, Frederick, things keep going missing around the house! And those noises—those inhuman noises! (*She weeps.*)

FREDERICK (*putting his arms protectively around her*): Don't worry, Babs. No one's going to harm you. (*Defiantly.*) And inhuman or otherwise, no one's going to drive us out of this château, not if Scotland Yard has anything to say about it!

LOPAKHIN: Scotland Yard? (*Exits hastily.*)

FREDERICK: There's something I don't trust about that fellow. Sometimes I wonder if he really is the young Belgian student backpacking his way around Europe that he claims to be. I mean for one thing he doesn't have a backpack. And he's been here for months. It'll take him another forty years to get round Europe at this rate.

BABS (*laughing*): Oh, Frederick, don't be silly! He's a dear, an absolute dear! He's terribly clever, and he knows ever so much about theater. (*Bashfully.*) He wants to put on a production of *Hamlet* in the village. He thinks I would make a perfect Ophelia.

FREDERICK: Babs, darling, you know the doctors forbid you from acting. Your health's far too fragile for that. Anyway, I think he's leading you up the garden path. Who's going to go to a theater production in the village? The damn peasants?

BABS (*wounded*): Why must you always undermine me?

FREDERICK (*taking her hand*): Oh, my sweet Babs, I'm only trying to protect you. You're such a naïf. Anyway, I need you here with me. I couldn't possibly run the château on my own.

BABS: Sometimes I despise this château.

FREDERICK (*simply*): It is our destiny. (*He goes and stands meditatively under the large portrait of their father hanging over the fireplace.*) Ham-

let, eh? "To be or not to be." It really is the question, when you think about it.

> (*There is a thunderous noise overhead.*
> BABS *rushes to* FREDERICK'*s side.*)

BABS: Oh, Frederick! I'm so frightened!

FREDERICK (*pulling a fencing sword down from the wall*): Don't worry, Babs, I'm here!

> (*The door bursts open and* INSPECTOR DICK ROBINSON, SCOTLAND
> YARD, *comes in, with* HORST *and* WERNER *caught under either arm.*
> LOPAKHIN *slouches in after them, looking disgruntled.*)

INSPECTOR DICK ROBINSON: Well, we've solved the mystery of the noises and the missing eggbeater. Bosnians, hiding out in your attic.

FREDERICK: Great Scott!

INSPECTOR: It's not uncommon, sir. Too lazy and undisciplined to get their own house in order, these parasites come over to proper countries to eke out a living—or in this case, seemingly, to drive good honest aristocrats out of their châteaus.

BABS (*covering her eyes*): Oh, they're hideous! I can't bear to look at them!

INSPECTOR: Don't worry, Ma'am. Where these miscreants are going, no one will be troubled by them for a long, long time.

HORST (*sneering*): Up yours, copper.

INSPECTOR: Why, you impudent— (*Makes to strike him.*)

FREDERICK: Stop!

(Everyone turns to FREDERICK *in surprise.)*

FREDERICK: Maybe they are lazy and undisciplined. But society is to blame too. These men deserve a second chance. I want to offer them a job working on my vineyard.

INSPECTOR: These are dangerous men, Your Excellency . . .

FREDERICK: Maybe so. But it's what Father would have wanted. It's what this vineyard means. *(To the* BOSNIANS.*)* What do you say, lads? It's tough, backbreaking work, and you won't get rich from it. But are you game?

(The BOSNIANS *disengage themselves from* INSPECTOR ROBINSON *and cross the floor to kneel at* FREDERICK's *feet.)*

BOSNIANS: My liege.

FREDERICK *(laughing)*: Arise, arise! We're not stuffy around here. Well! It looks like we'll have a harvest after all!

LOPAKHIN *(to himself)*: Gah!

BABS: Oh, how wonderful!

(The door bursts open. It is MAM'SELLE, *the comical French maid.)*

MAM'SELLE *(dramatically)*: Your Excellency, I have kicked the dog.

INSPECTOR *(startled)*: I beg your pardon?

BABS *(laughing)*: Don't worry, Inspector! She means she has cooked the duck!

FREDERICK: Oh, Mam'selle—you are a duffer!

328 · *Paul Murray*

> *(They all laugh and leave together, except* LOPAKHIN,
> *who remains in the room.)*

LOPAKHIN: Well, "Your Excellency," it looks like your old-fashioned brand of idealism has won the battle. But I know your Achilles' heel now—your fragile sister, Babs . . . and I won't rest until I have her, and your precious vineyard is nothing but rubble . . .

I THREW MYSELF into my work. What else could I do? I must have called the house a hundred times; Bel wouldn't even come to the phone. Depending on whom I talked to, she had just stepped out, or wasn't feeling well, or was in the bath; she seemed to be perpetually in the bath these days. Beyond that—whether she had swallowed her pride and returned to playing *Ramp*, repeating her small act of rebellion nightly in front of an audience, or whether she was cloistered away in her own misery, shunned by the others—I had no idea. "She left her bag here," I'd say. "Tell her to call me if she wants it dropped over." They'd promise to pass on the message, and that would be all I could do until the next day, when the process would be repeated.

As for Mirela, whenever she answered the phone I hung up straightaway; even though a part of me burned to talk with her, plead with her, in the same way that murderers are said to feel compelled to revisit the scene of the crime. I couldn't go out to the house myself for fear of running into her; so, as November stretched on toward Christmas, and the streets filled up with fairy lights and shifty-looking men selling spruces and pines from the backs of flatbed trucks, I buried my guilty conscience in work, and I tried not to think about anything else.

Fortunately there was plenty of work to occupy me. November–December is the busiest time of the year for those of us in the Yule Log business, and Processing Zone B was pushed to the limit. Everything seemed to be operating at double speed. Cigarette breaks were abandoned for the month, and we often worked overtime so that we could meet our quotas: Edvin, Bobo, Pavel, Arvids, Dzintars, and me bent silently, conscientiously over our machines, while the trucks waited rumbling at the loading bay and Mr. Appleseed patrolled the tiles with his pointer held behind his back. By now I had picked up a smattering of Latvian and mastered the vagaries of the sugar-frosting machine to become an exemplary Bread Straightener; I can point to my own modest part in Processing Zone B's late rally to overtake C shift and claim the Productivity Hamper. Not only that, but I used my position of influence and good command of spoken English to raise staff grievances and try to improve conditions for the workers. Over lunch, while Mr. Appleseed was ranting about how he'd never have believed there could possibly be a crowd of wasters worse than the Latvians until he'd met these new Estonian bastards, I would delicately and imperceptibly steer the conversation around to the showers.

"What about the showers, Fuckface?"

"Well, there aren't any . . ."

And Mr. Appleseed, to give him his due, listened, and promised to bring it up at the next management briefing. Meanwhile, I agitated among the workers themselves, disseminating ideas I had heard the builders talk about back in the house. It wasn't always easy. Most of the time they would just look at me as if I'd proposed we all relocate to the moon. "Don't you want a job?" they would say. "Do you want them to send us all home?"

"Of course not," I'd say. "I'm just saying we need to organize ourselves to make sure, you know, we don't get sold down the river. To get a fair shake of the stick."

"What river?" they'd say. "What stick?"

But I persisted; and at times when it seemed especially hopeless I would tell myself I was doing it for Bel, offering it up to her like a kind of prayer, as if somehow it would reach her and steal over her and she would without quite knowing why stop despising me and want to talk to me again.

In the evenings I labored over my play. Practically speaking it was a lost cause, given the new regime at the theater; furthermore, ever since the Bosnians had been discovered, my villain Lopakhin had been upping the ante. Currently he was dancing such rings around Frederick that I was beginning to wonder if the latter was really up to the job. Still I pressed on, thinking that if I could just say what I wanted to say, here on a blank piece of paper, a miraculous change would be effected and the universe would be restored. And then one night, I suppose about two weeks or three after that wretched tryst, the telephone rang. Somehow I knew it was for me: I threw down my pen and dashed into the living room. But it was only Mother, calling to harangue me for not RSVPing to some dinner invitation she'd sent me. It was a stormy night outside and the connection was bad; the line woofed and hissed with interference, and I had trouble making out what she was saying.

"Which dinner?" I said.

"The *dinner*, Charles, for goodness' sake, the Telsinor dinner, the invitations were sent out over a week ago."

"Well I didn't get one," I said, riffling through the correspondence sitting in the fruit bowl: bills, bills, final demand . . .

"That really is most galling, because I entrusted them a week ago *at least* to that—" Here a roar of wind enveloped the building and the connection was submerged in whistles and pops. ". . . see to it personally that they were delivered right away."

"What?" I said, putting a finger in my ear. "Where are you calling from? You sound like you're in the middle of a hurricane."

"I'm on my mobile," she said. "It's new. I said I gave them to that friend of yours to deliver, I don't see why you shouldn't have got yours . . ."

"What friend?"

"Oh, that fellow. The postman, Macavity the Mystery Cat, or whatever his name is."

I experienced a familiar sinking feeling. "He's no friend of mine," I said.

"That is infuriating," Mother said again. "I shall have to look into it. Well, anyway, it's Thursday night at eight sharp, black tie—I *mean* black tie, Charles, it is a formal occasion, so none of your comedy dickey bows, if you please—"

"But what *is* it?" I broke in. "You still haven't told me what it—"

"*Telsinor*," her voice crackling down the line like an ancient gramophone recording. "I've said it three or four times, it's to officially launch the partnership with the Centre. Nothing overly grand, a dozen or so guests. However, Mr. O'Boyle has very kindly agreed to attend in person, so it will be an opportunity for us to thank him for all his generosity."

"Oh," I said unenthusiastically. I didn't see what point there was dragging me along, and I was about to say as much when Mother beat me to it. "I should add, Charles, that I had misgivings about inviting you. Grave misgivings, in fact. I had hoped, naïvely perhaps, that your stint at the Civil Service might teach you a thing or two about responsibility and pulling one's weight. But to judge by the incidents at the premiere, that has not been the case."

"What incidents? You can't blame me for any of th——"

"The Golem business, Charles, that's your little hobbyhorse, isn't it? But anyway, I don't intend to discuss the matter now, other than to say that what took place that night was inexcusable. You are a grown man living under your own roof, however, and if you insist on ignoring your Higher Power and taking the slippery slope to perdition, that is your business. It is no longer my place to intervene. What I will not tolerate is the deleterious effect you are having on your sister. You know quite well that she has had difficulties, and yet you continue to fill her head with romantic nonsense. But no matter"—raising her voice to drown out my protestations of innocence of any kind of influence over any aspect of Bel's life—"no matter, I decided I would invite you anyway, because I wanted to show Mr. O'Boyle our gratitude not only as a theater but as a *family.* Because this affects us personally, Charles. As you know, they are pledging a significant sum toward the renovation of the house. More importantly, it seems that they are willing to make a commitment to clear all arrears outstanding and secure it financially for the foreseeable future, meaning that the house will remain in the family name into the next century. Whether we *deserve* it or not is another question, of course. Nevertheless, I want the whole family to be there to commemorate the occasion, even those black sheep who seem to prefer to skulk about the peripheries. Also," she added judiciously, "what I have just said notwithstanding, I thought you ought to see your sister before she leaves."

A jolt passed up my arm. "Before she what?" I shook the handset as the connection descended again into fizzing. "Before she *what*?"

"——cially *keen* on it"—she resurfaced—"nevertheless it seems a matter of simple good manners as much as of maturity. Please stop whatting me, Charles, it's most annoying—"

"Sorry, sorry," I burbled, "but what was that you said? About Bel leaving?"

"Yes, leaving," Mother said impatiently. "Honestly, doesn't anything reach you in your little cocoon out there? She's going to Yalta for six months with the Kiddon girl. Some sort of a Chekhov master class. You know Bel and Chekhov."

My mind felt like it had been dropped into a hornets' nest, with far too many questions to sort into any kind of coherent order. "What?" I said faintly.

"Yalta, Charles, it's in Russia. She's been planning it for weeks. You see this is what happens when you cut yourself off—"

"But *when* is she— I mean to say—when?"

"Friday, I told you, that's why we're having the dinner Thursday night. A sort of a double celebration."

Blood roared in my ears. I sank to my haunches and leaned against the door. "The Kiddon girl had some friend at the opening night of *Ramp*," Mother was saying. "She approached Bel shortly afterwards and offered her a place on this excursion, although don't ask me why, after that performance—"

"For six *months*?" I whispered. "In *Russia*?"

"I know, it's costing an absolute fortune. I did have my doubts, especially as the girl seems barely capable of tying her shoelaces at the moment without it turning into a German opera. But the hope is that a few months in her own company might give her time to pull herself together and perhaps even rejoin us here on Planet Earth. And the Kiddon girl assures me that these people are quite reputable, it's quite prestigious, in fact—"

"Who?" I said.

"This body, I believe it's called the Knipper Foundation—"

"No, no, the—Kiddon, who is this Kiddon girl you keep talking about?"

"You know her, Charles, Kiddon—what is her name? Jessica. She was in school with Bel. Her father is some sort of a noise at Deloitte and Touche."

"Well, I've never heard of her," I said. "And if you ask me the whole thing sounds quite preposterous, letting Bel go flimmering off around Russia with some perfect stranger—"

"She's not a stranger, Charles, I've spoken to her on the telephone myself and she seems a very sensible and levelheaded girl who will I hope be a *good* influence on your sister"—putting just enough stress on the word to make her meaning clear. "Please don't be difficult about this. I do think it's for the best." She paused. "She hasn't been very happy here lately," she said.

"But wasn't she going to tell me?" My voice was giving way on me now. "I mean, wasn't she even going to say goodbye?"

"I don't know, Charles," Mother said wearily. "Why must you pester me with these questions? If you'd simply RSVP like everybody else it would save us all a lot of trouble. Now are you coming to the dinner or aren't you?"

"Well, yes, obviously, but—"

"Good. Eight sharp, remember." Mother's voice acquired a metallic echo as the reception began to break up. "*Formal*, Charles. And bring a guest. Candida Olé tells me Patsy's back from her voyages, it might be nice if you—" There was a far-off crash, and the line went completely silent.

TO THE CASUAL OBSERVER it might have appeared that I was overreacting. But I *knew* Bel—I was the only one who did; I was the only one who could comprehend what a gesture like this meant. Yalta, for heaven's sake! Who on earth ever went to Yalta? No, I could read between the lines. This was her fresh start, and she was making it alone; and even if she did come back in six months—six *months*!—she would not be coming back to us.

The rest of that evening is something of a blur. I have a vague recollection of going to the petrol station and buying four or five bottles of the abhorrent German Riesling, after polishing off that Bulgarian

Cabernet; I have a sketchy image of me sitting cross-legged on the living room floor in the wee hours of the morning, drinking the last dregs of some sort of unspeakable wine-in-a-carton I had found under the kitchen sink, presumably intended for famines or droughts or that kind of emergency situation, weeping deliriously as I went through her suitcase: spreading her clothes out over the carpet, tipping the contents of her little makeup bag onto the table—lipstick, vaporizer of Chanel something or other, crumpled tissue, the Telsinor phone everyone had been given, coins, the beads of a broken bracelet, and at the very bottom the silver disk she'd taken to wearing lately, winking at me in all of its childlike, ineffable simpleness, as if it held the answer to everything . . .

But it's quite possible I just imagined it; and the next thing I knew it was eleven thirty-eight on a Wednesday morning and I was standing with shaking hands by the conveyor belt, which had just come to a halt.

Everyone was looking at me, expecting that I had jammed up the frosting machine again; to me, too, this seemed like the most plausible explanation. But I hadn't. The machines had just stopped. And Mr. Appleseed, now that we cast about for him, was nowhere to be seen. We took off our gloves, shrugged and muttered. Then the intercom squawked and a voice boomed into the room, summoning us to the Bread-Cutting Zone for a meeting.

This caused even more of a stir. A meeting? We had never had a meeting before. I hadn't even known there was an intercom. It was rather exciting—a meeting, just like real workers! Chests swelled and voices bubbled in excitement as we filed through the double doors.

"Maybe they're giving us a pay rise," Bobo said.

"Maybe they're putting in a new vending machine," said gingery Arvids, "with proper snacks in it, and not just slices of bread."

By the time we arrived the Bread-Cutting Zone was already crowded with overalled figures—including, I saw to my surprise, C shift, who weren't supposed to start work for another six hours. The Daves, the two drug-addled teenagers who ran this section, were standing by a column, looking on with more than their usual degree of befuddlement. The sweaty bread mixers were there, hands covered in dough; the raisin-and-poppy-seed people; the lank-haired girls from the washing hall, even the men from Zone T, pumpernickel-bread division, who shrouded their work in a Masonic secrecy and who frankly we all found a little odd.

The hall was abuzz. Gossip and rumor climbed the walls and bounced from the corrugated roof. At the top of the room, plastic boxes had been arranged into a kind of dais; the great slicing machines stood solemnly on either side, their blades held motionlessly aloft, giving them the air of acolytes at some mystical ceremony. Just as the chatter reached a peak, there was a scuffling, booming noise. Instantly a hush fell. Mr. Appleseed had appeared on the dais. He was staring out at us in his customary cloven-hoofed posture, tapping a microphone. By his side was a metal device about the size of a smallish filing cabinet, with a spindly, clawlike appendage extending from the top. "Vending machine," I heard Arvids murmur next to me, but his voice was faint and discordant in the suddenly charged silence.

"Gentlemen," Mr. Appleseed croaked, "and ladies. Thank you for your attendance. Today is an auspicious day in the history of Mr. Dough. The company is about to take a great leap forward, and we are very privileged to be here to witness it." Here and there low voices could be heard translating for those whose English wasn't up to scratch.

"You have all worked hard today," he continued, "just as you do every day. You might not think I see it, or appreciate it, but I do. And I know I speak not only for myself but for the entire board of Northwestern BioHoldings Group plc and its shareholders when I commend you for your dedication and your spirit. Mr. Dough is not always the easiest environment to work in. The dust, the great heat—the conditions here are far from ideal, as has been pointed out to me in no uncertain terms."

At this a few people turned to grin at me or give me friendly punches on the shoulder, which in my fragile condition I did not appreciate.

"It is not a job for the weak-willed or the delicate. One might say that in a perfect world no one would have to do jobs as tough as yours are. It is unquestionably a job for men or, in some cases, women." He silenced a burst of applause with a raised hand. "But today, with the help of science, I am proud to tell you that we are one step closer to that

336 · *Paul Murray*

perfect world." To another round of applause, this one scattered and rather muted, he stepped behind the metal apparatus and pressed a button. Lights blinked, and the arm began to whir through the air. "Meet BZD2348," said Mr. Appleseed. "This particular model has been primed to perform all the tasks currently undertaken by the Yule Log Division. Observe." He placed an unfrosted loaf onto a tray protruding from one end of the machine. There was a grinding noise as the machine swallowed it up, a series of clanks, and then, mere seconds later, it spat it out again—not only sugared on top but neatly packaged in the festive Yule Log box. The machine's arm lowered. It hummed obsequiously. "Marvelous," chuckled Mr. Appleseed. "What this in essence means is that thanks to top-of-the-range German technology, a single device can do all the work of, in this case, five Latvians and Fuckface—but at four times the speed and a fraction of the cost."

A couple of stray handclaps rose and reverberated through the lofty chamber. Suddenly a gap seemed to have emerged between the six of us and the rest of the crowd. People were giving us funny looks, a mixture of sympathy, fear, and poorly disguised relief.

"Other models can be fitted out for baguettes, soda bread, pastries, and what have you," Mr. Appleseed called out, drawing the audience back to him. "By the end of the month, we hope to have Mr. Dough converted into a fully automated factory." There was a palpable drop in pressure as three hundred people drew their breath. "The installation begins today," Mr. Appleseed went on. "As of this afternoon, Mr. Dough will be closed, and it will remain closed until such time as the change-over is complete. So it remains only for me to thank you again for your months, and in some cases years, of dedicated service, and to wish you the very best for the future." He looked down at us, as if surprised to see that we were still standing there. "That is all."

No one spoke. No one moved.

"What!" I exclaimed.

"Fuckface? You have a question?"

"You mean to say you're firing us? All of us?"

"I'm glad you asked me that, Fuckface. It's important that we're all completely clear about this. The answer is that no, it is not correct to say we are firing you. Your employer is and remains the recruitment agency that leased you out to us. So a more constructive way to look at it would be to say that the agency has completed its contract with Mr. Dough. And you can all take pride in a job well done. I should add that anyone with a suitable qualification in IT is more than welcome to submit their CV for consideration for positions in our new Robot Programming Division. Are there any more questions? No? Good." He stepped down from the platform and, the machine trundling behind him, left by a door at the back.

As soon as he was gone the chamber filled with noise again. But although there was breast-beating, although there were lamentations and woebegone faces and even a few tears, still no one seemed exactly *surprised.* No one seized a box and began smashing up the slicing machines; no one grabbed the microphone and declared that he wasn't leaving until Mr. Appleseed's blood had been spilled and who was with him? Instead everyone simply seemed to accept defeat. Already a few people were shuffling out of the door we had come in. I was shocked. Were these the men I had worked with side by side on ten-hour shifts in the furnace of Processing Zone B? Was this the indomitable spirit that had won us the Productivity Hamper?

"We're not just going to let them get away with this?" I appealed to my comrades. "I mean, we're not just going to lie down like dogs, are we?"

"What else can we do?" said Pavel, moving toward the exit.

"I don't know," I said. "Couldn't we go on strike, or something?"

"We've already been sacked, Fuckface," Edvin pointed out. "There's not much point going on strike when you've already been sacked."

"Anyway, you have already done enough," gravelly voiced Dzintars chipped in surlily.

"Me? What did I do?"

"Always complain, complain. Never just do the job. Always Mister Moany-Moan."

"I was only trying to make things better for you," I protested. "You can't blame me for this."

"What do you know about how it is for us?" Dzintars growled.

"All right, all right," Bobo intervened. "No point fighting about this now."

"Maybe we could make a deal with, how you say, the Union of Robots?" chuckled Edvin.

"Well sarcasm isn't going to help anybody," I muttered. But my inflammatory rhetoric proved useless. Word had filtered back that the paychecks were being given out at the factory gate, and no one wanted to risk any trouble; though to be accurate people weren't lying down like dogs so much as filling their pockets with marzipan bread and Danish pastries and whatever else they chanced upon on their way back to the locker room. The factory was suddenly full of men in blue uniforms we hadn't seen before. As soon as the herd left an area, they would move in behind us to seal it off with plastic barriers. We were silent now, everyone retreated into his own thoughts. At the gate, another of the blue-uniformed men was handing out checks to the workers. Once they had been paid, few hung around. They would stand outside for a minute, talking and shaking their heads; then, in clusters of twos and threes, they would mooch off down the street. In a corner of the loading area near the back of the building, more uniformed men were taking roughly robot-sized boxes from an articulated truck.

Bobo, Arvids, and the rest of Yule Log Division were among the last to leave.

"Name?" The uniformed man had a jaw thick with stubble and a baton hanging at his side. I wondered if he and his cohorts had also been hired from the agency, especially for the occasion.

I gave my name. He found it on his clipboard and ran a line through it, then handed me an envelope. As I went outside to join the others, it struck me that Sirius Recruitment must have known about the layoffs in order to deliver the monthly paychecks several days early. I studied the figure at the bottom and did the arithmetic in my head; if I was correct, they had paid us up until eleven thirty-eight of that morning, and not a minute more.

"I don't believe it," Bobo said, looking blankly at the slip in his hand.

"I know, of all the penny-pinching . . . You know, I bet if you invited them to dinner they'd be exactly the type of people who not only would not bring any wine but then you'd find out they'd been *starving* themselves for three days beforehand— I say—" as the paper fluttered free from his hand. "What is it?"

He crashed down onto the curb and put his head in his hands. I chased after the check and caught it as it careened merrily along the gutter. Wiping away the dirt, I read at the top "BOBODAN 'BOBO' BOBEYO-VICH," and beside it a figure identical to the one on mine, comprising wages, overtime, back pay, money for untaken holidays. But beneath that had been printed "DEDUCTION: agency fee 1200.00 IE"; and beneath that "DEDUCTION: accom. 108 nts @ 8.58 p.n."; and then "DE-DUCTION: visa reg. & proc.; DEDUCTION: handling; DEDUCTION: airfares & insurance"; on and on they went, DEDUCTION DEDUCTION DEDUCTION, until one found oneself at the bottom of the page, where nestled in a little blue box sat neatly "NET: 000.00."

I whistled softly to myself. Then, hearing a noise, I turned to see the gate close and a heavy bolt slide into place. Two of the men stared at me with folded arms from the other side.

Arvids, Edvin, and Dzintars, who had been standing about in comparable attitudes of despair, now made a move to go. Pavel pulled Bobo to his feet, and they trudged off down the road; I trotted after them, worthless check crumpled in my fist. The sky was heavy and dull and cold. Trucks rumbled by in clouds of exhaust fumes that made my eyes sting. What was happening to my life? Was this how it worked in the real world? Was it nothing more than a sandstorm through which one walked with one's eyes closed, every moment obliterated by the next? We arrived at the crossroads where the Latvians would turn off for their barracks and I would continue on for the bus.

"What will you do?" I said. "Where will you go?"

"Call the agency," Dzintars said.

"Call the agency? After *that*?"

Dzintars shrugged.

"No agency, no visa," Edvin elaborated.

"But . . ." I stood there chewing my cheek. I couldn't just let them go, B shift couldn't be let just dissipate like ghosts in the afternoon, as if the last few weeks had never happened. And yet it appeared that there was nothing left to say, nothing except—

"Chin-chin." Bobo clapped me on the shoulder. "See you later, old sport."

"Chin-chin, Fuckface," the others said, nodding at me; then taking their Yule Logs out of their pockets, they set off up the hill.

(Scene. A crumbling château by the Marne. Enter FREDERICK, *a Count, and* BABS, *his tragic sister.)*

FREDERICK: I don't care what the bank manager said! I may not have any money left, but I'm still the Count, and I'm going to take on the dog-eat-dog world of the French wine industry and produce a half-decent Burgundy if I have to plant every grape myself!

*(*BABS *is weeping constantly.)*

FREDERICK *(seizing her arm)*: Damn it, Babs, can't you see? What we have here is a dream, and as long as we're together no bank manager can touch it, because it's a dream, I mean to say it's not just—

FREDERICK: Damn it, Babs, please stop crying

FREDERICK: Babs, you're probably wondering about the other night, well the fact is it was all a plot of Lopakhin's

FREDERICK: Damn it, Babs

FREDERICK: Damn it

—

"HOW'S THE OUL play goin, Charlie?"

"Hmm? Oh, passably well, passably well . . . Just taking a breather at the minute, obviously . . ."

"Oh, right," shifting uncomfortably from foot to foot. "Eh, I was just wonderin about that rent . . ."

"Rent?"

"Yeah, it's just that your man was on lookin for it again, gettin a bit narky . . ."

"Oh," I said spiritlessly, playing with a tassel. "Well, I'll write you a check later on, will that do?"

"A check, oh right, grand job," clearing his throat conversationally, "here, I was talkin to me mate what has the warehouse and he says there's a shift goin if you're—"

"Ha, no fear!" I said, looking back at the television.

"Oh right so." He continued to hover behind. "Eh . . . is that Bel's lipstick?"

"Yes, yes it is, as a matter of fact."

"What are you doin with it?"

"Oh, you know, just sort of holding it. Helps me focus."

"You all right, Charlie?"

"Me? Tip-top. Never better. Still, best get back to the old play, no rest for the wicked, ha ha . . ."

"Ha ha . . ."

The play wasn't going well, obviously; the play was going terribly. I didn't know how it had happened, exactly, but Lopakhin was running the show now, and every time I picked up my pen and tried to rectify matters, it only made them worse. For instance, Frederick had gone to Monte Carlo for a two-day cork makers' conference, but Lopakhin told Babs that he'd sold his half of the estate and run off to gamble away the proceeds—and Babs believed him, why did she believe him? So now while Frederick was footling about with tax concessions for a bunch of grasping Portuguese farmers, Lopakhin had his sister on her own and was spinning her such appalling lies—black was white, up was down, Frederick was a shady obsessive who was stifling Babs's acting and romantic career—that I sometimes felt quite unwell and had to go and sit in the dark for a while.

Nevertheless, it was all I had left. I had not called Gemma at Sirius Recruitment. My experience at Mr. Dough had soured for me the whole idea of working; or rather it had served to confirm what I suspected all along, namely that working for a living was a mug's game. "The way I see it," I said to the others, "if you're not rich, you're poor, and the only way to get rich is either to be rich already or take up some sort of a crime, like architectural salvage or robbing old ladies— No offense, I mean."

"Ah you're all right, Charlie," Frank said.

"Gnnhhhrrhh," snored Droyd from his stupor on the sofa.

"Or starting a recruitment company," I mused bitterly.

So, as outside the streets grew day by day chillier and darker, and the fateful dinner party floated before me like an uncontemplatable abyss, I whiled away my hours in my dressing gown in the armchair. I wrote a line of my play and scratched it out; I swamped myself in vast deluges of memory; I concocted plan after fantastical plan by which to force Bel to stay—including, but by no means limited to: skywriting a carefully worded apology in the area of sky adjacent to her bedroom window; feigning to have contracted a life-threatening illness; having my play finished, submitted, and produced to great acclaim at the Abbey, starring Bel Hythloday, ideally before Wednesday; ringing up Mother and proving to her by exhaustive analysis of her recent behavior that Bel was in no fit state to travel; actually contracting a life-threatening illness viz. Lassa fever by concentrated association with Boyd Snooks. But most of the time I did what I did best, which was nothing.

I thought sporadically of returning to my monograph. I had reached the 1950s now; all the films were in that lurid Hollywood color that made everything look at once gaudy and exhausted. Gene had stopped wearing makeup years ago, but the overripe tones saturated her too, accentuating the vacancy that grew at the heart of her performances. If she had been trying to hide herself in her earlier films, in those last four—*The Egyptian, Personal Affair, Black Widow, The Left Hand of God*—she was gone. Sleepwalking would be putting it kindly; everything about those performances pointed to a person who was no longer actually there—the inertia, the lifelessness of her movements, the opacity of the beautiful eyes.

The Left Hand of God would be her last starring role in a movie. As soon as the film was completed, she fled Hollywood and holed up in New York with her mother. The studios promptly suspended her for breach of contract and accused her publicly of prima donna tantrums.

Reporters hounded her; the telephone rang day and night until finally her mother disconnected it.

In the New York apartment everything became confused. She slept for days on end. She didn't recognize the faces of her friends. She had never been political before but now became obsessed with Communist plots: she thought the Communists were trying to poison her, she thought they were replacing the words on the pages of the books she read. She stopped eating, then went on a diet of chocolate and bread and butter and gained twenty pounds in a couple of weeks because she thought she was pregnant and eating for two. Every night she imagined she gave birth, and every night the Communists stole her child; or she dreamed that Daria was no longer in an institution but in the house of a couple living down the street. Her brother would find her in the middle of the night, banging on the neighbors' door, demanding that they give her her daughter back. At last she was committed to the Harkness Pavilion asylum, New York.

Electroconvulsive therapy—ECT—was at that time considered a breakthrough in the treatment of the mentally ill. By administering an electric shock directly to the brain, it seemed that doctors could temporarily jolt patients out of their psychoses. The shock made them forget everything; and as Gene commented, you can hardly be depressed about what you don't remember. She was given thirty-two of these treatments over a single year. Every time she woke up not knowing who or where or what she was. Gradually, some of her memories would come back; generally, childhood first, then adolescence, then the middle past. But the months and years preceding the treatment did not. They were simply gone—impersonally stripped away, as if they had never happened, so that years later, when she came to write her autobiography (entitled, self-deprecatingly, *Self-Portrait*), she had to rely on newspaper scrapbooks, letters, the testimony of friends.

Her life in the institution became one long gray anonymous blur, punctuated by the electric current. And in some ways it worked: She was pacified, docile; she knitted, made tables, scrubbed floors; she was happy to be relieved of the burden of her identity. But she remained in dread of the ECT sessions. She recounts one occasion, waking up in the usual state of utter limbo, and—although, of course, she did not know why—suddenly becoming so angry that she punched the nurse standing over her right in the jaw. In revenge, the nurse brought her to the ward where the hopeless cases were kept and left her there for the day. Gene herself was so far gone, however, that she mistook them for Method actors from the Stanislavsky school. She stood there and applauded, all day long. It struck me that it might not be such a great shift, from Hollywood actress to mental patient. The hospital, like the studio, exercised strict controls on every aspect of your image, your routine, how you thought and spoke and acted; the patients were like actors who had stumbled too far into the script and could not find their way back out. Perhaps this was why Gene was released when she was: She knew how the system worked, she knew what they wanted from you; and she had what she called her model's trick, the ability to change her look for whatever the scene demanded. Trader, outlaw, dust bowl Salome, frontier girl, aristocrat, Arabian, Eurasian, Polynesian, Chinese—she knew how to remake herself to order; she could make it look, given time, as if nothing was wrong. And no one could tell, or at least no one troubled to look at what was still transpiring beneath the lovely exterior.

But I could tell; and perhaps that was why, as the days tightened around us like a noose, the garishness and the threadbare plots of those late films seemed curiously to fit my wintering world of curtailed grays and blacks; her sleepwalking performances seemed, somehow, to strike a chord in me, and even to provide a sad strain of company.

THE NIGHT FRANK and Droyd had their set-to it started to rain and did not stop. It was as if the belly of the sky had been cut open; the water thrashed against the window with such vehemence that the outside world was obliterated. The walls of the flat shook and groaned in the wind, and at one point the entire building seemed to pitch forward, sending junk skating off the shelves to the floor.

I was sitting in my dressing gown, trying to watch the television. The reception kept going; every few seconds snow crunched up on to the screen like a nervous tic. Frank was in his bedroom with Laura, working on his bookshelves, which for all the banging they were making seemed to be progressing very slowly; although as Frank had no books anyway, I suppose there was no real hurry. There was a knock at the door, and Droyd appeared from somewhere to answer it. Three cadaverous young men were standing in the hall.

Droyd, I should point out at this juncture, was a changed man from the boorish lout who had first moved in. One hesitates, obviously, to blow one's own trumpet, or put oneself forward as a civilizing influence, but whatever the reason, it seemed he was thoroughly reformed. He scarcely played his music at all now; he would sit by the window or in front of the television peaceful as a lamb. In fact, one could almost say he was too quiet for a lad his age. He seemed to have abandoned his musical career and also appeared to *sweat* more than was customary. But this was to split hairs. All I knew was that he hadn't called me a shirtlifter or tried to steal my wallet in weeks.

Anyway, there we all were, and Droyd called to me from the doorway that he was going out to play football if that was all right, and I replied that I didn't see why not, not listening all that intently because one really had to concentrate if one wanted to hear the TV what with the reception, and that would have been that, had Frank not at that moment happened to come out and ask what was going on.

"Jus' goin out for a quick game of football," Droyd said, as a peal of thunder broke over the roof.

At first I thought Frank hadn't heard him; he was giving the cadaverous youngsters a long, hard look. But then he said, "Y'are not."

Droyd muttered something to his pals, who sloped off down the hall, then turned back to Frank. "Wha?" he said.

"I don't want you hangin round with them lads," Frank said.

"Wha?" Droyd said. "Why not?"

"Cos they're scumbags," Frank informed him.

"That's bollocks," Droyd said. "They're me mates."

"I don't care," Frank said. "They're scumbags."

"Ah for fuck's sake!" Droyd was not happy with this verdict. "D'you expect me to just sit around all day on me fuckin Tobler? Am I not even allowed have mates now?"

"Oh, let him go, Frank," I chipped in from the armchair. "It's a sin to keep a growing lad cooped up in here all the time."

"He doesn't mind bein cooped up when it suits him," Frank jibed. "He doesn't mind sittin around on his hole eatin me food when he's supposed to be out lookin for a job."

Droyd assumed an attitude of wounded outrage. "I *tried* lookin for a job," he said. "I *told* you, it's impossible to find one now, cos of all the foreigners. There's no *room* for the Irish anymore. Like I got on the bus the other day, an' I couldn't even sit down cos of all the refugees takin up the seats. What's that about, when the Irish can't get a seat on their own bus? *That's* what we should be worryin about, 'f you ask me. 'F you ask me, they should send the lot of them back where they came from. Like maybe not the Chinkies from the takeaway, or them lads from down the kebab shop, but the rest—"

"You can't blame the foreigners for you sittin round doin nothin all day," Frank interrupted this polemic.

"I don't do nothin!" Droyd protested. "I go out every day for me methadone, don't I?"

"Goin for your methadone's not a proper job," Frank said.

"Fuck's *sake*!" Droyd exclaimed wildly. "*He* doesn't have a job either, why don't you fuckin nag him for a change?"

"That's a completely different set of circumstances," I said. "That's a matter of principle."

"Do you *want* to end up like Charlie?" Frank demanded, not appearing to have heard this. "Is that what you want?"

"Just fuckin leave off, would you?" Droyd clutched his head manically. "You sound like me oul lad, fuckin naggin me and naggin me and all he ever done himself was go down the boozer and get locked—"

"I'm not naggin you, I just don't want you hangin round with them gearbags—"

"You can't tell me what to do!" Droyd cut him off. "You're not even me *mate* anymore. You used to be a laugh, but now you're just tryin to be posh, bein with that bird, an'—an' *him*," leveling a finger at me. "I mean it's not his fault he's like that. He was born that way. But you're fuckin *tryin* to be like that, and all you're doin is makin a laugh of yourself! Well I'm fuckin sick of it! It's fuckin depressin in this place! I had more fun in the fuckin nick! So stick it up your bollocks, Frank!"

—

HE DIDN'T COME HOME that night, or the night after.

"He'll be back when he's hungry," I said. "There's no point getting in a state."

"But maybe something's happened to him," Frank said anxiously, pressing his nose to the streaming glass.

"What could possibly happen to him? He can take care of himself. He's not a child, after all, I mean he's been in *prison*, hasn't he?"

Frank was not convinced. But to be truthful, I paid little heed to Droyd's disappearance. I was busy with worries of my own, with fretting and remembering and framing unworkable plans; and now I woke up to find only one day remaining before the dinner party and Bel's departure.

The rain was still beating down; it looked like a perfect day for sitting around in one's armchair feeling blue. I had an appointment at the hospital to have my dressing changed, however, so I caught a bus into the city and sat glumly on the examining table as the doctor unwrapped me and prodded me with blunt instruments and asked me if it hurt. It didn't. I was too lost in my own thoughts—of gray Russian skies and the wild endless steppes and how they compared to my dismal little oubliette in Bonetown. So when he said the wound had healed, it took a moment to register.

"What?" I said, snapping awake. "Healed?"

"Won't do any more good covering it up," he said. "Time to let the air at it. Hold on, let's give you a look at yourself." He went to his drawer and fetched a hand mirror and held it up in front of me. And there looking back at me was Charles Hythloday.

"Anything wrong?"

"No, no, I just"—I cleared my throat—"I seem to have *aged* rather."

The doctor laughed and told me that that would clear up in a couple of weeks, and he wrote out a prescription for various unguents and poultices. "Nice weather for ducks," he said as I left, nodding at the window.

It should have been something special, to feel the rain on my face again after three months of clammy bandages; it should have been an occasion, to be *me* again after all this time as a Nobody. But all I could think of was tomorrow, and Bel. As I came back down Thomas Street I was rehearsing the impassioned speeches I might make to her at the dinner; and some of them I found so moving that I didn't notice at first that what I vaguely remembered as a shortcut down behind Christchurch had instead led me into a maze of dilapidated flats. By the time I realized, and stopped to take my bearings, I was already hopelessly lost.

I retraced my steps but every time ended back in the same place. Everything looked alike in this rain, and there didn't seem to be anyone around to ask directions. Then as I took in my surroundings properly I began to *hope* there was no one around; and I remembered the story Pongo McGurks told about getting lost in this locale and being set upon by street Arabs, and how they'd put a penknife to his throat and told him they were going to sell his internal organs to Dubai; and only that on the spur of the moment he'd thought to tell them that he was a Christian Scientist and for religious reasons wouldn't be allowed to have the organs replaced, and persuaded them to make do with his Cartier watch and a couple of credit cards belonging to McGurks *père*, heaven knows what might have happened. Getting panicky, I picked a street at random, conjecturing that I might have more success this way than by deliberately trying to find my way out. But it quickly emerged that I wouldn't, and I had just stopped again to tell myself that the situation was more serious than I had first thought when a bony hand shot out of the shadows and tugged me down an alleyway. Before I knew where I was I had been bundled to the ground, and a skinny figure in a hood bounced down onto my chest. "Gis your fuckin money," he hissed.

"Don't hurt me!" I cried. "I'm Amish— No, wait, I'm—blast, what was it?"

"The *money*," he snarled.

"Right, right," I gabbled, fumbling for my wallet.

"Hurry up," cuffing me roughly.

"Ow!" I wept, finally locating the damn wallet and passing it up to him—and then at the last second pulling it back. "Just a minute," I said.

"Don't try anythin," he warned.

I squinted at him through the rain. "Droyd?" I said.

This gave him pause. "Yes?" the figure said warily.

"It's me, you idiot!" I expostulated, pushing his knee aside. Droyd appeared totally thrown by this. He sat up and blinked heavily. I realized that he had never seen me unbandaged before.

"It's Charles!" I elaborated. *"Charles!"*

He put his hand over his forehead a moment. "Ah fuck," he said. Then, without further consultation, he turned tail down the alley.

THE APARTMENT WAS already in a state of upheaval when I eventually got back.

"It's the landlord!" Laura shouted in my ear from the safety of the bathroom. "He called again about the rent!"

A loud crash issued from the next room. "I thought we paid the rent!" I shouted back.

"He says he's going to evict you!" Laura returned over the sound of the back coming off the dysmorphic sofa and a heartfelt "Fuckin—culchie—pig—*bastard*—"

"What's he doing in there?" putting my hands over my ears.

"Breaking things, maybe you shouldn't mention about Droyd—" She dropped her voice as Frank abruptly hove into view and demanded to know what about Droyd.

She was right; the news did little to calm matters.

"Ah fuck, Charlie!" he wailed. "This is very bad, this is very bad."

"Well I know, I mean I have the luxury of my own face for all of five minutes and then somebody's punching it—"

"Where did he go? Did he say where he was goin?"

"He was *mugging* me, neither of us had time to exchange pleasantries."

"But, like—" He tugged his hair desperately. "How did he look?"

I considered this. "Very focused," I said. "Obviously concentrating on the job at hand, and—"

"No, Charlie, did he look like— Did he look like he was *usin*?"

I didn't know quite what he was getting at, and before I could puzzle it out he had rushed off to his room, staggering back in a moment later with a green-and-white sock in his hand, to tell us that the money was gone.

Everything was gone, as a matter of fact; the apartment had been cleaned out. All of Frank's savings; anything of value that could be carried away from the salvage; the blighter had even made off with my penny jar. It occurred to me that the extent of the theft was such that it must have been proceeding over some time. Only then did we realize that this month's, last month's, maybe even before then's rent had never made it to the landlord.

"Ah Jaysus." Frank gasped as if he had been winded, dropping into the chair.

The phone began to ring.

"And now that I think of it, that story of his about the dog waylaying him on the way to the post office, and running off with the check for the electricity? That was pretty unlikely too . . ."

The phone stopped ringing momentarily, then started up again.

Frank didn't sleep at all that night; I knew this because I didn't sleep either. I sat at the kitchen table in the candlelight and listened to him in the next room, barging restlessly through the furniture like one of those lumbering, outmoded-looking mammals, a pangolin or a three-toed sloth. My play was laid out before me, not that I held any hopes for it now. Lopakhin had won, Frederick and I both knew it. The vineyard's reputation was in tatters. Lopakhin had photographed Frederick in what appeared to be a deep embrace with Babs and released it to the press. It was a total fabrication, of course: What had really happened was that Babs, believing Frederick to be gone forever, had signed her half of the estate over to Lopakhin and then in a fit of despair thrown herself down the stairs; and she would almost certainly have died had Frederick not happened to come back early from the cork makers' convention and found her lying there in the hall and saved her life by performing mouth-to-mouth on her. But this innocent act, in the hands of Lopakhin and his scurrilous friends in the newspapers, looked like it was going to be enough to ruin Frederick's name, on the very day he was about to unveil his new vintage Burgundy to the notoriously conservative French wine industry. The fiendishness of Lopakhin's plot seemed to have shocked him into a kind of stupor; and now all he did all day was sit in his study, sticking wine labels in his scrapbook and playing backgammon with the Bosnians, as if marking time until the inevitable end. It was depressing; I don't know why I didn't just leave it and go to bed. Perhaps I hoped that by simply staying awake I could somehow hold the world as it was: keep it in that dark, rain-filled moment, and stop the fateful day from coming.

Laura's pajamaed silhouette appeared in the doorway. "What are you doing up?" she said. "You should go to bed, there's no point both of you worrying."

"I'm not worrying about Droyd," I scowled.

"You're not?" she said, walking past me to the refrigerator.

"If you ask me, we should be counting our blessings." I spoke sotto voce so Frank wouldn't hear. "It takes a particularly low sort of a black-guard to steal a man's penny jar."

"Are you worried about Bel?" She opened the refrigerator door, and a neat rectangle of light unfolded over her face like a blank page. I began to reply and stopped. Somehow it had slipped my mind how simply, how matter-of-factly lovely she was; and for an instant I was seized by the old hope that I could blink my eyes and transport the two of us to another, less contrary world, a world that could fit that kind of beauty. "You should be glad about it," she said, pouring a glass of lactose-free chocolate milk. "It's the opportunity of a lifetime. Like she's so into it, all that acting stuff."

"I am glad," I said unconvincingly, then trailed off and restarted suddenly. "I say—do you remember a girl in your class by the name of Kiddon? Jessica Kiddon?"

Laura mulled this over, reciting the name under her breath. "No," she said at last. "Who's she?"

"She's the girl Bel's supposed to be going off to Yalta with," I said, frowning. "*Apparently* she was in Bel's class. But I don't recall seeing her in any of the yearbooks."

"It's a big school, though, Charles. Like who could possibly re-member a whole yearbook?"

"Mmm." I made an ambiguous, throat-clearing noise.

"But I'm sure there's nothing to worry about. Like I'm sure she'll be totally fine."

"Mmm," I said again, not intending for it to sound quite as bleak as it did. She drifted behind me and placed her hand on my neck. "Charles," she said gently, "did you ever hear that thing, if you love somebody, set them free? It was in that ad for ice cream? With the talking bear?"

Her fingers stroked my nape; I hung my head, and shut my eyes. The kitchen was filled with the rumble of the rain against the glass.

"It's like someone's angry with us," she said, as if to herself. Then she snapped her fingers and spun back round to me. "I've finally realized who you look like!" she said.

"What?" I said, startled.

"Without your bandages— It's been driving me mad since you came back from the hospital. It's that painting, you look just like that painting in your house."

"What painting?" I said. "There's lots of paintings."

"You know, that one of that guy. The one in the hallway. You look just like it." She laughed again, pleased with this observation, then cut herself short as Frank huffed into the room. He had a frazzled, wild-eyed, vaguely prehistoric look about him, rather like one of those cavemen that they find from time to time encased in ice.

"Charlie," he said, "we have to do something."

I thought this meant we were finally going to contact the authorities, and I began drawing up a list of stolen properties. But it wasn't what he meant. He was proposing that we ourselves go out and look for Droyd.

"You can't be serious," I said.

"We can't just leave him out there," he said. "We can't just leave the little feller out there roamin the streets, in the rain and the cold."

I protested; I pointed out that there was every reason why we should leave him roaming the streets, given that he had lied to us and misled us and stolen three months of rent and basically abrogated the social contract, not to mention the whole penny jar business—

"Will you forget about the fuckin penny jar!" Frank exclaimed. "Who else is goin to look for him if we don't look? No one, that's who. We have to find him, or—or before you know it they'll sling him back in jail!"

There had been four years' worth of pennies in that jar; but Frank was insistent, and eventually I caved in and agreed to help, if only because it was obvious that he had no idea how to organize a search. He seemed to think you could just go out and wander around. I told him that if there were to be any point to this at all, we had to be methodical and exhaustive. The last sighting of Droyd had been in Christchurch, and I surmised that he was probably still in the city, it being more plentiful in terms of old ladies and unwary tourists. The obvious strategy was to fan out over the center, but as there were only the two of us, we decided to take a side each: I the area south of the Liffey, and Frank the north, reconvening at lunchtime to compare notes. We left at first light.

The rain was still coming down, dripping from the fairy lights strung between the lampposts, from the tinsel and the Japanese lanterns, making the streets a carnival of jostling umbrellas. In spite of the hour and the weather, great throngs of people were pouring up and down the thoroughfare, laden with bags of Christmas shopping. The windows of the department stores glittered with kitchenware, electronic doodads, gorgeous mannequins swathed in opulent fabrics. The atmosphere was so dizzy and unreal that I began to get rather disorientated and to forget who I was looking for. I kept seeing Bel's face everywhere; I kept thinking that these people hurrying down the Royal Hibernian Way must be rushing to get ready for tonight, and picturing my dinner jacket waiting for me on the back of the bedroom door.

Still, by one o'clock, when I met Frank as arranged by the statue of that woman with the fish cart and the décolletage, I was able to tell him categorically between mouthfuls of my crepe that having comprehensively covered the southern metropolitan area I could confirm that Droyd was definitely not staying in the Conrad, the Westbury, or either of the Jurys Inns, and that he hadn't been in Tie Rack all morning. Frank turned a funny color when I told him this. I wondered if he was hungry, and I asked him if he wanted some of my crepe.

"Tie Rack?" he exclaimed. "Why the fuck would he be in Tie Rack?"

"I don't know," I said. "I thought he might spend the money on a tie." Tie Rack struck me as the sort of place someone like Droyd would buy his ties.

At this point the strain of it all became too much for Frank. He started going berserk. His speech does not bear repeating here: Suffice to say it was fuck this and fuck that, cunt this and cunt that, suddenly everybody was a cunt—but the general gist of it was that I must have been living with my eyes closed for the last three months if I thought any cunt in Bonetown ever had call to wear a tie except when they were up in court, or would ever in their entire lives get past the door of the Westbury, or had anything at all to do with any of that stuff; that Droyd had spent the money on heroin, that all there was to spend it on in Bonetown was heroin. "Heroin, Charlie!" he yelled. "Heroin! The whole fuckin place runs on heroin!"

I didn't reply. People were beginning to stare. He stopped waving his arms about and looked me full in the eye, quivering with anger. Then he took my crepe and threw it in the dustbin.

"Come on," he said, stomping off in the direction I had just come from.

The route we took can't have varied much, cartographically speaking, from my original exhaustive search earlier on, yet it seemed like another city, existing alongside the glossy one I knew. This city was composed of dead ends and blind alleys and back streets full of garbage bags, and had its own cast of inhabitants, who lived in a permanent stench of urine and decay and had to be nudged to life with a toe before one could question them as to Droyd's whereabouts. Sometimes they were too intoxicated to speak; sometimes they tried to make up stories in the hope of getting some change. Sometimes they didn't respond to the toe, and we would have to roll them over and squint at their grubby faces till we were sure they weren't him. The sheer volume of these wretched people was incredible. And as we made our way back down Grafton Street, I realized that they were here too, had been here all along, living their heroiny lives: slumped by cash machines, lurking in suspicious-looking groups around dustbins, making lunatic speeches to office workers who scurried by pretending not to hear, or simply ghosting wall-eyed through the crowd, with beakers from McDonald's and misspelled cardboard signs.

It was slow, painful work. As the day dragged on, and yet another pile of garbage bags disclosed yet another human form, it started to seem as if there could hardly be anyone left who hadn't, in some fashion, fallen through the cracks; and the city began to take on the appearance of a newspaper photo, when you look at it close up and at some unannounced point the image gives way, leaving you with a collection of unsignifying dots in a vast empty space; so much space that you forget there had ever been a picture at all. "He's not here," Frank said bleakly.

We trudged down the quays and caught the bus back to Bonetown. We sat on the top deck. Frank stared straight ahead, making the small-animal noises he made when he was picking his lottery numbers.

Laura had taken the day off work to stay in the apartment in case Droyd reappeared. But the only contact had been from the landlord. "I couldn't really understand what he was saying," she said. "But he was really angry. He kept going on about how no city slicker was going to make a laugh of him."

"Ah fuck," Frank said, collapsing into his armchair. "Ah fuck."

"If only I could get my deposit back from that stupid estate agent!" Laura said. "She won't give it back to me, Frank!"

"That's it," Frank said. "That's it. We're going to be fucked out."

I shook my head fatalistically. *"Plus ça change,"* I said, *"plus c'est la même chose."*

"Charlie, for once could you not talk French?"

"Of course," I said understandingly. "Of course."

There was clearly nothing more I could do here, and time was moving on. I excused myself quietly, leaving him sitting in his armchair with the vacant air of a man under hypnosis; I went to my bedroom and began to change into my evening wear. I had just run into the usual difficulties with my bow tie when there was a knock at the door. It was Frank, holding a length of wood.

"I know where he is," he said.

"You do?" I said, undoing the knot again. "I say, Laura, you couldn't give me hand with this, could you?"

"He's in Cousin Benny's," Frank said. "I know it. It's the only place left he could be."

"Ah yes, the infamous Cousin Benny." Laura pushed up my chin and adjusted the collar. "Well, give him my best if you see him, tell him not to worry about the—the mugging—"

356 · *Paul Murray*

"Charlie," he said, "I need you to come with me."

"Me?" I said.

"I can't go down there on me own. It's down the bad end. I need re-inforcements."

"Well, I'd love to help you, old man, but the fact is I can't, I mean I've got a dinner party to go to and Mother'll have conniptions if I'm late, I mean it's bad enough I'm not bringing a date . . . ," I tailed off feebly. Damn it, what did he want me there for? Didn't he know my track record in fisticuffs? How could there possibly be a bad end of Bonetown? Laura's cool green eyes looked into mine as she folded the tie over and back on itself.

"Hell," I said faintly.

"Right." He bounded purposefully out the door.

Laura tied the tie tight, and I felt something pressed into my hand. It was the stringless Dunlop tennis racket. "Good luck," she said and planted a kiss on my cheek.

We ran down the street with our jackets over our heads, dancing between ravines full of muddy water, over petrol rainbows and a moon-scape of scorched earth, until we came to a low concrete bunker. The steel shutters had been covered with many layers of graffiti; the pitted ground outside was littered with cigarette ends and broken needles. I had been here before.

"We're going in?" I said. "Into the Coachman?"

Frank turned to me and put his hand on my shoulder. "Charlie, I want you to just follow me and do exactly what I tell you, right?"

"Right," I squeaked. I gripped my tennis racket a little tighter. "Fine. Well. Once more unto the breach, eh, old chap . . ."

"And don't say anythin either, all right?"

We went through the door, which didn't immediately seem to make any difference to the volume of water falling on our heads. A dozen pairs of hostile eyes fell on us. I looked around dumbstruck. It was the sort of place Egon Ronay must have nightmares about: warped linoleum on the floor, too-bright lights, no furniture to speak of other than rickety stools and picnic tables marked Dept. of Forestry. At the bar were sitting six men with literally no foreheads, one of whom bared his teeth at us.

"All right?" Frank said. No one spoke. Casually, Frank passed his plank from one hand to the other, and we began to sidestep along the wall, as though skirting the rim of a volcano. From the bar, the eyes tracked us, but the men did not move. At last we reached a door marked "Gents" and pushed through. I heaved a sigh of relief and immediately wished I hadn't. There was an indescribably putrid stench that grew worse and worse as we walked along a narrow corridor and arrived at a steel door with a grille set at eye level. With an almighty clanging and booming, Frank started beating it with his plank, until the grille slid back to reveal a pair of moist black eyes.

"Yes?" a voice said.

"We're here for Droyd," Frank growled.

"Francy!" the voice said. "Is it yourself? Wait till I get these—"

The grille slid shut again, and a complex series of unlocking noises ensued. At last the door swung open. We were greeted by a thin man in his forties, with lank hair and bad skin and the general appearance of having recently taken part in an oil slick. Cigarettes of unequal length burned between the middle fingers of his right hand. "Long time no see, Francy." He nodded at me. "Who's this, your butler?"

"We're here for Droyd," Frank said before I could set him straight.

"Droyd, eh?" Cousin Benny stroked his chin thoughtfully. "Haven't seen him. Sorry."

"He ran off with three months' rent." Frank lifted the plank threateningly. "I know you been sellin him gear," he said.

Cousin Benny seemed to find this amusing. "Have you not heard?" he said. "Droyd's gone straight. Clean as a whistle." He shook his head and sighed. "No loyalty, these kids. Take the best years of your life, then they just chuck you aside . . ."

With a gurgle of anger, Frank pushed past him; I raised an eyebrow in apology and followed him in.

The first thing that struck one about the room was the smell: a moldering collection of various species of decay—food, bodily waste, rotting brickwork. There was no furniture or carpeting, just mattresses, mildewed mattresses strewn everywhere. It was so dark that it took a moment to make out the comatose forms on top of them, and another to see that most of these were children. There were fifteen or twenty of them, lying down or propped in corners, with drooping eye-lids and nodding heads, as if they were coming home tired out after a school trip. Many of them I recognized from throwing fireworks at me in the street, and with a sick feeling I glanced from mattress to mat-tress until I arrived at the two moonfaced trolley children, slumped with hands clasped and a blackened ampoule at their feet.

Cousin Benny had closed the door. He stood beside it, half-hidden in the sepulchral light, exhaling a huge cloud of smoke into the pall that hung over the sleepers. Everything was perfectly still; it was like some unholy parody of peace. I realized my hands were trembling and folded them behind my back. Then there was a gasp. Frank, who had waded out into the middle of the sea of bodies, darted over to the far wall. He bent down and rose again with a tracksuited form lying limply in his arms. It was Droyd, deep in a swoon, and looking, quite unexpectedly, like something out of a Pre-Raphaelite painting. "Fuck off," he mur-mured drowsily. "Fuck off."

When it was clear that he couldn't be woken, Frank slung him over his shoulder. Puffing, he turned to Cousin Benny in the corner. "I'm takin him, Benny," he said. "I'm takin him."

"Go ahead," Cousin Benny said. The twin plumes of smoke twirled up like incantations from his fingers. "He'll be back."

"Don't get in me way." Frank took the first steps toward a peeling door in the corner. "Watch him, Charlie." Swallowing, I brandished the tennis racket.

Cousin Benny smiled mockingly. "What's he goin to do, blackball me from his club?"

But as Frank stumbled over to the door, he withdrew to a safe dis-tance. "Take him," he called after us. "He'll be back. He's only a cunt. You're all only cunts. He'll try and clean up, and then somethin'll hap-pen and he won't be able to hack it, and he'll be back here with the money—"

I slammed the door shut behind me; and then, mercifully, we were back on the street. Frank laid Droyd down on the concrete, and we sucked in cold, wet air as if it were manna from heaven.

I noticed my right cuff link had come loose. I tried to fix it, but my hands were still shaking too much. It was damned annoying. My dinner jacket was by now completely soaked as well. I leaned against the wall and took deep breaths and waited for the shaking to stop. Finally it abated sufficiently for me to make the necessary adjustment. Then I clapped my hands together. "Right," I said.

Frank had sunk onto his haunches beside Droyd and was staring at his feet with an air of utter dejection.

"Not much of an afternoon," I said, "but all's well that ends well, I suppose."

Nobody said anything.

"That is, all's well that ends well," I repeated carefully.

"Charlie, what are we goin to do?" Frank said.

"Well, I'd better get a move on to that dinner," I said. "I'd ask you along only it's black tie, you see, and—"

"No, about the *money*, Charlie, about the fuckin rent."

"Oh, I don't know," I said vaguely. "Something'll turn up, I imagine."

Frank did not appear to derive much succour from this. A wave of impatience rose up through me. Couldn't he understand I had problems of my own? Couldn't he stop thinking about money for five minutes?

"Well maybe you've got this landlord character all wrong," I said. "Maybe if you just explain it to him, he'll understand. Explain that, you know, Droyd stole the money to spend on drugs and that you're very sorry but you'll get it to him as soon as you can. Didn't you say he was an ex-policeman? An ex-policeman's going to understand about these things, isn't he?"

Frank laughed hollowly for about five minutes. I simmered and kicked my heels and twirled the Dunlop tennis racket in my hand. Suddenly Frank reached up and grabbed it. "Charlie, you can get us some money can't you?"

"Me?" I said incredulously. "Where am I supposed to get you money?"

He rose to his feet and stood over me. "Charlie," he said, "this is no time to be a scabby bastard."

"I'm not being any kind of a bastard. I don't *have* any money," I said, backing away.

"But you have to," he insisted mechanically, advancing on me, swinging his tree-trunk arms. "You're from fuckin Killiney, you've all got loads of money—"

"Damn it, can't you think for just two seconds?" I shouted at him. "If I had any money at all do you think I'd be living here? In a slum? Do you think I'd be spending my day traipsing around looking at heroin addicts, or hauling people out of opium dens? I was supposed to be moving in with air hostesses! Air hostesses, Frank! From *Sweden*! I mean, did it ever once occur to you that this might not be my ideal living situation, trapped in a ghetto with a scrap merchant and a juvenile delinquent?"

For a moment, I was sure he was going to hit me. But he didn't. Instead his face seemed to sort of *crumple*; and covering it with his hands, he sank back down to the ground.

A small voice piped up; the rain had woken Droyd. "I'm sorry, Frankie," he said in slurred, slow-motion words, tugging Frank's elbow. "It's all about the music now, I swear."

"That's what you said the last time, you geebag," Frank said, grinding his teeth.

"This time I mean it," Droyd pronounced. Rain spilled down his lolling forehead. "I swear. Don't worry, Frankie, we'll get out of this fuckin kip. We'll go to Ibiza, an' we'll sit on the beach all day drinkin cans . . . an' all the birds'll be after us, cos we're the men . . ."

"Just shut up, you cunt. Can't you see I've fuckin had it with you, you fuckin juvenile delinquent." Frank sank his head in his hands and buried it between his knees. "We're fucked," he sobbed. "We're fucked."

I put my hands in my pockets and shuffled uncomfortably. Away to the east, somewhere beyond the power lines, the first guests would be arriving for dinner. If I left now I could still make the starters. Tomorrow, perhaps Frank and I could sit down together and figure out a plan; there was no point dallying any longer, getting into Mother's bad books on top of everything else.

I was just turning to say pip-pip and set off across the waste ground when suddenly I had a premonition. Suddenly, vividly, I could see myself, sitting at the dinner table and relating today's adventures to Bel. I was presenting it as a kind of a picaresque yarn about the difficulties I had had getting here tonight. But she didn't appear to be seeing the funny side; instead she was getting angry and launching into me as I tried to enjoy my duck terrine. *Frank puts a roof over your head,* she was saying, *and what do you do for him in return? You let Amaurot slip through your fingers, and now you're going to let them take Apt. C, Sands Villas as well?*

I glanced down. Droyd had fallen back asleep with his head on Frank's shoulder. *Look,* I told the premonition Bel, *Mother said eight sharp.* She had been very clear on that point, and Lord knows she was close enough to disinheriting me as it was. *And furthermore, what about you?* I said, pointing to the premonitory suitcases waiting in the hallway beneath the glass frieze. *I don't see what you're getting so high and mighty about, when you're traipsing off to Yalta. When do you think Frank and Droyd will get to go somewhere like Yalta? Never, that's when. They'll probably never get out of this godforsaken place.*

But none of this seemed to matter. She just looked at me in that way she had, and I looked down guiltily at my imaginary duck terrine.

And then I had an idea.

ADMITTEDLY IT DIDN'T seem like much of an idea at first, particularly when we turned out our pockets and found we had only four pounds seventy-eight in change (Frank's) and one unusually colored pebble from Killiney Beach (mine) by way of collateral. But after we had taken Droyd back to the flat and put him to bed in Frank's room and barricaded the door with the sofa and the tallboy and a set of dumbbells that kept falling off the bar and told Laura not to let him out no matter what, I brought Frank outside to the van to discuss it. He was understandably shaken by events, and before he'd listen to anything he insisted on smoking some of his hashish to calm him down. As I was feeling rather in need of calming down myself, and I hadn't any baccy, I took some of it too and put it in my pipe. Then, when we were both calmer, I outlined my plan.

"The best way to look at it," I said, "is that basically we have nothing left to lose. In a way that's a sort of an advantage, do you see? It means we can take bigger risks, because, I mean, how much worse can things possibly get?"

"I don't know, Charlie," he said doubtfully. "I just don't know."

"I'm good at it," I said. "Honestly. It's probably the one thing in the world I'm actually good at."

Frank shook his head, sending scurrying little puffs of redolent smoke.

"You'll just have to trust me," I said, and with a small but expressive moan, he handed over his last four pounds seventy-eight.

And even as we approached in the van, it was apparent that this was a fated night. The rain was falling vertically and bouncing off the glass roof, and the floodlights shining through it gave the dog track, as we neared it, a kind of a halo, so that it seemed to glow, like a magical city, as if everything that had happened in our lives were no more than a yellow-brick road bringing us here. Drawing up in the van in a humble and trepidatious silence, I had the most curious sense that things had come loose from their everyday fixtures. Colors seemed brighter, sounds deeper, starker; thoughts and memories, past and future, bled out of their confines into the air. The Roma women with gold teeth selling magazines in the car park, the inhuman voice announcing the next race over the loudspeaker—everything seemed to carry a secret marker; everything took on the glaze of destiny.

I managed to persuade Frank to stay up in the bar this time. A little table with two chairs waited for us right beside the window. Outside, the stands were full and the atmosphere electric—literally, as over the stadium thunderclouds swirled and massed. I ordered a Tom Collins and set to work.

2003 Masterpiece Ivor Biggun **Trouble in Paradise 5/1**
2018 Twink's Mother Dunroamin **The Great Pretender 8/3 on**
2040 Flashdance My Other Dog's A Mercedes **Liberty Bell evens**

Picking the winners did not require much divination on my part. If there were, as seemed increasingly to be the case, unearthly forces at work that night, they were making little effort to disguise themselves.

Instead they seemed to be using the dog meet to single me out and pillory me for my recent errors in judgment. Oh Brother!; Good-Time Charlie; I'm Off—in every race there was a barely concealed indictment, meant solely for me; and every indictment cruised infallibly to victory. The money poured in thick and fast, and after an hour and a quarter of it my nerves were in shreds. Needless to say, this was completely lost on Frank.

"All right, this next one"—he scanned the racing sheet—"looks like a straight fight between Brits Out and . . . You Tore Me Down." And he looked up. "What'd you think, Charlie, is it Brits Out or—?"

"You Tore Me Down, damn it!" I exclaimed miserably. "You Tore Me Down, what else could it possibly be? This whole program has been nothing but a—but a *witch hunt* . . ." rubbing my fists in my eyes.

"You all right, Charlie?"

"Of course I'm not all right, I mean a fellow makes one mistake and instead of letting him make amends everybody just wants to *gloat* and point the finger. What about Harry, why does he get off scot-free? Why don't they name a few dogs after him?"

"Charlie, I think all that ganja's makin you a bit paranoid."

"Don't be absurd." I tugged at my collar. "Damn it, why is it so hot in here? Don't you find it oppressively hot? I say, get me a Manhattan, will you?"

"You prob'ly shouldn't be drinkin so much on top of it either, Charlie."

"Don't touch that, I'm perfectly fine, anyway it's helping me concentrate, I said *don't touch it*—"

Frank shrugged and put his pencil in his mouth and looked through the next race as I snapped my fingers for the lounge girl. "Right . . . How's Your Billabong eight to one . . . McGurks Mutual Finance Limited five to one . . . Oh wait, Shit Creek nine to two on favorite. Shit Creek, ha ha . . ."

You Tore Me Down thundered home, and so did Shit Creek. Frank whooped and went to collect our winnings. I watched the clock over the bar. They would be finishing their soup by now. Would Bel be wondering where I was? Or would she be glad I wasn't there?

" 'Member the last time we were here, Charlie?" Frank sat down cheerfully with another wad of bills. "With Bel, that was a good laugh, wasn't it?"

"Mmm."

"It was that time she was tryin to get into that play," he reminisced. " 'Member? Fuck's sake. Mad about that fuckin play she was. I thought she'd top herself when they told her she couldn't be in it, she was that into it." He piled the money into a little stack and sat back in his chair with his arms flung expansively over the back.

"Damn Chekhov," I muttered.

"Dunno *why*, like. All it is is these Russians goin on about their fuckin orchard and tryin to ride each other. Beats me why she'd be so mad into it. Do you know why she was so mad into it, Charlie?"

"She was in it in school," I mumbled into my Manhattan. "She forgot her lines."

"Ah yeah, I wouldn't be surprised. Cos like, maybe in the olden days it was good, like before they had special effects and stuff. But *now*, I mean, it's just fuckin *borin*. Like you don't even *see* the fuckin cherry orchard. No, wasn't my type of thing at all . . ."

I tuned him out, watched the lightning play along the rooftop. The family of aristocrats returning to their old house . . . It was coming back to me, it's about to be sold off, but they don't do anything about it. I remember becoming quite fond of them; they were a lazy, amiable bunch, quite gay in spite of everything—that's the spirit, I remember thinking, sunny side up . . .

"All she ever talked about was that play," Frank recalled. "She even made me learn this speech to help her, that was like a whole fuckin page long. What was it it went like?"

It was the spring: Father hadn't been around, so Mother had dragged me along instead; we sat on stiff-backed chairs in the freezing auditorium, a dozen expensive perfumes intermingling over deeper, older school smells of Christmas tests, double gym, morning assembly, and "All Things Bright and Beautiful." Giddy children whispered, parents clutched mimeographed programs; Mother sat erect on my left, mouthing the words with Bel whenever she came on—she played an old maid, always fretting and nagging and waiting to be romanced by another girl in a hairnet with a false mustache on—

"Think, Anya!" Frank bellowed, making me jump in my seat. "Your grandfather your great-grandfather and all your forebears were serf owners that owned livin souls! Don't you see human beins gazin at you from every leaf and tree trunk, don't you hear voices—"

And then she forgot her lines. How had she forgotten them? When for the last two weeks she'd been doing nothing but wandering around the house with a towel over her head, mumbling away incessantly to herself like Franny Glass? And she had breezed through the first half with no trouble at all. Yet here she was center stage, with her mouth half open and her arms held out like a men's room attendant waiting for someone to hand them a towel and clearly no idea how to proceed—

"Don't you see human beins gazin at you from every cherry tree in your orchard?"

It didn't take long for the audience to cotton on, and for giggles and snickers to begin to escape the smaller members; I squirmed in my seat and felt my face go hot and wished I had the courage to just run up onstage and deus ex machina pull her out of their wretched play and disappear with her into the night. Someone, a teacher presumably, hissed the line from the wings, but she didn't seem to hear; she stayed frozen to the spot, like a deer caught in headlights. The actors tried to continue the scene around her, but it was impossible, ludicrous—and people were enjoying the spectacle now, they guffawed heartily as the teacher hissed out the line again, and the room filled with derisory applause as the curtain hastened down, and Mother's hands rested perfectly still and white on her purse—

"Yet it's perfectly clear that, to live in the present," Frank went on, "we must first at-atone for our past and be finished with it—"

"Give it a rest," I murmured, "there's a good fellow."

She had been furious afterward, Mother, I mean, even though the play had restarted five minutes later and Bel, though jittery, had managed to get to the end without any further hiccups, which I thought was a credit to her, and anyway surely these things were just an occupational hazard—there was no reason for Mother to say what she'd said,

and if you asked me it was no coincidence that it was the very next day
that Bel had got sick and the doctor had had to come—

"—and we can only atone for it by suffering—"

Because that trouble before the play, the shouting and the broken
crockery, that had been enough to put anybody off, and when Father
didn't come home we had driven to the school in a hissing white-hot
silence; but that's how it had all started, the sickness and the doctors
and then Father too, then two years of white coats and not sleeping and
drugs with unintelligible names and one's jaw hurting from clenching
one's teeth all the time—that's when it all began, at that infernal play,
why did she have to keep circling back to it, why couldn't she just forget it?

"—by suffering by extraordinary unceasing exer-exertion—"

"Damn it—"

"Forward, friends! Don't fall behind!"

"That's *enough*!" My hand came down so hard that the ashtray
skipped right off the table and exploded on the floor.

"Janey, Charlie, I was only havin a laugh."

"Sorry," I said curtly, knocking back my drink.

"Seriously, you feelin okay, Charlie?"

"No," I said. How could they just let her go, without saying anything? How could they pretend nothing was wrong, let it all happen
again, just so they could get her out of the way?

"You prob'ly just need a bit of food," Frank said. He turned to the
girl knelt sweeping up the shards of the ashtray and asked her to bring
over ten packs of peanuts.

I exhaled jaggedly. I felt small and spent; I didn't want to think
about it anymore. "How much money does this fellow want anyway?" I
said, gesturing at the heap of notes. Frank did some mental calcula-
tions, then started scribbling on a beer mat. It would take us all night at
this rate, I thought with a sinking heart; and by then she would be gone,
gone into the snowy wastes.

The mechanical voice announced the next race. I went to the bar
and ordered a Guinness for Frank and a dry martini for myself, with a
shot of Calvados while I was waiting. Outside the sky had cleared enough
to make room for a brace of stars, which swam about in a comforting

way. I returned to the table to find Frank wearing an odd expression. "Look," he whispered.

His arithmetic had carried him off the beer mat and onto a left-behind newspaper, and he was pointing to a line in one corner: something about An Evening of Long Goodbyes, which sounded vaguely familiar.

"It's that dog what Bel bet on the last time," he said. "Remember the one that bit that young lad?"

"Oh," I said. "So it is. I thought I recognized the name."

"Look at the odds, Charlie," he whispered. "They're astromonomical."

"Hardly surprising, after that last farrago. I'm amazed they're still letting it race."

"But think, right, if we put everything we have on it, we'd have enough for the rent, and the electricity, and the gas, and . . ."

"Yes, but you're forgetting, it wouldn't win, you see, that's why the odds are—"

"But if we put down say two hundred blips, then—"

"But it *wouldn't win*, damn it. If it were the only dog running it wouldn't win. That dog's a *born loser*, can't you understand that?"

With a hurt look, Frank retreated to his beer mats. I sat back splenetically with the form. An Evening of Long Goodbyes, indeed. Put all our money on that? After what happened last time? Funny I hadn't noticed it earlier, though . . . With a diversionary cough, I reached for the left-behind newspaper. Now this really was queer. Unless it was a misprint, it appeared that the bookmakers were giving outlandishly long odds not just against proven reprobates like An Evening of Long Goodbyes but against all of the dogs running in the 2130, bar one. This dog, one Celtic Tiger, was favorite by such a distance that a return on his victory would be minuscule; but his previous times seemed unusually slow.

The prudent thing would be to treat it as a low-risk investment: Bet on Celtic Tiger and take the minimal return. And yet— I looked over my shoulder around the bar: Business appeared to be proceeding as usual—and yet what if we *had* stumbled across some kind of gambling anomaly? What if there really *were* something in the air tonight? What if that something—or someone—were trying to reach us, help us, via the unconventional vehicle of An Evening of Long Goodbyes?

"What are you thinking, Charlie?"

I ran my eyes over and over the tiny text. But suddenly my gambler's intuition had deserted me. I had no idea what to do.

I took a deep breath. The prudent thing: Generally—although it might at times seem otherwise—I had always done what was prudent. I had clung to things—to people, beliefs, certain modes of living. I had tried to hold them still, I had tried to shore them up against the vicissitudes of fate. Where had it got me? Everything I had tried to hold had escaped me. Perhaps the secret was to do the opposite: Perhaps to keep the things one loved one had to gamble them; one had to give all the heart, live in the aleatory moment . . . I reached for the pencil and filled out the betting slip.

It was obvious as soon as the dogs were led out onto the field that we had made a terrible mistake. Immediately the stadium erupted. Chants rose up, flags were waved, ne'er-do-wells linked arms and jigged, all for the benefit of Celtic Tiger, a.k.a., we soon learned, The Bookie's Despair.

"Bollocks," said Frank.

It took two men to squeeze Celtic Tiger into its trap. It must have weighed a hundred pounds, consisting primarily of haunches and gnashing fangs; whatever biological connection it had to the greyhound family, it must have been pretty tenuous. The other dogs, who had evidently encountered it before, looked singularly depressed—apart from An Evening of Long Goodbyes, that is, who was gazing off hopefully at the concession stand. What really struck one was its air of unchecked malevolence. I had never experienced evil of such magnitude at such close proximity, apart from lunches with Mr. Appleseed. Yet in spite of this, Celtic Tiger seemed to inspire an almost religious fervor. The punters looked to it with the worshipful, desperate love of a parched country for the annual rains. "God bless you, Celtic Tiger," said a worn man next to us at the window, his weathered cheeks wet with tears. I realized that for these people, Celtic Tiger must be one of the few certainties in life: aside from death, of course, and nurses. The starter's gun sounded and the rabbit scooted away.

We cheered on An Evening of Long Goodbyes as best we could, but I doubted he could have heard us. Within seconds, Celtic Tiger was out on its own, prancing along taking the salutes of the crowd, while the other dogs remained behind at a respectful distance. It was like some kind of canine Nuremberg rally.

"This is a fiasco!" I cried. "Those other dogs aren't even trying! What's the point having a race if they're too afraid to overtake him?"

Just as I said it, a ripple of consternation ran through the stands. All of a sudden one of the dogs had broken away from the pack and was quickly making up ground—which wasn't hard, considering Celtic Tiger had all the zip of a Panzer tank.

"That's a brave dog," one of the punters next to us said grudgingly.

"It's not so much it's brave," his companion said. "It's more like it's forgotten what it's supposed to be doing."

"It's him!" Frank whispered to me.

I quickly apprehended what had happened. A chap in the front row of the far stand had unwrapped a sandwich, and An Evening of Long Goodbyes had caught sight of it. The spectators could boo and curse him all they wanted now. I knew that all he was thinking about was that sandwich, and he would not be diverted, not by them, nor by the finishing line which loomed up ahead, nor by those intimidating looks the larger dog was giving him as he drew up alongside it—

"That's it!" I pounded encouragingly on the glass, attracting glowers from the punters around me. "That's the stuff!"

—and abandoning all pretense of sportsmanship, Celtic Tiger burst its muzzle as if it were paper and fastened its jaws around its rival's throat.

"What!" howled Frank. "Referee!"

It was carnage. At first, some of the more bloodthirsty punters cheered it on, but quickly even they turned pale and went quiet, and the whole stadium was silent except for the yelps of An Evening of Long Goodbyes and the murderous snarls, snaps, and tearing noises produced by Celtic Tiger. "Why doesn't somebody *do* something?" I appealed. But no one did anything. Celtic Tiger wasn't even running anymore, it was being dragged by the smaller dog, who struggled gamely on toward his sandwich even with Celtic Tiger latched around his neck.

The other dogs had backed up into a small, uncertain huddle some distance down the track; some lay down or rolled over, their dolorous baying segueing into the groans of Frank and the small minority of unwise men who had bet against the favorite—as An Evening of Long Goodbyes, drenched in blood, froth dripping from his mouth, uttered a long-drawn-out moan and toppled over on his side.

The silence seemed to deepen; the punters buried themselves guiltily in their pints. I couldn't take any more. I staggered away to the bar, squeezed in beside a silver-haired gent, and with the small sum of money that was now all we had left, ordered myself a triple whiskey. So much for destiny, I thought bitterly; so much for giving all the heart. The world had made suckers of us again. Cousin Benny's words kept circling through my head: we were cunts, we would always be cunts.

A gasp went up at the window for some fresh outrage on the track. I took a slug from the glass without looking round, wincing pleasurably at the sour, familiar kick. To hell with the damned race. I had enough whiskey here to get stinking drunk. At least when I was drunk I knew where I stood, and I didn't need anybody's directions to get there. To hell with Frank, and the lousy dinner party; to hell with Bel too. Let her leave if she wanted to leave, let her write off the one person who actually cared about her, who didn't think of her as an eternal outpatient with impossible dreams . . . The punters roared in anguish.

"Sounds like someone's taking a beating," the silver-haired gent beside me remarked.

"Someone's always taking a beating," I muttered without looking up.

"I suppose that's true," the gent agreed.

I turned around. The smoke was making it hard to see, and the room kept spinning, but when I squinted I could make out a well-cut if somewhat *vieux jeu* worsted suit and a pair of wire-frame spectacles. I wondered what he was doing here with this rabble. He motioned the bargirl to refill our glasses and, as if in answer to my question, said, "Still, one has to take one's chances, doesn't one?"

"I don't see why," I said, clinking my ice cubes.

"Come on, Charles," he said with a chuckle. "You know why."

The room seemed to lurch, and a sweltering buzz rose up from my toes to engulf me. At that moment the crowd roared again, and the punters at the bar rushed over to the window. I found myself thrown forward; standing on tiptoes, I peered blearily over the mass of heads.

It appeared that Celtic Tiger, having vanquished his foe, had not gone on and finished the race like a sensible dog but instead had turned his attentions on the dogs grouped miserably together a hundred yards behind.

"For fuck's sake!" the crowd were crying, clutching their heads as the cowardly dogs turned tail and fled, with Celtic Tiger now in hot pursuit. "The other way, you prick! Run the other way!"

"Too much PCP," a whiskery geezer with defeated eyes observed beside me.

But that was not all. At the other end of the track—far away from where the stewards were trying to fend off Celtic Tiger with a steel pole—An Evening of Long Goodbyes was beginning to stir. At first no one noticed—everyone was too busy trying to convince the renegade favorite to rejoin the race—but then a lone voice cried out, "Hey! That thick dog's not dead yet!"

There was a pause and then a collective rustling, as people checked the number in the program, and then, sporadically, from one or two points in the crowd, the shouts came: "An Evening of Long Goodbyes! An Evening of Long Goodbyes!"

The dog's tail thumped once, twice against the ground.

Seeing this, more voices joined in. The shouts grew louder. "An Evening of Long Goodbyes! An Evening of Long Goodbyes!"

And slowly, painfully slowly, the dog picked himself up, until, on legs as frail and ungainly as a newborn calf's, rain pasting his fur to his bony head, he stood there blinking at us in wonderment.

The clamor was deafening. Men shouted and pummeled the glass and stamped their feet. "That's it!" they bellowed. "Go on, you cunt! Go on, Goodbyes!" Everyone was of one voice, as if the only reason any of us were there was to cheer on this chewed and rather mangy-looking dog, which seemed to feed on these waves of furious noise and energy and—as the cheering grew to a roar, as Celtic Tiger was ushered into a cage by two men with cattle prods—now wagged his tail and began to trot toward the finishing line.

"Sprezzatura," a voice in my ear said, and I looked round to see, in the midst of the churning punters and the pillars of smoke, a familiar gray emanation. "What?" I said faintly. He smiled hermetically and pointed out the window; turning, I saw the rainy stadium filled with men in top hats and tails, with black dickey bows and carnations in their buttonholes, cheering on the dog they'd bet against as the voice behind me mused, "What was it Oscar used to say? *In a good democracy, every man should be an aristocrat.*"

I spun round—there was so much I wanted to ask him, there were so many things I didn't understand. "Wait!" I cried. "Come back!" But he was already halfway to the door, hoisting onto his head, as he melted into the throng, what appeared to be a giant sombrero . . . And now, after a series of dramatic collapses, An Evening of Long Goodbyes finally hauled his carcass over the line, and the place went crazy. It was as if we had just won a war. People whooped and sang; they tore up their losing stubs and threw them in the air like confetti. Frank appeared, laughing, and caught me in a bear hug. "We done it, Charlie!" he exclaimed. "We done it!"

Someone must have overheard him, because before I could correct his grammar, we were picked up and borne along on a sea of strangers' hands to the betting hatch, where with the crowd amassed behind us, the clerk hastily agreed that it would be poor form to declare the race forfeit, and paid out our winnings on the spot. Everybody in the bar applauded; Frank asked if anybody wanted a drink, and it turned out that most people did; and everything was so breathless and euphoric that it took me a while to pinpoint that irritating bleeping noise. Finally I realized it was Bel's phone. I had brought it along to give back to her tonight. It appeared to be having some kind of an episode. I pressed some buttons to make it stop and it started talking to me—a girl's voice, someone looking for Bel.

"She's not here," I shouted, putting a finger in one ear. "She's at home."

"I can't get through to her at home," the girl said.

"They're having a dinner thing," I said.

"Oh. Well, can you pass on a message?" The girl had a husky, rasping voice, as if she made a regular thing of smoking too many cigarettes. "Will you tell her Jessica wants her to—"

"Wait, you're Jessica?" I interjected.

"Why, does my fame precede me?"

"It most certainly does," I averred. "I'd like to know what you mean, running off with my sister."

"I wasn't aware I was running off with anyone," the girl said. "Who is this, anyway?"

"It's Charles," I said.

"Oh," she said. "Bel told me about you," she added, rather pointedly.

"That's neither here nor there," I said. "The fact is, Bel is clearly not fit for— What did you mean by that last remark? What did she say about me?"

"All *sorts* of things," Jessica said rather light-headedly, as if she had never until now believed they could be true.

"Well, be that as it may," I muttered uncomfortably. "The thing about Bel is—"

"Aren't *you* going to this dinner?" she interrupted. "Or have you been blacklisted?"

"Yes, I am going," I snapped. "Look, just give me your damned message, will you?"

"Certainly," she said primly. She told me that their flight was at seven, so would Bel get a taxi for four, and pick her up on the way? I said I would pass this on; there was a pause, and just as I was about to look for the off button, the voice came again: "Charles?"

"Yes?"

"I don't think Bel *means* those things she says about you, you know."

"Mmm," I said ambiguously.

"And Charles?"

"What?"

"I promise I'll take good care of her in Russia."

"Oh." I was rather touched. Possibly she was making fun of me, but somehow I didn't think so; there was a warmth in her voice that was really quite appealing. "Well, thank you."

"You'd better get to your dinner before everyone's gone to bed," she said.

"Yes," I said; and then, "You know, when you get back perhaps we ought to go for a drink or something. I've written a play and there's a part you might be interested in . . ."

She laughed, and said she'd see. "But our paths will cross again, Charles, somehow I'm sure of that . . ."

I tucked the phone away, beaming to myself. That old Hythloday magic! I was back in business!

It was now quite late. I went to find Frank and told him I was getting a taxi back to Amaurot. However he insisted on driving me over himself. This struck me as a damned decent gesture, and as we left I had another of my ideas: "You know, why don't— Ow!"

"You all right, Charlie?"

"Obviously I'm not all right, who put all those stairs there?"

"I think they were there on the way in too."

"Yes, you're probably right," I admitted. "I wish . . . I wish they hadn't opened that second bottle of champagne, might have gone to my head a little . . ." He hoisted me up off the tarmac and closer to a ring of prettily spinning cartoon stars. "B' what I was saying was, why don't you come along to dinner too? I mean, you're not in black tie, but . . ."

"Van's over here, Charlie."

"But don' you worry about that." I dismissed these concerns with a wave of the hand; I was feeling magnanimous and iconoclastic, and suddenly no obstacle seemed insurmountable. "I'll explain about all that. Mother's an absolute, an absolute pussycat if you know how to handle her—and anyway, I'll just tell her that you're my *guest*, and a—a damn fine fellow . . ."

"Thanks very much, Charlie."

"Not at all, not at all—I say, look at that. Someone's left behind their astrakhan jacket."

The van's headlights had illuminated an especially desolate section of the car park, where in a patch of weeds lay a discarded heap of clothing. It appeared to be emitting sounds of distress. I couldn't remember if jackets typically did this or not.

"Just a second—" I got out and weaved my way over the unsteady gravel to the heap.

"What is it?" Frank called from the van.

"Hmm . . ." The astrakhan jacket looked up at me with a pair of hopeful brown eyes. A long pink tongue tentatively licked my hand. "It seems to be An Evening of Long Goodbyes."

"They must have dumped it," Frank said, coming over.

"*Dumped* it? Don't be absurd. How could they have dumped it? Why, that dog's a hero—a hero!"

"Don't think it's goin to win many more races, though, Charlie."

He was right. The dog's flanks were streaked with blood. One of his legs was badly chewed, and his eyes and snout bore the gouge marks of Celtic Tiger's teeth. He laid his head back on the ground, panting rapidly.

"But that's— I mean to say, of all the . . ." I scratched the back of my neck and lapsed into a confounded silence. "What are we going to do? I mean we can't just leave it here."

"Ah Jay, Charlie, I thought we were in a hurry."

I held up a finger for silence. My mind was clamoring at me to make a connection: something to do with the greyhound and the reflection of the moon in this long, kidney-shaped puddle—

"Aha!" I fumbled about in my pocket until I'd found what I was looking for: the pale disk of metal Bel had become so enamored of; now I knew what it was.

"What is it?"

"It's a dog tag, old sport."

"What, like a soldier has?"

"No, like a dog has." It was the same one Bel had bought with her pocket money years and years ago, along with a red-leather collar and leash. It had been meant for the spaniel we hadn't been let keep, the one she'd worried over so; she'd been going to get its name engraved on it, if we'd ever got so far as to give it a name. Someone must have unearthed it in the attic.

"What would Bel be doin carryin that around, though, Charlie?"

"Shh," I said, blinking back the haze of alcohol that ringed my brain, trying to puzzle it out. I didn't know why Bel was carrying it around. It had to mean something. Was it that she'd never got over losing that spaniel? Had she been pining for it all this time? Or was it something more complicated? Did it have something to do with Mother? Or me? I frowned, swaying on the tarmac. Bel's understanding of the world was byzantine at the best of times, and often there were complex movements involved, such as things being signs, or standing for other things that to a normal person they had obviously nothing to do with. But the fact was that here was a dog being offered to us on a plate: not a spaniel, admittedly, and possibly requiring some minor surgery—still, given the fateful quality of the night so far, it seemed remiss simply to ignore it.

"Charlie—ah, Charlie, what're you doin?"

There was blatantly not time to explain this to Frank.

"Ah here, you're not puttin that wet thing in my fuckin van—"

"Talisman," I huffed, "lucky—symbolical—might bite Harry—"

"Bark!" barked An Evening of Long Goodbyes.

"Bark, that's right, good boy, we're going for a ride in Frank's van, aren't we? Yes we are!"

"For fuck's sake"—as he unlocked the loading doors and I stowed the dog in the back, where he curled up pacifically in a nest of altar cloths and priests' vestments Frank had taken from a church that was being turned into a shoe shop. "Charlie, are you thinkin if you give her a dog Bel'll forgive you for boffin that one-legged bird?"

"I wish you'd stop saying I *boffed* her, it really is a most disagreeable turn of phrase."

"Well, for ridin her then."

I thought about it. "Yes," I said. I studied the dog through the doors. He panted amicably at us. "Although," as Frank closed the doors up, "you know, An Evening of Long Goodbyes is such a cumbersome name. We ought to give him a new one."

"Yeah, like I was thinkin maybe that's why it ran so slow, cos like it was draggin round all them words after it."

"Yes, quite, anyway, what I'm thinking is—Ozymandias."

"Oz-y-mandias?"

"You know, the poem. Ozymandias, king of kings, look on my works, ye mighty, something something, I forget the rest—has a kind of a grandeur to it, don't you think? Kind of a *presence*?"

"I dunno, Charlie, it sounds a bit gay."

"A bit *gay*?"

"A bit, yeah."

"Well what do you suggest?"

"How about Paul?"

"Paul? You can't call a dog Paul. Why would you want to call it Paul?"

"I had a mate once called Paul."

"So did I," I remembered; and we both reflected for a moment. "I suppose he does have a sort of a paulish quality. Well, maybe we should leave it for the time being. Bel might have her own ideas."

We got into the van. Frank stowed our winnings in the glove compartment and started the engine. "Funny to think she'll be leavin, though, isn't it, Charlie?"

"Oh, I don't know," I said. "I think maybe she'll be all right." For as the city began to unreel through the window, and with all that money in the glove compartment, it felt like there was time still to set things to rights, to turn the clock back on old hurts. The night seemed limitless and replete with possibilities; everything glistened with water as if it had just come into being. "Well who's this?" as a long brown nose poked between the seats and smiled doggishly at us.

"Bark!" he said, as we hit the motorway and picked up speed.

"What's he sayin, Charlie?"

"He's saying, 'Forward, friends! Don't fall behind!'"

"Bark!"

"That's right, old chap," I laughed, rubbing his chin. "That's right—"

CHAPTER FIFTEEN

All the excitement must have overtired me, because I nodded off on the way. I was having the strangest dream, in which we were all buried in a terrible avalanche; but then I woke up to find we had stopped outside the old house, and that the avalanche was nothing more than the rumbling of Frank's stomach.

I don't know who Mother was expecting at that late hour, but she seemed surprised to answer the door and find me there; in fact she turned quite pale, and her glass slipped out of her hand, sending sherry all over the floor.

"I'm perfectly all right, leave it *be*, Charles," she said, recovering herself. "I wasn't expecting any more guests, that's all. Didn't I tell you eight sharp? And honestly, is that what passes for a clean shirt with you these days?"

I began to explain about the rent and the race, but she cut me off. "Charles," she said, peering downward, "there appears to be something dripping on my foot."

"That's what I'm trying to tell you—Mother, I'd like to introduce the newest member of the, the gang—An Evening of Long Goodbyes."

"You're not planning to bring it inside, I hope."

"Well, yes, it's a sort of a bon voyage gift for Bel, you see—"

"Charles, if you think I'm going to let you take in some flea-ridden stray to die on my parquet when there are guests in the house . . ."

"It's not going to *die*. It's just had a couple of knocks, that's all. Give it some food and it'll be right as rain—won't you, old fellow?"

Mother sighed heavily and straightened up. Muffled sounds of merriment drifted past her from inside. "Where's Patsy?" she said. Raising her lorgnette, she stared into the shadows, then turned back to me. "Charles," she said sotto voce, "that is not Patsy Olé."

"No, Mother, it's Frank, you remember Frank—"

"Not the boy from the cloakroom?"

"Yes, yes, that's him."

The ends of her mouth took another turn south. "I know several people who would be very interested to hear his thoughts vis-à-vis the whereabouts of their handbags."

"Oh, that's just silly," I objected. "Frank's straight as a die. Why, just look at him . . ."

We considered Frank once more where he waited by the van. He waggled his fingers at us and grimaced horribly.

"I promise I'll keep an eye on him . . ."

There was a faint whistling sound as Mother exhaled through her nose. "Very well," she said. "But if there is so much as a hint of trouble . . ." She let the threat hang unstated in the air. "And take that *thing* in by the kitchen."

I wasn't sure whether she meant Frank or the dog, but I didn't press her. I gave Frank the nod; he lurched over, and picking up the stricken greyhound at either end, we navigated around the soggy garden.

Rococo Christmas decorations hung in every window, and every light in the house was on, throwing buttery light over the grass and the leafless trees of the orchard; the bottle green Mercedes sat proudly in front of the garage, like a mountain lion surveying its kingdom. From outside, the kitchen resembled a Greek funeral: black-clad caterers were rushing everywhere, carrying dishes and dropping pots into quivering mounds of soapsuds. No one paid any attention to us or to our strange cargo—not until we found Mrs. P., fiddling about in the alcove by the refrigerator.

"Master Charles!" she cried, throwing her arms around me. "You have a face again! Your beautiful face!" And then she caught sight of the dog. "Ay, Master Charles, you have run him over with the car?"

"No," I said, annoyed. "It's a bon voyage gift for Bel."

She said something in Bosnian, and Zoran, the round-headed son, came over and began pressing the dog's ribs with his fingers. "I am thinking this dog is, how you say, a goner?"

"He's not a goner. I wish people would stop saying things like that, you're *upsetting* him," although admittedly An Evening of Long Good-byes wasn't looking his best, lying there on the floor not moving. "He's had a couple of knocks, that's all. He just needs some food, and . . . what are you doing?" Zoran had attached a thin metal clamp to the dog's side and was rattling about in a case of sinister-looking instruments.

"It's all right," Mrs. P. whispered in my ear. "He is trained as a doctor."

This was news to me, as all I had ever seen him do was drink beer and play the trumpet badly; and An Evening of Long Goodbyes didn't appear too keen on those needles that were materializing out of the case. Still, Zoran seemed to know what he was about, and on considera-tion, it was probably better that the dog was patched up a bit before we surprised Bel with it.

"Charlie . . ." A feeble hand clawed at my sleeve.

"Oh, for heaven's sake, man, don't be so melodramatic— Mrs. P., I don't suppose there's any dinner left? Frank's feeling a bit . . ."

Mrs. P. was doubtful but said she would forage about and see what she could do. In the meantime, she directed us to clean ourselves up and join the others inside.

"Here, Charlie, how come Mrs. P. isn't invited to the party?" Frank asked as we came down the hall.

"Well she's . . . it's not that she's *not invited*, as such. She prefers to stay behind the scenes at these things. Hates extravagance, you know."

"Oh right. I was just wonderin what was she cryin about."

"Was she crying?"

"Yeah, when we came in."

"Probably chopping onions or something. Or maybe she's upset about Bel. She's very maternal, you know, cooks generally are . . ."

Individual voices could be heard as we approached the dining room, Niall O'Boyle's preeminent among them: "... new alloys we're using mean that when you drop it down the toilet, for example, it won't break, and if you stand on it—go ahead, stand on it—see? That's the future of communications you're standing on there. Or even, say, if you threw it against a wall ..." We pushed open the door to enter a seraglio of hushed lights and the most breathtaking golds and reds.

"Good Lord!" I said, taking Frank's arm. "Isn't this wonderful? I say, duck—"

"What?" Frank said, as Niall O'Boyle's phone came whizzing through the air to catch him square on the temple, and he toppled to the floor like a felled tree. Two dozen pairs of eyes lit on us, and at the head of the table Niall O'Boyle and Harry, the phone thrower, stood guiltily agape. Mother looked grimly at me. Hastily I picked the phone up and displayed its flashing screen.

"Still working, ladies and gentlemen." Everyone exhaled a happy sigh of relief and resumed their chattering.

"I was just trying to demonstrate," Niall O'Boyle blustered.

"He'll be all right," Mother assured him, drawing him back to his seat. "Bel, darling, get him some ice or something, will you?"

Bel rose reluctantly from the far side, the warm glow of the candelabra catching in a slender gold necklace around her neck. She too was dressed in black. She came round and knelt down beside Frank, who was writhing about with his eyes closed, babbling incoherently. "Where have you been?" she said. "What have you done to him?"

"I haven't done anything to him," I said. "It's been rather an exacting day, that's all."

"The pair of you smell like a distillery."

"Let's just get him some food ... Is there any food left?"

"There are truffles," Bel said. "And maybe some bisque?"

"What's bisque?" Frank said, opening his eyes.

We guided him to a chair. Bel went out and returned with an ice pack and a plate of leftovers that Mrs. P. had scraped together, which seemed to pacify him. I sat down opposite. I was feeling a trifle light-headed myself. I hadn't eaten anything since that crepe Frank had thrown in the dustbin, and I was beginning to wish I'd taken his advice and we'd stopped at the takeaway for chicken balls on the way back from the dog track. But it was too late now, so I made do with a bottle of smoky Rioja which was floating around, lit my briar, and took in the table. Mother was seated at the top, with the guest of honor, Niall O'Boyle, on one side and Harry on the other in that repellent country-squire waistcoat. Mirela was next to Harry; I did not allow my gaze to linger. Beside Niall O'Boyle was a woman in a rather unfortunate lavender jacket—his personal assistant, I discovered—and then Geoffrey, the woolly-headed old family accountant. I hadn't seen him since he'd executed Father's will. He looked uncomfortable, as if something were caught in his throat. Our place in the new order was plain; we had been given unglamorous seats in the middle, just at the watermark past which the company descended into hooting actors and stage managers.

"Must've thought we weren't coming tonight," I said to Bel jauntily. "Had rather an exacting day."

"What is that thing?" She reseated herself next to me with a choking cough. "Since when do you smoke a pipe?"

"I have a lot of time on my hands," I explained. "As I was saying, though, we almost didn't make it. It's been a perfect nightmare of a day. But I said to Frank, this is Bel's going away, and come hell or high water I'm going to be there."

"It smells repulsive," she murmured.

I was glad she was talking to me, even if she wasn't exactly turning cartwheels; but she seemed removed from things, and everything she said had a rhetorical ring, such that I began to feel foolish replying to her. Try as I might, I could not breach this porcelain reserve; not only was I unable to get onto the subject of forgiveness, and the manifold speeches I had prepared on that topic, but—once I had passed on Jessica Kiddon's message about the taxi and made a little small talk about the decor—I quickly ran out of anything to say to her at all; and frankly it came as something of a relief when Mother stood up and pinged a glass and I realized that, although we might have missed the food, Frank and I had arrived just in time for the dull speeches.

"Tonight," Mother pronounced, "is a night of hellos and goodbyes. In one way, it is a sad occasion, because we will be taking leave, if only for a short while, of our dear Bel, who is traveling to Russia in the morning. But in the main it is a joyful one, for tonight we mark the beginning of a new epoch—a new passage in the history of this marvelous old house."

We applauded dutifully.

"It is also an opportunity for us to say thank you—to Telsinor Ireland, and more particularly to Mr. Niall O'Boyle, whose personal vision and sense of social commitment, so rare in today's business world, have played such a part in creating this unique partnership." As Niall O'Boyle basked like a lizard on a rock, Mother asked us to reflect for a moment on the meaning the partnership—to be cemented tomorrow morning when the papers were signed—would have for the house. She outlined the plans to renovate the old west wing, expand the theater, begin the long-promised instruction of children from underprivileged parts of the city; she explained how, on a more personal level, the signing of the papers would at last secure the house financially, something that her late husband, for all his years of work, was never conclusively able to do—

"Charles, stop *twitching.*"

"It's Geoffrey, he keeps *staring* at me. He looks like he's suppressing the urge to bless himself."

"It's your face, Charles," Bel whispered back. "Haven't you seen it? You look exactly like—oh—"

Mother had moved on to the goodbyes part of the speech and was calling on Bel to stand up and take a bow. "Our loss is Russia's gain," Mother was saying. "Bel's devotion to the theater has never been in question. I can't think of any other girl who would come to her own going-away party dressed like Hamlet . . ."

Everyone laughed obligingly and clapped again. Frank leaned over to Mirela, who had left most of her food uneaten, and asked if she was planning to finish it. Niall O'Boyle rose and thanked Mother and began to read from flash cards handed him by his P.A. to the effect that Amaurot was more than just a house, it was a symbol, the symbol of an ideal, and how inspiring he personally found it to see this ideal being perpetuated by modern technology in the form of the Telsinor Hythloday Centre for the Arts. There was a fresh sally of rain against the window. To my left Bel fidgeted with a doily. The tubby stage manager was

rubbing his foot up and down the girl with barrettes' ankle and trying
to make her laugh.

". . . a central part of our project of renewal, who really *embodied*
these values we've been talking about, and more importantly used them
and shared those qualities with others in order to make the world a better place, a permanent monument to him."

Noisy applause here. "What did he say?" I whispered to Bel.

"They want to put up a statue of Father," Bel said, absently twisting
her doily into a garrote.

With this announcement, the speeches came to a close. All around
us, the table fragmented into a happy babel of conversation: But Bel
only continued to retreat into herself, watching the proceedings as if
they were occurring on the other end of a microscope. It didn't matter
what I asked her about—Yalta, *Ramp*, Olivier's legal travails—she would
answer politely in as few words as were humanly possible, and then
withdraw into silence. It was like being seated next to a vacant lot.

I decided it was time to bring out the big guns. When Mrs. P. came
in to ask about coffee (Frank was right, I realized, she did look rather
out of sorts), I had a word in her ear. A few minutes later, An Evening of
Long Goodbyes nosed into the room, bandaged up and looking much
improved.

"Well!" I said. "Look who it is!"

"Who is it?" Bel barely lifted an eyebrow.

"Don't you recognize him?" I said, seeking to disengage the dog's
head from its reproductive organs momentarily so she could see him
properly. "It's that dog you bet on at the races that time, remember? An
Evening of Long Goodbyes. You thought it was romantic."

"What's it doing here?" Bel said.

I stifled my exasperation. "Well, it's for you, obviously. I mean it's a
bon voyage gift."

"We robbed it from the car park," Frank chipped in unhelpfully.

"We didn't *rob* it," I said. I explained about the race and the dog's
heroics earlier that evening. Bel still didn't seem to understand how
this related to her; she nodded neutrally, patting the smooth area between the dog's ears, and made some remark about not knowing if
Aeroflot allowed dogs on as hand luggage.

"You're coming back, aren't you?" I said, beginning to feel a little browned off. "I just thought it would be nice to have a dog about the place again. I remembered how you used to dote on that spaniel . . ." This I felt sure would elicit a response, but her face remained blank as the silver tag nestled in my pocket. I thought about producing it as evidence of her obsession, and thereby proving that the dog was a good present, Aeroflot's luggage policy notwithstanding; but I checked myself. I had done my best to make amends. If she was going to be infantile, that was her business. She returned to her reverie. I fell into a grumpy silence of my own. From the other side of the table, Frank resumed his muttering, mingling it with superstitious glances at Bel of the kind a savage might throw at a bicycle. Oh yes, we made quite a party.

"You know," Niall O'Boyle was telling Mother, tilting his chair back from the table, "I've always fancied one of these big houses. A man could get some thinking done in a place like this."

"Oh, these old piles are far more trouble than they're worth," Mother laughed. "Don't be fooled. So much work just to keep them going, and it's only on nights like this that they truly come into their own." But even as she said it, her eyes roved over the lavish appointments and sparkled with approval.

"It's those Slavic cheekbones," the lavender-jacketed P.A. said, stroking her wineglass and gazing at Mirela. "They photograph so beautifully . . ."

"I'm calling it *The Rusting Tractor*," Harry said to Geoffrey. "It's about a young woman moving from the city to an isolated village in Connemara, one of those places that's totally stuck in the past, you know, no Internet access, two TV channels— Anyway, she gets in a fight with the locals because she wants to put a mobile-phone mast up on her land, because I don't know if you've been to the west but the coverage is really appalling out there, but to them this is a kind of sacrilege, because, you know, the 'Land,' capital *L*—"

"Charlie!" a hoarse voice called from across the table. "What's he talkin about?"

"I think he's talking about mobile phones," I said.

". . . so what develops is a conflict between the quote-unquote 'new' Ireland, the Ireland of technology and communication and gender equality, and the 'old' Ireland of repression and superstition and resistance to change, which is represented by the rusting tractor . . ."

"Why does he keep doin that thing with his fingers?"

"Oh, it's a sort of inverted commas," I whispered. "Just ignore him. It's patent nonsense anyway. Mobile phones, the very idea is absurd. People don't want to be bothered with phones when they're out and about. That's the whole reason they leave their houses."

"It's like a strobe light goin off in me brain," Frank said through clenched teeth, holding his head with his hands.

"What?" I looked over at him. Sweat stood out on his forehead, and his eyes were doing this alarming trick of rolling back in his head. He was definitely behaving more sociopathically than usual. That blow earlier must have dislodged something. "Look at all these bastards," he said, gazing saturninely up and down the table.

"Eat your truffles," I said hurriedly, pointing to his plate. "And maybe you shouldn't drink any more." I poured his glass into mine.

I haven't mentioned it up to now for fear of sounding immodest, but ever since I sat down Mirela had been staring at me. At first it had been in the form of plaintive, mea culpa–type looks whenever Harry's head was turned, which I had politely ignored. Yet she persisted, and as the night wore on, they had increased in urgency—flickering constantly from the other side of the table as if she had some message she was attempting to send via a Morse code of blinks and flashes, until they came to resemble the entreaties of one of those silent-movie heroines who has been tied to a train track. But now, as the clock struck for midnight, she seemed suddenly to resign herself. She slumped down in her seat; at the same moment, a wineglass pinged, and Harry got to his feet.

"Friends . . . friends." He held up his hand for quiet. "You'll forgive me if I detain you with a few brief words of my own." His doltish hair looked even more snaky and annoying than usual. An Evening of Long Goodbyes began to growl. "Shh," I said. "Bad dog. Be quiet," slipping him a truffle when Mother had stopped looking.

"We've heard a lot tonight about 'new visions,' 'rebirths,' and 'new beginnings—' "

"Gnnnhhhh." Frank ground his fists into his temples.

"So in keeping with the general theme of the evening," Harry continued, "and with no further ado, it is my pleasure to inform you that at half past eight this evening, Miss Mirela Pribicevic agreed to give me her hand in marriage—"

Before he had finished the sentence, the female contingent of the table erupted and rushed over to swamp Mirela in squeals and embraces. "How wonderful!" Mother clasped her hands to her cheeks as her eyes welled up with tears. "Oh, how wonderful!"

My first thoughts were for Bel, and I swung round with my arms half outstretched, I suppose in case she might be about to swoon. But she was looking on placidly as if this were happening far, far away, to a group of people she had never met; and I was forced back to face my own emotions.

It was funny; if someone had put this situation to me hypothetically five minutes earlier, I'd probably have replied, quite honestly, that I didn't think it would bother me in the slightest. Yet as I watched Mirela now, I felt as cold and sick and hollow as if I had been dealt a mortal blow. As I watched her emerge from the scrum of well-wishers, pink and fresh-faced and laughing and looking very much like a girl in love, everything she had said to me in our few contradictory exchanges ran through my mind; and in that moment, I realized with a terrible sense of finality that I had no idea, and I never would have any idea, how this world worked or what went on in the hearts of its inhabitants; that it was and always would be utterly opaque and mysterious to me, and that whatever happened from now on would not make any difference, because it would never come any closer.

"Charlie," Frank confided sweatily, "I'm not feelin meself."

"Me neither, old chum," I said. "Me neither."

Harry, meanwhile, had lied about a few brief words. Instead he was using his announcement as a springboard for more speechifying. "On the occasion of this double union"—he raised his voice over the hubbub—"I would like to say a word of thanks. You hear a lot these days about how the notion of 'the family' is one that can't exist anymore in our fast-paced modern world. But from the first day I came here, after Bel asked me to join the theater group she was just starting, a family is exactly what it's been. And it's made me realize what a family can be.

Coming from a typical middle-class, 'petit bourgeois' background, I suppose I had a fairly low opinion . . ."

From his position facedown on the empty plate, Frank informed me that he couldn't take much more of this.

". . . realize that the family can be something *political, radically* political, can be a force which can be posited *against* the controlling groups of our time, a "free space" where differing opinions can come together . . ."

I gulped back a fresh glass of Rioja and felt a cold sweat break over me like a kind of necrosis. *You can't stop life from happening*, that's what Mirela said, that night in Frank's apartment. It would carry you further and further away from yourself; it would make its way into your past and transform that too . . .

". . . learn that the market, like a gun, isn't anything *intrinsically* good or bad, that we can use it for good, we can join forces with it. And just as we have grown, so Amaurot has grown with us . . ."

And meanwhile all anyone did was make speeches! It felt like he was dancing up and down on our grave, he and market forces, he and the asset strippers, he and the Golems of progress, and yet no one *did* anything, no one gainsaid or challenged him or said, It isn't right, these things you're saying *aren't right* . . .

". . . a house weighed down by, or rather trapped in, its own history, to recontextualize it, realign it with modernity, and basically haul the place into the twenty-first century—"

I was reaching the point where I didn't think I could physically stand any more; and evidently someone else in the room felt the same way, because suddenly a loud, exasperated voice called out, "Oh, balls!"

Everyone went quiet. Harry adjusted his bow tie and said "Excuse me?" as if to offer the perpetrator a chance to exculpate himself. But this protester was not to be silenced. "Balls!" the voice cried again, even louder than before. I tittered to myself; and I was so enjoying seeing Harry squirm that it took a moment to realize that I was standing up, and that, furthermore, the entire table was staring at me.

Bother.

"Charles, leave the room, please," Mother said.

"No," Harry interjected. "If you don't mind—let's hear what Charles has to say."

I wiped my palms on my trousers, unexpectedly finding myself addressing the table at large. "Well, I mean to say," I stammered. "I mean . . . well, a house is a house, isn't it? It's a place people live in. I don't see what the twenty-first century's got to do with it. I don't see why, just because you've put up some new wallpaper, you should be allowed to claim the place in the name of the *future*, like some sort of . . . you know . . . time-traveling . . . pirate."

"That's Harry for you," chuckled Niall O'Boyle. "I like a man who's got his eye on the future. Because that's where it's all going to happen, mark my words. The past is one thing, but the future, that's where the money is."

"I'm not trying to step on anybody's toes," Harry said. "I'm just saying you have to move with the times. It's in everybody's interests. You have to admit this place was falling to pieces before we came."

I thought back to that golden age when it was just Bel and me and the drinks cabinet. "It wasn't," I said.

"It was," he reiterated. "The paint was peeling, the floors were rotten—your mother told us that while she was in hospital the bank had practically called in the sheriffs to repossess the place . . ."

"That was all a misunderstanding," I claimed.

"But you blew up the Folly for the insurance," Harry pursued, fingering the buttons of his lawyer's waistcoat. "I mean—you tried to *fake your own death*. How can you say the house was better off then?"

I blinked stuporously and cast about me for support. Bel continued to gaze dreamily into space like a patient under ether in the dentist's chair. Frank was lying inert on the table like a giant rag doll, as he had been for the last five minutes. All the others waited for my response, their eyes holding me pinned like so many skewers. "We knew what we were doing," I mumbled.

There was a momentary delay; then, as one, the guests around the table burst into laughter. It was warm and full; everyone joined in, even people I had never met before, like Niall O'Boyle's P.A.; even Mother, her anger dissipating in the general gaiety. Harry threw his hands up humorously as if to say, I rest my case; I slunk down in my seat and thought that maybe I was just a dope—in all likelihood I was, I wasn't debating the matter: But still it didn't seem right that a man should be made to feel like this, not in the dining room of his own childhood home.

And then, abruptly, mechanically, Frank lifted his head from his plate. With a glazed yet curiously purposeful expression, like a man acting with orders from on high, he rose and tucked in his chair; then he crossed the floor and began strangling Harry.

For a couple of seconds we sat watching dumbly as plates flew, glasses smashed, chairs tumbled. Then the girls began to scream. At the same time, the bit-part actors at the end of the table hurrahed and stood on their seats to get a better view; the dog barked; Mirela turned gray; the businessmen puffed themselves up and waved their hands about—

"Do something, Charles!" Mother shrieked. "Do something!"

"Right," I responded, getting to my feet. "Who's for brandy? And I believe we have some cigars . . ."

"CHARLIE?"

"Yes, Frank?"

"You awake?"

"Yes, Frank, I'm awake."

"Where are we, Charlie?"

"We're in Father's study. You had a sort of a funny turn."

"Oh right. I gave your man a box." There was a pause; the darkness recomposed itself over the shelves, the vials and periodicals and thick portfolios of photographs. "I'd say he wasn't expectin that."

"No, I don't suppose he was."

"Your ma was awful angry, wasn't she? Like sayin she was goin to get us arrested and stuff."

"Oh, Mother says these things, you know . . ."

"Sorry, Charlie. I dunno what happened. It was like I wasn't in control of me own mind."

I charitably let this pass.

"He kept goin on and on with all that shite. It was drivin me mad. And I couldn't just let him make a laugh of you."

I coughed. "Well, I don't know that he was making a *laugh* of me—"

"Like I wasn't just goin to let him make you look like some geebag that didn't know his arse from his elbow."

"Well . . . well, thanks, old man."

Silence.

"Charlie?"

"Go to *sleep.*"

"Fuckin cold in here, isn't it?"

" . . ."

"Charlie . . . d'you ever see a ghost here? I bet there'd be loads of ghosts in an old gaff like this . . . Fuck"—the camp bed creaked painfully—"just like that bit in Bel's play, like all these faces like *starin* at you from the fuckin trees and shit—"

"Look, there aren't any ghosts, all right?" I said irritably. "If there were, Harry would have roped them into serving dinner, or helping in his wretched play. Lord knows if I was a ghost I'd have fled the minute he walked in the door."

"Ah yeah, I s'pose . . ." He laid himself gingerly back down. I turned back to the window. I was at my old vantage point behind Father's desk, where I'd used to look out at the Folly and occasionally see an angel, or an actress. There weren't any angels tonight; we had used up our quota, probably, or else they had hitched a ride with the ghosts.

We had ruined the dinner party so thoroughly, so unequivocally, that even after the furor had died down and the paramedics had gone, the wisest course of action had still seemed to be one of ignominious retreat. I wasn't at all sure that Mother had been joking about pressing charges, so with Mrs. P.'s help I had smuggled Frank up here, and here the two of us had stayed. Only now, as I sat at the windowsill, did it occur to me that this was the end—that our parts were, at last, played out. Tomorrow was already today. Bel would leave for Yalta, and Amaurot would be reborn as the Telsinor Hythloday Centre for the Arts. Our contributions had made, when it came to it, not the slightest bit of difference.

I had been utterly defeated on every front; I should, at that moment of all moments, have been steeped in despair. And yet, as I sat at the window, I did not find myself despairing. For out of the gloom, the hopelessness, the humiliation of the day, certain images kept defiantly floating up: Frank with Droyd in his arms, lurching out of the stinking basement; Frank thumping the Plexiglas, cheering on the dogs; the glorious moment of Frank, tongue tucked between his teeth, crisply punching Harry on the nose. I didn't ask for them; they didn't appear to change anything; yet there they were, floating up out of the darkness before my eyes, over and over again, and with them now something Yeats had said once: "Friendship is all the house I have."

I frowned out through my ghostly reflection at the swaying trees, the rain. *Friendship is all the house I have.* It wasn't a line I'd given much thought to before. Still, you could see what he meant, given all the problems one encountered with actual houses—heating bills and mortgages and wayward domestics, rack-renting landlords, actors moving in, all that. What kind of house would my friendship make? The day's events paraded palely by again, like the tapestry of a long-ago battle. On the evidence it seemed that, for all my aspirations to the courtly life, I hadn't provided much protection from the elements. Bel, Amaurot, Droyd, and the Latvians . . . the closer you looked the more it appeared that, in terms of houses, it was your Charles Hythlodays who were the seedy, overpriced flats with wobbling walls and dubious plumbing; while it was the Franks of this world—even if they thought a French press was some sort of ungentlemanly wrestling move, even if they were under the impression that Stockhausen was a Swedish furniture shop, even if one had heard them with one's own ears telling Droyd when he asked that Donatella Versace was a Teenage Mutant Ninja Turtle—it was the Franks who were the grand old mansions overlooking the sea. And it struck me that the last time we all of us had been happy—really happy, even if we hadn't been aware of it—was when Frank and Bel were still together.

"I say . . ."

No response.

"Frank?"

"Whhnnnhhh?"

"You know, I've been thinking. Bel's only going for six months. It's not such a long time really . . ."

". . ."

"I was just thinking that if—if you ever wanted to, you know, give it another shot with her . . ."

"Yes, Charlie?"

"Well, I might be able to put in a word, that's all." I had never dreamed I would be saying this; and yet suddenly I could picture it so clearly—me restored to my room, the theater disassembled and scattered to the four winds, Bel and I laughing gaily as Frank attended to any heavy lifting work that needed to be done around the house, as all the flurrying elements of our lives drifted back down into place, like the flakes in one of those little snow globes . . .

"Cheers, Charlie," Frank said. "You're a sound man."

"Well, it's the least I could do. I mean I should have mentioned it earlier."

"Yeah." He scratched his nose thoughtfully. "'Member, though, how you were sayin that about plenty of fish in the sea?"

"Yes?"

"Yeah, cos like, eh, me and Laura, we've been, eh, you know . . ."

"You've been what?"

"Well, like, you prob'ly noticed she's been around a good bit lately . . ."

"I thought she just liked DIY," I said in a small voice.

"You don't mind, do you? I wuz worried you might have a bit of a boner for her yourself."

"Not at all," I said; as the restored Amaurot receded over the horizon into the Land of Might-Have-Been, and with it the bounteous Laura, her grabulous melons . . . "I'm delighted, old chap. Delighted."

"Yeah, cheers, Charlie. I'll give her one for you, ha ha."

"Yes," I said faintly.

Mercifully his breathing deepened into snores; and after I had listened to the snores for an hour or so, I decided that maybe what I really wanted was a drink; so I rose again and went downstairs.

The caterers had gone home hours ago. Everything was tidied away. The long table had been stripped of its trappings, the chairs ordered with geometrical precision around it; the blood splashes from Harry's nose had been mopped up, the dishes washed and dried and stacked in the cupboard. Father waited, waited, in his frame in the hallway. Without knowing why, especially, I began to go from room to room, picking things up and putting them down again. In the vague blue darkness, everything seemed to tingle; I felt a little like the Prince in *Sleeping Beauty*, creeping through the slumbering castle, observing the secret life the objects led while everyone lay in their enchanted sleep. Then I found myself beside the drinks cabinet, and thought that seeing as I was in the neighborhood, I might as well make myself a gimlet. After a moment's thought, I decided that it ought really to be a double. Then I took the bottle and put it in my pocket.

Bel was in the drawing room on her own, staring out the window with the lights off.

"Didn't think I'd find you still up and about . . ." I attempted a jolly, avuncular tone.

"The taxi's coming at four. There hardly seemed much point going to bed."

"Interest you in a . . . ?" I held up my glass and jingled the ice cubes. She looked round.

"How can you still be drinking?" she said affectlessly, returning to her vigil.

"Years of practice, I suppose . . ." I took a seat on the chaise longue. A pink vinyl suitcase rested at one end. Outside thunder groaned and the sky lit up silver. "Lord, what an awful night. Don't know if your plane'll fly if it keeps up like that."

"It'll fly," Bel said.

"Aha," I returned emptily. I shunted myself forward, attempting to balance my drink on my knee.

"Glad I caught you, as a matter of fact. Didn't get much of a chance to say goodbye earlier on, what with all the fuss and all those paramedics swarming around. Cripes, you'd think even a hemophiliac would be able to deal with a bloody nose, ha ha . . ." She didn't appear to have an opinion on this. I rubbed my hands together miserably. "Wanted to ask you how you felt about the Harry and Mirela thing too. Must have been a bit of a shock for you, after all."

The slender shoulders shrugged indifferently. "She's marrying him for citizenship. If he doesn't know that now, he soon will."

"Ah. Well, that's good, then." I cleared my throat. "Dinner seemed to go fairly painlessly otherwise, didn't it, apart from the—the fighting I mean . . . The statue, for example, I thought that was a nice touch."

This at least evoked a response. "A *statue*," she murmured, staring out at the night. "A *statue* . . ."

I took a good draft of my gimlet. "Look here," I said. "I don't want to beat around the bush. Maybe you want to hear this and maybe you don't, but you ought to know that what happened between Mirela and me, it was a mistake. I had— That is, I didn't—" I broke off, trying and failing to untangle the words that were coiling up in my brain like Silly String.

"What happened between you and Mirela is entirely your own business," she said.

"Oh," I said unhappily. "Good. Because I thought, you know, I was worried you might be going to Russia because of me, ha ha."

She shook her head, came away from her curtain, and plucked an azalea from an enormous bunch on the table. "Think of Russia as a last hurrah," she said. "A whistle-stop tour of my childhood dreams, before I settle down and marry money." She clasped the stem between her two hands and waved the flower at me. "It's late, Charles. You should go to bed."

"Right, right," I agreed, clambering off the chaise longue. "Well, bon voyage," I said, then, impulsively, went over to hug her. It was awkward and stiff; I felt her body pulling back. "Right," I said again, and backed falteringly out of the room.

"Oh, Charles?" She stopped me as I reached the door. "That tag, do you have it?"

"What? Oh . . . yes." I fumbled about in my pockets. "I have your phone too, if you want it."

She told me that she wouldn't need that. "I would like the tag though. Just as a memento. Silly, I suppose."

"No, no . . ." I found the dog tag and flipped it in the air like a coin; as I caught it I laughed. "When I think about how you used to worry about that dog, night and day. You always were such a worrier. It was as if you thought your worrying was all that held the world together, and if you stopped for a split second the whole thing would just fly apart. I never did understand it, those were such happy days . . ." Bel had picked up several more flowers now and held them in a fan across her face. "Do you remember"—I chuckled—"how we used to pretend your mattress was a raft, and the stairs were a river, and we were sailing away escaping from the serfs? And how we'd act out scenes from *Eugene Onegin*, and you'd get cross because you didn't think I was sad enough when you told me you didn't love me?" The fan nodded infinitesimally, swayed by the lightest of breezes. I rubbed my chin excitably. "Remember how we used to help Father inventing makeup? He'd give us poster paints, you'd get yourself up as Tinker Bell, and I'd be Bela Lugosi. I was absolutely convinced there was a fortune to be made from this untapped market for Bela Lugosi makeup— What is it?"

Bel had lowered her fan and was looking at me with a kind of impatience. "It wasn't always happy days," she said. "There were things to forget, too."

"How do you mean?"

She rolled her eyes. "Nothing," she said. "It's late, that's all. You should go to bed." Then, pretending not to notice me stare, she held out her hand. "The tag?"

I closed my fist around it and lowered it slowly down by my side.

"Don't be childish, Charles, just give it to me."

"First tell me what you meant."

"Nothing, I didn't mean anything . . ." She had turned an angry beetroot color.

"It wasn't nothing, if it was nothing you wouldn't have said it, and what do you want this old thing for anyway, it hasn't even got a name on it . . ."

"Oh, for God's sake, just *keep* it then!" She wheeled away, exasperated. Immediately I felt sorry and lunkish, and I was just about to apologize and hand it over when she spun round, catching me unawares—

"Ow—what are you *doing*?"

"Give me it, Charles," digging her nails in my hand to try to get me to release it. I pushed her away; she pressed her elbow into my chest for leverage, and we tussled for another minute before I twisted her arm to disempower her but did it too hard so she was thrown back onto the drawing room floor.

"Oh hell . . ."

"Get off me—"

"I didn't mean it, I was just—"

"You were just *drunk*, you're *always* drunk." She wriggled away from my outstretched hand to lean against one leg of the chaise longue.

"Sorry," I said again. "It's not broken, is it?" She didn't reply, just sat folded up by her suitcase, nursing her wrist.

"It wasn't deliberate," I said, feeling guilty. "It's just, I don't see why you always have to run things down . . ."

"Oh, Lord—just leave me alone, will you?"

"You do, Bel. I mean maybe you don't notice, but—"

She looked up with tears of pain in her eyes. "Why do you keep *doing* this to me?"

"Doing what?"

"Why do you keep making me have the same conversation again and again and again?"

"I don't."

"You *do*, with your happy memories and weren't-we-blessed, you make it seem like this whole time I've been living in a totally different *life* to you, you have no idea how it makes me *feel* . . ."

"What are you talking about?"

"The way you talk about *us*, the way all your stories are about when we were little children, like nothing ever happened after we were ten years old, and everything bad you can just paint over and for*get*—"

"I'm not painting over anything."

"Me in the hospital, why don't you ever talk about that? Didn't that happen? It was you who called the ambulance, wasn't it? Or did I imagine it?" The embers from the fire cast a deep red, livid glow over her face: she rubbed her wrist agitatedly, brushed her nose with her sleeve.

"It was a painful period in our lives," I said. "Just because I don't talk about something doesn't mean I've forgotten it, or *painted over* it . . ."

"You do!" She struggled to her feet, the injured wrist held in one hand giving her a martyred aspect.

"Even tonight when I'm *going* you come home with some stray dog you found half dead because you don't want me to remember the first one, because you think you can just erase the memory when the whole point is we shouldn't be trying to forget it, we should be remembering it and what a rotten thing it was for Mother to take a little puppy and—"

"It was just a bon voyage gift," I protested. "It wasn't supposed to be some kind of existential—"

"It was, Charles, it always is, and then you start in on me with remember this remember that and everything you don't want to remember either just disappears or else you twist it around to make it fit this *illusion* you live in, just like the rest of them with their *statues* and their *tradition* and perpetuating Father's *legacy*—but it's worse when it's you, because you were here, you know it's not true."

It was late, and I should have known to leave her be. In a very short period of time she had worked herself into quite a state. But I was a little the worse for wear myself by this point, and suddenly I had had enough of her put-downs; so I told her rather harshly that I hadn't the faintest clue what she was talking about.

She ground her hand against her cheek frustratedly. "*This*, Charles. The whole house. All the lying and pretending and putting on masks, everybody doing whatever they can to avoid having to actually confront reality, everything paid for by conning old ladies into thinking they can be young again—it's a total fiction, all of it. That's all it's ever been, it's what the house was *built* on." She paced out to the fireplace and back, circling like some tormented moth. "And now it happens all over again, with Harry and Mirela, and this phone company using us to make itself look like *something* instead of a bunch of Scandinavian venture capital. And Mother trying to look like she cares, and more lying and pretending, and *that's* Father's legacy, Charles, that and a hundred bank accounts that we don't even know where they are, and yet you still won't admit it, even when you know what went on up there, Jesus Christ you know how he *died*, and then you think to ask me why I'm going to Yalta— God, when I think of spending another *second* here . . ."

In the window lightning snapped, transforming the room momentarily into an engraving. "Are you finished?" I said quietly.

"Yes I'm— Why, wait, where are you going?"

"I'm going to wake Mother," I said.

"What?" She scurried round and interposed herself in front of the door. "What?"

"I'm going to get Mother, and then I'm going to call the doctor," I said, setting her aside. "You're hysterical."

"I'm not hysterical," Bel said, shocked. "Why do you think I'm—"

"You're hysterical, and I'm calling the doctor. You're not in any shape to be going anywhere."

"That isn't *fair*, Charles, just because I tell you something you don't want to hear doesn't mean I'm hysterical"—she stretched out a hand, which I dodged easily—"just because something happened once you can't keep—"

"I'm sorry," I said stolidly. "I have to do it."

"But it isn't— Wait!" springing back nimbly to block my path again. "Wait, Charles—Charles, wait—" She hung her head, pinched her nose with one hand, took a deep breath. "Wait, there's no need to drag Mother out of bed. You're right. I'm overwrought. It's been such an exhausting day. I'm sorry. I just need a minute to calm down, that's all. Why don't we just"—she cast about her, then caught sight of the bottle poking out of my pocket—"why don't we just sit down, and pour ourselves a drink, and calm ourselves down."

She tugged at my shirt buttons pleadingly. I wavered. Her eyes seemed chaotic and far too white; still, a drink would really hit the spot about now.

Bel fetched a glass and poured a healthy shot for herself, then one for me. We sat on the chaise longue and sipped and looked out at the storm, as placid and genteel as if we were taking tea on the lawn. Unprompted, she began to chat about this master class in Yalta, and how the residence had been Chekhov's country house when ill health forced him from Moscow; how he'd lived with his actress wife, Olga, and written his last play, *The Cherry Orchard*, there; how on his birthday he'd returned to Moscow for its first performance and had a coughing fit when the audience called him out onstage; how he'd died peacefully two months later, at the age of forty-four. And what she'd said, or almost said, a moment before, hung undispellably in the room, invisible and odorless as asbestos. And after we'd lapsed back into silence, and sat there a while longer, I said, "Do you remember the night of the school play, Bel?"

"Mmm?" she said absently.

"When you did *The Cherry Orchard*, and you forgot your lines. You went totally blank, do you remember?"

"Of course I remember," she said.

"I was telling Frank about it, and I realized I never did ask you what happened."

"I don't know," she said. "I suppose I mustn't have learned my part very well."

"You had that big fight with Mother," I said. "And the next day you got sick. But we never talked about it."

She looked at me curiously. "I have a better idea, Charles," she said, getting up. "Go to bed. Drink your drink and go to bed, and to-morrow you'll have forgotten all about this."

"I thought you said we ought to be remembering things."

The vodka made the air seem close and velvety like a cushion. Be-hind her the sky sparked silver again and reeled into darkness, and I thought suddenly of Gene Tierney waking up in her hospital bed after her electric-shock treatment not knowing where, or who, she was.

"You know what happened," she said quietly.

"Tell me again."

She chewed her knuckle thoughtfully. She looked at the clock, the dying embers in the fire. "I suppose it doesn't matter," she said. "You won't believe me anyway." She picked up the azaleas again and went to the curtain, beating them rhythmically against her palm. "But it wasn't that night everything happened," she said. "It was a few days before-hand. We all got half days that week, so we could go and practice our lines. It must have been a Wednesday, because the maid was off. I was in my room, going over a couple of scenes, when I heard this— I don't know how to describe it. In my memory it's just this sound of . . . trou-ble. I didn't know what it could be. There wasn't supposed to be anyone in the house. I opened the door to see what it was, and I found this girl, standing there, totally naked. Just standing there, it was like something out of a dream. She had this blue eye shadow on and she was staring right at me, but I don't think she knew I was there. I don't think she knew where she was. Her eyes were just these blanks. For a minute we stood there blinking at each other, and then Father came round the corner and she bolted off down the stairs. I was left there looking at him. I think I said something like 'What's up?' And he grabs me and goes, 'Christabel, there's been an accident, I need you to help.' He kept saying it over and over. He wouldn't let me go. There was no accident, obviously. But whatever had happened the girl was in hysterics, and she wouldn't let him go near her. So I had to go and look for her. She was in the utility room, wedged in behind the dryer, you know where Mrs. P. keeps the ironing board? I found her in there, and Charles, all I wanted to do was get in beside her, she looked so small and thin, so defenseless, like a little animal. Wearing nothing at all except this eye shadow, all this dark blue eye shadow, that made me think of those scary Egyptian goddesses, Isis and Nepthys and those ones? But I talked to her and took her to the bathroom and washed her and calmed her down. She was okay after a while. There was nothing really the matter with her. She'd just freaked out. She was just so *young*. She went upstairs to put on her clothes and I called her a taxi. Father stayed out of sight. Then she was gone, and I went back to my room to read my lines, and it was like nothing had happened. He didn't say anything to me about it, and I didn't intend to tell anyone else. Not to protect him, necessarily. More that I thought if I didn't tell anybody it would feel less like something that had really happened. But of course I couldn't stop thinking about it. Suddenly it was like everything in the house revealed this new meaning. The locked doors, the photographs. I'd stand in my room and look at all the things he'd given me, the clothes, jewelery, perfume, and I'd think, did he give the same things to his—to the models? Did he pick up three of everything at the airport? Or did he see something looked nice on some girl he was . . ." She paused decorously.

Outside the night shuddered and boomed. "And then I started throwing up. I couldn't keep anything down. Mother thought it was nerves because of the play. Maybe it was, partly. And the night it was on, she was so sweet, telling me not to worry and how she'd played Varya when she was a little older than me and then before I could stop myself it all came out. I was crying and everything just came out. I didn't think how she'd react. Or I thought she would want to know. I mean I thought that that was the whole point of the truth, that you told it. And you know she was always the one chasing after us to stand up straight and tuck in our shirts and not steal Thompson's apples. For a while when I'd finished she didn't say anything. I remember she was standing beside the sink with her mouth closed, and I was sitting at the kitchen table in this ridiculous Russian ball gown just wishing she'd say something. But then when she did I wished she would stop because it was so horrible. The main thrust of it, though, was that I had made the whole story up. She was so *angry*—so angry I was worried she might damage herself, and I started thinking that I *must* have made it up, and I wondered why I would do such a horrible thing, which is when everything got confusing."

She stepped across to the mantelpiece and trailed her fingers over the marble; I lifted the glass to my lips and found it was empty. I reached for the bottle.

"If I hadn't told her, everything would've been fine. She knew anyway, that's what I realized afterwards. Everybody does it. It's a part of the fashion world. They take these fourteen-year-old girls away from their homes, they turn them into fantasies, they make them famous and rich and in return . . . Well, who could resist it, making love to an actual work of art, to your very own creation? It's a kind of a *droit de seigneur*, I suppose. And then they wonder why two years down the line their artworks are anorexic or swallowing razor blades. But of course Mother knew about it. I presume they'd come to some kind of arrangement. Or maybe she didn't care what he did, so long as it was discreet. All she wanted was to have the city at her feet again, everybody paying her compliments like in the old days. Like at that dinner party tonight, she was so happy. She was even thinking of giving you a room in the new wing, Charles, if you hadn't made such a mess of things. But she never forgave me. I broke the rules. Everything's fine as long as nobody tells. Everyone knows and everyone pretends not to and that's how the world keeps turning. But once the truth starts coming out, the entire artifice crumbles. There's too much at stake for that to be allowed to happen. That's what she was trying to tell me the night of the play. And you know, she always did say an actress should never concern herself overly with the truth." She cupped her hands round her vodka glass and hunched her shoulders. "But I never was much of an actress."

She paused and drank and refilled the glass. I wanted to stand up and say something, but there was a weight pressing down on my chest and I was having some kind of problem with my vision. I didn't seem to be able to make out the whole room; instead individual areas were being illuminated one by one, like lights in a pinball machine—the pink vinyl suitcase at my right foot; the hounds tearing at Actaeon; the swell of green metal over the front wheel of the Mercedes outside the garage; Bel's legs white as candlesticks under the whipping black dress as she came back and stood in front of me.

"But you know all this," she said. "I know you know. Maybe not all of the details, necessarily. But enough. That's why you've been falling over yourself trying to get out of the place, first that half-witted plan to go to Chile, and then when that didn't work you storm out after some tiff with Mother? Because she told you to get a job, you leave your ancestral home and move in with Frank?"

She sat down next to me on the chaise longue. "Don't you see, though, that's why I get angry with you, because you pretend not to know, because you act like you think everything in the world's just a *digression* from the grand, noble lives Father had mapped out for us, and that if you ever *did* anything or became *part* of anything, you'd be betraying him. But there is no map, Charles. There are no values. All Amaurot ever was was somewhere to fill up with his delusions and walk around with his head in the clouds, pretending the world outside didn't exist. I'm not judging him for it. But none of this means anything at all. Except maybe money."

The balls of my fingers were sweating, and the glass kept wanting to slip away from them. The mad skirl of the storm came rushing down the chimney. It felt rather as if we had arrived at the end of the world; and all that was left now was this drawing room, this chaise longue, her body beside mine. Summoning all my energies, I heaved myself forward, like some old dinosaur struggling out of the swamp, so that my forearms leaned on my thighs; then, clearing the dust from my throat, I said in a slurred voice: "Poppycock."

I might have gone on. I might have told her that I'd never in my life heard such vile trash; I might have gone through her points and refuted them one by one. But I found that the effort of sitting up had exhausted me; so I set my glass down by the suitcase and sat staring sourly at the floor, ignoring her gaze on my cheek.

"Geoffrey's been arraigned," Bel said; her voice had regained its parsed, melodious distance. "I'm sure you've heard. One of Father's companies turned up in this offshore thing the government's investigating. They haven't traced it as far as us yet. But it'll hardly take them long. It's pretty obvious once you start looking at the books. Front companies, holding companies, dummy accounts, leading here, there, into the ether. Donations to these mysterious charities, trust funds— you must have wondered what happened to your trust, Charles, you must have realized even you couldn't have drunk it all."

I said nothing; eventually she sighed and got up and went to the curtain again, as she had been when I came in.

"I mean it doesn't matter," she said. "The place'll go on regardless, and get stronger and stronger. They'll create synergies and put up statues. How could you ever stop something as big as that?" She looked round at me over her shoulder. "So you can wake Mother now, if you want. Tell her I've gone crazy again."

I still did not reply; I was thinking of something else now.

"But, Charles, promise me one thing. When I'm gone, promise you won't come back here. Even if Mother offers you a room. There isn't going to be any more face painting, do you understand that?" She crossed the floor, frowning to herself. I suppressed a giggle. She hadn't noticed, but there were two of her now, pacing along side by side. The room was beginning to wheel slowly, in a cozy, rockabying sort of a way. "And you have to stop falling in love with beautiful girls you don't know anything about . . ." A chorus line of Bels lifted their hands and pushed the bangs out of their eyes. "Because what you have to remember, if there's one thing, it's that everybody's human, that's the first thing they are, whether they're beautiful or not, or rich or poor, or actresses from the 1940s or Frank . . . They're all humans, the first thing they are is human, do you see? Do you see, Charles?"

I was only dimly aware of the kaleidoscope Bel that shimmered up and waited expectantly at my foot. I was thinking of that time when she was seven, when she'd watched the documentary about the famine in Ethiopia and decided she was going to make a cake to send over to them. "Do you remember, Bel? Everyone was out and the kitchen went on fire, and Father said, when the firemen had gone, Father said"— hooting with laughter now—"he had a good mind to ask the blasted Ethiopians to send some of their food to *us*, seeing as we'd have to eat takeaways for the next month . . ."

The shimmer paused, then said quietly that she remembered. The clock struck something or other, and she said she really did have some things to do.

"Yes," I said, rising unsteadily and sinking again. "I might just need a—a small hand, however . . ."

She took my wrist and hauled me up. When I had found my feet, she draped my right arm over her shoulders and linked her own arms tightly around my waist, and in this fashion we made our way down the hall, with her slight frame braced against mine, adjusting itself forward, backward to counter my errant center of gravity. It seemed, as we began our ascent of the stairs, that I could hear the sound of chopping wood somewhere; but Bel was already huffing under my weight, so I didn't mention it. Probably just some left-behind spook, I thought, as she hefted me onward; probably just some Golem, dragging its sad, sleepless feet of clay through the darkened grounds.

The next thing I knew, we were standing outside Father's study door. "Well," I said to the place where I thought she was standing.

"Yes," she said.

"Give my regards to old Chekhov."

"Of course."

There was an awkward lacuna; suddenly I was aware of something having been brought up that had been left unresolved—or was it something left unsaid that should have been said? I couldn't remember, so hazarding a guess I said, "You know, that business we were talking about before. You and I finding a place to live, so forth. We should have a talk about it when you get back, thrash out something definite."

"Of course," she said again: no more than a smudge now, a thumb-print on the photograph of the night. She planted a kiss on my cheek. "Goodbye, Charles."

"Goodbye," I said. But she had already vanished down the stairs.

I tripped into the study and took my share of the blankets back from Frank and fell instantly into a dreamless sleep; as Bel returned downstairs, went out to the garage, climbed into Father's Mercedes, and drove it at full speed into the garden wall.

"Why should people be trapped with just one face?" Father liked to say. "Or stuck in just one life?"

The mask, he'd say, was something that you wore but was opposite to you; because it was not wholly real, it could withstand pain that you could not; because it was not wholly human, its beauty was not diminished by age or feeling. Father's hands never smelled of the same thing twice; and fragrances hung in the house like sweet invaders, like opulent chains of memories that no longer belonged to anyone.

We'd encounter his models on their way up or down the stairs, in the ordinary prettiness of their unmade-up daytime faces; it was always a shock to find them in the magazines a few months later, and see what Father had made from them. Louche, tomboy, prissy, gauche; Cleopatran, Regency, Berlin decadent; flappers and hippies and Arabian princesses—he mined their faces for stories and myths and desires old as history, or older, like seams of rare ore that lay buried in the earth of their youth.

In the magazines, the faces of these transient girls had a power, a power that my father could summon and balance, like those old music hall acts that spun plates on sticks. They could call into being any age or emotion or state of mind; and everything around them would be transformed too, turned from diffuse, unwieldy life into a story, something with direction and significance. Looking out from the glossy pages, their faces seemed to promise everything; they promised that you could become anything; they promised that they would take you with them, that you could leave yourself behind.

SHE HAD PROBABLY gone right through the windscreen, the forensics man said; through the windscreen and over the wall into the sea. An old car like that wouldn't give you much protection in the event of a collision. Examining the wreck, he hadn't found any reason why it should have taken off like that—but then again it was so badly damaged it was hard to tell; and anyway these old cars always had their own idiosyncrasies. They were museum pieces, really, they weren't meant to be driven.

Mother thrived in certain kinds of adversity. For the following week, as the rest of us stumbled around in a daze, she handled the policemen and detectives who swarmed about the house—answering their questions, providing copies of old medical reports, making sure they got lunch. When the crash was placed at roughly half past four, it was she who remembered that the taxi had been supposed to come on the hour; it was she who put forward the idea that Bel, realizing it wasn't going to arrive in time, had in a panic decided to take the antediluvian Mercedes to the airport, only for it to spin immediately out of control on the wet grass. The police agreed subsequently that this was by far the most likely explanation.

They took statements from all of us but most of the time stayed out in the garden, taking photographs of the garage, measuring the doorway with tape, making plaster casts of the tire tracks that led over the lawn through splintered wood and split branches to where the car sat in a spray of ground glass and broken stonework, salt air blowing through the smashed windscreen, by the low wall that bounded the bluff from the steep drop down to the sea: only a few feet, coincidentally, from the spot where Father would take Bel and me on long-ago evenings, to look down at the waves and recite to us: *Come away, O human child! To the waters and the wild.*

There were divers too, with a boat, but the water at the base of the cliffs was so choppy that it was impossible to conduct a proper search. We would have to wait, they said meaningfully, and we nodded comprehension. All this time I was expecting her to walk in the door, laughing, and explain that it had all been a prank, a setup, a misunderstanding. But she didn't; nor did she wash up on the shore; and after a week the coroner filed a verdict of death by misadventure.

At the service at the tiny church, her absence only added to the already sharp air of unreality. There was a curious sense of rehearsal to the proceedings (but for whom? for what?); people were wary with their grief. Mother worked hard to counter this and give the occasion the appropriate gravitas. The actors in their orgy of lamentation; the college friends from Trinity; the girls I knew from her school yearbooks, already marked a little by time; the countless oafs, oiks, nitwits, and pettifoggers she had dallied with against my advice; the litany of bumptious uncles and dreary second cousins, headed by that poisonous maiden aunt of Mother's, who seemed to come alive only at times like this; friends of the Family, with a capital *F*: society types one had met only once or twice, the shiny-headed fellow with all the supermarkets, a couple of the lesser Smorfetts, the Earl of somewhere or other, who at a do many years ago had been sick down Mother's décolletage— she greeted every one of them with a smile and a heartfelt word of thanks; she was so good at these things.

That night she assembled the theater people and told them that the family would prefer to be left alone for a while; and it was only when they had gone that I realized "the family" now meant just the two of us, and our slight retinue.

The house seemed to grow bigger in the silence of the succeeding afternoons, bigger and colder, no matter how many fires were lit; one felt, as one rattled purposelessly through it, a little like an Arctic explorer trekking through some icy wasteland, where the only sources of warmth were endless cups of tea and the convalescent dog licking one's hand. Vuk and Zoran had retired to the garden shed, where they could be heard very quietly rehearsing "You Are My Sunshine"; Mirela stayed in her room and did not come out. It became possible to spend the whole day without speaking to anyone.

Occasionally I'd meet Mother in her dressing gown, on the stairs or in the hall with a whiskey glass in her hand, and we'd exchange a few desultory lines about the cobwebs, or the dust. Mrs. P. cooked meals that nobody ate, that sat all night long on the dining room table; she cleaned and dusted and hoovered from dawn till dusk, but it didn't seem to make any difference. Every day more of the house was given over to shadows. Older forces were reasserting themselves now; we did little to resist.

Most of the time I'd sit up in Bel's bedroom and flick through her yearbooks, or old photographs predating her ban. In one of them she sat with her arms thrown around the anonymous dog, as if pleading, on its behalf, for mercy; and I wondered if she'd never let go of that child-hood idea of the world as a place where nothing could be held on to, where every step was on thin ice, where every sunset might be the last; if we'd never managed to convince her otherwise. Sitting there in an aureole of pale November sunshine, I'd look around the room as if see-ing it for the first time, as every surface—the rosewood doors of the wardrobe, the ruched velvet of the curtains, the satin sheen of a half dozen formal dresses—became a tableau on which her image appeared and fled from just as my eye lit on it, dancing capriciously from point to point until I was too dizzy and tired to chase it anymore and I laid my head down on the pillow, with the sunshine like a friendly palm on my cheek, and the smell of her so close; and then I would smile, for how silly it seemed, here among her warm sheets, that she could be gone, how like a storybook with the wrong ending, here on the mattress that was the raft we had sailed on so many Sunday afternoons, down tum-bling rapids and shady meanders, to St. Petersburg and Timbuktu, to Narnia and Never-Never Land . . .

Until one day I went in, and the things had gone back to being merely things. It was as if overnight some spirit had left them; I found myself in a roomful of anonymous objects, a rabble of wood and plastic that no longer had anything to do with anything, waiting to be gone through and put in boxes, or thrown away. That was when I realized I had to go.

By chance, the day I chose to return to Bonetown was the day the builders came in bulldozers to demolish Old Man Thompson's house, and found Olivier's body hanging from the remotest end of the veranda. He had been there for some time; the auction house people must have missed him when they were clearing out the interior. The builders had to cut him down. They were rattled, and they left off work for the day to come in and sit in our kitchen. They hadn't heard about Thompson's death, or the rival claim for the estate that Olivier had refused to challenge. I explained it to them and they shook their heads. "It would have had to've been knocked down whether your man had sold it or not, Mr. H. That place is only waitin for a stray spark to go up like a matchbox. You know the way with these old places. Just to put in new wiring you'd have to rip up so much of it it's hardly worth it. Cheaper in the long run to knock it all down and start again. No point gettin upset about it."

The new development was being called Romanov Arbour: five luxury residences with gym and sauna, each one named after a different Russian writer: the Pushkin, the Tolstoy, the Gogol, and so on. They had already been presold for record sums.

"Computer money, Mr. H.," the builders said. "Give these people a place with an electric fence and a foreign-sounding name, and the sky's the limit." They didn't like it, but as they said, you couldn't get too upset about these things: especially being a builder, especially in Dublin. Anyway, this was their last job. They had saved enough money to get out of the rat race.

"Out?" I said.

"Mexico," they said. In the new year they were taking their equipment and moving out to join some crowd who had set up their own state in the jungle of the Chiapas mountains. The leader wore a black balaclava that he never took off. "He says it's a mirror," the builders told me, "for the faces of the dispossessed."

"Must get awfully stuffy, though," I said. "You know, it being the jungle and everything."

"Someone's got to do it," they said, climbing into their bulldozers. "So long, Mr. H.! *Viva la revolución!*"

I never thought of Bonetown as anything more than a temporary solution. Yet the longer I stayed, the more the idea of living away from Frank came to trouble me. It wasn't that he said anything, nor indeed that he did anything; it was more the basic fact of him that was reassuring. He seemed to prop things up, somehow; he was like a buttress, holding up a very important wall. It seemed to make a kind of sense, moreover, being back amid the junk, the discarded pieces of failed lives. So I brought over the piano from home in his van and squeezed it into the living room, and in the evenings after work—as Droyd, to whom Frank was teaching the rudiments of panel beating, hammered away at the kennel he was making for An Evening of Long Goodbyes, and Laura hung pictures of flowers in wooden frames from Habitat, or combed the day's salvage for treasures that might fit the color scheme she was devising for the apartment, and beneath the window the pushers pushed and the addicts groveled, and Frank snored gently, patriarchally, in front of the muted television news—I tinkered with fragments of melodies that had come to me, or that perhaps I had heard somewhere before: on Bel's record player, maybe, the Dylan fellow, or the woman with the grace notes who sang the song about the dishwasher and the coffee percolator. And one day I stopped at the front door and, with the lipstick I had never given back to her, added to the graffiti a bright red C.

"Charm the Homeless," read a reedy voice behind me. I turned to see a scruffy boy in a sweater. It took me a moment to recognize him without his trolley and his accomplice; and before I could ask him where they had gone, he had scurried away.

I had taken that job, in Frank's friend's warehouse. I worked the late shift, from two o'clock till half past ten, readying everything for pickup the next day. The warehouse was the distribution center for a company that manufactured uniforms. They made them in Africa, then shipped them here to be delivered to various points about the country. My job was to separate them into individual orders: with my billhook plucking each item from rails that went all the way up to the ceiling, packing the goods into boxes I had assembled earlier, checking off names and addresses against triplicate order forms. The only other worker was a deaf-mute called Rosco, who generally left me alone. It was peaceful there, among the aisles of empty pants and jackets—like a museum, I thought, a museum of the present. Usually by nine o'clock or so, everything was done; and when I had swept the floor and assembled a few dozen boxes for tomorrow, I would retire to a chair and a rickety writing desk I had stowed away at the end of the nurses' aisle; and hidden by their crisp white hospital skirts and tunics, begin to write.

ON CHRISTMAS EVE 1958, the day before she was to return to Hollywood after her four-year absence, Gene Tierney suffered her most total breakdown yet. She had been fine: She had convalesced with her mother in Connecticut; *Life* and *Time* had written articles about her to the tune of "Reborn Star" and "Welcome Home for Troubled Beauty." But the night before the flight, quite without warning, she dissolved utterly; and instead of California, she woke—like Dorothy returning from Oz—and found herself in Kansas. This was the Menninger Clinic, her third and last institution. The doctor who ran the clinic didn't believe in ECT. Instead, Gene was encouraged to do what she wanted, and what she wanted to do, it turned out, was knit. She knitted rugs and pillows. She knitted throws and shawls and full-length dresses. She knitted and knitted for months on end, and gradually, she was restored to herself.

When she finally made it back to Hollywood in 1962, the studio system that created her was long gone, and because of her history, the insurance companies wouldn't cover her to work. It was Otto Preminger—who'd directed her in two of her best films, *Laura* and *Whirlpool*—who bailed her out, threatening his producers that he would quit the picture if she wasn't given a part, insurance or no insurance. She was given the part; her cameo in *Advise and Consent* allowed her to complete her contract with Fox. After that she retired to Houston and married a millionaire and never set foot in an institution again.

The doctors speculated that her problems might never have surfaced if she hadn't chosen to act. She had grown up a society girl, and to society she returned; it was only when she stepped before the camera that everything went haywire. It seemed to me, though, that this was missing the point. There were her men, for one thing. "For a beautiful intelligent girl," Dana Andrews tells her in *Laura*, "you've certainly surrounded yourself with a remarkable collection of dopes." She'd always had a weakness for aristocratic types—the disinherited Russian count, the presidential candidate, the billionaire gadabout, others: Howard Hughes for instance, before he crashed his plane in a street in Beverly Hills. They wanted her for the same reason as the studios: her stellar beauty; and just as she did for the studios, she morphed and mutated and recomposed this beauty into the precise form of their desires, until there was nothing of her left.

These relationships, however, were merely variations on a theme that had been set long before with her father, Howard Tierney Sr. Growing up, Gene had worshiped him. He was without doubt a compelling figure: the stern moralist who brought her to church every Sunday; the financial wizard who had built his family two houses, enlisted them in the best country club in Connecticut, endowed them with servants, horse, boat, sent his daughter to a Swiss boarding school with the daughter of Marlene Dietrich and the future wife of a maharajah.

She worshiped him, and through the thirties she watched him dwindle to a man so crippled by debt and the Depression that he took to carrying a gun in his pocket so that if the worst came to the worst and they had nothing left, he could kill himself and the family could claim on the insurance. When Gene first decided to act—after that fairy-tale discovery on the Warners lot, on the holiday across America with Pat and Howard Jr. and Mother—it was with the intention of helping the family, helping him, restoring him to what he had once been.

And so he brokered her first deal, while warning her against the meretriciousness of the movie business; when her mother moved out to Hollywood to chaperone her, he stayed in New York and set up the Belle-Tier Corporation to manage her earnings. She lived within the parameters he set—she drove a small car, made her own clothes—and everything was dandy, until she eloped with Cassini and her mother flew home in disgust to New York and found that her husband had been having an affair with her best friend, whom she had charged with "taking care of him" while she was away. The best friend was the daughter of a railway tycoon and had a fortune of her own; in her, Howard Tierney Sr. saw at last a way out of his debts. In fact, this relationship had been going on for some time; in fact, the reason he'd sent his young family on that fated holiday across America in the first place was so that he could spend the summer alone in New York with her; and now, fresh from denouncing his daughter to the press, he announced he was divorcing Gene's mother and marrying her best friend.

It would be an understatement to say that Gene was disillusioned to find her father had feet of clay. But there was more to come: because when she demanded a new deal with the studio, so that her salary went straight to her and not to the company her father had set up, he sued her for fifty thousand dollars for breach of contract; and when she won the suit, and for the first time saw a statement of her savings at the Belle-Tier Corporation—of all the money she had earned in Hollywood and obediently sent on to her father, who had administered it with such draconian rigor—it came to zero, naught, nothing; there was nothing in the account.

She saw him only two more times. Once, she was under sedation and didn't recognize him. The other time he came to her house and said, as he left, "Well, Gene, I suppose we both got what we wanted."

Hence, surely, the succession of millionaires, the trade-off of her beauty for the security of knowing that no matter how else they betrayed her, she would never have to see them diminished like that; she would never have to see them dismiss the maid, or sell the crystal piece by piece, or carry a gun in case the worst came to the worst; no matter what else happened, there would always be security, there would always be enough to pay her hospital bills, her daughter's hospital bills.

One would have a strong case for arguing that it was the men in her life—the lovers, the father, the directors, producers, critics—who destroyed it. And yet when you looked at the broad sweep they appeared more as agents, collectively, of a darker, wider force of ruin that pursued her. It was as if her epic beauty somehow angered the gods and drew down a suitably Promethean punishment; and the girl behind the beauty—the nice girl from Connecticut who at the end would wonder whether, if her life had been a movie, she would have been cast to play her part—found she had wandered off the lot into a Greek tragedy.

Sitting amid the uniforms in the cavernous warehouse, I tried not to think about this. I tried to concentrate on the good things: the Oscar nomination for *Leave Her to Heaven*, in which out of nowhere she gives a performance of jealousy and insanity and anomie that is quite chilling; the premiere of *The Razor's Edge* in New York City, the first big premiere after World War II, when she'd walked a red carpet in a black tulle dress in front of thousands of fans . . .

But I couldn't help but hear echoes of another life: in Gene's mother, Belle, in the Belle-Tier Corporation her father had sucked dry, in *A Bell for Adano*, Belle Starr, whose heroine's name she'd chosen for an alias when she eloped with Cassini to Las Vegas; and I wondered if she'd ever, in the midst of those dreams and hallucinations, thought of the girl who would come fifty years later, who would also sit in a hospital ward and wonder who she was . . . And in the end I decided it might be kinder to forget, to let her disappear back into the twilight of late-night broadcasts, of dusty stills in the back of dusty junk shops patronized by lonely men with too much time on their hands. I put my notes in a shoe box and stowed it under the davenport in my room.

I ASKED FRANK one time if he could remember how *The Cherry Orchard* had ended. After some deliberation he said that, as far as he could recall, they all just leave.

"They all just *leave*?"

"Yeah, 's far as I remember."

"What kind of ending is that?"

"Dunno, Charlie. Must have been the only one he could think of."

The Amaurot Players never reconvened. The papers had never been signed, and the lavender-suited P.A. had taken Harry aside after the funeral and told him that Telsinor were pulling out of the deal. No one was pointing fingers or making judgments, she said; still, the company had a responsibility to listen to its shareholders, and in the shareholders' eyes these recent events were simply not in the spirit of youth and change and communication that Telsinor represented.

Initially there was some talk of looking for funding elsewhere, but it quickly petered out. Nobody's heart was in it anymore. Soon everyone went their separate ways. Harry made some sort of a statement claiming that the theater was an elitist art form and that the Internet was the only medium capable of expressing truly revolutionary ideas;

he got a job writing copy for the Snickers website, and to my knowledge *The Rusting Tractor* was never produced.

Mirela seemed to have taken the crash especially hard. For weeks afterward she barricaded herself in her room; she would not speak to Harry, and the engagement was quietly forgotten. She left the house shortly afterward. For where I did not know: Mrs. P. would not speak about her. I never saw her again, at least not in the flesh.

It was only a short while after that Vuk and Zoran's application for asylum was turned down. The former Yugoslavia, in the eyes of the Irish government, was no longer sufficiently dangerous to merit their staying on here; the next thing we knew they were heading back to Croatia with Mrs. P. It all seemed very sudden. The truth of it, though, was that the citizenship issue was only an excuse. Mrs. P. had been pining to go back home since the day she arrived, and the "recent events" had only bolstered her resolve.

"To her it doesn't matter there is nothing left there," Vuk said to me. "Always she is thinking only of my father, who was lost, and she does not want to live away from."

"What about Mirela?" I said. "Is she going too?"

"Ay, Mirela," he sighed. "Maybe she is right. Maybe it is better to stay here, to forget. But Mama is determined." He tapped his head and grinned. "We go with her, make sure she doesn't go too crazy."

I knew Mother must be lonely in the house on her own. I had been nagging her to get in someone new, but she didn't listen. In fact, I was never sure how aware of my visits she was. She confined herself to one or two rooms these days, leaving the rest of the house to the great drafts that roamed through it. I would find her sitting by a cold hearth, with a glass in her hand and cinders all over the floor. We would talk, or rather I would listen as she talked: about the old days, invariably—Trinity College, the Hunt Ball, Father, and her star turns in this or that production. Sometimes I would try to get her to talk about Bel, but whether it was real or put on, I could not pierce this cloudy nostalgia. Once only, when I asked her straight out about the night of the school play, did it seem that the cobwebs fell away. She paused, ran her finger around the rim of her sherry glass, and then said, "A true actress, Charles, never lets herself be seen. Every time she walks on stage, she creates herself anew, using what's around her; and when she walks off she divests herself of it just so"—lifting her arms and shrugging off an imaginary gown. "Her life is merely a peg on which to hang it. But Bel, you see, Bel . . ." She paused once more, and smiled sadly. "Bel always insisted life skip to her tune. She never would learn the value of compromise. So like her father in that way, making things harder than they already were . . ."

The fingers ran around the glass; then, abruptly, she brightened. "But in the *old* days, Charles, how jolly it was. Now, of course, it's all little people and their rules. But then . . . but then, when the house was full of life, when the grooms would bring round the brougham, and the maids would present in their frocks, and curtsy at the knee, and the valet and the chauffeur and the cook, and every room bustling with life . . ."

"No, Mother," I contradicted gently. "That wasn't here. We never had all those people working for us in Amaurot."

"I don't mean us, Charles," she said irritably. "I mean in the old days. The last century, before we ever arrived. Now we're starting a new century, of course," she added with disdain, and her eyes glazed over as she poured herself more sherry, absently tilting the bottle up and up till the drink trembled right at the rim of the glass. "But how jolly it must have been, how jolly . . . ," shaking her head and smiling fondly and not noticing as I raised the latch and let myself out into the gusty hall.

I couldn't get out to her as often as I should have liked, and I did worry about her. I rang the Cedars once, to inquire about the possibility of having her return there, just for a short while; but there had been some sort of trouble with the last check, so I let the matter drop.

Thus I passed my new life. My work hours meant that I rarely had to speak to people, and the quiet order of it suited me; it was like swimming underwater, through the ruins of some drowned city.

And then one night I got a call.

It was one of those bitter, sleety winter nights, so desperately cold that in the warehouse even the uniforms seemed to shiver on their rails and yearn to clap their hands together, if they'd had hands. I had gone into the village on my eight o'clock break in search of coffee to warm myself up. There was nothing visibly out of the ordinary when I got back. Rosco was working at the far end; the pile of cardboard boxes was just where I had left it. And yet the air seemed somehow *heightened*, hyperreal, as if the focus wheel had been turned and a new clarity been added. I waited a moment there at the door, looking over the cold hall, then realized that a phone was ringing.

With a tight feeling in my chest, I tracked the sound: past the foreman's cabin, past the shuttered doors, down the aisle of nurses' uniforms till I came to my writing desk and lifted a pile of order forms to find Bel's phone.

I had kept it more as a souvenir than anything else, a souvenir or a pet. Droyd had showed me how it worked, how to unlock it and keep it fed; but I never used it, other than to wonder at its little green display, and hardly anyone ever called me. Yet here it was singing away. I picked it up and pressed a button, and a voice said, "Charles?"

The entire warehouse, the entire world, the particles in the air seemed to freeze and hang motionless in suspension.

"Hello?" the voice said.

"Yes, yes, I'm here," hurriedly.

"I was hoping you'd pick up," the voice said.

I sank onto the chair.

"Why aren't you saying anything?"

My heart was racing, that was why. I wiped a frost of sweat from my forehead and said, with some effort, "Is this you?"

"Of course it's me, don't you recognize me?"

"No, I— damn it"—the damn phone was so *small*, it kept losing itself in my hand—"damn it, we all thought you were—"

"I suppose that was the idea."

"That was the . . . ?" rising again, caught in a bewildering mixture of emotions that ranged from relief to gratitude to apoplexy. "We've been so *worried*—not even worried, we've been— I mean of all the wretched, selfish . . ."

There was a silence at the other end. For one terrorized instant I thought I'd scared her off. Then the voice said, "I know. I'm sorry. But I didn't think you'd think— I mean I thought you'd work it out."

"Work what out?"

"The name."

"The name?"

The name, she repeated, the name, come on, Charles. And slowly it stole across me. Jessica Kiddon: Jess Kiddon: Just Kidding.

"MacGillycuddy," I breathed.

"Maybe I should have gone with Tempora Mores," Bel mused.

Just kidding: It was one of his conceits, I'd have recognized it a mile off; and once I did I couldn't believe I hadn't guessed before. I should have known he'd be in this up to his neck; I should have known that banishing him from our lives was like asking a genie to kindly get back in its bottle, or trying to shoo a charging bull with a big red rag. Before she said another word, several unexplained phenomena suddenly became clear. The dinner invitation that hadn't arrived; the mysterious school friend who wasn't in the yearbook; the chopping noise I had heard that night, clearing a path through the trees for the car, to the same cliffs MacGillycuddy had been so determined I fall off instead of exploding myself. There was no master class in Yalta; there was no Jessica Kiddon. Bel had lifted the entire idea from me and my abortive flight to Chile—which, given the uncomplimentary things she'd said about it at the time, I thought was pretty rich.

In fact her plan, as she explained it to me that night, was significantly more detailed than mine. It had to be, she said; she hadn't had any money of her own, and the only way to fund her escape had been to create this new persona, the respectable girl who could persuade Mother to part with the necessary sum. Furthermore, familiarizing us all with the fictitious Jessica (I thought here of our flirtatious conversation after the greyhound race and blushed) would lend her both time and a means of muddying the waters after her initial departure. The idea was to travel to Russia in her own name, under cover of the Chekhov trip. As far as we were concerned, Jessica would be with her and everything would appear aboveboard. It was only when she was over there that the phony papers, passport, et cetera that MacGillycuddy had arranged would come into play. The way she had set it up, she would then have a six-month window (the length of the spurious class) in which she could merge into Jessica—Jessica, who had no roots, no background, could disappear quite easily and never be traced—and let Bel Hythloday simply melt away, without any of the mess or pain or logistical headaches of an actual faked death, a drowning or an explosion or a car crash.

But she *did* crash the car, I said, confused. What was the point of setting up such an elaborate plan, doing all that groundwork, and then at the last minute abandoning it in favor of a crash—inflicting all that chaos on us, all that pain?

"How's the theater?" she asked lightly, suddenly, changing the subject. "How's Harry and Mirela and all those plans for Amaurot?"

I was rather thrown for a moment. Because the theater was gone, of course. The plans for Amaurot—the refurbishment, the statues, the marriage of art and commerce, Harry and Mirela's engagement—all of these things had been destroyed along with the bottle green Mercedes. But only then did it dawn on me that this could have been deliberate: that the crash could have been a deliberate act of sabotage, severing the house from its future and leaving it in darkness as surely as if someone had cut the power; or a stay of execution, whichever way you chose to see it. I kept quiet as this thought established itself, and all my other thoughts reordered themselves around it. Then I said, "Everyone's fine. Everyone's right as rain."

I got to my feet and walked over to the warehouse door. "What's it like over there, Bel?"

"You'd like it," she said. "Everybody drinks a lot of vodka." She laughed, and I laughed too, cradling the phone against my jaw and scanning the car park outside, because in the movie of our lives, that's surely how the scene would play; I'd see her looking at me from a telephone kiosk mere yards away . . .

"Are you ever coming home? May I remind you there's no place like home?"

"Maybe someday," she said. "Or maybe someday you'll come over here. But I ought to go now. Let you get back to your work."

"Well . . . thanks for calling." I turned back inside, to the Perspex roof, the silently hanging garments.

"My pleasure."

"Happy New Year, old thing."

"Happy New Year, Charles."

OR MAYBE IT DIDN'T happen like that at all. Maybe that was just a silly fantasy I made up myself; maybe we had already received a very nice letter from a former school friend of Bel's who had waited for Bel to come that night, who had rung the house but not been able to get through and in a panic had taken a taxi out to the airport herself, had taken the plane alone and arrived alone in a resort town in Russia where the news was waiting for her, where she watched for a week as a blizzard raged outside her window until the roads were clear enough so she could turn around and come home again, too late though, too late for the funeral. Or maybe it was just a wrong number on the phone that time, or it was Frank, calling to see if I wanted him to pick me up a kebab when he and Droyd were down at the kebab shop, or someone else, Patsy Olé for instance, asking if I'd like to meet up later on.

You can take the alternative if you want, with the endless dreams of seaweed-braided arms, the countless glimpses of her in clouds, billboards, the faces of strangers. But this one is the version I prefer: the one where she lies awake at night, drawing up her plans; where she is set free from her life, from her unspellable name, and spirited away; in the MacGillycuddian universe, where people disappear only to resurface elsewhere, with French accents and false mustaches, where everything is constantly changing and nobody ever dies.

"WHY DO THEY CALL IT being on your uppers? Surely uppers ought to be good things. Upper class. Upper hand. Surely you're on your downers, if you have no money."

"I don't know," I said.

Patsy and I were walking along the strand behind the warehouse. It was late and impossibly cold, and the night scrolled up over the sea blue and starry like cheap paper scenery. Patsy was still wearing her foam antlers from work. She had come back from her Grand Tour to find the family embroiled in one of those ghastly tribunals; her father was up in Dublin Castle practically every week, answering questions about these supposed payments, and meetings he'd had three or four *years* ago, how was he supposed to remember that? "And in the meantime all the accounts have been frozen. So here I am, serving coffee and damned panini to idiots."

"It can't be that bad."

"It is. It's a nightmare. It's a nightmare from which I am trying to awake." She pulled on her cigarette. "*An*tlers, Charles. What kind of despot *forces* a person to wear antlers? In Nazi *Ger*many they didn't make people wear antlers. Someone ought to write to Amnesty International."

"I think they're rather deer."

"Charles darling."

"Sorry."

"I expect it'll blow over soon enough, though," she said, exhaling a long plume of smoke. "I mean that's the beauty of white-collar crime, isn't it? Nobody really minds."

"It must be dreadfully hard on you, all the same," I said gently.

She clapped her hands together meditatively. "I know Daddy's no saint," she said. "But Charles, who is? You have to get your hands dirty if you want to succeed in life, don't you? And anyway, do you know what these tribunal lawyers get paid? They get paid *heaps* more than Daddy paid himself. Someone should haul *them* up in front of some old judge." She sighed. "It's so wretchedly tiresome. All Daddy seems to do anymore is run around the house looking for bits of paper and burning them in the back garden. You should have seen our Halloween bonfire this year, Charles. It was like the Towering Inferno. *And* he's taken my credit cards." She flicked her cigarette out to the sea. "It's all so un-*speak*ably tiresome," she said, narrowing her eyes in judgment of the whole of civilization.

We walked on a little farther. Somewhere along the way, her hand found its way into mine, and we swung them back and forth against the cold, like children.

"What about you?" She gave me a sidelong glance.

"I don't know," I said. "My heart will go on, I suppose."

She gazed reflectively at the misty banks of rain blowing in from the sea. "It's this damn country," she said. "How's a person supposed to live in a country where it rains all the time?" She sighed. "Maybe Hoyland has the right idea—I saw Hoyland the other day, was I telling you? *He* thinks we should all just give up on this ghastly place. Move to some tropical island, and start our own superior society there. You know, we could have a beehive, and a polo ground and so forth."

"*Nine bean-rows will I have there*," I recited absently, "*a hive for the honey-bee . . .*"

"What?"

"Oh, sorry. Yeats. Sorry. Had sort of a similar notion, back in the 1900s. Couldn't stand this place. Had this idea of a magical mystical Ireland, wanted everyone to come along. Utopian sort of a thing. Didn't work, needless to say. Never does."

"You'd have to get someone in to clean, obviously . . . ," Patsy said thoughtfully, stroking her chin; then throwing her hands up: "Oh, it's hopeless, it's all perfectly hopeless!"

A billboard on the road above overlooked the strand. It showed a beautiful girl in ragged, dusty clothes. Her face was stained with grime and tears; she stared out impassionedly from the rubble of a bombed-out city. CAN'T WE TALK ABOUT IT? the slogan read at the bottom of the billboard, with the Telsinor logo in the right-hand corner. I used to know that girl, I said to Patsy.

The wind blew; the water crashed. The headlands to the east and west threw their arms out around the sea, as if to hold in place something that really, really wanted to go. Like a photograph, I thought: like those pictures in the yearbooks, the girls in their plaits and ponytails who had stared out at my friends and me as we huddled round behind the cricket pavilion; who were embarked on digressions of their own now, but would remain with us, to be guessed at and sighed over, in the shape of that split second before the shutter fell; before the shutter fell and the camera clicked, and everybody laughed and clambered over each other, and giggled off into the next lost frame of their lives, and the next, and the next.

ACKNOWLEDGMENTS

Much of the material relating to Gene Tierney is based on Tierney's autobiography, *Self-Portrait* (Berkley Books, 1980), written with Mickey Herskowitz.

The title was inspired by the song "An Evening of Long Goodbyes" by Rachel's, from their album *Selenography*, on Quarterstick Records. With thanks and respect to Rachel's.

For their support and generosity during the writing of this book, I would like to thank my parents, Christopher and Kathleen Murray, as well as Simon Prosser, Natasha Fairweather, Juliette Mitchell, Sarah Castleton, Lee Boudreaux and all the wonderful people at Random House, Andrew Motion, John Boyne, and everyone who helped with the early chapters, especially Tim Jarvis, Andrew Palmer, and Neil "Stewarty" Stewart. Neel Mukherjee and Chris Watson provided a home away from home and some fine cuisine. Thank you to Miriam McCaul for keeping the world turning and the sun shining.

AN EVENING OF
LONG GOODBYES

Paul Murray

Q: How did you come up with the premise of *An Evening of Long Good-byes*? What inspired you to write it?

Paul Murray: Well, I was about eighteen months out of college, and after suffering through a series of minimum-wage, go-nowhere jobs, I decided to take myself off to Barcelona, with the grand idea of writing a novel while teaching English on the side. I quickly discovered that Barcelona was full of people who had come to write their novels while teaching English on the side. The already fraught situation was exacerbated by the fact that no one in Barcelona wanted to learn English. I ran out of money after a few weeks—I ate nothing but pasta, I couldn't afford the subway, so I had to walk everywhere. It was a scary and deeply unromantic situation. *An Evening of Long Goodbyes* began one night in the deepest, darkest throes of my stay there. I was living with a makeup artist and I think I had drunk about half a bottle of wine, both of which elements feed into the narrative in interesting ways. It started as a short story and was really just a piece of escapism, a fantasy about being at home in a big house with peacocks and food, with a lot of jokes to cheer myself up.

Q: What was the writing process like? Did you write many drafts or struggle with any sections? How long did it take you to complete the novel, and how did your vision of it change during the writing?

PM: It took about three years from start to finish. Like I say, it began as a story, so I was surprised as anyone when it finished up as a novel of four hundred-odd pages. The first draft took about six months—I ended up scrapping the whole second half. I don't know how many drafts there were all told; with computers, one draft just segues into another. Rewriting is a really important part of the process. Obviously the first draft, when you're in the grip of the muse, is crucial, but it takes a lot of editing to make that look like a book, as opposed to the ravings of a madman. You have a shape in your mind for the book, but you can't realize it directly—instead you have to keep pruning and reshaping. It's really like chipping at a block of marble. I'd love to be able to write one draft and have it be perfect, but it seems like the only way I can work is to rewrite obsessively.

Q: Who are your literary influences? Did you draw on other writers' work while you wrote *An Evening of Long Goodbyes*, or refer to works for inspiration? Are you influenced differently by Irish writers than by American writers?

PM: I don't know that I *drew* on anyone, as such. Everything I read influences me in some way—teaches me a lesson, or awakens me to a new technique, or alerts me to a flaw—but I think it happens at quite a subliminal level. I mean, if I'm reading a book, I'll just lose myself in it, if it's any good; I won't go through it looking for pointers. But I'll hope that something will seep down into my writing. A lot of reviewers have compared the book to P. G. Wodehouse, which is very flattering but I'm not really that familiar with his work. In fact, a lot of the comparisons have been to writers I've only come to subsequently: Evelyn Waugh, for instance, or Kingsley Amis. In Ireland, we're spoiled for writers, of course. In college I studied Joyce and Beckett, who remain two of my heroes. But later writers I neglected. I had formed the impression, rightly or wrongly, that Irish writing had become rather reserved and formal, rather *literary*, and wasn't taking the risks that gave me a rush in the modernists. By "risks" here, I think I mainly mean humor. What I love about Beckett is that one minute he can be dealing with grand existential themes, and the next someone's pants will fall down. It's an obvious slapstick gag, but it's very important, in political and literary and any other terms you care to mention, that that gag is there. I read a lot of American writers, and in some ways I think they're the true inheritors of the Joyce-Beckett tradition, or antitradition—that sense of freedom, iconoclasm, inclusiveness. Thomas Pynchon was a huge influence on me—again, a writer unafraid to deal with the most complex, dark, and difficult themes, and weave into them incredibly funny, silly, even infantile jokes. But there are any number of American writers I love. Edith Wharton. George Saunders. We could be here all day.

Q: Why did you choose to write in first person?

PM: It was more a case of it choosing me. I just started writing one night and the voice was there and it was strong enough from the very beginning to sustain us both. It was enormous fun to write as Charles, to say things like "Great Scott" and "noisome." And writing in first person you can get that much deeper into the character's thoughts; in third person there is much more distance. If the book had been written in the third person, Charles might well have seemed unbearable.

Q: Who was the most difficult character to write? Who came most easily to you?

PM: I was fond of all the main characters, and most pretty much arrived fully formed. Charles was simultaneously the easiest and the hardest to write. Because everything was coming through him, and because his voice was so distinctive, it gave the book—which has a lot of material to keep in the air—a structure and a sense of focus that otherwise might have been hard to achieve. But the flip side is that it also made the writing quite difficult, because Charles is so clueless and such a solipsist. So if there was some delicate emotional nuance happening, I would have to find some alternate means of presenting it, because

Charles himself wouldn't be sufficiently aware to notice it. Everything had to be rendered in this anachronistic, emotionally stymied way and it could sometimes be really frustrating. These are the kinds of things you don't think of when you start writing a book.

Q: *An Evening of Long Goodbyes* contains elements of comedy, sadness, satire, and political commentary. How would you characterize it over-all? Did you set out to create any sort of social message for your readers?

PM: I didn't set out with the express intention of writing a comedy. I had a fair idea of what was going to happen at the end, so I was aware all the way through of the darkness under the surface. I think it's quite a sad book, in many ways. It's true, though, that there is a lot of comedy, and I think some readers are surprised by the turn it takes later on. But I don't think a book ought to be limited to one genre, as comedy or tragedy or whatever. Without wanting to get too grand about it, that's not the way life works, is it? It doesn't divide itself up neatly into humorous part, tragic part—it's more blurred than that. When things seem outwardly perfect, we can find ourselves despairing, and conversely, when things seem at their absolutely most hopeless and desolate, we can find our-selves laughing at the silliest joke. And I think it misrepresents experi-ence and is even sort of dangerous to insist that serious subjects must always be treated seriously. The importance of humor is primarily to puncture fixed ideas—to make us step back and realize that our situa-tion, whatever it may be, is, in the grand scheme of things, always con-tingent and arbitrary and ephemeral. And that helps us to deal with our emotions and to keep going. Holding on to one perspective, on the other hand, whether it takes the form of grief or anger or a particular political standpoint, is often destructive to us and to those around us.

For the same reason, I didn't want my book to have a message. My guiding light when writing it was to be true to the characters and let them go where they wanted to go. If I had wanted to play the situation purely for laughs, it would have meant keeping the characters one-dimensional, and, for better or worse, I liked them too much to do that. Likewise, if I'd been using them to make some sort of a satirical point, I would have had to subordinate them to that. I preferred to have whatever message there might be come from the characters, rather than the other way around.

For all that, there is a good deal of satire of the New Ireland and the economic boom. But the cupidity and cynicism and foolishness at the time was so astonishing that all you had to do was write down what you saw and let them hang themselves.

Q: What do you think fiction can achieve that nonfiction cannot?

PM: That's a tricky question. I don't really read nonfiction apart from research, and though I often enjoy it, I'm always reading fiction at the same time. I've never really thought about why fiction should be such a staple. I just know that I need it. It's like food. Off the top of my head, though, I guess fiction allows for a much greater degree of empathy between the reader and what's happening on the page. Biographers and historians are always going to be hamstrung by the facts and the need to be faithful to the real version of events. And they can't presume to know what's going on in someone's head. Those are two almost insurmountable obstacles to creating something interesting right there. Because fiction deals with the imaginary, it can, paradoxically maybe, give a much fuller account of what it's like to be here and be alive, because it allows for a kind of holistic approach. You know, you can go off on digressions about daffodils or a red wheelbarrow or whatever, and the reader will work with you to incorporate it into the story and into the world you're trying to create. Whereas if you're writing a biography of Lyndon Johnson, no matter how much such and such a part of his life may remind you of how you feel when you see a red wheelbarrow, the reader is always going to want to know what the hell it has to do with Lyndon Johnson.

Q: You fictionalize two historical figures in your novel: Yeats and Gene Tierney. Why did you pick these personalities?

PM: I wasn't quite sure when I was writing it, but in retrospect I think it was because of the limitations of Charles's voice I mentioned above. He's a naïve and unperceptive character, but he's also quite guarded, especially when it comes to talking about his family. I think he knows more than he lets on, but he's turned his life into this kind of performance that allows him not to see it. Bringing in these real-life figures was a way of illustrating elements of his and Bel's characters that I wasn't going to be able to voice through him. Shortly before I started writing the book I'd done some research on a biography of George Yeats, W. B.'s wife, in the course of which I found out a lot about his life—these aristocratic, antimodern urges of his, which chimed with what I wanted Charles to express.

Gene Tierney I'd been interested in for a long time. Her struggles prefigured Bel's in some way, and Charles's obsession with her was a good way of expressing his fears for Bel, which most of the time he's in denial about. Both Yeats and Tierney were romantic figures too, which fitted the basic tenor of the book: one the romantic artist and one the artist's subject, if you like. It gave me an avenue to explore some of the politics of a romantic outlook.

Q: What was your reasoning in creating two different possible endings to *An Evening of Long Goodbyes*?

PM: Well, I don't want to show too much of my hand here. John Fowles does a similar thing in *The French Lieutenant's Woman*, which I remember talking about in class once. Maybe that's where I got the idea. I suppose the novel is all about illusions, true and false versions of reality, how ultimately you have to create your own way into reality, artificial though it may be. I think that's something Charles manages to do but Bel doesn't. And I envisaged the book as a kind of performance that Charles is giving for the reader. But he's not going to give everything away. It seemed, after so much smoke and mirrors, far too clunky to come down and say exactly what happened, there was a happy ending or there was a sad ending. I like that the reader can decide for him or herself what happens, and I like that it's never really final. I change my mind on it too, all the time.

1. Masks, disguise, and role-playing have major significance in *An Evening of Long Goodbyes*, as do references to photographs and films. Is identity in real life as fluid as it appears to be here? Do you think this confusion about identity affects people in their twenties more than it affects other age groups?

2. The biography of Gene Tierney appears at intervals throughout the book. How does this material fit with the rest of the novel? What is it intended to signify? The use of real-life figures in works of fiction is becoming more and more common. Is this simply a device that authors use to make their fictions seem more credible? Or are they merely looking for ready-made stories? Would you argue that Paul Murray's inclusion of Gene Tierney is exploitative?

3. Some readers prefer the first, arguably more comic section of the book, prior to Charles's move to Bonetown. Others find Charles difficult to identify with at this stage of the book, and find him, and the novel, more likable after he moves in with Frank. If the novel had ended

at the close of chapter four, how would it compare with the novel in full? How important is it to a novel's success that the main character be likable? Does humour entail likability, or can it become an obstacle to the reader taking the characters seriously? Does the comedy throughout enhance or work against the tragic denouement?

4. To what extent does the novel accord with Yeats's idea of the mask—that to live fully, one must create a persona that is the total opposite of one's actual identity? Can it be argued that Charles's character is a construction, a persona that enables him to adapt to the real world in a way that Bel cannot? What do you think might happen to Charles at the end?

5. To what degree can this be said to be a novel about grief, specifically the family's mourning for their dead father? What picture of Charles's father emerges over the course of the book? What would he have thought about Frank?

6. Charles is on the receiving end of the process of modernization that is overtaking Dublin, while Frank makes his living from it. Although he is one of the kindest characters in the book, is Frank's involvement in this process problematic? Does pragmatism lead in the end to conservatism? If someone is kind to those immediately around him, is it fair to criticize his actions on a larger scale? At what point does idealism, like Bel's, become a bad thing?

7. *An Evening of Long Goodbyes* is a late example of a "big house" novel—traditionally set in the manse of a family of the Anglo-Irish ascendancy, with the native Irish featuring as comical interludes, or as exemplars of a more primitive but more spiritual outlook. How does this novel conform to the genre, and how does it subvert it? How plausible is the novel's claim that both rich and poor are placed in the same position by the forces of globalization?

8. Over a handful of years, Dublin changed from a run-down backwater with high emigration and high unemployment to one of the richest (and most expensive) cities in Europe. Does the novel give a uniformly nega-

tive impression of this transition? Is this fair, given the improvements on the lives of many of its inhabitants? Does the relationship between Laura and Frank at the end of the novel, representing the new and old Dublins, offer a sign of hope for the future?

9. The largely comic antics in the book take place against some serious real-life events—which the protagonists, for the most part, ignore. Is this an accurate reflection of how world-historical events affect our lives? Does fiction dealing with serious events, especially real-life events, have a responsibility to be serious? Or is comedy at times an appropriate response?

10. At the end of *An Evening of Long Goodbyes*, Charles offers us a choice between two different endings. Are both versions plausible? What does your own choice entail for your reading of the novel? Why does Murray use this strategy? How does Charles's refusal to tell us the real version of events influence your view of what already happened?

PHOTO: © CORMASCULLY.COM

PAUL MURRAY was born in Dublin in

1975. He studied English literature at

Trinity College and took a master's in

creative writing at the University of

East Anglia. A former bookseller, he lives

in Dublin. *An Evening of Long Goodbyes*,

his first novel, was shortlisted for the

Whitbread Prize, and earned Murray

a nomination for the Kerry Irish

Fiction Award.

Printed in the United States
by Baker & Taylor Publisher Services